A Dream of Death

A Dream of Death

A Kate Hamilton Mystery

❧

CONNIE BERRY

CROOKED
LANE

NEW YORK

Published in the United States by Crooked Lane Books, an imprint of The Quick Brown Fox & Company LLC.

Crooked Lane Books and its logo are trademarks of The Quick Brown Fox & Company LLC.

Library of Congress Catalog-in-Publication data available upon request.

ISBN (hardcover): 978-1-68331-987-0
ISBN (ePub): 978-1-68331-988-7
ISBN (ePDF): 978-1-68331-989-4

Cover design by Lori Palmer

Printed in the United States.

www.crookedlanebooks.com

Crooked Lane Books
34 West 27th St., 10th Floor
New York, NY 10001

First Edition: April 2019

10 9 8 7 6 5 4 3 2 1

For my parents

They were right, my dear, all those voices were right
And still are; this land is not the sweet home that it looks,
Nor its peace the historical calm of a site
Where something was settled once and for all. . . .

—"In Praise of Limestone," W. H. Auden

Chapter One

~

I never wanted to return to Glenroth.

Three years had passed since Bill's death, and the veneer of coping I'd laid over my grief was as thin as eggshell porcelain and every bit as breakable. It didn't take much—the smell of the sea, hearing a snatch of a Scots accent, finding one of Bill's distinctive doodles on a scrap of paper—and there I was, back in the land of memories and regrets.

That was the problem. On the Isle of Glenroth, memories and regrets lay as thick on the ground as yellow gorse in autumn.

Still, a promise was a promise. Even one I'd never intended to keep.

"Going somewhere fun?" my mother had asked.

"Scotland. Glenroth, actually."

There'd been a moment of tactful silence. "Sure that's a good idea, Kate?"

Of course I wasn't sure. Especially at the moment. Thick curtains of fog swirled across the deck of the car ferry, swallowing the landing ahead. I was the only passenger, and I'd been instructed to set my emergency brake and remain in the driver's seat for the duration of the twenty-minute voyage. The boat lurched, and I gripped the wheel of the hatchback I'd hired at the train station in Fort William, grateful

1

for the metal railing dividing the deck of the small craft from the icy depths of Cuillin Sound.

With a long blast of the ship's horn, the fog parted and the Isle of Glenroth rose before me like Brigadoon materializing in the Highland mist. Trees lined the banks, their bare limbs dark and lined with snow. An old movie in black and white.

The bell sounded, and I started my engine.

"Take care, lass," the burly ferryman called through my partially open window. "Roads 're slick."

My second warning. The man at the car-hire desk had made a point of telling me about the "wee airly storm" that had blown through the Inner Hebrides the previous night, surprising the islanders with a layer of wet snow. "Could I talk ye into waitin' till mornin'?" he'd asked in a wheedling tone. When I explained that I'd learned to drive in snowy Wisconsin, he'd shrugged. "Whit's fur ye will no go past ye." In other words, *What will be, will be.*

I closed the window, tasting the salty tang of the sea on my lips. Ahead to the north, I could just make out the rocky peaks of Skye. Behind me, although I couldn't see them, were the islands of Rúm and Eigg. The car bumped over the ramp onto solid ground. Twenty-two hours after leaving Cleveland's airport, I'd arrived—by plane, train, automobile, and ferryboat—on the small Hebridean island where my husband was born. And where he died.

I tapped my brakes and coasted to a halt at the blinking stop sign. A splash of red caught my eye: *Fàilte gu Eilean Glen Roth.* Then, in English: WELCOME TO THE ISLE OF GLENROTH. POPULATION 238. Precisely the same as my first visit twenty-five years ago. However did they manage it?

Beside me on the passenger's seat lay my canvas carry-on. At least I had the essentials—overnight stuff, toiletries in the regulation quart-size baggie. No clothes, though. In less than four hours I'd be expected to appear at the Tartan Ball in something formal and festive. Thanks

2

to cruel fate, or an inattentive baggage handler in Cleveland, all I had were the jeans, white T-shirt, and quilted jacket I'd thrown on that morning.

The narrow road rose steadily, leaving the mists below, but given a latitude roughly equivalent to Hudson Bay, the afternoon light was already slipping away. In Glenroth Village, ancient stone cottages, now island shops, huddled together along the High Street—Wee Dram, the island's purveyor of spirits; the Tartan Gift Shop; the Bonnie Prince, the pub where Bill and I had hung out on my first visit years ago; Flora's Café. A sign over the café door featured the pretty face of Flora MacDonald, the girl from Skye who had saved the Bonnie Prince by disguising him as her maid. If the Glenroth islanders were guilty of shamelessly exploiting their Jacobite heritage, I couldn't blame them. The tourists ate it up.

Today, signs of Halloween adorned every shop—jack-o'-lanterns, giant spiders, even a friendly ghost or two. Lights were on at Ferguson's Sport Shop. I slowed the car. What if my suitcase *didn't* arrive on the very next flight as the lost-luggage lady in Glasgow promised? Ferguson's front window displayed a baffling mix of sea kayaks, fly-fishing gear, and sportswear. I pictured myself arriving at the ball in a Scotty Dog T-shirt and black sweatpants with I ♥ GLENROTH appliqued in fluorescent pink tartan down one leg. Seeing the look on Elenor's face might be worth it.

A mile or so past the village came the moment I'd been dreading, the first one anyway. The sign for the Harborview Hotel & Marina read CLOSED FOR THE SEASON. *Drive past. Focus on the road.* But my eyes moved of their own accord to the bathing huts strung like buoys along the rocky strand below. Gone were the gaily-colored umbrellas. The kiosk dispensing soda and ice cream was boarded up. Snow lay on the pier, as soft and cold as a grave blanket.

The memory struck me like a rogue wave. Bill's hair streaming water, the paramedics, Elenor's shrieks. My vision blurred.

The white car appeared out of nowhere. I slammed on the brakes, feeling them judder on the slick asphalt. *Crap, crap, crap. I'm going to hit him.*

Wrenching the steering wheel to the left, I held on as my car slid off the road and plowed into the soft, snowy earth. I jammed the gearshift into park and pounded the steering wheel. If I'd believed in omens, which I didn't, I'd have turned right around and—

Someone tapped on the driver's side window. The lunatic driving the other car. He bent down to peer at me and made a rolling motion with his hand. Tall, lean, dark hair flecked with silver. I lowered the window an inch or two. The wind whipped my hair.

"Are you injured?" The voice was low, concerned, and unexpectedly English.

"I'm fine, no thanks to you. Why did you pull out in front of me?"

"Why didn't you slow down? The speed limit's twenty-five. You must have been doing at least fifty."

We glared at each other. He said, "Try backing out."

I turned the key and put the car in reverse, feeling the tires spin.

"Not like that," he said. "You're digging yourself in further. Gently. Try to rock it."

I did, feeling absurdly pleased when it made no difference.

"I'll see if I can free the tires. Do you have a shovel?"

I gave him my best scornful look. "It's a rental."

He crouched near the front of my car, clearing snow and mud with his bare hands. A few minutes later he straightened his back. His hands were lobster-red, the knees of his crisply pressed trousers wet and soiled. "Now put it in reverse and go gently. I'll push."

Even with the man's added muscle, the car refused to budge. This wasn't getting me anywhere. "Look," I said, sounding more confident than I felt. "I appreciate your help, but the rental company will send someone."

He dashed toward the road. For a moment I thought he'd bolted, but I glimpsed him in the rearview mirror, waving with both arms.

I got out of the car and stood shivering in my quilted jacket. A pickup truck pulled next to me on the verge. The window rolled down and a familiar head appeared. Long face, lantern jaw. "Need help, miss?"

My heart leapt. "Bo, it's me, Kate."

Bo Duff jumped out of the pickup, all six foot five of him, and caught me up in one of his massive bear hugs. "Mrs. Bill, you came back." Bo was fifty-seven, exactly Bill's age if he'd lived. His voice was deep, his Scots accent thick, but his eyes were as wide and innocent as a child's.

I almost melted. "I did come back, and seeing you is the best part."

A lopsided grin split his face. "Got the photos. Best present I ever got in my whole life."

I'd sent him an album filled with childhood photographs of the two of them, Bill and Bo, fishing, kayaking, wrestling on the lawn of the Adventure Centre.

"Shoulda written." Bo shoved his big hands in the pockets of his parka. He wore baggy cords and a pair of enormous rubber wellies. His long hair had thinned at the crown since I'd seen him last, but his face was unlined, his cheeks pink from the cold.

"Doesn't matter." I took his arm.

The mist had gathered into a fine drizzle, drenching the already melting snow.

"I don't mean to interfere," the Englishman said, "but it's starting to rain. Do you think you can pull her car out?"

"Aye, that's what I do." Bo spooled out his winch cable and attached it to the rental car's undercarriage.

The Englishman slid into the driver's seat.

What—am I helpless? My annoyance flared and settled. The man had a moral duty to help me. The accident was his fault. Mostly.

In less than five minutes, my car was free and parked safely on the side of the road. The Englishman pulled out his wallet. "What do I owe you?"

"It's a freebie." Bo grinned. "Mrs. Bill's my friend." He bent to look in my eyes. "Are you sad still? Do you miss Bill a lot?"

"I remember the good times, and that makes me happy." A lie, but sometimes the truth isn't helpful. "How are you? Still living on the croft?"

"A'course I am." His smile faded. "I'm grand."

"I'm here till Sunday. How about we grab a meal?" I made a note to find out more about that unconvincing *I'm grand*.

Bo's face lit up. "The pub? We went there with Bill. Remember?"

How could I forget? Bo had single-handedly devoured two Highland game pies with neeps and tatties. We'd plugged the juke box with coins and danced like kids to the Isley Brothers. I smiled at him. "Call you tomorrow."

He climbed into his pickup. "See you later, alligator." Bo adored rhymes.

I answered as Bill always had. "In a while, crocodile."

He tooted his horn and drove off.

The Englishman turned to me. "I ought to have introduced myself. My name is Tom Mallory."

"Thanks for your help, Mr. Mallory. I should go." I slipped my hands in my pockets to keep them warm.

"The name's Tom, and before you do, let me check for damage." He examined the rental car from all sides. "Brilliant. Nothing visible anyway." He pulled out a handkerchief and wiped his hands before extracting a card from a leather wallet and handing it over. "Contact me if you find something amiss later. My mobile number's there, at the bottom. You keep the leading zero when you're in—"

"I know how to make a phone call," I said. Prickly, I know.

His card bore a crest over the words Suffolk Constabulary,

Bury St. Edmunds. Beneath that was his name: Detective Inspector Thomas Mallory, CID. What was an English detective doing in the Inner Hebrides in late October? Tourist season was over.

"Your friend with the truck. Is he all right? I mean—" He stopped, unable or unwilling to put his question into words.

"He's fine." I felt protective. Why should Bo's condition have to be explained to a total stranger? "My husband was born on the island. He and Mr. Duff grew up together."

Confusion lingered on his face, and I relented. "Bo was born with a genetic syndrome, mild cognitive disability, some social deficits. He's a mechanical genius, and the best friend my husband ever had." I had to blink hard to clear my eyes.

"The Bill he mentioned. Your husband?"

"He died here three years ago."

"I'm sorry." He narrowed his eyes. "You're certain you're all right?"

"It's the island. I haven't been back since . . . since it happened." *Terrific.* Now I was explaining my own life to a stranger. I straightened my shoulders. "I'm Kate Hamilton. And you were right. I wasn't paying attention."

He flashed me a disarming half smile. "And I apologize. I did pull in front of you. One of the hazards of driving in unfamiliar territory."

"You're a visitor, then."

"As you are, I gather. Staying with family?"

"With my husband's sister." Why was I telling him all this? And why was he asking? I looked at him properly now. Midforties. About my own age. Aquiline nose, high cheekbones. He wore a brown waxed cotton field jacket with a corduroy collar, the pricey, English-country-set kind. I could picture him with a monk's cowl draped over his forehead, but his face was saved from asceticism by that disarming half smile and hazel eyes that crinkled at the corners.

"I really should be going." I felt myself on the brink of a blush.

"Please call if you find damage. Anything at all."

I got back in the driver's seat and spent several minutes retrieving the contents of my handbag from the floor of the car. I'd been in Scotland less than half a day, and I'd already lost my suitcase and nearly wrecked the rental car. And that wasn't the worst bit.

Now I had to face Elenor.

Chapter Two

❧

Twenty minutes later I made the sharp left turn at the south end of the island. Stone columns flanked the drive. A brass plaque on the left read GLENROTH HOUSE HOTEL. ELENOR SPURGEON, PROPRIETOR. An identical plaque on the right advised visitors to KILL YOUR SPEED.

The drive curved to the right and entered a manicured forest of pine, beech, and alder with an underlayer of rhododendrons, their leathery leaves scrolled and frosted with snow. A stocky man stood in one of the planting beds stringing tiny lights, his shoulders and flat cap beaded with rain. He stared as I drove past, acknowledging my wave with a barely perceptible nod.

I rounded the final curve and caught my breath. The ancient seat of the Glenroth MacDonalds still had the power to enchant. Scots Baronial. Four stories of local stone coated with harling, the traditional lime-based rough cast, rendering it impervious to the wet Highland climate. The house sat in a wooded glen, so perfectly situated the structure might have emerged, full-blown like Venus, from the native bedrock. Three flags flew from the gabled rooftop—the Union Jack on the left; St. Andrew's Cross, the Scottish national flag, on the right; and in the middle, highest of all in case anyone questioned where their loyalties lay, the banner of the Jacobite Rebellion, a white rose on a red field.

Several panel vans bearing the imprint of Posh Nosh Catering hunkered near the wide entrance. Otherwise the gravel lot was empty. I pulled into a spot facing the front garden.

I sat for a moment without moving. Retreat was still an option, but not one I'd be proud of later. And I'd come so far.

Grabbing my carry-on and slinging my handbag over my shoulder, I dodged the raindrops and dashed up the steps to the entrance. Pushing open the door, I caught a hint of lemon wax and something else, something warm and savory. Pastry? Cheese?

The reception hall was as lovely as I remembered. Marble blocks in a black-and-white checkerboard paved the floor. A wide staircase rose from the center of the room toward a broad landing, where it turned and climbed to the guest rooms on the upper floors. An enormous painting of Charles Edward Stuart in full Highland dress hung on the wall to my left. His head was bare, revealing his famous red curls. Glenroth House fiercely promoted the local legend that Bonnie Prince Charlie had spent his final night in Scotland, the nineteenth of September, 1746, in one of the house's many bedrooms. The fact that not a single historian endorsed this theory had done nothing to dampen the fervor of the island's faith.

A young, dark-haired woman sat behind a French ladies' desk to the left of the staircase. She rose and held out her hand. "Welcome to Glenroth House. You must be Elenor's sister-in-law. Kate, isn't it? I'm Becca Wallace, the receptionist." Her accent bore a trace of Irish, more Galloway than Highlands.

"Kate Hamilton." I set the carry-on down and took her hand.

"Elenor said to expect you. She told me about your husband's death. How awful for you."

I hate the obligatory expressions of sympathy. *You're too young to be a widow* or, worse, *I know how you feel*. One woman had actually said, "Things happen when they're supposed to, I guess." I'd felt like slapping her. People aren't supposed to become widows at the age of forty-three.

I smiled and changed the subject. "How long have you worked at the hotel?"

"Near eighteen months now. We're all fairly new, except Agnes MacLeod, of course. She's been around since the hotel opened. But then you know that." Becca Wallace tucked her black-coffee hair behind her left ear. On the right it fell in a glossy curtain, almost concealing a thin white scar that tugged at the corner of her mouth.

"Did the airline call?" I asked. "My suitcase didn't make it."

"I'm afraid not." Becca's brows drew together. "Do you have something to wear tonight?"

"Makeup and shoes."

Her mouth twitched. "I have a black dress you could borrow."

I glanced at her tiny figure. "Kind, but I don't think I'd fit."

Becca examined me. "Let's see what Nancy can do." She picked up the desk phone and pushed a few buttons. "Nancy, Kate Hamilton is here. They've lost her suitcase. Any ideas for tonight in case it doesn't arrive in the next couple of hours?"

In moments, a solidly built woman in a white chef's apron bustled through the door from the rear of the house. Early sixties was my guess. Her hair was threaded with silver and held back with tortoiseshell combs from which a few unruly tendrils had escaped. "Welcome to Glenroth, dearie." The smile was sunny, the accent pure Highlands. "I'm Nancy Holden, the chef." She untied her apron and pulled the loop over her head. "I'll take you to your cottage, shall I? Then we'll sort you out something to wear tonight. Just in case."

"I can't put you out like that. You're getting ready for the ball."

"Nae, lass. No trouble a'tall."

A cold draft swept through the room. Detective Inspector Tom Mallory shut the entrance door behind him and wiped his shoes on

11

the brown coir mat. He'd changed his ruined trousers for jeans. He stared at me. "I thought you were staying with family."

"I am," I said, surprised to see him too but enjoying his confusion.

"You've met, have you?" Nancy asked.

"Not officially." Tom ran a hand through his damp hair. "We, ah, ran into each other."

"Kate, this is Tom Mallory," Becca said, "our only guest at the moment. Besides you, of course. Mr. Mallory, this is Kate Hamilton, Mrs. Spurgeon's sister-in-law."

"Ah, yes, I see." He flashed me that charming half smile. "You've come for the ball. I'll see you tonight then." He laid an envelope on Becca's desk. "Promised my mother I'd write."

"Friend of Elenor's?" I asked when he'd gone.

"I don't think so." Becca slipped the envelope into a wire organizer. "She invited him to the ball, though, since he's staying at the hotel. We explained it's a local Chamber of Commerce event, but he seemed pleased to have been asked."

And Elenor would be pleased to have an attractive man to flirt with, even one a good decade younger. Not that I was one to quibble about age. Bill had been eleven years my senior, a fact that had caused my mother some initial angst. "Mr. Mallory and I are the only guests? I thought Elenor gave special rates to partygoers who wanted to spend the night."

Nancy and Becca exchanged glances.

"No more special rates." Becca flicked another look at Nancy. "And the locals aren't keen to pay full price."

I knew all about the prices Elenor charged, even for family. That's why Bill and I had stayed at the Harborview that last summer. "Is Elenor here?"

"Oh, aye," Nancy said, "but she'll no' be for long. Getting her hair done up."

"I should say hello."

"Of course, dearie." Nancy patted my arm. "Fetch me when you're ready. You'll find me in the kitchen."

Elenor's living quarters occupied most of the ground floor of the east wing. I faced the glossy white door and bit my lip. Three years of estrangement loomed between us, broken only the previous week when Elenor had telephoned in a panic. "I'm in trouble, Kate, and I don't have anyone else in the whole world." She hadn't actually said *now that Bill's gone, thanks to you*, but she didn't need to. I knew that's what she meant. Elenor was always great at guilt.

I knocked and the door opened in a cloud of flowery scent.

"Darling, how marvelous of you to come."

I gaped at her. Was this the same woman who'd told me I'd ruined her life and she'd never speak to me again?

Elenor was in the process of getting dressed. She wore a slim tweed skirt and a silky camisole. Her blonde hair was caught in a ponytail that made her look more thirty-something than fifty-three. She took my hand and pulled me into the flat. "Too bad about the weather. We haven't had snow like this since I was a girl."

"I've been worried about you," I said.

"You have?"

"You said you were in trouble. You said you needed help."

"Oh, I do. Only I have to be at the salon at four. But come look at something—while I finish dressing." She took my hand again.

I hated to be suspicious.

She led me through a pale blue-and-white living room and bedroom to a bathroom tiled in finely veined white marble. A table draped with a white bath towel held a small footed chest, a *casket* it would have been called in past centuries. The case appeared to be constructed of satinwood, but it was difficult to tell because the entire surface, top and four sides, was inlaid with designs in what looked to me like rosewood, mahogany, ebony, and a lighter, fine-grained wood. Boxwood, perhaps, or holly.

The first sign was a tingling in my fingertips. I felt blood rush to my cheeks. My mouth went dry and my heart raced. I knew the symptoms. I'd had them from childhood in the presence of an object of great age and beauty. My father, who'd taught me about antiques, had called me a *divvy*, an antique whisperer, drawn to the single treasure in a houseful of junk, able to spot a fake at fifty paces. An exaggeration, of course.

"What do you think?" Elenor was buttoning up a soft cashmere sweater. She looked as pleased with herself as a tabby presenting her human with a fat, furry mouse corpse.

"It's extraordinary." I moistened my lips and bent for a closer look. I'd seen some fabulous examples of marquetry in my time, but nothing like this. Tiny, fantastic creatures frolicked in a field of vines, berries, curling leaves, and stylized roses, all bordered with a fine checkered banding. The effect was magical, as if the work had been done by elves.

"The form says eighteenth century," I said, "but it's certainly not typical. The designs are curious. Almost oriental. Where did you find it?"

"That's the secret." Elenor tapped the casket lightly. "This is where it all began. I'll tell you the whole story after the ball. You can give it a proper going over then."

My stomach clenched. Is that why Elenor had insisted I come—not because she needed my help, not to heal old wounds as I'd hoped, but to do an appraisal? Never mind that I had an antique shop to run in Ohio. Never mind that I was in the middle of preparations for the prestigious Western Reserve Antique Show. Never mind that returning to Glenroth would rake up emotions I'd worked so hard to bury.

"You want a valuation." I fought to keep my tone neutral.

Elenor fastened a gold chain around her neck. "No. Well, yes, I wouldn't mind that actually. But there's something else. I want you to see it and tell me what you think."

Someone knocked. "Oh, for pity's sake." Elenor *tsk*ed and rushed off.
I heard the door open and Elenor say, "What is it now?"

"Do you want two or three servers pouring champagne tonight?
The caterers want to know." I knew that voice. Agnes MacLeod, Elenor's old friend and the hotel manager.

"Were three included in the proposal?"

"I don't know."

"I pay you to know these things, Agnes. How many did we have
last year?"

"I don't remember."

"*I don't know. I don't remember.*" Elenor mocked the words in a
high-pitched singsong. "Well, I suggest you find out, because if they
charge extra, it's coming out of your salary."

The door slammed and Elenor reappeared, finger-ironing her
forehead with small, swirly circles. "Stress causes wrinkles. Did you
know that? Sometimes I wonder why I put up with that woman."

Put up with that woman? Agnes MacLeod had been Elenor's loyal
friend for more than twenty years. She'd given up her teaching career
to help Elenor run the hotel.

"I'll get my coat." Elenor stopped and turned back. Her eyes glistened. "I am glad you're here, Kate. We haven't always seen eye to eye,
but I do need you. Something's going on and it's scaring me."

"Scaring you? Have you called the police?"

"I can't do that." Her eyelashes brushed her cheek. "I found something, and—oh, it's a long story, and there's no time now." She made
a helpless gesture and turned toward the bedroom, calling back over
her shoulder, "I left something for you in your cottage. A package.
Promise me you'll open it straightaway. It's important."

"Of course." I turned back to the casket. The old wood seemed to
glow against the white backdrop. I ran my fingers over the smooth-as-
silk joins.

Who made you? What stories could you tell?

"Come on, come on." Elenor slid her arms into the sleeves of a white mohair coat. "I'm going to be late."

I drew back my fingers in confusion. A word had formed in my head. Or the shadow of a word.

Murder.

Chapter Three

A steady rain dripped from the turrets and sheeted off the old window glass. Nancy Holden raised a green golf umbrella as we hurried down the front steps of the house and along the path to the sea. My mind was stuck on that curiously embellished casket. And *murder*.

I don't want to give the wrong impression. I'm not a psychic. I have no paranormal powers. I don't actually believe in such things. Nevertheless, I admit to having experienced something similar before. Nothing as definite as a word, mind you—just an impression, of joy or sadness or longing, as if the emotional atmosphere in which an object existed had seeped into the joints and crevices along with the dust and grime. The first time it happened I was a child, holding a crude wooden doll in my parents' antique shop. "Dolly was made a long time ago," my mother had said, "in a faraway place with no toy stores." I was wondering why the doll's owner had been so careless as to lose her when I felt a powerful surge of loneliness. Had the doll really been lost, or had she been discarded, unloved?

I'd never told a soul. Not my parents, not even Bill. Dismissing thoughts of ESP or second sight, I'd written these experiences off as the products of my overactive imagination, filing them away under the category of Unexplained Things like déjà vu and why men can never find anything in a refrigerator.

But *murder*—where had that word come from? Elenor's fear must have triggered it.

Nancy took my arm under the umbrella. "Where did you and your husband meet?"

"Cleveland. Case Western University. I was a graduate student. Bill was a law professor. Almost the first thing he told me about was this island. And the history of the house."

"Did he find it strange when Elenor turned their family home into a hotel?"

"He never said so, but then we were only here twice after the hotel opened, once for the grand opening and then three years ago when he—"

"Aye. I know, dearie." Nancy squeezed my arm.

I loved her for that.

Nearing the sea, the gravel path split in two. "Frank and I live there." Nancy pointed to a small stone cottage with an attached carport. "I'm sure I can find you something bonnie to wear."

"Thank you." I hoped I sounded gracious. If Becca's clothes were too small, Nancy's would be several sizes too big. I pictured myself arriving at the ball in a matronly knit two-piece. And I'd be obligated to wear it, now that Nancy was taking so much trouble.

"Follow the path to Applegarth," Nancy said. "If you give me your car keys, I'll have my husband drive your car around."

I stopped walking. "Elenor put me in Applegarth?" The name conjured images. A chill breeze off the water. The smell of a turf fire at night and strong coffee percolating in the morning. The feel of Bill's flannel shirt against my skin. The narrow, creaky bed.

"Is something wrong?" Nancy looked alarmed.

"Bill and I spent our honeymoon in Applegarth twenty-four years ago. Before the hotel was a hotel."

Her face relaxed. "Lovely." She rushed off, leaving me with my memories.

I stood on the path. No one would blame me if I asked for another cottage, or even one of the guest rooms in the main house. *Coward's way out.* I continued up the flagstone path.

The sound was what I remembered most about Glenroth—the steady pulse of the sea, the rush of the wind. Applegarth stood on a low rise overlooking Cuillin Sound. Unlike the estate's original stone outbuildings, the ex-caretaker's cottage was a relatively modern structure, timber clad, painted white with dark-green shutters. Framed by pines, the cottage matched the picture in my mind, and yet there was a subtle difference—like a long-lost photograph, the image both familiar and utterly alien.

A wreath of twisted bittersweet hung on the door. I opened the door and looked around in amazement. The simple kitchen I remembered was now a sleek modern space with granite countertops and a small cast-iron Aga. A king-size mahogany four-poster stood in place of the old iron bedstead, barely wide enough for two. Almost nothing remained of the cottage I remembered. Even the simple fireplace had been refaced with local stone. I dropped my carry-on, pulled out my cell phone, and punched the numbers.

"Hello," came a cheerful voice at the other end. "This is Linnea Larsen."

I smiled. Mom always answered her calls that way. "Well, I made it," I said, tucking the phone between my cheek and shoulder and beginning to unpack the welcome basket on the kitchen table. "Everything all right at the shop?"

"Splendid. I sold a Georgian teapot, a pair of gilt metal sconces, and that early Qing dynasty celadon vase."

I could hear the satisfaction in her voice. She was in her element. "You're the best in the business, Mom."

"How was the trip?"

"Long." I told her about the lost suitcase and the dense fog, deleting the near accident and the English detective.

"I'm surprised you went," she said. "You never liked Elenor."

I considered protesting, but what was the use? Mom could spot a fib faster than a certified appraiser could spot a flea-market forgery. "She's not making it easy. First she calls and tells me she's in trouble but can't explain because it's too complicated to go into over the phone. Now I've come all the way to Scotland, and she can't explain because she's late for a hair appointment. I feel manipulated."

"So why are you there?"

Ouch. My mother always puts her finger on the sore spot. "Elenor is Bill's sister," I said virtuously, tucking a bag of fresh-roasted coffee beans next to the fancy coffeemaker.

"And that obligates you to do whatever she asks forever?"

"Of course not, but I'm curious. Elenor's up to something. I want to know what it is."

"*Up* to something?" I heard the spark of interest in my mother's voice. She never could resist a mystery.

"She showed me a casket. Eighteenth century, I think, but it's something special, unusual. When I asked where she got it, she went all mysterious and said she'd tell me after the ball."

"Could you email me a photo?"

"First chance I get." I'd known Mom's curiosity would be piqued. Both my parents had loved the antique business, but it had been my mother who'd done the research, applying near-Sherlockian principles of observation and deduction to prize out the interesting details the customers loved.

"I ran into Bo Duff. I'm taking him out for a meal." I opened the refrigerator and found a dozen plump brown eggs, a block of farmhouse cheese, and a packet of locally made sausages.

"Give him my love."

"Mom. You've never met him."

"That doesn't matter. Give him my love anyway."

A series of beeps reminded me that I'd stupidly packed the charger cord in the outside pocket of my suitcase. My lost suitcase. "I think I'm losing you. I'll—" The call dropped.

I slipped the phone into my handbag. Mom wouldn't fret if I didn't call her back right away.

I'd inherited a lot from my mother—her passion for history, her natural curiosity (bordering on nosiness, some have thought), her dark mahogany hair and blue eyes. *Blue as the waters of the fjords*, my father used to say. What I had not inherited was her unflappable conviction that things generally turn out all right.

Because they don't.

I transferred my carry-on from the kitchen floor to the bench at the foot of the bed. Unzipping the top, I pulled out a pair of flannel pajamas, my quart-size plastic bag of toiletries, and a small silver frame, which I placed on the bedside table. The frame held a photograph of Bill in faded jeans and an old plaid shirt—his fishing uniform.

A wrapped package lay on the quilted counterpane. I untied the ribbon and peeled back layers of tissue. Inside was a book, a novel, *The Diary of Flora Arnott, Volume One*, by Dr. Hugh Parker Guthrie. The dust jacket pictured a raven-haired girl in a white Regency-style gown, a tartan shawl around her shoulders. The name Guthrie was familiar. I'd met a woman named Guthrie at the grand opening ten years ago, a pompous widow from one of the island's oldest families. She had a son, if I remembered correctly, off teaching history at some university near Aberdeen. I turned the book over. The author stared back at me through wire-rimmed glasses. *A real-life unsolved murder mystery*, declared the blurb. *Beginning in the Scottish Lowlands and ending on the Isle of Glenroth, we follow the short but remarkable life of Flora Arnott, who sacrificed everything for the sake of the man she loved.*

I thumbed through the book, finding an inscription on the title page: *For Kate, who knows the story*. I did know the story. Everyone connected with Glenroth knew it.

Bill and Elenor's childhood home had been the seat of the Glenroth

MacDonalds since the fourteenth century. After the defeat of the clans at Culloden, the estate was forfeited to the British Crown and granted to a Loyalist from Dumfries who planned to raise sheep on the island. Finding Highland life too rigorous, he sold the house and land to Abraham Arnott, a fellow Lowlander. Abraham never lived on the island, but in 1809 his son James brought his bride, Flora, to Glenroth. Their happiness ended less than a year later when Flora was murdered.

Dr. Guthrie had turned a piece of island history into a novel. Good for him.

From within the pages, papers fluttered to the floor. I picked them up, unfolding a sheet of the hotel's letterhead. The handwriting was Elenor's. *Kate, I really am in trouble this time. I need your advice, but read this book first.* The last words were heavily underlined. *Don't let me down. E.*

Her usual theatrics? I had dreaded Elenor's phone calls when Bill was alive. There was always some calamity. Like the time she forgot to pay her income taxes for two years. Like the time she had an affair with the headmaster of her school and lost her teaching position.

The second paper turned out to be a photocopy of two old newspaper articles.

The Hebridean Chronicle
9ᵗʰ March 1810

A shocking double murder was committed on Saturday last, 3ʳᵈ March, north of Angus Ransom's tavern on Glenroth. At dawn on the 4ᵗʰ a cabinetmaker on his way to Skye discovered two bodies on the road near the peat bogs. Mrs. Flora Arnott, wife of Capt. James Arnott, lay on the road, her neck pierced by an arrow. The body of her companion, Miss Gowyn Campbell, was found partially hidden in the brush. She had been stabbed in the back with a Highland dirk. How the women came to be there remains a mystery.

Capt. Arnott's settlement on the Isle of Glenroth has long been a point of contention with the local clansmen, who claim Glenroth House as sacred to the memory of Charles Edward Stuart. In a related development, an anonymous source reported the disappearance, the very night of the murder, of a young negro in the Capt.'s employ, the former slave known as Joseph. If anyone has seen such a person, he is urged to contact the Sheriff in Inverness.

Capt. Arnott remains in seclusion, from which he has issued a proclamation offering a reward of £100 to anyone who can shed light on this despicable deed or give any clue whereby the perpetrator or perpetrators may be brought to justice.

I rotated the page ninety degrees to read the second article.

The Hebridean Chronicle
18th January 1811

News has reached this desk of the tragic death of Capt. James Arnott of Glenroth. Searchers found his body in the woods near his estate on New Year's Day.

Readers may recall the shocking murders last spring of the Capt.'s young bride, their unborn child (as was later learned), and her companion. Sadly, that crime remains unsolved. The Capt.'s friends had hoped that his marriage last August to Miss Eliza Brodie would bring him a measure of comfort. They now fear the shock of his first wife's death may have permanently unbalanced his mind.

I frowned. No one had ever mentioned the existence of original accounts of Flora's death.

Someone rapped on the door.

"Your Fairy Godmother," Nancy Holden called out. "Bearing ball gowns."

Chapter Four

I turned up the collar of my jacket and dashed toward the hotel. The temperature had dropped, and the rain had turned to icy pellets bouncing off the gravel path. Another storm was on its way.

As I neared the house, pathway lighting gave way to flickering gas lamps that washed the facade with liquid gold. Candle flames danced in the windows. Plug-ins, I supposed, but they looked authentic. With a little imagination, it could be 1810. How extraordinary, I'd thought on our honeymoon, to live in a house mentioned in the history books. Bill had treated it with the inconsequence of familiarity. He'd been happy to sell his share to Elenor. I'd been happy, too. His share had paid for our lovely old Victorian in Jackson Falls and was currently putting our children through college.

Headlights swung an arc across the parking area. I shielded my eyes as a silver sedan careened toward the Carriage House. Someone had missed the speed warning.

Brakes squealed. A horn blared. Car doors slammed.

An older couple walking up from the self-park area met me where the paths converged. "Did you see that?" the woman asked.

"What happened?" I slowed my pace to walk with them.

"A near accident," the woman said. "A BMW and one of the valet cars."

"BMW's fault," added her companion, a man in a dark kilt and hose flashed with red ribbons. "She nearly broadsided him."

The woman *tsk*ed. "Nasty mouth on her, that one."

We'd reached the stone steps.

"What do you expect?" the man said. "Lady of the Manor."

* * *

The gathering room was a long rectangle, high ceilinged and dominated by the original inglenook fireplace. Tall windows looked out on a formal garden. Stone archways led to the main dining room, added along the rear of the house during Elenor's renovations.

Partygoers balanced plates of hors d'oeuvres and gestured with their drinks. I scanned the faces. Some looked familiar, but I've always been terrible with names. I plunged into a sea of tartan, avoiding a waiter carrying a tray of champagne flutes.

"Kate, over here." Becca Wallace's short red kilt showed off a pair of shapely legs.

"I think Elenor nearly broadsided someone with her car just now."

"I'm not surprised. She's a demon behind the wheel."

"But why is she so late? It's after seven."

"Grand entrance. Gets more attention that way."

"Is that your family tartan?" I asked, indicating her red kilt.

"Goodness, no. It's the staff uniform. We're expected to wear our kilts to all official events." She stepped back to look me over. "The dress is gorgeous. Fits you like a glove."

"A tight glove. I keep reminding myself to take shallow breaths." The dress Nancy and I had agreed upon—a strapless black taffeta with a full skirt and deep pockets—belonged to Nancy's married daughter, currently pregnant and living in Dundee. Nancy had managed to close the zipper on the third try. She'd added a tartan sash and pronounced it perfect. I slid my hands into the pockets and fanned out the skirt. "Makes me feel like a fifties film star."

A young man with rimless glasses and a thatch of sandy blond hair joined us. Becca slipped her hand through his arm. "Kate, this is my friend Geoff. Ignore the glassy stare. It's the dress."

Geoff turned pink and shoved his glasses higher on his nose.

"Kate is Elenor's sister-in-law," Becca told him. Then to me, "Geoff is a curator at the West Highland Living History Museum in Fort William."

Someone behind me swore. I turned to watch a middle-aged man in a tuxedo struggling to maneuver a wheelchair through the doorway. The occupant of the wheelchair, a silver-haired woman in a tartan shawl, pointed a lacquered fingernail toward the far end of the room. "Bar's over there." He bent to flip a lever, and the chair lurched forward. Instantly the man was cornered by two women dressed in matching tartan skirts, velveteen jackets, and black tam-o'-shanters dotted with decorative lapel pins.

"That man looks familiar," I told Becca.

"That's Dr. Guthrie, our local celebrity. He's written a novel about island history."

I took in the small nose, round pink cheeks, and slanting chin. The photograph on the book jacket had flattered him wildly.

"The woman in the wheelchair is his mother," Geoff said. "Closest thing Glenroth has to landed gentry these days."

The pompous widow. I remembered the blue eyes and silver hair but not the wheelchair. "Why are the women talking to him dressed alike?"

"The Arnott twins, Penny and Cilla." Geoff grinned. "Penny's the one on the left."

Penny Arnott was tall with a square jaw and jutting chin. Cilla was short and plump with a heart-shaped face and dimples. They had identical pageboy haircuts, but while Penny's hair was a coarse brown streaked with gray, Cilla's was pure white, fine as corn silk.

"I remember now," I said. "Bill pointed them out once. His father bought the estate from their father fifty years ago."

"I wonder if the twins realize that." Becca flashed me a wry smile. "They act as if they still live here. One day they'll probably find a couple of unoccupied bedrooms and move back in. Come on." She took my arm and steered me toward the fireplace where the twins stood warming their backs.

Hugh Guthrie had excused himself. Or escaped.

"Hello, Penny and Cilla," Becca said. "I'd like you to meet Kate Hamilton."

"The sister-in-law?" One of Penny's unruly eyebrows waggled. She held up two bony fingers, crossing them. "Close, are you?"

It took me a moment to figure out what she meant. "If you mean close to Elenor, we don't actually see each other that often. I live in the States."

Penny's mouth turned down, as if she doubted the truth of my assertion.

It might have been the heat of the fire or possibly my overactive imagination, but I felt as if she'd moved into my personal space. "Tell me about your pins," I said, taking a step back. The pressure of Becca's arm told me I'd made a mistake.

"The red one with the white rose is for the Defenders of Scotland." Cilla pointed at one of the larger pins on her sister's tam. "Women's Auxiliary."

Penny closed her eyes as if accessing her hard drive. "Our ancestor, Colonel Abraham Arnott, fought bravely at Culloden. One of the survivors. Returned to the West Indies after the defeat. His son, James, settled here in 1809 and—"

Penny had a peculiar, elliptical way of speaking. Captain Hook with a Scottish brogue. I stifled a giggle. All she needed was an eye patch.

It took us a full ten minutes to extricate ourselves.

Geoff handed us each a glass of champagne. "Another five minutes and I'd have staged a rescue."

I sipped my champagne, feeling the bubbles tickle my nose.

An enormous man with dark, wavy hair circled the hors d'oeuvres table. He wore a tuxedo with a green-and-blue tartan cummerbund and matching bow tie.

"That's Jackie MacDonald, right?" I whispered to Becca.

"Well spotted, Kate, although Jackie is rather hard to forget."

I took another sip of champagne.

Tom Mallory stood in a circle of women near one of the stone archways. Seeing me, he waved. It looked like a *come save me* wave, the kind Bill used to do when cornered by a pack of academics chasing some theory to ground. More likely, Tom expected me to join his admirers. I gave him a brief smile.

It was nearly eight when Elenor finally swept in. She wore a blue velvet, off-the-shoulder gown with a wool sash in the soft blues and greens of the Ancient Hamilton hunting tartan. Her hair was gathered at her neck in an elaborate knot. Spotting me, she sailed over.

"Thank you for the book," I said. "Where did you find the newspaper—"

"Shhh, not here." She flapped her hand as if erasing my words in the air.

A gong sounded.

"You're with me at the head table." Elenor took me by the elbow and propelled me toward the dining room. I glanced over my shoulder.

"See you later," Becca said. "Peasants sit near the kitchen."

Fires blazed in huge stone fireplaces at each end of the dining room. Round tables had been laid with crisp white linen and centerpieces of white roses and purple heather. A banner hung over the band platform: WELCOME TO THE TENTH ANNUAL TARTAN BALL.

I found my place next to a woman already seated, a thin woman with a long neck and dark hair molded to a small round head. The name that popped into my head was *Olive Oyl*. "Hello," I said, praying her real name would come to me.

"Oh, Kate. Remember me? Dora MacDonald, Jackie's wife. We own the Tartan Gift Shop."

Of course. How could I have forgotten? Privately, Bill and I had called them Olive Oyl and Bluto.

Dora downed her champagne and plunked the glass on the table near several empties. Jackie appeared and handed his wife another flute. "Wee Kate," he beamed. "Grand to see you again, lass."

Across the table, Hugh Guthrie was attempting to position his mother's wheelchair.

"You make such a fuss, Hugh." Mrs. Guthrie grabbed the wheels of her chair. "Now hand me that napkin and sit down."

Guthrie sat between his mother and Elenor, looking as if his license to exist had just expired. The remaining two seats at the table were claimed by Penny and Cilla Arnott.

"Has everyone met Kate Hamilton?" Jackie asked.

Guthrie rose, holding his napkin. "Hugh Guthrie. And this is my mother, Margaret."

"We've met," Margaret said in a rich alto voice. She eyed my bare shoulders. "You must be chilly, dear. Let me know if you need my shawl."

Ooo, nasty. "How sweet."

Jackie stepped up to the microphone. *Tap, tap, tap.* His white teeth gleamed in the spotlight.

Dora leaned in my direction. "Still gorgeous, isn't he?"

"Very handsome," I said truthfully.

"He got his looks from his mother. She was a MacDonald, too, from another branch of the family. Jackie says we should be living in this house." She poked me with a sharp elbow. "But not around Elenor or the Arnott twins."

Jackie unhooked the microphone. "As president of the Chamber of Commerce, I welcome you to the Tenth Annual Tartan Ball. We have a lot to celebrate. This year's tourist season has broken all records, and we know who to thank for that, don't we?" He raised his glass and saluted the head table. "As of October first, *The Diary of Flora Arnott* has sold more than twenty thousand copies. Our island is quickly becoming a pilgrimage site for the growing ranks of Flora-philes. He raised his glass again. "*Sláinte*. God bless Hugh Guthrie. And God bless Flora Arnott, may she rest in peace."

"Sláinte," echoed the crowd.

Hugh Guthrie appeared to shrink in his seat.

Spoons clinked on water glasses. Jackie MacDonald resumed his seat at the head table between his wife and Elenor, who made room for the big man by moving her chair so close to Dr. Guthrie she could have eaten off his plate.

Margaret Guthrie scowled.

Waiters appeared with the main course.

Jackie tucked a napkin in his collar and turned to me. "I still think of you as a new bride. How are you getting on?"

"Poor Kate." Dora's eyes glistened with sympathy or alcohol or both. "It can't have been easy, raising those children by yourself."

I forced a smile. Why was I always *poor Kate*? "Eric and Christine are both in college. Doing well. No significant others." I crossed my fingers under the table. Christine's history with men ranked somewhere between Miss Havisham and Monica Lewinsky.

Later, as the waiters cleared the main course, Jackie took the stage again and the guests settled in for the evening program. "Our first order of business tonight is to announce the winners of the Eighty-Second Annual Glenroth Archery Tournament. Ladies and gentlemen, I give you our new champions"—the band played a drum roll—"Frank Holden and Dora MacDonald."

I blinked as the audience exploded into applause.

Dora stood and swayed briefly. Stabilizing, she made her way to the podium, where she joined a man with a wrestler's build and short-cropped gray hair, the man I'd seen working in the planting beds. Nancy Holden's husband, I presumed.

Trophies were presented. Speeches were declined.

"Now please," Jackie said, "everyone rise for the traditional toast."

The crowd, having imbibed freely by this time, stood as best they could, locking arms and swaying together. It wasn't easy with Dora MacDonald leaning on me.

Bonnie Chairlie's noo awa', we sang. *Safely ower the friendly main; Mony a heart will break in twa', should he ne'er come back again.* I knew the words by heart. Bill would sing them after a couple of glasses of red wine. *Will ye no come back again? Will ye no come back again? Better lo'ed ye canna be, Will ye no come back again?*

"Raise your glasses," Jackie said, "to the prince across the sea, Charles Edward Louie John Casimir Sylvester Severino Maria Stuart. *Sláinte mhor.*"

Glasses clinked. Eyes misted over. Sláinte mhor, *To the health of the woman*, the coded Jacobite toast, referring to Charlie disguised as Flora MacDonald's maid. Humiliating, I'd have thought, but all accounts said Charlie donned the skirt, shawl, and cap quite cheerfully.

"'Tis now my privilege," Jackie said as the audience took their seats, "to introduce tonight's special guest from the Noble and Sacred Order of the Forty-Five. Please welcome—"

A woman with bony shoulders and a beaklike nose made her way to the platform. Jackie handed her the microphone. I'd missed the woman's name. Dora MacDonald had knocked over her glass of champagne and borrowed my napkin to soak up the mess.

"As you know," said the woman in a fluty voice, "the Noble Order exists to honor the heroes of Culloden and to cherish in our hearts the memory of our glorious and rightful king. Each year we choose a worthy recipient for our grant program, and tonight we are pleased to present to the Isle of Glenroth Historical Society a check for twenty thousand pounds to be used for the erection of a statue—"

Cilla Arnott squealed. Penny dabbed her eyes with her napkin.

"—honoring Glenroth's illustrious son and savior of this historic house, Captain James Arnott. Not only did Captain Arnott's father fight with the Bonnie Prince at Culloden, but he himself fought in the war on Scottish shipping interests in the Caribbean."

Huh? I had a graduate degree in history. Was the woman talking about pirates?

Cameras flashed at the tableau surrounding a huge cardboard check.

"Accepting on behalf of the Society," Jackie said, "are Miss Penelope and Miss Priscilla Arnott. Ladies? Any remarks?"

Cilla shook her head.

Penny leapt onto the platform and pounced on the microphone. "Tonight's honor—long overdue, I might add—is the fulfillment of a dream conceived by our father more than sixty years ago. To see our esteemed ancestor honored in a way appropriate to his exalted place in our island's history is entirely—"

Dora MacDonald listed slowly in my direction, her chin coming to rest on her right bicep. "Twins'll never stop talking about this. 'S been their life's dream."

I crossed my legs, smoothing the crisp taffeta skirt over my knees. As I did, I felt something in one of the pockets. Reaching in, I pulled out a scrap of paper on which someone had printed two words in large capital letters.

GO HOME.

Chapter Five

I stared at the words in disbelief.

Had someone slipped the note in my pocket without my noticing? Possibly. The gathering room had been jammed, and there'd been a crush funneling into the dining room. But why would someone want me to go home? I bit the corner of my lip. That didn't make sense. More likely the note had been in the pocket of the dress all along—a joke, meant for Nancy's daughter. I slipped it back in the pocket. I would show it to Elenor, though, just in case.

Penny Arnott concluded her speech, and the Highland Rovers launched into a Celtic folk tune. A number of couples stood up to dance, including Elenor and Jackie MacDonald, who turned out to be remarkably light on his feet. Was Dora the jealous type? If she was, it didn't matter. She was snoring softly.

The twins were in their own world, whispering happily behind their napkins.

A waiter tried to set a dessert plate in front of Margaret Guthrie, but she pushed it away impatiently. "I didn't ask for this."

Too bad. She could use a little sweetening up.

Hugh Guthrie kept glancing toward the exit. I half expected him to slip under the table like my kids used to do when they wanted to escape boring adult conversation.

The band, who'd transitioned to contemporary classics, was sliding into Etta James's *At Last*. Lights from the chandeliers twinkled over-head. Couples swirled on the dance floor. I experienced a pang of jealousy. Widowhood stinks.

"Care to dance?" Tom Mallory held out his hand.

My heart thumped alarmingly. The last time I'd danced with anyone other than Bill was—well, too long ago to remember. Taking his hand, I followed him onto the dance floor.

He slipped an arm around my waist. "That's quite a dress."

I felt myself blush. I'd never have worn a dress like that to the faculty club dances. But then the faculty club had been overstocked with Margaret Guthries.

"What do you think of Glenroth?" I asked a shade too brightly.

"Quiet. Just what the doctor ordered."

"You should see it in summer. The beaches are packed. Some of the locals open their homes for bed and breakfast."

"And Glenroth House?" He pulled me in for a turn, avoiding a couple whose dancing skills were more exuberant than skillful.

A bubble of pleasure caught in my throat. "The hotel attracts mostly English and Americans," I said, trying not to sound breathless. "The upscale crowd—you know, showing off their designer sportswear and comparing investments over cocktails in the garden. Once a week everyone dresses up and pretends they're lost in the Highlands, like in *Brigadoon*. Not that it doesn't sound appealing. Lost in the High-lands, I mean." I was chattering.

"At the moment I much prefer being here."

Good-looking and smooth.

His hand was warm on my back. He smelled nice, a kind of mas-culine, woodsy scent that made me think of bonfires and starry nights. I closed my eyes and rested my cheek against his shoulder.

Someone tapped my arm. "Cutting in, dearie. Hope you don't mind." One of Tom's lady admirers smirked wickedly. The lady's part-ner, a man in a red tartan bow tie, held out his hand. "Shall we?"

"Do you mind if I take a rain check?" I hoped I wasn't offending him, but my conscience had been bothering me. Agnes MacLeod and I weren't exactly friends, but I knew she'd feel slighted if I didn't make an effort to speak with her.

I located the staff table near the double doors to the kitchen. There were only six of them at the table, including Geoff, Becca's guest. Less than half the number of staff members I remembered from the grand opening. As I threaded my way through the crowd, I saw Becca whisper something in Geoff's ear. He threw back his head and laughed. A man in love, I thought with another pang of jealousy.

A striking woman with high cheekbones and smooth olive skin sat on Geoff's left. A thick ebony braid fell halfway down her back. Gold hoops hung from her ears. Like the other staff women, she wore a red tartan kilt, but on her it looked almost exotic. I wondered if she was Romani, a gypsy.

Nancy Holden looked lovely, her hair tamed into a sleek twist. Her husband, Frank, ran a finger between his neck and the collar of his shirt. He leaned toward her and spoke something in her ear before leaving the table, his trophy in hand.

Agnes MacLeod had teased her hair into a frizzy gray nimbus that, together with her sharp nose and receding chin, gave her the unfortunate look of an elderly hedgehog.

I gave the group at the table a cheery wave.

Nancy welcomed me. "I believe you know everyone except Sofia." She indicated the exotic-looking woman next to Geoff. "Sofia, this is Kate. She was married to Elenor's brother."

Sofia looked at me through her long, dark eyelashes and bestowed a smile worthy of a princess.

I gave Agnes a hug and took the seat next to her, the one vacated by Frank Holden. "How have you been?

"What?" She tipped one ear toward me.

"How are you?" I shouted over the band.

"Me? Oh, I'm dandy." The sour expression on her face communicated the opposite. "No one told me you'd arrived."

If Agnes had a fault, it was a tendency to assume she was being overlooked. "I saw Elenor, but only for a minute." I had decided not to mention the argument I'd overheard, but it occurred to me that Elenor, who liked nothing better than rubbing things in, might mention it herself. "I couldn't help overhearing your conversation about the champagne pourers. I'm sorry. You didn't deserve that."

Agnes snorted. "Take the extra charge out of my paycheck? Ha-ha. What Elenor pays me wouldn't keep a teenager in bubble gum."

She was making a joke of it, but I could tell she was hurt.

The music ended. Couples stood on the dance floor waiting for the next song to begin when Elenor appeared at the microphone. "Please, everyone, return to your tables. I have something important to say."

I stood to leave, but Agnes pulled me down. "No, stay."

"Dear friends." Elenor's hair shone white-gold in the spotlight. "I have two announcements, both of which will come as a surprise. First, I have decided to sell the hotel."

Silence descended, broken only by the sound of chairs scraping the floor as people turned toward the bandstand for a better view. Elenor smoothed her tartan sash. "On January first, this wonderful hotel will become part of Stately Homes & Castles, a chain of country house hotels based in Switzerland. I intend to stay on until spring to help with the transition."

"Doing what?" Agnes muttered. "Getting your nails lacquered?"

Agnes always did have a wicked sense of humor. She made me laugh. But this bitterness was new. Agnes used to orbit around Elenor like a soft, adoring moon.

Heads turned toward a commotion at the head table. Dora Mac-Donald staggered to her feet and pointed a shaky finger at Elenor. "Swiss people? From Swi'zerland? What about Scottish Night at the hotel an' all those kilts we sell?"

"Nothing to worry about, Dora." Jackie tried to pull her back into her seat. "If we have to, we'll just exchange those kilts for lederhosen."

Dora shook him off. Outrage seemed to be sobering her up. "In case you hadn't noticed, Elenor, the Tartan Gift Shop is how we make our living."

Murmurs of agreement rose from the audience.

"See? I'm not the only one. But you don't care, do you?" Pink splotches flared on Dora's cheeks. "As long as you're happy, everyone else can go and take a flying—"

Jackie stood and clamped his massive hand over Dora's mouth. "Time to go, I think." He began marching her toward the exit.

Dora wasn't finished. "We all depend on the hotel," she howled over her shoulder. "Do you have any idea how much we've invested in tartan clothing and fabric and gifts and—" Her words faded as she and Jackie disappeared through the stone archways.

All eyes pivoted to Elenor. She cleared her throat. "There will be changes, naturally. The new owners will have their own ideas, their own people. But there's nothing to worry about, I promise. The excellence of Glenroth House, its famous cuisine and outstanding reputation, will continue."

"How very comforting," Agnes said tartly.

"And now for my second announcement," Elenor said, "which will explain *why* I have decided to sell the hotel." She extended a slim arm toward Hugh Guthrie at the head table.

He joined her on the platform with the look of a prisoner awaiting sentencing.

"Hugh and I are to be married." Elenor beamed. Guthrie studied the top of his left shoe. "In April, right here at Glenroth House."

What? I realized my mouth had dropped open, and I snapped it shut.

"Hugh's publisher has arranged a book-signing tour. It will be our honeymoon. When we return, we intend to make our home in

Edinburgh, where Hugh will complete the manuscript for his new book. And . . ." Elenor drew the word out provocatively. "I promise you're in for *quite* a surprise."

Guthrie looked surprised himself.

"The only thing left is to make it official." Elenor threaded her hand through his arm, possibly to prevent his escape.

Guthrie gawked at the audience. At last he reached into the pocket of his tuxedo jacket and extracted a blue velvet ring box, which he surrendered into Elenor's grasp. She opened the box, slid a ring on her left hand, and held it up for everyone to admire. An enormous diamond caught the lights over the bandstand, reflecting them around the room like a mini disco ball.

Someone began a slow clap.

I peered around heads to view the head table.

Cilla Arnott appeared to be sobbing into her napkin. Penny, red-faced, was patting her back. Margaret Guthrie sat as still as a wax figure, but the set of her shoulders radiated disapproval.

As if things weren't bizarre enough, the band began to play "Going to the Chapel."

Elenor held up both hands. "Before we celebrate, there's someone Hugh and I wish to acknowledge." She turned toward the head table. "Margaret, may I call you Mother now?"

Every head in the room swiveled toward Margaret Guthrie, sitting like a ramrod in her wheelchair. She looked as if she'd just taken a swig of sour milk.

"Even though Hugh and I will no longer be living on Glenroth," Elenor said, her eyes glittering, "we will always have your welfare uppermost in our minds. Wherever you choose to live—now that Hugh will no longer be able to care for you himself—please remember that we will do everything in our power to make the days you have left happy ones."

I heard a few audible gasps. Guthrie pulled a handkerchief from his inside pocket and mopped his face.

Margaret Guthrie reared up like a cobra in her wheelchair. "You are too hasty, my dear. I'm certain my son has agreed to no such plans." She turned to Hugh. "Take me home now. I'm tired."

The audience held its collective breath.

Hugh Guthrie stood motionless, a pile of metal shavings between two powerful magnets. He looked at Elenor, then at his mother, and seemed to quail. Releasing himself from Elenor's grip, he stepped from the platform and hurried to Margaret's side. The wheelchair squeaked through the stone archways toward the exit. Moments later we heard the thud of the heavy front door closing, followed shortly by the roar of an engine and the crunch of tires on gravel.

Elenor still held the microphone, her face frozen in a smile.

The band began to play "Some Enchanted Evening." Clearly one of the musicians had a wicked sense of humor, too.

"I should go to her," I whispered to Agnes.

By the time I made it to the head table, Elenor was already seated. With the MacDonalds and the Guthries gone, only the Arnott twins remained. Penny glared at Elenor—in furious disbelief, if I read her expression rightly. She threw her napkin on the table. "Party's over, Cilla. We're going home."

I moved next to Elenor at the big, empty table, scrambling for words of comfort. As it turned out, I didn't need them. Without a word, Elenor rose and walked from the room, her head held as high as Mary, Queen of Scots' on her way to the scaffold.

I watched her go. Two things were clear: first, Elenor had just ticked off the entire island; and second, that talk we were supposed to have was not going to happen tonight.

* * *

It was after midnight when Nancy and I finally made our way from the hotel toward Applegarth Cottage. Snow was falling thickly now, ankle deep on the path. I carried my heels, thankful for the pair of molded rubber wellies Nancy had loaned me. "Once in a decade," she said, shaking her head. "Must be that climate change they talk about."

She took my arm. "Unusual evening."

"Very," I agreed, thinking a more accurate term would be *bizarre*. After Elenor's departure, half the guests had followed suit, citing headaches, unreasonable childminders, and the impending storm. The other half, true Scots, stayed till the end, grimly determined to squeeze every penny's worth out of the price of admission. I danced with the man in the red tartan bow tie and most of the remaining male guests as well. All but Tom Mallory. He'd escaped soon after Elenor, just my luck.

I stayed to help Nancy with the cleanup. Becca had been given the night off on the strength of Elenor's earlier promise to chip in. Obviously that wasn't going to happen, so I'd insisted. Cleanup went quickly. The caterers packed up and headed out while the ferry to the mainland was still in operation. Agnes stripped the table linens and helped Sofia sweep the oak floors and mop the puddles in reception. Nancy and I dealt with the mountain of dishes and silverware, stacking the commercial dishwashers three times. Frank, after delivering the last of the valets, doused the fires and secured the bar. Then he headed out to do some task Nancy seemed to consider unnecessary or unwise. "At this time of night?" I heard her ask him. I didn't hear his reply, but I saw her lift her hands as if to say *so be it*.

Agnes and Sofia finished up around eleven fifteen. Sofia headed for the Lodge, the dormitory Elenor had built to accommodate the seasonal workers. Agnes went to her flat directly above Elenor's on the first floor—what we Americans call the second story.

Nancy and I were the last to leave. As Nancy stopped to turn the heavy lock on the front door, we saw lights from Elenor's flat spilling out on the snow below her windows.

"Poor thing must have fallen asleep with the lights on," Nancy said. "Probably cried herself off."

I doubted that. More likely Elenor was awake and plotting painful ways to murder Margaret Guthrie. Where the pathway split, Nancy and I parted company. She hugged me. "Thank you, Kate." She looked exhausted.

Five minutes later I opened the door to Applegarth Cottage, flipped on the lights, and stood for a moment, unable to comprehend what I saw. My handbag, which I'd left on a kitchen chair, lay on the floor, the contents strewn everywhere. I ran into the bedroom. My carry-on, which I'd zipped and tucked under the bench at the foot of the bed, sat in the middle of the floor, the zipper open.

It took a moment for my brain to catch up. Then I got it.

Someone had searched my cottage.

Chapter Six

〜

My first thought was for my wallet. I spotted it under the kitchen table.

My heart sank. There went my credit cards and the two hundred pounds I'd taken from the ATM at the Glasgow airport.

Wrong. Every card, every bill was still there.

What was the intruder after if not money?

My second thought was to run to the Holdens' cottage for help, but then I remembered that Frank might not have returned from wherever it was he'd gone, and what could Nancy do? Besides, the intruder might still be out there in the dark. The safest thing was to stay put and use the telephone. I raced around the cottage, making sure the doors and windows were locked and the curtains tightly drawn. Then I located the hotel directory. A section labeled SECURITY/EMER-GENCIES listed three numbers—the emergency services on Skye, the police station on the mainland at Mallaig, and one of the hotel's extensions with the words 24 HOURS in parentheses. I dialed the hotel and got a recording: "You've reached Glenroth House. Please leave a detailed—"

I hung up and dialed again. Someone had to be awake at the police station.

It took some minutes to get through to the constable in charge. When I explained what had happened, he told me the entire area was under an amber snow alert. Ferries had ceased operation at eleven and the causeway between Skye and the mainland had been shut down shortly after that. The Isle of Glenroth was cut off. Could I wait until morning? I said I could and accepted his offer to have the duty clerk call back at intervals to check on me. Then I climbed into bed and lay in the dark, listening to the rafters creak and the wind rattle the downspouts. The digital clock on the bedside table flicked from 12:44 to 12:45.

The air was cool, the duvet soft and warm. I'd thrown my clothes, the only ones I possessed at the moment, in the washer/dryer, and the soft *thrump thrump* should have lulled me to sleep instantly. Not a chance. Thoughts of the intruder circling the cottage alternated with images of Elenor's face when the man who loved her had sided with his mother.

If Guthrie did love her, that is.

One of the dark thoughts plaguing my mind after Bill's death was the idea that he'd abandoned me. I knew it wasn't true—Bill hadn't wanted to die—but the notion refused to budge, looping through my brain like one of those blasted earworms. I stretched out my arm, resenting the emptiness. Bill should be there beside me. He was the reason I'd come to Glenroth in the first place.

The memory returned, as vivid as the scent of the musk roses I'd planted near our front porch in Jackson Falls. Bill and I were sitting on the glider. Fireflies winked in the warm July evening. My feet were in his lap. "You will look out for Elenor," he'd said in his soft Scottish burr, "if anything happens to me."

I'd pulled away. "What do you mean? Nothing's going to happen, is it?"

"Not if I can help it. But promise me, Kate. Please."

So I did, and two weeks later he was gone.

The dryer stopped. The clock on the mantel ticked like a metronome. The bedside clock flipped to 12:50. I should have been sleeping. Instead I was waiting for phone calls from the duty clerk at Mallaig. Oh well. I was never going to sleep anyway.

Hugh Guthrie's book lay unopened on the bedside table. I sighed and flipped on the lamp. I really must stop making rash promises.

Hazelbank House, Lochweirren, Ayrshire
26th September 1808
To-day is my 15th birthday & Father declares I must marry. He has given Grandmother an allowance for gowns & instructed Mrs. Poole to train Gowyn to attend me. My hair, which he called wild, is to be arranged in the latest fashion. No longer am I free to wander the estate, nor am I to ride Turk without a saddle. I am to be a Lady, groomed, gowned, and paraded about like one of the Duke's prize racehorses

Father, having no son to take charge of me should he die, pretends to be concerned for my welfare, but I know it is pounds & shillings he wants. Through a series of foolish ventures, Father has lost both his own modest fortune & poor Mamma's greater one. He paces the house in a black despair while daily the Post brings fresh demands. He is convinced that an influx of cash will set things right & I am to be the means of this happiness, for Father (it is plain) hopes to prevail upon a wealthy son in law. It is hard having no Mother to advise me.

To-night, as a kind of rehearsal, I was dangled before Sir Charles Murray, who is fond of saying he would be 6th Duke of Atholl were several of his relation to perish together. He himself is quite venerable, a widower with several children, the eldest a girl near my own age. At dinner he thought to impress me with tales of his exploits in Malta. He has a long red face & a kind of braying laugh that puts me in mind of a donkey. He also has twenty thousand a year, which makes Father quite in love with him.

After dinner, pleading a sore head, I made my escape & met Gowyn in the garden. She presented me with this diary, fashion'd herself from writing paper & stiff board covered in red calico from my old summer frock. The rest she is cutting up for a pieced quilt, which shall be mine, says she, when I am betrothed. I cannot help wondering how long she has been privy to a scheme communicated to me only this morning.

The next entries concerned preparations for Flora's debut, a time-consuming affair and an expense her father resented but agreed to on the grounds (as Flora's grandmother put it) that the first step in making hare stew is to catch the hare. A month after Christmas, Flora made her entrance into society at a ball given by the Murrays of Ashley Park, a fifteen-mile journey from Lochweirren.

21ˢᵗ January 1809
    The servants went by Post on Wednesday. Grandmother & I arrived the following day in her ancient barouche, frozen solid, limp as rags & bruised from bumping along the Turnpike, but in state nonetheless, pretending the journey had been pleasant & the shocking fortune spent on my gowns had not reduced Father to the borrowing of a carriage. To-night I wore my ivory silk with Mamma's pearls. Grandmother says a good figure will go a long way, but I wonder how far a fine bosom & narrow waist can take me in the absence of a dowry.
    Sir Charles claimed the first dance but soon huffed & puffed, begging that I excuse him as his new slippers were causing him pain. My other dancing partners were a distinguished lot. Several spoke nonsense. Two trod on my feet. One, the younger son of some Viscount or other, had sense enough but as little interest in the game as I & we satisfied ourselves by saying very little

*through a Quadrille & a Reel. I fear what Father will say when
I return home without a proposal of marriage. If I were to meet
a gentleman of sense & character, I would accept him gladly
enough.*

I marked the page and closed the book. Until tonight, Flora's story
had been no more than a sad tale of long-ago events. People don't cry
over the death of Joan of Arc anymore, do they? But Hugh Guthrie
had brought Flora to life. She was now a living soul, a flesh-and-blood
girl who'd known loss, who'd coped with her circumscribed role in
society with intelligence and humor. Was this why Elenor had insisted
I read the novel? Was seeing Flora in this new light a preparation for
whatever it was she wanted to tell me? In September 1808, Flora was
fifteen, a child determined not to be a pawn in her father's financial
schemes. In September 1809, she stood in what was now the gathering room of Glenroth House and pledged her hand and her heart to
Captain James Arnott. Five months later she was dead. Why?

I leaned back against the soft pillow and let my thoughts drift to
that woodsy scent and charming half smile. *Stop it*, I scolded myself.
I knew nothing about the tall Englishman with the smooth dance
moves—or was that precisely why I had allowed myself to think of
him? Our lives were on different tracks, headed in opposite directions.
The chance of our paths crossing a second time were slim to none.

Chapter Seven

❧

Saturday, October 29

I flung my hand out of the warm cocoon of the duvet. The shadow of a dream, dark and menacing, hovered beyond reach. My eyelids flickered as the events of the previous night came back with a rush—the Tartan Ball, Elenor's announcements, the intruder.

I squinted at the clock: 9:12. *Yikes.* I had to get up and get dressed. The constable at Mallaig had promised to send someone out that morning, rather halfheartedly, now that I thought of it. Maybe I had overreacted. Nothing had been taken. No one was hurt.

I slid out of bed and padded to the window in my bare feet. A fresh layer of wet snow flocked the pines. The turquoise sea had turned the color of oxidized silver. This morning I'd tell Elenor about the intruder. And the note in the pocket of the dress. Assuming she was in the mood to talk. I stretched and stiffened my resolve. In the mood or not, she owed me an explanation.

A waffle-weave robe embroidered with the hotel logo—a thistle— hung on the back of the bathroom door. I layered it over my pajamas and headed for the kitchen. The fireplace was already banked with logs. Removing the spark screen, I struck one of the long wooden matches and turned the starter key, hearing the soft *wh-oosh* as the gas ignited. When the kindling caught, I turned off the gas, replaced the screen, and sat on the hearth, letting the flames warm my back. I should phone Bo Duff right now, before he headed out for the day. Lunch or dinner, his choice. Unless Elenor had other plans. If so, there was always Sunday. My flight to London didn't leave till eight PM. I'd spend a few days with Christine in Oxford, then fly home for some time with my mother before she returned to Wisconsin.

Bo's number was listed in the slim island directory. After ten rings, I hung up. If he didn't answer, he wasn't home. Simple.

I poured a cup or so of coffee beans into the automatic grinder and breathed in the rich, earthy aroma. My grandmother used to say Norwegians were born with coffee in their veins. She also used to say, "Only dead fish follow the stream." I still don't understand that one, but it reminded me I was starving. I'd barely eaten at the ball the night before. There'd been no room in that sexy black dress. I found an enameled skillet and fried up two thick slices of streaky bacon and two large eggs with deep orange yolks. I was finishing the last bite when the cottage phone rang.

"Mrs. Hamilton? This is Detective Sergeant Bruce of Police Scotland."

"Oh, yes. I thought you'd call this morning."

"You did? Why is that?"

"Well, because of the intruder."

"I don't know anything about an intruder. I'm calling about another matter. Could you come to the hotel, please? As quickly as you can."

"Why? What's happened?"

"I'd rather speak with you in person."

"Tell me now. I insist."

"Elenor Spurgeon's body was found this morning. I'm sorry. She's dead."

*   *   *

Elenor dead? *Dead?*

I took the steps two at a time, nearly sliding on the slick stone. Had she fallen? Suffered a heart attack? The policeman said her body had been found near the Historical Society. That made no sense.

A howl pierced the air. I pushed open the big entrance door to find Agnes MacLeod sprawled in Becca Wallace's desk chair. Becca was fanning her with a file folder. Nancy held her hand. "There now, dearie, there now." Nancy looked up, her face pale. "Kate. You've heard."

A man in a black police uniform leaned against the newel post at the foot of the staircase. His face was deeply lined. "Mrs. Hamilton?" He flashed me his ID badge. "I'm Constable Mackie from the police station at Mallaig. The detective inspector is with someone at the moment. He'd like a word in the conservatory at ten thirty."

"Of course." I glanced at the long-case clock. Just after ten. I didn't know what to do. My tongue felt thick. My feet were rooted to the floor. I made a strangled sound and clutched my throat. *Elenor's really dead.*

Nancy rushed over. "Catch your breath now, lass."

I swiped at my eyes. "I think I'm in shock."

Constable Mackie stepped forward. "Do you need help?"

"I'm all right. I just need a moment to . . ." To what? I couldn't finish the sentence.

"Try to remain calm. I've asked Miss MacLeod here to have a look at Mrs. Spurgeon's flat."

"Why me?" Agnes's eyes slewed from the officer to Becca and Nancy. "I don't know anything. How could I? I was in my apartment. I was asleep. I was—" She stopped midsentence, and the effect was like a race car driver slamming on the brakes in the middle of a lap.

"Ready now, Miss MacLeod?" Constable Mackie helped Agnes to her feet. She followed him with the look of a prisoner headed for the gallows. I noticed she was limping.

"Come into the kitchen, Kate," Nancy said. "Coffee's on."

A fire smoldered in the kitchen hearth, filling the room with the distinctive toasty, smoky smell of peat. A carton of eggs and a loaf of bread lay abandoned on the counter near the sink. Becca sat at a long oak table near the fire. I slid in next to her.

"Did that sergeant tell you what happened?" Becca asked. "All we know is that someone found Elenor's body this morning."

"That's all he told me too."

Nancy reached for a cup and saucer. "Frank's with the detective inspector now." The cup clattered on the saucer as she handed it to me.

"Detective inspector?" I was confused. "Do you mean Tom Mallory?"

"Oh, no—this one's from Police Scotland. Detective Inspector Devlin."

"Why did they want Agnes to look at Elenor's flat?"

Becca passed me a pitcher of cream. "They said someone had to do it. To see if anything is missing, I suppose. I've never been in Elenor's flat, so I wouldn't know."

"Nor have I." Nancy took another cup and saucer from the shelf. "Sofia used to clean for Elenor, but she's"—Nancy and Becca exchanged glances—"well, she's in no state to be questioned at the moment. We sent her to the Lodge. That left Agnes."

Why was Sofia in no state to be questioned? I picked up my cup. "Elenor and I were supposed to talk this morning." I choked on the words and reached in my handbag for a Kleenex. "I can't believe she's dead."

"Nor can we," Becca said. She seemed unusually calm to me, but I know people react to a crisis in different ways. My son, Eric, goes silent. My daughter, Christine, goes into hysterics. My mother listens. Then she asks questions.

Nancy handed Becca a cup of coffee. "I was afraid something terrible would happen," she said darkly. "The curse."

"Really, Nancy." Becca rolled her eyes. "That's daft, and you know it."

Instead of taking offense, Nancy seemed to take heart. "You're right. Of course you are."

A curse? I couldn't let that drop. "What are you talking about?"

"The Arnott curse," Becca said. "Because of those murders—Flora Arnott and that other woman, Gowyn somebody."

"Gowyn Campbell," I said. Bill had never mentioned a curse.

Nancy wrapped the loaf of bread in a tea towel. "People say the house is cursed, Kate. Two murders—three if you count the child—and a suicide."

"But that was a long time ago. Even if there were such things as curses, would it skip two hundred years?"

"It didn't," Becca said. "Not that I believe it, you understand, but the Arnotts have suffered an unusual number of tragedies over the years. Someone made a list once—disease, insanity, freak accidents, deaths in war, in childbirth. Even a duel back in the mid-1830s. It's a miracle they survived at all, but each generation managed to produce a male heir."

"Until the twins," Nancy said. "The last of the Arnotts. Some say it's revenge."

"For what?" I asked.

"For taking land that had belonged to the MacDonalds since the dawn of time."

Becca scoffed. "It's marketing, Kate. Gives the island a mystique."

"Not all marketing," Nancy said. "Stories of a ghost have been around for generations."

That I knew to be true. "Bill told me about the ghost of Flora Arnott, searching for the nursery that would have held her child. Elenor had terrible nightmares as a child. She said she saw the ghost, and no one could talk her out of it."

"Oh, aye." Becca said. Once again, she and Nancy exchanged glances. "Did you know Elenor claimed to have seen the ghost recently, several times? One moment there'd be a dark shape, the rustling of fabric, the smell of wet wool. Then the shape would vanish."

Nancy turned pale. Did she believe in ghosts? Scotland teems with them. Wee Annie of Mary King's Close who might take the hand of an unsuspecting tourist. The Warrior of Culloden, the tall Highlander who tramps endlessly through the moors. The Green Lady, harbinger of doom for the Burnett family. Queen Victoria claimed to have seen that one herself.

I figured we had enough horrors at the moment, so I steered the subject away from ghosts. "That police sergeant, Bruce, said Elenor was found near the Historical Society. Why would she go there in the storm?"

"And if she set her mind to go"—Becca set her cup in the saucer—"why not take the car?"

"The Carriage House was locked, for one thing," Nancy said. "She'd have had to find the key and back the car out herself. Or wake Frank."

Becca looked thoughtful. "I suppose. And the Historical Society is only a fifteen-minute walk by the forest path. But still—in the snow?"

We fell silent.

Nancy sighed. "Poor wee Agnes is taking it the hardest."

I agreed. I'd seen the shock in Agnes's eyes. I'd also seen something that looked a lot like panic.

Chapter Eight

*

I arrived for my interview with the detective inspector a few minutes early, wondering how he would expect me to react to Elenor's death. I was shocked, of course, and saddened, the sadness one always feels for the senseless loss of life, but I wasn't bereaved and couldn't pretend to be. What I did feel—I'm not proud to admit it—was frustration. Elenor's hints of danger and secrets had piqued my curiosity. Now I might never know what she'd gotten herself into. All I could do was tell the police everything and let them sort it out.

The conservatory was a large, leafy space made of glass, perfect for catching the afternoon sun. Today the sky was sullen. Three men sat on wicker chairs. One of them I knew—Tom Mallory. The other two, both in dark suits, would be DS Bruce, the man I'd spoken to on the phone, and the detective inspector. What had Nancy called him— Dalton? Davis? The three men acted like old friends, but then policemen everywhere probably have an instant bond, a secret handshake or something. Seeing me, they rose.

Tom crossed the room. "Kate, I'm so sorry about Elenor. Are you coping?"

His kindness touched me. "I'm fine. I just need to know what happened."

"Don't worry. They'll get to the bottom of it." He gave my arm a squeeze and left.

One of the men in suits stuck out his hand. "Detective Inspector Rob Devlin, Police Scotland, Major Investigations Team." Devlin had a swimmer's body with a long torso, broad shoulders, and a bullet-shaped head—shaved, I guessed, to disguise premature baldness. He offered me a chair, perching himself on the arm of a wicker sofa.

He was chewing gum, his speech punctuated with snaps of emphasis. "The police station at Mallaig got the call at seven this morning, when the body was discovered." *Snap.* "MIT was called in—Major Investigations Team. Standard procedure for homicides these days." *Snap.*

Homicide? The room tilted. I gripped the arms of my chair. "Elenor was murdered?"

"I'm afraid so."

I swallowed hard. *Just breathe.*

"Do you need something? A glass of water, perhaps? Take your time."

"I'm fine," I said again, forcing a smile.

"You spoke with Detective Sergeant Bruce earlier."

Bruce nodded, eyelids at half-mast.

Devlin extracted a pair of half-moon glasses from his breast pocket and perched them on the end of a long nose. He consulted a small black notebook. "We'll start with some basic information. Your husband was Mrs. Spurgeon's brother. He passed away, ah . . . three years ago. And you live in Ohio, is that right?"

"Yes, Jackson Falls, near Cleveland." The information must have come from Agnes or Becca. "My husband was a law professor at Case Western Reserve University."

"You have two children. Also in Ohio?"

"Eric's a graduate student at Ohio State, but he's in Italy right now, doing research. Christine attends college in England."

"Do you work, Mrs. Hamilton?"

I'm an antiques dealer and appraiser. I have a shop in Jackson Falls."

"I believe your husband was part owner of the hotel."

"No. Bill had nothing to do with the hotel. The property belonged to their family. He and Elenor owned everything jointly until twelve years ago, when Elenor bought out his share."

"Hard feelings?" *Snap.*

"Of course not." How could I explain Bill's blindness when it came to Elenor? He would have given her the property if she'd asked.

"You and Mrs. Spurgeon were close then, friendly?"

I took a breath. This was where the tell-him-everything part came in. "We weren't close. She resented me for taking her brother away, which wasn't true. I thought she was difficult and self-centered." I searched Devlin's face for disapproval but found none. He'd make a great poker player.

"When did you leave the party last night, and where did you go?"

"I helped with cleanup. Then Mrs. Holden and I walked together to our cottages—a little after midnight, I think."

"Without speaking to Mrs. Spurgeon?"

"She left the party at nine. I'm sure someone told you what happened."

"The reaction to her announcements—yes." He ran a hand over his bald head. "Any idea who might have wanted your sister-in-law dead?"

Besides half the island? "None at all. I hardly knew her."

"Had Mrs. Spurgeon told you in advance about the sale of the hotel?"

"No, and I didn't know about the engagement to Dr. Guthrie either. As I said, we weren't close."

"When was the last time you spoke with her? Before yesterday, I mean."

"My husband's funeral three years ago. She came to Ohio. We'd had no contact after that, until last week when she telephoned."

Devlin dragged the sofa forward to avoid a drooping palm frond.

"Why did you come to Scotland, Mrs. Hamilton? You say you and your sister-in-law weren't close. You hadn't spoken in three years. Yet you traveled all the way from Ohio for the Tartan Ball."

Put like that, it did sound suspicious. "I was shocked when Elenor phoned. She said she was in trouble and needed my advice. She begged me to come. I felt obligated."

Obligated. The word my mother had used and I'd denied.

I pulled Elenor's letter from my handbag. "I found this in a book Elenor gave me."

Devlin took the letter, frowning as he scanned it. "What sort of advice did Mrs. Spurgeon want?"

"She never got a chance to tell me." I shifted in my chair, feeling guilty. I always feel guilty when I'm being watched for signs of guilt.

"Tell me about the book," Devlin said.

I'd brought the novel, too, and handed it to him. "The book was written by Elenor's fiancé. She asked me to read it."

Devlin studied the cover. "And you think this book is connected to her death?"

"Elenor wasn't the book-club type. She would have had a good reason for wanting me to read it." My ears burned. I sounded like one of those eccentric villagers in a British cozy mystery, the ones who provide the red herrings.

"And have you read it?"

"Just a few pages last night."

Devlin returned the book and the letter. "Well, if you find anything relevant, let me know." He'd managed to sound both attentive and condescending. "Were you concerned about Mrs. Spurgeon's safety?"

"I should have been. Elenor told me something was scaring her. Her exact words."

"But she didn't tell you what."

"No. I should have insisted she give me a clue right away, but Elenor loved drama. She wouldn't have wanted to spoil a good story."

"Have you mentioned this to anyone?"

"Just my mother, but she's in Ohio."

"Don't mention it to anyone else. Now, what's this about an intruder?" *Snap.*

I inched forward in my seat. Until that moment I hadn't connected the intruder with Elenor's death. "Someone searched my cottage last night. I reported it to the police at Mallaig, so when Sergeant Bruce called this morning, I assumed the call was about that."

"When did you call Mallaig?"

"I'd just gotten back from the ball, so twelve twenty, maybe?"

Devlin made a note in his book. "How did the intruder get in?"

"The cottage wasn't locked."

DS Bruce sniffed. If it was meant as a comment on my naïveté, he'd schooled his face into a careful neutrality.

"So you called the police station at Mallaig."

"I thought I should tell someone."

Devlin nodded at Bruce, who left the room.

"Why not first notify the hotel?" *Snap.*

That gum was getting on my nerves. "I tried to. I got voicemail."

"What was taken?" Devlin licked his index finger and turned a page in his notebook.

"Nothing. My money and credit cards were still in my wallet, and there wasn't anything else to take. No jewelry or anything." I explained about the lost suitcase.

"Someone searched your belongings but left your cash and credit cards untouched. What do you think he was looking for?"

"I don't know. Maybe I scared him off. It's strange."

"Yes, strange." *Snap.*

He thinks I imagined it. Or made it up.

DS Bruce returned and whispered something in Devlin's ear. The corner of Devlin's mouth twitched. "Constable Mackie verified your call last night."

Light dawned. I wasn't being interviewed. I was being questioned. Well, I had a few questions of my own. "You haven't told me how Elenor died."

Devlin studied my face. "I can give you a bit more information, but you'll have to keep it confidential. Just until we know what's relevant. Can you do that?"

I nodded.

He closed his black notebook. "Mrs. Spurgeon was shot through the neck with an arrow."

I grabbed my throat. "But that's what happened to Flora Arnott."

Devlin pulled off his glasses and stared at Bruce. "Someone else on the island was murdered? Why wasn't I informed?"

Bruce shrugged. "No report of another death, sir."

"Not recently," I said. "March of 1810. That's what the book is about, a well-known episode in island history. Flora Arnott was shot through the neck with an arrow. No one ever knew who or why. She lived in this house. Don't you see? Someone has recreated a historic murder."

"Two hundred years later?" Devlin pinched the bridge of his nose. "Fascinating, but a bit late for a copycat crime."

"I agree. But why would someone kill Elenor in that particular way unless they were trying to make a point?" I was beginning to feel frustrated. "There must be easier ways to kill people. Not everyone would have the skill and strength to kill someone with a bow and arrow." As soon as the words left my mouth, I pictured Frank Holden and Dora MacDonald receiving their archery trophies.

"Actually, any number of people could have done it," Devlin said. "Archery seems to be an obsession on the island. Are you familiar with the archery school at the Adventure Centre?"

I nodded. "My husband was a camper there for years."

"The Adventure Centre sponsors public archery classes and an annual competition. The arrow that killed your sister-in-law had their signature red-and-yellow feathers."

"Fletching, sir. The feathers are called fletching," Bruce said, earning a sharp look.

"But hitting a target block isn't the same as hitting a moving person," I said.

Devlin held up a finger. "Ah, but Mrs. Spurgeon wasn't moving. She was sitting, leaning actually, against the stump of a tree." *Snap.*

"In the snow? Why would she do that?" The room swayed. I dug my fingernails into my palms. "Do you know when it happened?"

Devlin hesitated as if deciding how much to say. "We don't like to speculate until after the postmortem, but given the snowfall beneath the body and other physical signs, the police surgeon estimates death between twelve thirty and two AM. We have corroborating witnesses for the earlier time—the ladies who live across from the Historical Society." He consulted his black notebook. "The Arnott sisters. I'm afraid we woke them up."

I pictured the twins in flannel nightgowns and mobcaps, tying up matching woolen robes as they opened their door to the police.

"The sisters noticed lights inside the Historical Society at twelve thirty. They have a clear view of the road from their house, and they swear there was no body outside then. Good news for you, Mrs. Hamilton. Unless the sisters are mistaken or the postmortem examination changes things, you couldn't have done it."

I have an alibi. First time in my life I'd had occasion to say that.

Devlin nodded at DS Bruce, who read from his own black notebook. "The Mallaig Police Station received a call from Applegarth Cottage at twelve twenty AM. Mrs. Hamilton said it wasn't an emergency and left a message for the constable on duty. He returned her call at twelve thirty. The conversation lasted for approximately ten minutes. Mrs. Hamilton asked them to send someone out." DS Bruce managed to convey scorn without moving a facial muscle. "They explained the island was cut off, and the constable offered to have a duty clerk call back at intervals. Calls were made and answered at one fifteen, one fifty, and two thirty."

I was warming to that intruder.

Devlin removed his glasses. "You might have driven to the Historical Society, of course, but your car hasn't moved since before the storm. We checked. And you might have made it there and back on foot, if you hurried. But the snow had tapered off by then, and you would have left tracks. There weren't any."

Good point. "What about the Historical Society? Did you find tracks there?"

"Unfortunately not. By the time we arrived this morning, the road had been plowed and the walkways shoveled. A pity."

"We did find strands of purple wool," Bruce added, "caught on a bush near one of the west-facing windows."

"No proof they're connected," Devlin snapped. "But there were two recent sets of shoe prints inside the building. One set matched the boots Mrs. Spurgeon was wearing at the time of her death. The other was made by a pair of molded rubber boots, size ten, manufactured at the Mucky Duck factory in Fort William." *Snap.*

I was impressed. "How do you know that?"

Devlin's mouth twitched again. "The logo and size are molded into the soles. It's an important piece of evidence, though. The tread on a shoe or boot wears in a unique way. Almost like a fingerprint."

I couldn't help wondering why he was telling me all this. Because he'd decided he could trust me, or because he wanted to gauge my reaction?

"What about DNA?" I asked. I knew absolutely nothing about DNA, but wasn't that what the police always checked for?

"We know our jobs, Mrs. Hamilton." *Snap.* "The Historical Society is a public building, and DNA analysis can take weeks. I'd like to think we'll clear things up before that."

"You think the killer is still on the island?"

"No one left the island after eleven last night. We set up checkpoints this morning at the ferry terminals at Mallaig and Skye. Trust me—whoever committed the crime is still here."

Was that meant to reassure me? "Is it safe? I mean, with a murderer on the loose?"

"I don't believe you're in danger."

How could he be so sure? I started to ask why, but he held up a hand. "Hold that question for now, hmm?"

"Do you have a suspect?"

"A person of interest. That's all I'm allowed to say. We're taking statements. We'll fill you in as we can, but remember, strict confidentiality. If you think of something you haven't mentioned, let me know immediately." He held my gaze for a moment before flipping a page in his notebook. "Now, a few more questions. According to Miss MacLeod, Mrs. Spurgeon received a phone call at eleven thirty last night." One corner of his mouth went up, not quite a smile. "You, by any chance?"

"No." The implication struck me. "It must have been the murderer."

"Assumptions, Mrs. Hamilton." Devlin shook his bullet-shaped head.

"But that means Nancy and I were still in the kitchen." An icy hand clutched my heart. "We might have just missed her."

"Did you hear the telephone?"

"I don't think so. The big dishwashers were going."

"Was the front door locked when you left?"

"Yes. Nancy locked it. We saw lights on in Elenor's flat."

"Did you notice prints in the snow?"

"No, but we weren't looking for them. You said you found shoe prints at the Historical Society. Have you checked the other members of the Society?"

"Ma'am, please." He waggled his finger in my face. "Amateur detectives are popular in crime fiction, but this is real life. Leave the investigating to us, hmm?"

The rules were becoming clear: *Answer when asked. Do not offer unsolicited opinions.*

"There is something you can do to help us." Devlin smiled at me like a Little League coach handing out ribbons for participation. "I'd like you to take a look at Mrs. Spurgeon's flat. Tell us if anything appears, ah, unusual or out of character."

"I thought Agnes MacLeod did that."

"No help," DS Bruce said drily. "Hysterical."

"Are you free after lunch?" Devlin asked. "Around one?"

"I'm free anytime until my flight tomorrow afternoon." The moment the words left my mouth, I realized that wasn't going to happen.

"Oh, you won't be leaving just yet." Devlin reached into his suit jacket and pulled out a sealed plastic bag containing an enormous diamond ring.

I blanched. "That's the ring Dr. Guthrie gave Elenor last night."

"She was wearing it at the time of her death."

"Not a robbery, then."

"No." He sounded disappointed. "The ring will be kept in evidence for now. I trust you have no objections."

"Me? Why would I have objections?"

"Because you are the executor of Mrs. Spurgeon's estate. We spoke with her solicitor an hour ago."

"Elenor named *me* as her executor?"

"You didn't know?"

I shook my head. Devlin was saying something about releasing the body and preliminary arrangements, but I was having trouble taking it in.

Elenor had been murdered, and in spite of Devlin's skepticism, I couldn't shake the feeling that her death was connected in some way with the death of Flora Arnott.

How in the world could I fulfill my promise to Bill now?

Chapter Nine

I found the hotel kitchen empty. Nancy and Becca were gone. The coffeemaker was turned off, the cups washed and left to dry on a wooden rack. The only sound was the ticking of the long-case clock in reception.

Time like an ever-rolling stream . . .

The words of the old hymn popped into my mind. How many minutes, hours, days had that old clock marked? Years rolled by, then decades and centuries, and every morning the hands of the clock turned anew, as if it were possible to record over the failures and griefs of the past.

The turf fire had died down in the hearth. I found a poker and prodded what remained of the crumbling peat, watching the embers flare and settle. If the past could be rewritten, I'd go back to that horrific July day three years ago and change everything—the bitter words, the guilt, the final, irreversible blow.

That wasn't possible. All I could do was forgive and move forward.

Well, that was easy. *Conquering Grief and Guilt in Two Simple Steps.* Now I could tackle other challenges, like solving the mystery of the Bermuda Triangle and finding the remains of Jimmy Hoffa.

A thin light slanted through the south-facing windows. I moved to the sink and looked out on the broad stretch of lawn sloping down to the cliff edge. Last night's snowfall was already melting. The trees dripped. Puddles had formed on the flagstone patio.

DI Devlin was counting on a quick wrap-up—a disgruntled islander with a violent temper and a predictable motive. Nothing to do with convoluted things like island history and the death of a young Lowland girl two hundred years ago. Only Devlin hadn't seen the look on Elenor's face when she had made me promise to open the package right away. He hadn't heard her say about the casket, "This is where it all began."

When I got on that airplane in Cleveland, I had imagined that Elenor and I could forgive each other and start again, for Bill's sake. Instead, she lay dead in a morgue in Fort William. The time for helping Elenor was past. The most I could do now was make sure her killer was caught and punished. Not for Elenor's sake. Not even for Bill's sake. For my own. But what could I do? All I had was a conviction that Elenor's death was connected in some way with island history. I'd promised Devlin I wouldn't share the little information I had with anyone. I would keep my word, but I hadn't promised not to ask questions. A few innocent questions. The trick would be knowing the right questions and the right people to ask.

Someone on the island knew something, and the most likely person was Agnes MacLeod.

"You okay?" Becca Wallace stood framed in the doorway to the reception hall.

"Oh—yes. Is Agnes still in her flat?"

"Nancy tucked her in a half hour ago with a thermos of tea and a hot water bottle. If she took one of her sleeping pills, we won't see her again until suppertime, or possibly breakfast."

The phone in reception jangled and Becca dashed off.

I shrugged on my jacket. My conversation with Agnes would have to wait.

Plan B was Nancy Holden.

* * *

Twenty minutes later I sat at a scrubbed pine table in the Holdens' compact kitchen. Crisply ironed curtains framed a wide, multipaned window overlooking the sea. A scalloped shelf displayed photographs of a pretty child at various stages of development. Frank and Nancy's daughter, the owner of the sexy black dress.

Nancy struck a match and lit the candle in the center of the table. The sharp tang of sulfur faded into cinnamon and apple pie. I could tell Nancy had been crying, but her voice was steady. "How did it go with the detective, dearie?"

"Looks like I'll be staying awhile. I'm the executor of Elenor's estate." Surely *that* wasn't breaking a confidence.

Nancy filled a fat brown teapot from a steaming kettle. As the tea steeped, she set out mugs and small plates. "Did the police tell you anything more than we've heard?" She pronounced the last word *haired*, and it reminded me how I'd missed hearing the Scots accent since Bill's death.

"They'll know more after the autopsy," I said, not wanting to lie but remembering my promise. Nancy poured tea and, without asking, added generous spoonfuls of sugar. I took a sip. Strong and sweet. The British answer to every crisis.

"Frank's been shooing reporters away all morning, the wee scunners," Nancy said. "They're very determined." She placed a basket of scones on the table and sat across from me, lacing her fingers around her mug. She looked solid, reliable—a woman used to taking care of others, a nurturer. She would protect those she loved, fierce as a mother bear.

Nancy stared at her mug. "There will be rumors, of course. There always are in a small community." She looked up. "It was kind of you to come, lass."

Nancy's sympathy nearly did me in. If you want to help someone through a hard time, do not be nice to them. "I keep thinking," I said in a squeaky voice. "If I'd gone to Elenor after the party, I might have been able to—" I stopped, unable to finish the sentence.

"To prevent her death?"

I shook my head. It was all I could do *not* to say that she and I might have missed Elenor by minutes. "I don't mean that. Oh, I'm not sure what I mean. Elenor and I were sisters-in-law for almost twenty-five years, but I never really knew her. She wasn't easy to know."

"She wasn't easy to work for, either." Nancy's chin went up. "Of course, Frank and I got along with her. We did our work and stayed clear of the drama. I'm sure it won't affect us." She offered me the basket of scones.

I took one, warm and fragrant. "You mean the new owners. They'd be crazy to let you go."

"Ah, well. Better bend than break, my ma used to say. If things don't work out, Frank and I can always go to our daughter in Dundee. She'll have a wee one by March. Our first grandchild." Nancy smiled.

"Were you shocked that Elenor sold the hotel?"

"Surprised." Nancy turned the gold band on her finger slowly. "What shocked me was the engagement. I know Elenor and Hugh worked together at the Historical Society, but there wasn't a romance going on." Her brow creased. "Only there must have been."

I took a bite of my scone and almost swooned. "Nancy, these are incredible."

Nancy's face went pink, making her look about twenty. "Baking is my therapy. When Frank finds me at home with flour on my hands, he asks what's wrong."

I took a second bite, resisting the urge to scarf the whole thing in one go. "Elenor's first chef was French. He was supposed to have won some major competition, but I don't remember him producing anything like this." I picked up the crumbs with my finger and stuck them in my mouth.

"I was hired when the fourth French chef resigned," Nancy said. "Shortly after your husband died, it was. Elenor was a right mess. She and her brother must have been close."

Close wasn't the word I would have chosen. *Codependent*, maybe, but what did it matter now? "You've been here almost three years. I'm impressed."

Nancy topped up our mugs. She added another spoonful of sugar to hers and stirred. "Frank and I were working at a resort on Skye when I saw Elenor's advertisement. To be honest, I think it was the Highland accent got me the job. She encouraged me to chat up the guests, especially on Scottish Night. I'm part of the entertainment. Everyone wears fancy dress—kilts, sashes, tams, the whole kit. Mostly purchased at the Tartan Gift Shop."

"No wonder Dora MacDonald isn't happy about the new Swiss owners."

Nancy covered the teapot with a quilted cozy. She hesitated, as if coming to a decision. "You dinnae have to tell me, lass, but Elenor's death wasn't an accident, was it?"

I said nothing, a tacit confirmation. Is it my fault if people guess?

"Do they have a suspect?"

"They're taking statements. First step, apparently."

Nancy's gaze shifted to the window. "That detective asked me who might have wanted to prevent Elenor from selling the hotel, or marrying Dr. Guthrie."

"What did you tell him?"

Nancy shrugged. "Everyone on the island would have tried to stop the sale if we'd known. Glenroth House is a part of island history. Local businesses depend on the connection with Bonnie Prince Charlie. And now, since Dr. Guthrie's book, wee Flora. But the contract was already signed, lass. And the only person opposed to the marriage, as far as I know, was Margaret Guthrie."

"She did make her point, didn't she?"

Nancy carried our dishes to the sink. She rinsed them and dried her hands on an embroidered tea towel. "If you ask me, Margaret didn't want to lose her live-in caregiver. But what could she do? Hugh's a grown man."

"Had Elenor been worried about something recently? Had you noticed a change in her behavior?"

Nancy leaned against the sink. The question seemed to interest her. "Well, her memory was getting pretty bad. She was always mislaying things. Keys, reading glasses. We'd all have to stop what we were doing and help her look. Then she started saying people were stealing things—from the hotel and from the Historical Society as well. A fortnight ago she had a deadbolt installed on the door to her flat. I thought she might be experiencing some form of paranoia."

I thought about the marquetry casket and did a quick mental edit. "Was there something in particular Elenor might have wanted to protect?"

Elenor frowned. "Not that I know of. We assumed her fears were general and irrational. But then something *was* stolen. An antique silver tray. Lovely it was, too. We kept it on the Irish cupboard in the butler's pantry. One day it was there. Next day it was gone. We searched everywhere."

"Did you report it to the police?"

"Elenor wouldn't allow it. Bad publicity, she said, and she was probably right. Guests like to believe they're safe here." Nancy folded the tea towel and hung it over the edge of the sink. "You know what's odd, though? When Frank arrived at the hotel this morning, he found the main door ajar. Snow had blown in all over the marble floor."

That was odd. I'd watched Nancy lock the door with my own eyes. Had Elenor left the house in a panic later that evening, or had someone else, my intruder, for example, lured her out in order to get inside and steal something—like the casket? The thought that I might never see the beautiful casket again brought a surprising pang of regret.

Nancy sat at the table and slid a basket full of towels to her feet. "Elenor's always been difficult. You know that, Kate. But lately she's been almost irrational. She insisted she heard footsteps at night, like someone creeping around the house."

Careful. Mysterious intruders were definitely on the don't-talk-about-it list. "A guest who couldn't sleep and decided to wander?"

"We've had no guests in the main house since the first of September. Our autumn visitors seem to prefer the cottages." Nancy transferred an armful of towels to her lap and began folding.

"Let me help." I gathered some towels myself, making a mental note to ask Agnes about footsteps in the night.

"It wasn't only the fear, though." Nancy added a neatly folded hand towel to the growing stack. "Elenor's never been oversensitive to people's feelings. You know that as well. But lately she seemed to go out of her way to wound people."

"What do you mean?"

"The August bank holiday, for example. Our last big weekend. The hotel was full—we were swamped—and Agnes assigned one of the summer staff girls to clean Elenor's flat instead of Sofia. Elenor hit the roof. She said, right in front of everyone, that Agnes was either taking advantage of their friendship or getting too old for the job. Agnes wouldn't admit it, but she was hurt by that. Really hurt. Then last week Elenor fired one of our part-time gardeners."

We'd come to the bottom of the laundry basket. Nancy's hands dropped to her lap. "Such a sweet man, Kate. He was trimming hedges in the garden, and the noise startled one of our autumn regulars, an old dear. She'd dozed off, and her teacup smashed on the stone patio. She insisted it was her fault, but Elenor blamed Bo. Not only did she fire him, Kate, she humiliated him."

"Bo? Bo Duff?" A sliver of ice pierced my heart. "I know him, Nancy. He *is* a sweet man. He tried to save my husband's life. Elenor knew that."

"Frank was the one who persuaded her to hire Bo. Now he's right sorry for it. Bo didn't deserve that treatment."

Any regret I might have felt over Elenor's death was evaporating. Bill had seen Elenor as vulnerable and insecure. I'd seen her as selfish and manipulating. The Elenor Nancy had just described was cruel.

"That's not the worst." Nancy shot me a guilty look. "Frank asked Bo to help him park cars last night. He shouldn't have done it, not after what happened, but Bo needs the work, and nearly everyone still on the island was a guest at the ball. There was an accident—a near one, anyway. Elenor was driving. Flying like a demon, Frank said. She nearly crashed into Bo, driving one of the valets. Elenor blew up. She slammed out of the car and screamed at him. She told him he was useless, and if he ever stepped foot on her property again, she'd have him arrested."

I felt sick.

"Anyway," Nancy stacked the folded towels in the basket, "the police said we should contact them if we think of anything relevant."

"Have you?"

"Only an odd comment Elenor made last week. Wednesday, it was. She'd been impossible for weeks, snapping everyone's head off, criticizing everything we did, especially Agnes. But at dinner she was different. Nice, chatty. She stayed for a second cup of coffee while I cleaned up. We were talking about Dr. Guthrie's book and how the Flora legend has brought money to the island. She got kind of dreamy—'away with the fairies,' my gran used to call it. She said, 'Sometimes it's better not to know.' I asked her what she meant by it. She said it wasn't important, but I got the impression that it was important, that there was something she was mulling over. Do you think I should mention it to the police?"

"Probably." I could only imagine how DI Devlin would receive Nancy's airy-fairy story. I waited a beat. "Nancy, who do you think killed Elenor?"

Nancy brushed some invisible crumbs off the tablecloth. Something had flicked behind those clear, gray eyes. "I haven't a clue." She untied her apron and laid it across the back of her chair. "I should get back to the kitchen."

The cottage door opened. Frank walked in, holding his cell phone. "I've been trying to reach Bo all morning. I cannae find him."

Chapter Ten

I made myself a mug of tea, my fourth shot of caffeine that morning, and sat near the still-smoldering fireplace in Applegarth Cottage. I'd canceled my flight to London and been surprised to receive a credit against future travel, the single bright spot in an otherwise dreadful morning. The other piece of good news was they'd found my suitcase. The bad news was they'd found it in the Dominican Republic. On the very next flight to Glasgow, they'd promised.

My suitcase was the least of my concerns. I was worried about Bo. I told myself I was blowing things out of proportion. Frank had been puzzled by Bo's whereabouts but not overly concerned. Bo probably had a job today—pruning someone's rose bushes before winter set in or jumping a dead battery. He could do just about anything physical or mechanical. I pressed the still-warm mug to my cheek.

The day I first met Bo was one of those blue-sky days they put on Scottish calendars. Bill and I had just arrived. He wanted me to see the island, to meet Elenor. The sky was cloudless and the breeze stiff enough to blow away the midges. The weather was unusually warm, and we'd taken a picnic lunch down to the beach at Glen Corry. Bo was there, a big man in his early thirties. Bill's age. I could picture Bo now—baggy swim trunks tied high on his belly, long wet hair plastered against his skull. He pointed at us and came galloping across the silver sand in his big bare feet. He'd been swimming. I recognized the signs at once. *Cognitive disability* is what they call it now. Bo was obviously high functioning. Like my brother, Matt, had he lived. A smile split Bo's face, and he gave Bill a big, damp bear hug. "No way, José," he said, grabbing Bill by the shoulders and looking him up and down.

Bo spent the afternoon with us. He and Bill played like boys, racing through the tidal pools, scrambling up the sandy dunes. King of the Hill. It wasn't hard to see the bond between them—on Bo's part adoration, and on Bill's part a complete lack of condescension. I learned later that Bill had taken Bo under his wing one summer when they were kids, shielding him from the island bullies. *Daftie*, a big kid from Glasgow had called Bo. Bill had punched the kid, giving him a bloody nose.

Good for you, Bill Hamilton.

I added my mug to the breakfast dishes in the sink and located the scrap of paper on which I'd written Bo's phone number. I dialed again. Same result. He wasn't there.

Putting thoughts of Bo aside, I turned my mind back to the main problem. Elenor. As I replayed my conversation with Nancy, I realized that Elenor's problems (her current ones, anyway) seemed to have begun about a month ago. She'd been more irritable than usual and had taken it out on her staff, especially Agnes. Nancy had wondered if Elenor was experiencing some form of mental breakdown, but the symptoms—forgetfulness, bad dreams, mood swings, obsession with security—could also have been caused by fear.

Something's going on here, and it's scaring me.

When I'm confused, it helps me to put my thoughts on paper. I found the small notebook and pen I always keep in my handbag. Turning to a fresh page, I wrote *Questions* at the top.

1. *Who or what was E afraid of—theft of casket? Who knew it was in E's apt?*
2. *Agnes is the only other person who sleeps in the house. Did she hear footsteps?*

3. *What caused E's mood to change so dramatically on Wednesday (per Nancy)?*
4. *Is Nancy hiding something?*

I tapped the pen against my chin.

5. *Why did E go to the H.S. and whom did she meet? (Mucky Ducks, UK sz 10)*
6. *Where did E get the newspaper clippings about Flora Arnott's murder?*

That last question could probably be answered quickly. Old copies of *The Hebridean Chronicle* would be archived somewhere, kept in a repository, either on microfilm or digitized and stored in an online database. With my phone dead and without my laptop—no reason to bring it, I'd thought—I'd have to use the cottage phone.

A magazine holder on the kitchen counter held several phone directories. In the one for the South Highlands, I found a listing for the University of Strathclyde. After explaining my question, I was directed to the Digital Resources office. A pleasant female voice answered my call.

"I hope you can help me," I said. "Do you have copies of *The Hebridean Chronicle* from the 1800s?"

"Ah, *The Chronicle*. That depends. The paper was published weekly, but only for several years. Can you give me specific dates? I'll check our listing."

"I'm interested in two dates." I consulted the photocopy. "March ninth of 1810 and January eighteenth of 1811."

Computer keys tapped. "Oh, dear. I'm afraid we don't have the issues you're looking for."

"Would there be copies somewhere else—another library, for example?"

"Afraid not. Not even the National Library of Scotland has copies. *The Hebridean Chronicle* folded in August of 1812 after a devastating fire. Nothing survived. The copies we hold were donated by a woman on the Isle of Lewis who found them in her grandparents' attic."

"What about one of the local historical societies, like the one on the Isle of Glenroth, for example?"

"All the historical repositories in Scotland share information. If additional copies of *The Chronicle* exist, we'd know about it."

I thanked her and hung up. Wherever Elenor had found the articles, it wasn't an official archive. But that didn't mean unofficial copies didn't exist. I took out my lighted magnifying glass and examined the photocopy. Apart from significant yellowing, the newsprint appeared to be in surprisingly good shape. No holes or creasing, no major foxing, but the edges were irregular, as if they'd been torn rather than clipped. To the last question in my notebook, I added, *Ask Dr. Guthrie about old newspapers*, underlining it twice.

Fresh air nut that I am, I'd cracked the window over the sink, and the curtains billowed slightly. I still had half an hour before lunch and decided to make use of it. Agnes MacLeod wasn't the only person who might know something about Elenor's fears. Using the slim island directory, I looked up *Guthrie*. Only one was listed.

A young girl answered. "Dr. Guthrie isn't available. Sorry."

"This is Kate Hamilton, Elenor Spurgeon's sister-in-law. Will you ask him to phone me at Glenroth House? If I'm not here, he can leave a message. I'll call him back."

I replaced the receiver.

I'd have to tell my children about Elenor's death, of course, but there was no hurry for that. Eric and Christine had hardly known their Aunt Elenor, and she'd never shown the slightest interest in them. One person, however, I needed to tell right away.

I picked up the cottage phone again, trying not to think of international phone charges.

"Hello. This is Linnea Larsen."

"Hi, Mom." My voice caught. *Dang it.*

"Kate—darling. What's wrong?" I could picture her face, lines of worry on her brow.

"I'm fine," I said for the ninth or tenth time since arriving on the island. "It's Elenor. She's dead."

There was a moment's silence. "Tell me what happened."

My mother let me talk, as she always did, without questions or interruptions. I told her everything, including the note in the pocket of the black dress and the searching of my cottage.

Finally I took a breath. "It's Nancy's story about Bo Duff I can't get out of my mind. How could Elenor treat him like that? It feels like watching someone strike a child."

"Perhaps for Bo, the hurt faded quickly. Have you spoken with him?"

"I tried to call him. He's not answering." My shoulders tightened. I'd been telling myself not to worry, but I was worried. Things happen to the people you love.

"When are you coming home?"

"After the funeral, I guess, although I don't know when that will be. I won't be able to visit Christine now. And if you need to get home, just say so. I'll call one of my part-time helpers to fill in."

"I'll stay as long as you need me. When will you learn your duties as executor?"

"Monday, probably. I have to set something up with Elenor's solicitor."

"You will lock the cottage from now on, won't you?"

"Of course, but I'm not in danger."

"Think about what you just told me, Kate. Do you know why Elenor wanted your help?"

"No."

"Do you know why she was murdered?"

"No, but—"

"But you believe the two are connected."

I was silent.

"Someone else may believe they're connected, too, darling. Promise me you'll be careful."

After we hung up, I sat at the kitchen table and watched the wind ruffle the sea.

Years ago I'd typed up handouts for Bill's ever-popular class on Investigative Techniques. A line came to mind: *Most violent crimes are personal. Begin with those closest to the victim.* Those closest to Elenor lived on the island, worked at the hotel. Elenor's killer might be someone I knew, someone I'd thought I could trust.

Reasons to dislike Elenor were as plentiful as cold germs in January. But none, as far as I knew, had the slightest connection to the death of Flora Arnott. I thought about the casket and the word that had formed in my mind: *murder.* Had it been a warning?

Get a grip. I pulled my quilted jacket from the closet.

If there was a link between Elenor and Flora Arnott, something that led to Elenor's death, the answer would come from research, not talking furniture.

* * *

I set out for the hotel at twelve forty-five. Nancy had insisted on preparing lunch, saying that everyone needed to eat and she needed to keep busy. What I needed was answers.

The ever-present wind carried the briny smell of the sea, layered with the mustiness of fallen leaves and the raw dampness of melting snow. I turned up the collar of my jacket, not that it helped. If my suitcase didn't arrive soon, I'd have to go shopping.

Nearing the main house, I saw Agnes. She stood on the service drive near the post box, rubbing her arms against the cold and shifting from foot to foot. She hadn't taken a sleeping pill after all. I was about to call to her when the rear porch door opened and Nancy waved me inside. "Come in, lass. Warm your wee bones." She took my jacket and hung it on one of the brass hooks in the back hall.

The kitchen was fragrant with the aromas of peat and baking bread. Sofia stood at the kitchen sink, rinsing leaves of romaine lettuce. She was taller than I'd realized. Today she wore a long black wool skirt and a denim shirt with the sleeves rolled up. Her eyes were as dark as obsidian over bruiselike shadows that suggested anxiety. Or insomnia. "You have my sympathy," she said, pronouncing it *zeempaty*.

The first words I'd heard her speak. Eastern European? "Thank you," I said. "It was a shock."

"A shock, a beeg surprise." She reddened. "'Scuse my English."

"Your English is wonderful. Where are you from?"

"I was born in Bulgaria, but I am in this country for many years." She returned to her task, transferring the lettuce to a large ceramic bowl and placing it on the counter.

The back door opened and Agnes appeared, wiping her sturdy shoes on the rug. She pulled off her dark woolen coat and hung it on a hook. "The post," she said, handing a packet bound with a thick rubber band to Nancy.

"Do you think I forget?" Sofia asked. "I was going now."

"No need to get hostile," Agnes snapped. "I was just passing the letter box."

No you weren't, I muttered silently. *You were waiting for the mail delivery.*

Sofia's lip quivered. "Is my job."

"Never mind." Nancy put her arm around Sofia's waist. "Agnes is tired."

"I'm not wired," Agnes said. "She's the one who's wired."

"*Tired*," Nancy repeated. "Honestly, Agnes, if you don't get your hearing tested, we're going to have to buy you an ear trumpet."

Agnes scowled.

Nancy and Sofia laid out a buffet lunch on the long oak table near the hearth. Along with the romaine salad and a lemony dressing, there was a loaf of freshly baked whole-grain bread and a soup of winter squash and apples. Becca joined us, and Nancy ladled a generous portion of soup into her bowl, topping it with a dusting of nutmeg.

Most murders are personal. Begin with those closest to the victim.

I looked at the three women and lost my appetite. That was a first.

Apparently Agnes and Sofia weren't hungry either. They sat staring into their soup.

Sofia sat slightly apart from the rest of us, as still as the doe rabbit I'd found nesting under my porch one March, nearly invisible in her spring camouflage. I'd given her privacy, rejoicing over the tiny balls of fluff that bounced across my lawn five weeks later.

Sofia's coloring didn't lend itself to invisibility.

"Where's Frank?" I asked, breaking the silence.

"Looking for Bo," Nancy said.

Again I felt that frisson of fear. Why was Frank looking for Bo if he wasn't concerned?

Agnes stirred her soup in little figure eights. Getting people to talk wasn't going to be as easy as I'd imagined.

I tried a new tack. "What will happen to the hotel between now and January when the new owners take over?"

That did the trick.

"We carry on as usual," Becca said. "We've got a genealogy seminar in two weeks. No time to cancel now. Christmas is fully booked."

"And we do have a guest," Nancy said. "Poor wee man takes a holiday from crime, and next thing you know there's a murder."

No one batted an eye at the word *murder*. Either Nancy had filled them in or they'd figured it out on their own.

Nancy cleared her half-eaten bowl of soup. "What will you do this afternoon, Kate?"

"DI Devlin asked me to meet him at Elenor's flat. Later I should work on emails." I turned to Becca. "My cell phone's dead, and the charger's in my suitcase. Would you mind if I used your computer?"

"Of course not. It's always on during the day. No password. Use it whenever you like."

"Did Elenor have a laptop?" I was pretty sure I knew the answer. Elenor had been a dyed-in-the-wool technophobe. She didn't email or text. She barely returned phone calls. "If you want to contact Elenor," Bill quipped once, "you'd best send a herald on horseback."

"Elenor didn't trust computers," Agnes said.

Nancy covered her face with her hands.

"What's wrong?" I pushed back my chair.

"Nae, lass." Nancy waved her hand. "It's the uncertainty, the way we're all looking at each other. Things will never be the same."

"You're right about that," Agnes said. "By May we'll all be gone."

Nancy stared at her. "What do you mean?"

"The new owners will 'bring in their own people'?" Agnes put air quotes around the phrase. "Think about it."

"She didnae mean replacing us." Nancy shook her head. "No' without giving notice."

"Maybe she meant the new owners will bring in a larger staff," Becca said.

"That's right." I nodded. "You could use more help, couldn't you?"

"We get along grand as we are," Nancy said. "Locals help in the off-season. They're glad for the extra income. During the season we have the wee summer girls, a whole busload from the Ukraine this year." Nancy put her hand on her heart. "They come to learn English and get work experience, but they get homesick and stop by for cookies and hugs."

"If it's cookies and hugs they want, they should stay at home with their mothers," Agnes said. "They're here to work, and most of them aren't qualified. I guarantee the new owners will do a more thorough job of vetting than Elenor did."

Sofia stood, waving away help as she succumbed to a paroxysm of coughing and ran from the room.

"Was that really necessary?" Nancy asked, the first time I'd heard her angry.

"It's the truth. Face it." Agnes stood. "If you want me, I'll be in my flat." She stumped out of the room, the Eeyore-like cloud over her head almost visible.

Nancy's cell phone rang. She picked up. "Did you find him?"

She listened for a moment before ringing off. Her eyes were wide. "That was Frank. Bo's pickup is at the croft, but he's not there."

Chapter Eleven

∼

I stood outside Elenor's flat while DI Devlin used two keys from a set on a jeweled key ring to open the double-locked door.

Now I really was worried about Bo Duff. He knew I was going to call him today. He was looking forward to our pub meal. Besides, where would he go without his truck?

Calm down. There'd be a simple explanation. Maybe someone picked him up.

Devlin handed me a pair of latex gloves. "We have to wear these. Regulations." He slipped a pair on his own hands with practiced ease. On my hands, the gloves looked like oversized balloons. I rolled the wrists to keep them from falling off.

"Ready?" He gave me a tight smile.

"As I'll ever be."

"Let me know if anything strikes you."

At least he wasn't chewing gum this time.

Devlin opened the door into Elenor's small foyer. A jacket and furled umbrella in Burberry plaid hung on a brass coat tree.

Elenor's living room looked more like a furniture store than a home. Everything matched impeccably. Yesterday her personality had filled the space with sharp angles and saturated colors. Today the angles seemed blunted, the colors bleached.

A white sofa and matching love seat faced a gray-veined marble fireplace. Between them, a square glass coffee table held a heavy art-glass bowl in swirls of cerulean and white and an oversized book enti-tled *One Hundred Years of Fashion & Style*. I ran my gloved hand across the top of a sofa. "No one's dusted in a long time. That's not like Elenor. She was fussy."

In the dining area, a pendant lamp hung over a round table draped in a subtle blue-and-white print cloth. On the table stood an open cardboard box on which someone had scrawled *Historical Society* in thick marker. I peered inside. The box was filled with kitchenware—utensils with chipped Bakelite handles, an aluminum percolator, an iron pot. Someone's castoffs.

I suppressed an urge to dash into the bathroom to see if the casket was still there. Instead, I followed Devlin into Elenor's pristine kitchen.

He opened the built-in refrigerator. "Didn't cook much, did she?"

"I wouldn't either if I had Nancy Holden to cook for me."

In the bedroom, Elenor's bed was loosely made with a pale-blue damask coverlet. Expensive, custom-made. A framed photograph of Bill, the one I'd sent her for Christmas the year he died, rested on the bedside table. One of the hotel's signature waffle-weave bathrobes lay across a chaise lounge covered in the same pale-blue damask. Elenor's blue velvet dress and Hamilton tartan sash lay in a careless heap on the floor. I imagined her dematerializing, leaving them to collapse in place.

A handbag in soft cream-colored leather lay on the bed.

"Take a look inside," Devlin said.

I did, finding the usual items—sunglasses, Kleenex, a comb, sev-eral tubes of lipstick, a powder compact, an assortment of pens, and a leather organizer well stocked with cash and credit cards. I shook my head. "Nothing unusual."

Elenor would have hated the idea of people picking through her things. I half expected her to march through the door, eyes blazing, demanding to know exactly what we thought we were doing in there.

A vanity table with an oval mirror and a small plush bench filled the space between two tall windows. The middle drawer hung open, exposing a hodgepodge of creams, foundations, lipsticks, eye makeup. The glass top held a lighted makeup mirror, a prescription bottle, several expensive-looking flasks of perfume, and a blue velvet ring box.

"May I?" I indicated the ring box and Devlin nodded. The box was empty, but gold lettering under the domed lid spelled out PATERSON & SON, JEWELERS, INVERNESS.

The prescription had come from a local chemist in Mallaig. The label read ESZOPICLONE. NO REFILLS. I opened it and tipped several round blue tablets into my hand. Each was marked *S193*. "What's eszopiclone?"

"Let's find out." Devlin typed something into his cell phone. A moment later he read aloud: "Eszopiclone may be effective in the treatment of insomnia where difficulty in falling asleep is the primary complaint. If drug therapy is appropriate, it should be initiated at the lowest possible dose to minimize side effects."

"Sleeping pills." I tipped the blue pills back into the bottle and closed the cap.

"Was Mrs. Spurgeon in the habit of taking sedatives?" Devlin asked.

"I don't know. She's been under stress."

Devlin gestured around the bedroom. "Any thoughts?"

"Yes, actually. It looks to me like Elenor was already undressed when the phone rang. Someone insisted on meeting her at the Historical Society, so she threw on some clothes and redid her makeup. That tells me the caller was a man."

"Romantic evening?"

"No. If she were leaving for a romantic evening, she would have taken her handbag."

"Why's that?"

"Lipstick, compact, comb." *Men don't have a clue.* "The fact that she left it behind tells me she was planning to come right back."

Devlin raised an eyebrow, and I couldn't help a brief gloat.

"Take a look in the bathroom," Devlin said.

I breathed a sigh of relief. There it was, the casket, resting on its towel-draped plinth. I ran my hand over the velvet-smooth surface, half dreading and half desiring a repeat of the experience I'd had the day before, but today the casket was keeping its counsel.

"Some kind of chest, right? Looks old." Devlin perched on the edge of a claw-foot tub so large you could swim laps.

"I saw it yesterday when I arrived. It's probably eighteenth century, and technically, it's a casket."

"Small for a casket, unless you're talking a pet hamster."

"Not to bury someone. That's a coffin. A casket is a case for valuables—documents, coins, jewelry. The decoration is called *marquetry*, inlaid designs using the grain and colors of thin veneers, usually wood, but sometimes other materials like tortoiseshell or ivory or precious metals. The workmanship is exceptionally fine." I looked up, wanting him to understand. "This piece is valuable. Museum quality."

"Why keep it in the bathroom?"

"I assume Elenor set it up to be photographed. I can think of three reasons she might do that: to document it for insurance purposes, to inquire about its *provenance*—its history—or to offer it for sale. May I check the underside?"

"Help yourself."

"British cabinetmakers of the period rarely marked their pieces, but you never know." I lifted the casket, judging the size-to-weight ratio, one of the indicators of age and quality. The piece might have been made by one of the famous London houses—Sheraton, Chippendale, Hepplewhite—but their work was well documented, and I'd never seen anything remotely like this casket. I considered the lesser-known houses—Frederick Beck, maybe, or Ince & Mayhew—but even that was unlikely. Holding the key in place, I turned the casket over, feeling something shift inside. The underside of the casket was beautifully constructed, the boards fitted side-to-side to minimize shrinkage and expansion. "No marks," I said, replacing the box on the table, "but there's something inside." I turned the key and lifted the lid.

Within the faded red-leather-lined compartment was a copy of Guthrie's book. I opened the cover and found an inscription: *To Elenor with love, Hugh.*

DS Bruce poked his head in the room. "Message, sir."

Devlin excused himself and stepped out.

I looked at the casket, then at the book in my hands. What was it about Elenor and that book? *Look for the details*, my mother would say. *When you see things together, things that shouldn't be together, there's always a connection.*

Once, in a box of old pearl buttons, my mother found an unused train ticket. Stoughton, Wisconsin, to Chicago, dated 1932. "What do you think the woman was like who owned this button box?" she asked me, then about fourteen. "Why would she keep a train ticket in with her buttons?"

"Stuck it in there one day and forgot about it?" I hadn't especially cared.

"No, look. The buttons are sorted and sewn onto pieces of muslin. The needles are pinned into squares of felt in order of size. This woman was orderly. And she's saved thread, winding it around bits of folded paper, so she was thrifty, too."

"What do you think?" I asked, interested in spite of myself.

"I think she was a seamstress, and she saved up money for a long time to get away from her small town and start a new life. She hid the ticket in a place no one would look. But she never had the courage to go. Or maybe"—my mother's eyes had brightened with a happier thought—"she met a wonderful man and decided she didn't want to leave after all."

Mother, the eternal optimist. But she was right about noticing details, things that shouldn't be together. That principle had come in handy when I was raising my children. Finding crumbs in the pocket of Christine's pink jacket after the cookies I made for the school bake sale vanished. Noticing the smear of lipstick on Eric's collar after the junior high youth group hayride. They'd called me Sherlock Holmes.

So why had Elenor put Guthrie's novel in the marquetry casket? What was the connection?

"Sorry." Devlin returned to the bathroom. "That was Mrs. Spurgeon's doctor. He began prescribing the sedatives six months ago when she said she couldn't sleep. Lately she's been asking for more. He was concerned about addiction."

Addiction? I'd known Elenor to overindulge in alcohol on occasion but never drugs.

Devlin glanced at Guthrie's book, still in my hands. "We've already examined the book. Take a look at page 112."

I turned to that page, finding in the margin a notation in Elenor's handwriting: *HS6uprtgrnlft51bluedn3rd.*

"Mean anything to you?"

"Some kind of code?"

Devlin snorted. "And here's me without my secret decoder ring."

I bit back a remark about boys who never grow up. "I'm serious. When we price antiques at the shop, we use a code to record the price paid and the date of acquisition. If it's a consignment piece, we include the initials of the owner. *HS* could mean Hewie Spurgeon, Elenor's husband. He died in a plane crash more than a decade ago. Maybe he left a safe deposit box somewhere, or a Swiss bank account."

"We're checking that." Devlin sounded testy.

No unsolicited opinions. I'd broken the rules again.

"Is it all right if I ask my mother to do some research on the casket? She's an expert. I'd like to send her photos."

"The crime scene team should be finished later today. After that, help yourself. Just don't mention it to anyone."

I replaced the book and closed the lid. As I did, I stepped on something, a paper clip, pulled apart to make a tool. Knowing that old lock mechanisms can stick, I hoped Elenor—impatient as she was—hadn't caused damage. I turned the key a few times, and the mortise moved up and down, smooth as silk. I laid the clip on the porcelain sink.

"There's something else I want you to see." We returned to Elenor's bedroom.

Devlin pulled out the bottom drawer of Elenor's desk and removed three sheets of plain white writing paper, each with its own envelope. He laid them on the desktop. Three messages had been printed by hand in capital letters.

The first sounded almost biblical: *DECEIVERS WILL PAY FOR THEIR SINS.*

Devlin cocked his head. "Mrs. Spurgeon didn't tell you she was being threatened?"

"No. She said she was afraid. She didn't tell me why."

"Does the message have any significance to you?"

"It's a veiled threat, obviously. When did she receive it?"

"Postmarked in Fort William on October third, so possibly the fifth."

I read the second message: *MY HOUSE SHALL NEVER BELONG TO STRANGERS.*

"*My* house?" I said. "Sounds like someone pretending to be Flora Arnott."

Here was a possible link between Elenor's death and Flora Arnott, but instead of shedding light, it only deepened the mystery. "I think someone was trying to frighten Elenor out of selling the hotel to that Swiss company. The problem is no one admits knowing the hotel was for sale."

I read the final letter, postmarked October seventeenth. This one upped the ante: *ENJOY THE BALL, ELENOR. IT WILL BE YOUR LAST.*

I felt a chill.

Three letters, each mailed in Fort William on a Monday, a week apart. Elenor would have received the final one—I counted the days—on Wednesday, the nineteenth. *The nineteenth.* A memory pricked at the back of my neck. "Look at the date," I said, tapping the postmark. "October nineteenth. The day Elenor called the antique shop, begging for my help."

Devlin made a note in his little black book. Then he gathered up the papers and slid them into an evidence bag. "We'll have the printing analyzed. You'd be surprised what an expert can glean, even from block letters."

Block letters? The jolt of recognition came like a punch in the gut. "Wait a minute. I received a note like that. In block letters, anyway." I told him about finding the note in the pocket of the borrowed dress. "I assumed the message wasn't for me."

"Do you still have it?"

"It's in my handbag in the kitchen. I'll get it."

I returned in minutes and handed him the folded paper.

He read it and looked up. "Someone told you to go home. Why?"

"I don't know." My standard answer. But should I have known? Had I missed something?

Devlin put the note in another evidence bag, sealed it, and scrawled some words on the outside. He gave me his card. "If you receive any further communication, or if anything happens that doesn't feel right, call me immediately."

DS Bruce appeared in the doorway. He waved a piece of paper triumphantly. "Got it, sir. Name of the plow guy. They're sending a couple of constables to pick him up."

Chapter Twelve

I climbed the stairs to Agnes's apartment and knocked softly on her door. No answer. I knocked again, more loudly. "Agnes, are you there? It's Kate."

"Come in." She sounded sleepy.

Agnes's flat was identical to Elenor's in layout. What drew my eye were the paintings. Agnes collected landscapes in oil, mostly mid- to late-nineteenth century I judged. Not masterpieces but skillfully executed.

Where Elenor had a dining room, Agnes had made a library. That's where she sat, prostrate in an overstuffed chair, her eyes covered with a damp cloth. Two tall windows admitted the dull afternoon light.

"Should I come back later? I see you're resting."

"Nesting?" Agnes grabbed the cloth and struggled to sit up. "I'm trying to pull myself together. Come, sit." She slid an accusing look in my direction. "I suppose you knew all about the sale of the hotel."

"I didn't, actually. I don't even know why Elenor wanted me to come."

Agnes's nut-brown eyes fluttered. "Maybe she hoped with you here, the serfs wouldn't organize a lynching party."

I marveled again at the change in Agnes's attitude. I'd met Agnes more than twenty years ago when Elenor (Elenor Hamilton then) had been hired as the sixth-form English teacher by St. Hilda's School for Girls near Aberdeen. Naturally she couldn't cope, so Bill and I had left our two toddlers with my mother and flew over to help her find a flat, set up a bank account, and settle into her new job. She'd made quite a splash. The dress code at St. Hilda's tended toward boxy business suits and sensible pumps. Elenor—platinum blonde, pencil thin—wore cashmere and Italian wools and silk blouses in luscious colors. The other teachers were jealous, of course, especially when Elenor chose Agnes MacLeod, the primary school art teacher, as a special friend and confidante. Why Agnes was singled out as the recipient of Elenor's favor was obvious to me if not to anyone else. Elenor needed to be adored. Or at least envied. Agnes fit the bill on both counts, following Elenor around with a kind of starry-eyed gratitude. It made me sick.

Disaster was inevitable. Elenor was intelligent and knowledgeable in her field, but she had little interest in the students and cared nothing about the traditions and reputation of the school—St. Hilda's one unforgivable sin. Then there was The Scandal. Both Elenor and the headmaster were dismissed, and back we flew to pick up the pieces.

Elenor's teaching career was in shambles. She'd never get a recommendation from St. Hilda's. She didn't need one, as it turned out. Two weeks after her dismissal, Elenor met multimillionaire Hewie Spurgeon, sprinting from girlfriend to wife to merry widow before the year was out. After Hewie's death—he crashed his Gulfstream IV twinjet, making Elenor the fortunate fourth (and final) Mrs. Hewie Spurgeon—she counted her millions and declared that her life's dream was to turn her family's estate on the Isle of Glenroth into an upscale country house hotel. And Agnes MacLeod would help make that dream a reality.

Little Agnes had traveled a long way from hero worship to contempt. Realizing the situation called for diplomacy, I said, "I figured if anyone knew what's been going on around here, it would be you."

The implied compliment brought a flush of pleasure. "What do you want to know?"

"Had anything happened lately that caused you concern?" I wanted to say *like threatening letters* but waited for her answer.

"I don't think so." The corners of Agnes's mouth turned down.

"What about Elenor's behavior? Did anything strike you as strange?"

"Stranger than usual?" Agnes pursed her lips. "She's been going on about people stealing things. Did Nancy tell you about the missing silver tray? Elenor blamed me. What was I supposed to do—post an armed guard? I told her it was dumb to keep something like that on display. She never listened."

"The tray was valuable?"

"Geoff Brooker said it was made in London by Hester somebody. He showed us the marks on the bottom."

I knew all about Hester Bateman, the eighteenth-century silversmith who had taken over the family workshop after her husband's death. A tray by Hester Bateman would be valuable indeed.

"The tray was engraved," Agnes said. "*Y* for Young—Flora's maiden name—and *A* for Arnott. Workmen found it in the attic when we had the roof repaired a few years ago. There was a wee article about it in the newspaper. The twins thought it should go to them, but Elenor's solicitor said that legally it went with the house. We use it sometimes to serve tea in the conservatory. Guests love the Flora connection."

So it wouldn't be easy to shift locally. I knew from experience that easily identified pieces stolen in one part of a country are usually disposed of in another, even sold abroad. "Was anything else stolen?" I wondered if Agnes's version of events would agree with Nancy's.

"Not from the hotel," Agnes said, "but Elenor insisted someone was stealing things from the Historical Society, too, although I can't make out how anyone would know. Have you seen the place? More car-boot sale than museum."

"What do you think happened to the tray?"

"Who knows?" Agnes said tartly. "Maybe the ghost of Flora Arnott took it."

"Bill told me about the ghost."

"Did he tell you she still walks the halls? Pure blather, of course, but I'm certain that's why Elenor wanted me to live in the house. Afraid to be alone. She claimed she saw disappearing shadows, heard creaking floorboards."

"Did you ever hear footsteps?" Foolish question. With Agnes's hearing, an entire platoon of ghosts could troop through the house undetected.

Agnes *tsk*ed. "This is an old house. Windows rattle, things settle."

"You're not a believer in the Arnott curse?"

Her upper lip curled in disgust. "Ghosts, curses, superstitions. Elenor's way of getting attention."

"I don't think she enjoyed the attention she got last night. Did you have a chance to talk with her after the party?"

"No." Agnes plucked a bit of invisible fluff off the arm of her cardigan. "I finished my work and came straight up to bed. Well, I might have turned on the telly to relax a bit first. I'd been awake since dawn. Never even stuck my nose outside the house after lunch."

"The police said you heard Elenor's phone ring at eleven thirty. You didn't know she went out?"

"I heard her phone ring, yes. You can, you know, in an old house. I knew it was eleven thirty because the weather presenter had just signed off, but once I take my sleeping pill, I'm out like a light." Agnes's eyes were little round moons in a full-moon face. "In fact, I had a bit of a lie-in this morning. Nancy had to wake me up when the police came to tell us Elenor was"—she swallowed hard—"dead. I didn't find out she'd been murdered until Nancy told me. The police made me wait all that time, wondering. It was cruel."

Her choice of words surprised me. Overly cautious, maybe, even insensitive. But cruel?

"Did Elenor ever mention old newspapers?"

Agnes's face went blank. "If you mean Historical Society stuff, you'll have to ask Dr. Guthrie."

"Did you know Elenor was in love with him?"

"I'd have sworn in a court of law she wasn't. Guthrie isn't her type at all. Elenor liked a challenge." Agnes tapped the side of her nose. "Not *strictly* available, if you know what I mean."

"I know about the headmaster at St. Hilda's."

"*And* Hewie Spurgeon. He was still married when they . . . got together." Agnes struggled to sit up. "Elenor craved excitement. Secret meetings, forbidden fruit. Or maybe the pleasure of being adored without the commitment."

The comment was so insightful I had to adjust my assessment of Agnes. She must not have been quite as starry-eyed as I'd thought. Elenor did crave attention. I'd always thought it was the reason she resented me. I'd knocked her off center stage in Bill's world.

"I told her she was playing with fire," Agnes said with the knowing air of someone who's had vast experience with the opposite sex. "She laughed it off, but I got the idea there'd been a pregnancy."

I blinked. This was the last thing I'd expected to hear. "Are you telling me Elenor had a child? An abortion?"

"I don't think she would have done that." Agnes chewed her bottom lip. "Look, I don't know for a fact she had a child. It's an idea I got from something she said once."

Bill had never mentioned a pregnancy. Of course he wouldn't if Elenor had sworn him to secrecy. But if Elenor had a child somewhere, then I had a niece or nephew. Eric and Christine had a cousin. There would be records.

I refocused on what Agnes was saying.

She lay back, half closing her eyes. "The second year after Elenor came to St. Hilda's, she invited me to spend my summer holiday with her on the island. When the hotel was still her family home. But my father got ill, and I had to leave. Elenor stayed alone, which she never liked. Later she told me she had an affair with a married man, a much older man. It broke up his marriage. There was a child involved."

Something stirred in my brain. Was I wrong after all about the connection with Flora Arnott? A broken marriage could be a motive for murder years later, especially with an unexpected pregnancy. "But Elenor would have returned to teaching at the end of summer. How was she able to hide a pregnancy?"

"That's the thing. She was present for fall term but left school after Christmas for a special course at London University. At least that's what we were told. We were allowed to take a sabbatical every ten years. She said she talked the headmaster into waiving the rules so she could go early. Created quite a fuss among the faculty, as I remember."

I remembered it, too. Bill had sent her money. Had it really been to cover the cost of housing in London or to offset the costs of a pregnancy and adoption? With Bill gone, I'd probably never know. "Was her lover someone from the island?"

"Elenor never said who the man was."

"What happened?"

"Happened?" Agnes opened her eyes. "Nothing. Elenor wasn't serious about him. What I mean is, I can't see Dr. Guthrie as a challenge, can you? Now his mother—that's another story."

True. I thought about the face-off between Elenor and Margaret Guthrie at the Tartan Ball. Boadicea versus the Queen of the Amazons. "Why was Margaret Guthrie opposed to the marriage?"

"You mean apart from the fact that they sprang it on her like that? Frankly, though, I don't think she'd have accepted the engagement under any circumstances. They say Cilla Arnott took a shine to Hugh Guthrie once, years ago. Margaret Guthrie put a stop to it. Weird relationship there, if you ask me."

"What's Hugh Guthrie like?" I was poking at shadows, hoping to hit something solid.

"Born and bred on Glenroth. The Guthries were one of the families who settled here with James Arnott in 1809. Hugh's mother is one of the Aberdeen Parkers, the fishery people who got in on North Sea oil in the late sixties. They say he has a whopping trust fund. They also say he's been a disappointment to his mother."

"Why?"

"The Parkers are a prominent family. Very proud. Hugh never made a name for himself academically. He's considered an expert on those ancient stone circles, but he never promoted himself. No ambition."

"Writing a book's pretty ambitious."

"A bit of a fuss?" Agnes cocked her ear.

"Am-bi-tious."

Agnes looked thoughtful. "He's writing a sequel. There's even talk of a movie." She spread out the damp cloth, smoothed it, and rolled it into a fat sausage. "One thing bothers me. That constable—Mackie—told us Elenor's body was found just after seven this morning. But Bo Duff begins plowing early. Four AM. Never varies. He would have passed the Historical Society around five. If he saw a body, he would have called the police."

A trickle of fear ran down my back. If Bo Duff plowed the island roads, then he was the one who'd inadvertently destroyed potential evidence the night of Elenor's murder. And he was the person the deputies were on their way to pick up right now.

I shook off the worry, or tried to. Agnes was right. Bo was kind, caring. No way would he find a body and fail to tell someone.

Agnes ran her fingers through her hair, revealing several angry scratches on her forehead.

"You've hurt yourself," I said.

"Hurt myself? Oh . . . aye." Agnes finger-combed her hair over her forehead. "Bumped into a door, if you can credit it."

I couldn't credit it, but I let it go. "What will you do now? Will you stay on at Glenroth House?"

Agnes snorted. "We'll all be turfed out. If Elenor had an ounce of decency, she'd have tried to save our jobs. Did you know she promised me part ownership in the hotel? That's why I gave up my career, my future. I even cashed in my pension to tide me over—just until things got going and she could afford to pay me more. That never happened. And then, after all I'd done for her, she ups and sells the place."

And then she ups and dies.

Red splotches flared on Agnes's neck. "What did she expect me to do—hand out trolleys at the Poundstretcher in Portree?"

I rowed back into safer waters. "Couldn't you go back to teaching? Or work in an art gallery? You're clearly an expert. Your paintings are wonderful."

"Art is my passion." Agnes unrolled the sausage and pressed it against her neck.

"You must have been collecting a long time."

"Oh, no. Just since we moved to Glenroth. I had a furnishing allowance. I chose not to use the fancy decorator from Edinburgh and bought paintings instead. They belong to me. It's in my contract."

So, Agnes wasn't going to be left a complete pauper. The collection would fetch a good sum at auction. Not enough to retire on, but it would be a start.

"That was generous," I said. Foolishly.

"Generous? *Elenor*?" Agnes's face went bright red. "I was the one who did all the work. All the ideas were mine—all the good ones, anyway. She couldn't have pulled it off without me. And not once in eleven years did she so much as give me a raise." A tear spilled out and ran down her cheek. "Never even said thank you." Agnes dabbed her eyes. "Only took me twenty years to figure it out. We were never friends. I was convenient, someone to keep around until my usefulness wore off."

Probably true. Once the hotel was sold, Agnes was expendable. "Elenor always was better at making enemies than friends."

"I'll tell you one thing," Agnes sniffed. "I wouldn't want to make an enemy of Margaret Guthrie. That woman is scary."

"What do you mean?"

"I'm just saying. You don't poke a tiger with a stick."

I collected my handbag. "Don't get up. I'll let myself out."

Agnes's dark woolen coat hung on a hook in the foyer. Something stuck out of the pocket—the cuff of a glove. A purple knitted glove. Like the strands of purple wool the police had found outside the Historical Society?

I felt the cuff. Soaked through. A pair of molded rubber wellies sat on the floor in a slowly evaporating puddle.

Never even stuck my nose outside after lunch.

Agnes lied.

She had gone outside before lunch today to collect the mail, but she'd been wearing shoes, not wellies, and I would have noticed purple gloves. Unless she had gotten up at the crack of dawn for a snowball fight with Frank Holden, she'd been out in the storm last night.

"Everything all right?" Agnes called from around the corner.

"Just leaving." I plucked a bit of damp purple fuzz and stuck it in my pocket.

I pictured the angry red scratches on Agnes's face.

Had Elenor poked a tiger? Which one?

Chapter Thirteen

~

I was overjoyed to see my suitcase on the bench at the foot of my bed. Frank Holden must have delivered it while I was with Agnes.

The first thing I did was locate my charger cord and plug in my cell phone. Then I unpacked my clothes, smoothed out the wrinkles, and hung them in the closet.

My thoughts circled back to that wet purple glove.

Agnes had been out in the storm the night Elenor died, I was sure of it. And it wasn't only the wet gloves and wellies that convinced me. Those little round eyes. The set of her shoulders. Agnes wasn't a natural liar. She was probably telling the truth about hearing Elenor's phone ring at eleven thirty, though. The police could check that. Maybe the caller was Agnes herself, confronting Elenor with the broken promise of partnership. But why would the two of them leave in the middle of a snowstorm to fight about it?

When Nancy and I left the hotel that night, we'd seen lights on in Elenor's flat, but that didn't mean she was there. I should have asked DI Devlin if her lights were still on when the local constable arrived before dawn on Saturday.

I folded my cherry wool sweater and tucked it in the top drawer of the high dresser.

Agnes's resentment was understandable, but had she been angry enough to kill Elenor? I could just about imagine her slipping poison in Elenor's drink. I couldn't imagine her shooting Elenor with an arrow and watching her die. Maybe my suspicions were unfair. Even if Agnes had followed Elenor to the Historical Society that night, it didn't mean she killed her. Besides, as Devlin pointed out, there was no way to determine that the purple fibers had been caught on the bush the night of the ball. Maybe Agnes had visited the Historical Society earlier. Maybe someone else on the Isle of Glenroth wore purple knitted gloves. Maybe the Arnott twins knitted them by the dozen and gave them away as gifts.

I zipped up my now-empty suitcase and slid it under the bed. If I showed DI Devlin the strands of purple wool, he'd accuse me of playing amateur sleuth. Well, to be honest, I was, but was it my fault if people left clues dangling out of coat pockets?

I peeled off my jeans and T-shirt and changed into my jogging clothes—black leggings with a microfleece, an old Case Western sweatshirt of Bill's, and my trusty Nikes. I needed to clear my mind.

A well-worn footpath followed the sea from below the hotel to Crabby Point. That's what Bill had christened it, anyway, in honor of the curmudgeon who'd stationed himself daily at the end of the jetty to shake his fist at boats venturing inside the breakwater. The jetty was gone now, and so was the old man.

Time, like an ever-rolling stream, bears all its sons away.

Time had borne Bill away. Now it had borne Elenor away, too, except that in Elenor's case, someone had shoved the hands of time forward a couple of decades.

A flock of greylag geese flew in formation, honking encouragement to their leaders.

I followed the track from the rear of Applegarth toward the low cliff edge. Applegarth was the smallest of the hotel's guest cottages. The others were tucked in the woods east of the main house, stone structures with steeply pitched roofs and leaded windows, the stuff of fairy tales—Snow White, Cinderella, Hansel and Gretel. Romantic, if you ignored poisoned apples, wicked stepmothers, and old ladies with long, sharp teeth.

The melting snow had left icy patches. I picked my way cautiously down the stone steps to a rocky cove. The path, cushioned by white crushed-coral sand, skirted the edge of the dark-turquoise sea. Fingers of amber kelp rose and fell among the rocks. Sea spray whipped my hair and wet my face. I pulled up my hood.

A question niggled at the back of my mind. Could Bo have missed Elenor's body in the predawn shadows?

I lengthened my stride, taking in the scent of fish and peaty earth. Two dark smudges on the southern horizon picked out the small islands of Rùm and Eigg. In the distance, a colony of spotted seals lay like giant sausages on the half-tide rocks. Several raised their whiskered, doglike faces and barked. I was headed north. In a mile or so I'd be able to see the tip of the Sleat Peninsula on the Isle of Skye.

The narrow beach widened, and the footpath snaked through a sliver of forest skirting the sand. I pushed myself into a jog, feeling the pleasurable burn in my thighs. Bill and Elenor had loved the sea as children. They'd waded in the tidal pools and collected mussels, cleaning them in seawater and boiling them over a beach fire. Jackie MacDonald's ancestors had revered this island as well, their devotion fueled by legend.

A bonnie prince. A lost dream. *Will ye no' come back again?*

The land was thick with memories, the kind that never die but go dormant, waiting for someone to remember and mourn.

Would I ever stop mourning?

A riptide of sorrow took my breath. I stopped running, gulping in the cold, salt air and trying to regain my equilibrium. The wind tore at the hood of my sweatshirt.

The day Bill died, a gusty wind blew in spurts from the southwest. We'd come to Glenroth by ourselves—a second honeymoon, Bill said, except we were staying at the Harborview instead of Glenroth

House. Fine with me. Better, in fact. That evening we'd decided to eat at the Bonnie Prince. "We might run into a few of the lads," he'd said, and I could tell he hoped we would. I hoped so too, for his sake. The next day we'd planned to take the ferry to Skye and hike to the chilly, sparkling blue Fairy Pools near Glenbrittle.

I was unpacking when Bill returned from what he'd promised would be a quick visit to the hotel, just to say hello. "Sorry, Kate." He reached out to touch my hair. Sunlight picked out the lines around his eyes and mouth, and I remember thinking he'd been looking tired lately, older. "We'll have to postpone the Skye trip. Elenor needs my help in the morning. It may take most of the day. A problem with one of her suppliers."

"Can't it wait?"

"She says not. We can go another day, can't we?"

I'm not proud of my reaction. I flung the shirts I was holding onto the bed and turned to face him. "Why do you always put Elenor first? She probably manufactured the problem to sabotage our time together. I wouldn't put it past her."

"That's unkind, Kate. And selfish."

"Are you going to put me in time-out? You're not my father, Bill."

That's when I saw Elenor standing in the cottage doorway. The look of triumph on her face told me she'd heard every word. And relished it.

Bill grabbed his blue windbreaker. "I'll take my sister home. Then I'm going sailing."

Later I sat, fully dressed and miserable, in one of the canvas loungers along the strand. A paperback novel, an Agatha Christie, lay in my lap. I read the same page three times before closing the book in disgust.

I'd have to apologize to Elenor. No getting around that. But first I'd apologize to Bill, the minute he came in. Even if Elenor had purposely ruined our day, it wasn't his fault. Bill's kindness was one of the things I most admired about him. I couldn't stop him loving his sister. I didn't want to. The problem was mine. I had to fix it.

The sea shimmered in the afternoon light. Waves folded upon themselves along the silver sand. Bill was tacking back and forth in his single-hand dinghy about a half mile off shore, his red life vest a bright dot. I watched the sail luff and fill again as he brought the small boat about into the wind. A strong gust threatened to topple my umbrella. I reached to steady it. Then I grabbed my binoculars and turned the focus.

The sail snapped as the boom swung free.

Bill? What's wrong?

A sharp crack rang out jerking me back to the present. My head turned instinctively toward the sound, but all I saw were trees, ferns, lengthening shadows. Silence.

Did predators still live in these woods?

Something rustled, and this time I caught a dark shape melting into the foliage.

That was no animal.

I turned toward the hotel, striding quickly as images flipped through my brain. Terrible images. The dead bodies of Flora and Gowyn near the peat bogs. Bill, lying cold and still on the pier. Elenor, seeing the face of her killer as he (or she?) drew back the bow.

Spooked now, I began to run, but the section of path was uneven and the light was fading faster than I'd imagined. I narrowed my eyes, scanning the track for roots or stones—anything that might trip me up. Someone had lain in wait for Elenor at the Historical Society. Was that person stalking me now?

"Kate, watch out."

My head shot up just in time to see Tom Mallory before I barreled into him.

"Blimey," he said, catching me and holding on until I regained my balance. "We *will* keep running into each other."

"Sorry," I managed to get out between breaths. "I wasn't paying attention. Again."

He wore dark athletic pants and a lightweight black hoodie in some kind of thin, synthetic fabric. His hair had fallen across his forehead. "Training for a cross-country?"

"I thought—" I felt foolish now, but I hadn't imagined that dark shadow. "Well, to be honest, I thought I saw someone in the woods near the path. With all that's happened, it frightened me."

He looked at me sharply. "What did you see?"

"A shadow." That sounded terminally lame, even to me.

"An animal? A deer?"

"It didn't look like an animal. I got the idea someone was following me."

Tom nodded, probably deciding if I was given to hysterics.

He glanced at the sky. "It's getting dark fast. Come on. I'll walk back with you. Nearly time for dinner anyway."

True, and if Tom had set out for a run, he'd started a bit late.

Chapter Fourteen

～

I left Applegarth at six thirty and followed the mushroom lights toward the hotel. My experience in the woods had left me feeling vulnerable. And more than a little silly.

Movement in the distance caught my eye. A dark figure strode away from the house toward the wooded glen. My stalker? Flora's ghost? With those long legs, it looked more like Sofia.

I picked up my pace. I couldn't claim to have seen a ghost, but I was certainly racking up dark figure sightings.

On the far side of the parking lot, DI Devlin and Tom Mallory stood near one of the hotel's gas lamps. Devlin gave Tom a playful shove, knocking him off balance. They'd become buddies pretty quickly—that all-cops-together thing again, I supposed. They noticed me, and something in their faces told me I'd been a subject of conversation.

I ran up the steps.

"Hey, Kate." Becca Wallace sat at her desk. "You got your suitcase at last. Love the outfit."

"Changing clothes was an amazing experience." I wore the skinny black ankle pants and cherry-red cashmere sweater Christine had given me for my last birthday. Charged on my Visa.

"Mrs. Guthrie called." Becca handed me a pink slip.

Can you come tomorrow afternoon? the message read. *Please let me know.*

Becca let me use the desk phone. Margaret Guthrie was home, and I accepted her invitation for "tea and light refreshments" at three PM on Sunday.

"Give me a moment. I'll take you to your table," Becca said.

As she busied herself with the papers on her desk, I examined one of the few original pieces in the house, a portrait of Captain Arnott's only child, a son by his second wife. He stared at me with stern, thin-lipped disapproval.

"Favored his mother," Becca said wryly, shoving a notebook in the top drawer of the desk. "There's a framed silhouette of the second Mrs. James Arnott in the Snug. She looks as disagreeable as he does. Not that I blame her. She married the captain and became his widow before this lad was even born."

"At least she got the house."

"Yes. This is a wonderful house." Becca swiveled her chair toward me. "Full of surprises. You know about the secret staircase, right?"

"First thing Bill showed me. I thought I was supposed to be admiring the Georgian woodwork, but when we got to the third-floor landing, he pressed on one of the raised panels and it swung open. Like a fairy-tale castle, except for the spider webs." I shuddered. "I've got a thing about spiders."

"The spider webs are gone, I promise. We take guests up there sometimes if they ask. Of course Elenor never would. She had a thing about the attic."

The phone rang and Becca picked it up. "Glenroth House. May I help?"

I pictured the large, open space under the eaves where I'd seen a hodgepodge of old furniture shrouded in dusty sheeting, mostly inferior stuff from the thirties and forties. I'd also seen a large number of crates and boxes, neatly sealed and stacked. The attic air that June day had been hot and dry, faintly musty with a finish of mothballs. For the budding antique dealer in me, perfume. "Did you and Elenor play up there as children?" I'd asked Bill as we made our way down. He'd grinned. "You'll find this hard to believe, but Elenor and I were more interested in the sea and the woods. We played outdoors with the island kids. Mostly boys, as I remember. Half the boys on the island were in love with Elenor."

But who had Elenor been in love with?

* * *

I followed Becca into the west wing and along a corridor to the library, a large room facing the front of the house. Floor-to-ceiling bookshelves flanked the fireplace and continued along the wall nearest the door. Three tall windows provided a view of the parking area and curved drive. A narrow refectory table held a selection of cheeses, what looked like homemade crackers, and two bottles of wine. I examined the labels—a Cabernet from France and a pale Riesling from Austria.

A table was set in front of a crackling fire. "What's this?" I asked, fearing I already knew the answer.

"Mr. Mallory will be joining you. You don't mind, do you?"

"Mind? Of course I mind. And more to the point, so will he. He'll assume I set it up." I groaned. Most of the single men I knew in Ohio wore the perpetually suspicious look of game animals on a private hunting preserve.

"It's only dinner."

"This feels awkward, Becca. I know Tom and I are the only guests, but I had no idea we'd be sharing a table. I'd rather eat in the kitchen, or in the cottage. I can cook for myself."

"Too late." Becca whispered and slipped out the door just as Tom Mallory entered.

"Good evening, Kate. You look wonderful."

He looked wonderful himself. Tonight he wore another pair of beautifully tailored trousers, this time with a kind of marled blue V-neck sweater over an open-collared white shirt.

He bent to kiss my cheek. "No further incidents? You're all right?"

I nodded and layered a sliver of cheese on a cracker. "I keep imagining I'll wake up and everything will be back to normal."

He held up one of the stemmed glasses. "Red or white?"

"White, please." As he poured, I thought about my mother's flexibility. One of her gifts. "Accept what you can't change," she would tell me now. "Look for the silver lining." As far as I knew, my mother had coined that phrase. The silver lining here was an opportunity to find out more about the mysterious detective inspector from Suffolk, England. I took the glass from his hand. "Your card said 'CID.' That's Criminal Investigation Division, right?"

"Right." He handed me the glass. "Coppers in plain clothes."

"I'm not a geography expert, but isn't Suffolk north of London?"

"Right again. East of Cambridge, south of Norfolk. Along the coast, if that helps. I work out of Bury St. Edmunds, about fifty miles inland."

"Is that where you live as well?" I took a sip of the Riesling. Crisp, citrusy.

"I live in Saxby St. Clare, a village thirty miles south of Bury." He poured himself a glass of the Cab. "We have a post office, a petrol station, a Tesco, and three pubs—all the necessities."

"As lively as the Isle of Glenroth after tourist season then." I cringed. "Apart from the murder."

"Let's not talk about murder," he said, making things worse. "How do you like your cottage?"

"Lovely. They all are. Elenor spent a lot of money on renovation."

"I'm in Tartan. First one east of the main house. Two bedrooms, two baths. I'm rattling around there on my own."

I was about to ask him if he'd come on holiday when the library door swung open and Sofia entered with a tray stand. If Sofia was the person striding away from the house earlier, she'd made it back in no time flat.

"Sit, please." Sofia set up the stand near the hearth and disappeared.

Tom pulled out my chair. I sat, feeling as awkward as a middle-schooler at her first boy-girl dance. "This wasn't my idea, by the way."

His eyes crinkled at the corners. "Too bad. I was hoping it was."

I pictured my mother, doing one of her I-told-you-so looks.

Sofia returned with bowls of fresh green salad and a basket of warm rolls. After filling our water glasses, she left again, shutting the door behind her. The feeling of awkwardness returned. What would we find to talk about for the next hour or so?

Quite a lot, as it turned out. Like me, Tom was single. His wife, Sarah, had died of ovarian cancer five years earlier when their daughter, Olivia, was thirteen.

"Eric was in college and Christine in high school when Bill died," I said. "At least he was there when they were growing up. How did you manage?"

"My mother moved in after Sarah died. For Olivia's sake. My job doesn't run to regular hours."

"Your father?"

"Dead."

"Brothers and sisters?"

"None. What about you?"

"My father died when I was seventeen. My mother lives in what's called an active retirement community in Wisconsin. She's staying at my house in Ohio at the moment, keeping my antique shop open."

"Siblings?"

"I had a brother." I watched a log collapse in a shower of embers. "He was a Down's child."

"He died?"

"When I was five. He was born with a serious heart defect. Lived eleven years. Longer than expected, I'm told."

Tom handed me the basket of rolls. "Tell me about your children."

"Well, Eric's getting a master's degree in nuclear physics. This quarter he's doing research near Turin in Italy—something to do with spent fuel rods and deep bore holes." I put up a hand. "Don't ask. That's all I know. Christine is studying medieval history. More my field. She's in her second year at Magdalen College, Oxford."

Tom looked surprised. "She's at Magdalen? I was at Trinity. We don't get many American undergraduates at Oxford."

"My husband was an undergraduate there."

"Which is why you know how to pronounce the name."

Magdalen College, I'd quickly learned, is pronounced *maudlin*. Something to do with the pronunciation of vowels in the Middle Ages. "Yes. I think the locals were disappointed. They enjoy pretending not to understand the American tourists."

Tom laughed. "Unforgivable snobs."

"We took the kids to England after Christine's sophomore year in high school." I fished in my handbag for a photo. "Magdalen was having an Open Day, so we went—just for fun—and Christine fell in love with the school. She loved her father very much."

I handed him the photograph I'd received in September. "My daughter." I pointed to a young woman wearing what looked like mummy wrapping over low-slung, shredded jeans. "That's Tristan, her boyfriend. I'm trying not to worry."

The couple stood, arm in arm, on the banks of the Cherwell, Oxford's iconic river. Christine looked deliriously happy. It was impossible to tell how Tristan felt. He was tall and brooding with dark hair that fell heavily across his eyes. He wore tight jeans and a shrunken military jacket with a striped scarf wound tightly around his neck.

"Lovely girl, Kate. She has your coloring. If Christine is reading medieval history, she should visit Suffolk. There's a wonderful fourteenth-century church in Thornham Parva and an early guildhall in Lavenham."

He pulled out his phone and showed me a picture of Olivia, taken recently, he said, in East Africa. "She's working in an orphanage. Taking her gap year before starting university."

"She's beautiful," I said, and meant it. Unlike her father, Olivia was fair with a pale oval face, enormous eyes, and a full mouth. She held one little fellow, naked, skeleton thin, with the distended belly of the chronically malnourished. Several other children clung to her long skirt and gazed into the camera with huge, black-velvet eyes.

Tom folded back the linen on the bread basket. "Olivia sat for her A levels last spring. She did well enough to get a place at Cambridge, but I worry about her." He chose a roll and reached for the butter. "She tends to be too serious."

Hmm. One thing I didn't have to worry about with Christine.

Tom poured us each a second glass of wine, and by the time Sofia reappeared with the main course, I was feeling distinctly mellow. Nancy had prepared sliced filet of beef on a bed of wild mushroom risotto with green-sprigged baby carrots and small, buttery Brussels sprouts tucked artistically on one side. I fantasized about hiring her to cook for me in Ohio. And her husband, Frank, could whip my yard into shape. Perfect.

The logs settled with a pop, sending sparks flying upward. *I'm enjoying this*, I admitted, reminding myself that my goal hadn't been to enjoy myself but to find out about Tom Mallory. Was his presence at the hotel when a murder occurred a coincidence? Odd that he'd spend a whole week alone on a small island. Maybe he was antisocial, a charming hermit.

I watched him take a sip of wine. "What brought you to Glenroth? Had you met Elenor somewhere?"

"I came for a homeland security conference in Edinburgh. Olivia's in Africa, my mother's visiting family in Devon, so I decided to take a holiday. I ran into Rob Devlin at the conference. He's the one who suggested this place, the hotel."

One mystery solved. Tom and DI Devlin had met before.

Tom swirled the wine in his glass. In the firelight, it looked like melted rubies.

"You're not a suspect, then," I said, trying to be clever.

"Everyone is a suspect, Kate. I have an alibi. Sofia spent the night in my cottage."

"She did?" I managed to maintain my composure, but *really*. Tom and Sofia?

"It's not what it sounds like." He glanced at the library door. "She came to my cottage last night, late, but not to see me. I'd placed my lunch tray on the bench outside the door as instructed. She'd forgotten to collect it earlier. Apparently Agnes is a stickler about lapses like that. Sofia intended to take the tray away quietly, but a glass fell and shattered. I heard the crash and went to see what happened. She'd cut her finger pretty badly, so I insisted she come in to rinse it off and apply a plaster. I could see she was shaken, so I made her sit on the sofa and gave her a glass of wine while I cleaned up the mess outside. When I came back, I found her sleeping, so I covered her with an extra blanket and went to bed. When I woke this morning, she was gone. Told me later she left at five with a headache and a stiff back."

"Why was she upset—the sight of blood or the sale of the hotel?"

Tom took a forkful of risotto. "The prospect of having to find a new job, I think."

I took this as my cue to turn the conversation to Elenor's death. "How is it that someone you know was assigned to investigate the murder? Coincidence?"

"Not exactly. I saw lights early this morning and went out to see what had happened. Habit, I suppose. A constable from Mallaig arrived first, followed by a crime scene manager from Skye and someone from CID in Fort William. When I heard about Elenor's death—clearly murder—I called Rob Devlin. He's part of Scotland's Major

Investigations Team. Basically they pack a bag with a few days' worth of clothes and head to wherever they're needed. He'd just wrapped up a case in Inverness, so he was close."

"I saw you talking to him earlier. Does he have news?"

"Early days yet, Kate. They're taking statements."

"Are they focusing on anyone?"

"Like who?" He looked at me speculatively.

"No one in particular." I flushed and popped a baby carrot in my mouth. Oh, I'm slick.

"He told me about your intruder. And your theory—the similarity to the death of Flora Arnott."

"Did he also tell you I'm on leave from the asylum?"

Tom smiled. "No, he didn't. And I assure you, they will follow every line of inquiry. Elenor made enemies. The police will begin there and expand as they learn more."

Apparently the ban on sharing information didn't apply to fellow policemen. "I'm surprised to hear you speak so openly about the murder. Devlin threatened to have me drawn and quartered if I breathed a word to anyone."

"I'm not speaking openly, Kate. I'm speaking to you."

"But how do you know these things?"

"I'm helping with the investigation."

Had I heard him right? I'd watched my share of British police procedurals. "As in 'helping the police with their inquiries'? I thought you said you weren't a suspect."

He looked amused. "As in helping Police Scotland with the investigation, Kate. They're shorthanded. I called my guv. He gave his permission."

"Your guv?"

"My boss, Chief Superintendent Rollins. Devlin asked me to read the evidence reports and the interviews they've taken so far to see if I could find discrepancies. Or anything I could add. My impressions of the staff, what I'd seen and heard. He also asked me to keep you informed—to be a liaison—which is what I'm doing right now."

Really? More likely, Devlin had asked him to keep an eye on me. Fine with me. Information can go both ways. "They should be looking into Elenor's state of mind these past weeks. She was obsessed with security. She knew she was in danger, and I think it had something to do with Dr. Guthrie's book."

"Devlin told me about the threat letters," Tom said, "and I agree with you. They will follow every lead, but investigation takes time."

Police-speak for *Leave this to us, miss.*

"I know investigation takes time, but Devlin needs to know that people around here aren't telling the truth—at least not the whole truth." I wanted to tell him about Agnes and the purple gloves, but the words refused to form. "Do you know if lights were still on in Elenor's flat when the police arrived this morning? That could help pinpoint when she left the house."

Tom put down his knife and fork. "Look, I know you're trying to help, Kate, and I understand your frustration. But you must be patient. Give Devlin time to do his work. You mustn't get involved."

I started to protest when the library door opened and Sofia pushed a rolling cart through the jamb. The cart held a French press filled with coffee, two cups, and two ramekins of something that looked like soufflé.

"Cranachan," Sofia said. "Famous Scottish dessert. Whiskey, honey, oatmeal, raspberries." Her eyes were fixed on Tom.

I couldn't blame her for that. But Tom was looking at Sofia, too, and some message passed between them. Had her night on his couch really been as innocent as he claimed? Why did that irritate me?

I waited until Sofia was gone. "Look. Elenor was my sister-in-law. She asked for my help, and she was murdered. Can you blame me for wondering why?"

"Of course I don't blame you, but that doesn't mean you can

involve yourself in the investigation. It's not safe. What if the killer sees you as a threat? You mustn't interfere. Leave it to the police. They'll decide who's telling the truth and who isn't. They don't need your help."

I glared at him. He glared at me. Spoons tinked against china.

What business was it of his to tell me what to do? The police did need help. They were just too pigheaded to admit it. I folded my napkin and stood. "You know, I can't eat another bite. I'll say good night."

Tom got to his feet. "Let me see you to your cottage."

"No, thank you. I'm absolutely fine."

I left him standing there, a napkin in his hand and a puzzled look on his face.

Chapter Fifteen

❧

I shut the cottage door behind me and kicked off my heels. Tom Mallory was even worse than DI Devlin.

My cell phone was now fully charged. I unplugged it and turned it on. The screen lit up with a series of pings. I'd had a text from Christine (miracle of miracles) and five missed calls, four from a number I recognized, a client with more taste than money and a nasty habit of taking oil paintings on approval and returning them the morning after a big dinner party.

She could wait.

I opened the text from Christine: TRIS + I HAVE NEWS, HOPE U R NOT UPSET.

Upset? My heart lurched. Was she talking about a wedding? Dear Lord, not a baby.

Fear turned to guilt. *News* wasn't necessarily a prelude to disaster. I wanted to text back WHAT NEWS? in shouty caps, but I hadn't raised Christine for nineteen years without learning a thing or two. Questions were interpreted as intrusion. Expressing concern was the kiss of death. I had to walk on eggshells with Christine.

I punched in GREAT, CALL SOON. Murder isn't something you put in a text.

I scrolled back to the other missed call. *Strange.* The number was

Scottish. Someone in Scotland had called my cell phone at 12:48 AM on Saturday morning. There was a message.

I listened, transfixed.

The voice was Elenor's.

Grabbing my handbag, I found DI Devlin's card.

* * *

"It's definitely Elenor's voice. But she sounds strange. Kind of slurry." I stepped back as Detective Inspector Devlin barreled through the door of Applegarth Cottage.

His shirt was rumpled, his tie askew. Dark circles had appeared under his eyes. I wondered how long he'd been away from home.

I put my cell phone on speaker.

"Kate . . . need you . . ." The voice caught. "'S okay . . . help's coming. Need you to keep something . . . hidden . . ." We listened until the time ran out, but there were no more words.

"Are you sure it's Mrs. Spurgeon?" Devlin took the phone.

"Positive." I shivered. "Did you hear it, right at the end? At first I thought it was the movement of air or the rustling of fabric, but when I listened again, it sounded more like a footstep."

"Forensics will analyze it." He dropped the phone in an evidence bag and wrote out a receipt. "We should be able to return it to you in a day or so."

"Elenor said help was coming. Do you think she called 999?"

"We'll check." He eyed the door.

"There's something I need to tell you about Agnes MacLeod. Did you know she has a pair of purple knitted gloves? I saw them. They were wet and—"

"We'll check on that, too."

"But I took—"

"Please, Mrs. Hamilton. Leave this to us. Try to relax. Get a good night's sleep." He backed out, pulling the door firmly shut.

I stared furiously at the closed door. Did the man ever let anyone finish a sentence? I could bring him a signed, notarized confession and he'd probably say, "We'll check on that."

His taillights disappeared into the darkness. Snatching the strands of purple wool from my jacket pocket, I held them mutinously over the wastebasket. But I didn't drop them. Instead I carried them to the kitchen, where I sealed the wisp of purple wool in a plastic baggie and tucked it in the outside pocket of my handbag.

Ten minutes later I slipped between the smooth cotton sheets, switched on the bedside lamp, and opened *The Diary* to the page I'd marked.

In early February, events took a troubling turn for Flora. At a country dance given by a neighboring family, old Sir Charles Murray, in the middle of a Scottish reel, proposed marriage. Flora refused him as tactfully as she could, but her father, exasperated by the sums spent on his daughter's fruitless entrance into society, blew up.

4ᵗʰ February
Hazelbank House
> *This evening I was called to Father's study and made to account for what he called my unreasonable willfulness. He will not let Sir Charles go, clinging to his fortune like a sailor with only a plank between himself & a watery grave. "He is very old, Father," said I. "I cannot marry him. I shall not change my mind."*
>
> *"Will ye not obey me?" said he, calling me a most obstinate & ungrateful child. Thinking to frighten me into submission, he brought his fist down with such a blow that poor old MacPherson burst in, fearing Father had succumbed to a fit. Father vows to lock me in my chamber until I come to my senses & accept Sir Charles' proposals. He has persuaded this credulous gentleman that I, being full young & inexperienced in the ways of the*

world, am merely reticent & will acquiesce in the end. If Sir Charles is fool enough to believe this fiction, I shall regret the pains I took in my refusal to avoid mentioning his age.

Father is desperate & thus dangerous. I fear no one can defy him.

In the end, however, Flora's grandmother summoned the courage, if not to defy, at least to divert.

1ˢᵗ March 1809
Edinburgh

Father at last has given up hope of Sir Charles, or rather Sir Charles has given me up as a hopeless cause. In any case, Grandmother pleaded with my Aunt Grantley for aid & I am now installed in her townhouse on Queen Street in Edinburgh. This good lady has the distinction of marrying off three daughters to gentlemen of fortune & breeding & is presently waging a campaign on behalf her youngest, Adeline, a sweet, compliant girl of seventeen.

Last evening we attended the Assembly Rooms on George Street. Among those present was one who claims an acquaintance with Father. His name is Capt. James Arnott, lately returned from the Indies where his own good Father operates a sugar plantation. This I learn'd from Adeline, who says a vast fortune is entailed upon the Capt., but he is considered by some not quite respectable.

Respectable or not, Capt. Arnott has the very good sense to be both rich & handsome & so made quite a stir among the young ladies who passionately wished him to quit the gambling tables & stand up with as many of them as possible.

Lady Grantley arranged an introduction. I found him to be

perfectly amiable. We danced two dances. I declined a third, reminding him that he was neglecting the other young ladies. 'And why should I not,' said he, 'when you are the handsomest lady in the room?' He then bowed, quite gallantly I thought, and said that while he did not seek society's good opinion, he did seek mine & would obey my command. But what do you think? He did not dance after all & spent the rest of the evening standing near one of the chimney pieces, observing me with a look that made me blush.

My Aunt seems inordinately pleased with herself.

12th March 1809
Hazelbank House
I return'd to Lochweirren five days ago & found Father curiously silent about my prospects. You may imagine my surprise, dear diary, when a letter from Capt. Arnott arrived by post. Having completed his business in Edinburgh, he declar'd his intention to pay his respects to Father & to me. Shall I admit to being flatter'd?

Yesterday he arrived. Father welcomed him with excessive courtesy & after offering refreshment, gave me leave to show him our garden. I thought this strange as I could offer him only crocus & snowdrops, but the Capt. seemed to take a great interest. As we walked, he told me about the islands where he spent his youth. Flowers there, said he, grow in wild abandon. The breezes are warm & scented with jasmine. Women wear colorful lengths of cloth & adorn their hair with orchids & hibiscus. He took his penknife & cut a lavender crocus, tucking it in my hair. I am certain I blushed.

The Capt.'s connection with Father must stem from some business dealing, for this morning the two closeted themselves in

Father's study. To-night my theory was confirm'd when Capt. Arnott inform'd us that he intends to make his home permanently in the Indies.

I am heartily ashamed of myself. Capt. Arnott has come to Hazelbank, not because of any special regard for me but to seek Father's advice. The bitterness of my regret takes me quite by surprise.

13th March 1809

I am greatly perplexed. This morning, as the weather is crisp & fine, the Capt. begged me accompany him riding, declaring his wish to admire our lovely hills & woods. Gowyn came along as chaperone altho she is not over-fond of riding. We stopped to rest the horses along the riverbank & the Capt. told me tales of his youth in the Indies & of his mother's death of fever when he was but a lad. I told him of my own dear mother's death but a year ago. 'Our sorrow is a bond betwixt us,' said he, taking my hand in his & pressing it to his heart.

This evening we were join'd by the Vicar & his wife. After supper the party withdrew to the music room where Capt. Arnott requested I play for him on the pianoforte. He chose 'Fairwell to the Banks of Ayr' by Mr. Robt Burns. I, knowing he is to leave Scotland for-ever, nearly wept.

I am convinced his feelings for me are genuine, but fate is cruel & I must not allow myself to hope. In two days' time he will be gone for-ever.

14th March 1809

All is changed! This morning the Capt. asked to speak with me in private. Grandmother sat by the fire with a shawl over her lap, but was soon snoring so loudly I wonder'd if the Capt. had slipped a dram of whiskey in her tea. He sat on the rosewood *chair & bade me stand be-fore him that he might admire my gown. He made me turn round to show it off & remarked that I had grown quite womanly for one so young. He should not have taken the liberty—indeed he should not!—but I have forgiven him. He has not had the benefit of society.*

Grandmother stirred in her chair & he put a finger to his lips. Then he gave me what he called tokens of his esteem—a fine emerald ring that belong'd to his poor mother & a miniature of himself on ivory surrounded by seed pearls, lest I forget him. Dear diary, can you not guess the end of the tale? We are betrothed! The wedding is to take place on an island west of the Highlands where the Capt. has begun the renovation of a house fine enough, says he, for a queen. We shall make our home there, until we are granted the blessing of a child. Then, when the child is able to travel, the Capt. will take us to live in paradise!

"You must give me a son, dearest one," said he. "And if the child is a girl?" I asked, teasing him. But his expression turned dark & so I said, "We shall have a dozen sons if it pleases you. Or perhaps one daughter to keep me company." Then he smiled again & all was well.

To-night I showed his likeness to Gowyn. She says he looks like a pirate. I daresay he does, but a bonnie one. Capt. Arnott is the finest & handsomest gentleman I have ever known. I would follow him to the ends of the earth.

The betrothal was sealed, Guthrie explained in a footnote, when James Arnott was thirty-four and Flora Young fifteen. I think that's illegal today. Flora was clearly smitten, but what could have possessed her father to allow the engagement? He must have known he would never see his daughter again. Guthrie's story disturbed me. Maybe it was Flora's innocence, her naïve assumption that the new life she'd embraced would be an adventure, that marriage to a man she'd known for so short a time would be perfect. But then I—and all Guthrie's readers—knew the dark thing that was coming.

I marked my place and flipped off the lamp. Nothing I'd read so far shed any light on Flora's murder. More to the point, nothing I'd read so far had any bearing on Elenor's life or death. Had I missed something?

Start with what you know, my mother always says. Well, nearly a full day after Elenor's murder, I could say a few things with confidence.

One. Elenor's death wasn't a random act of violence. It was personal.

Two. According to Agnes, Elenor received a phone call at eleven thirty the night of the ball. She'd dressed and walked to the Historical Society. To meet someone?

Three. The person Elenor met wore Mucky Ducks, size ten.

Four. Elenor was alive, if not exactly well, at 12:48 AM. That's why the twins hadn't seen a body at twelve thirty. There wasn't one yet.

Five. Elenor said someone was coming to help. Who was it, and why hadn't they arrived?

Six. Her slurry voice. Was she drunk, or had she suffered one of those ministrokes? The autopsy would tell that, but even if she had, it was an arrow through the throat that killed her.

Seven. She wanted me to keep something for her. She used the word *hidden*. Did she want me to hide something, or was it hidden already? If so, where? No answers there either, except that if Elenor had whatever-it-was with her when she died, her killer must have taken it.

Eight. And here was the cobweb's connection to Guthrie's novel. Someone had been threatening Elenor, playing on her superstitions about Flora Arnott and her ghost. The obvious reason was to prevent the sale of the hotel, but who knew a sale was a possibility?

Nine. The casket and the puzzling notation in Guthrie's book.

No one at the hotel had mentioned the casket, and I wasn't allowed to bring it up.

Ten. Only Elenor heard footsteps, and only Elenor saw a ghost.

I yawned. Eleven . . . was there an eleven? My brain was getting fuzzy.

I'd almost drifted into sleep when the phone rang. I rolled over and reached for the receiver. "Hello?"

"Detective Inspector Devlin here. I've sent a car to pick you up. We have Bo Duff at the police station in Mallaig. He's asking for you."

Chapter Sixteen

Frank Holden stood beside me in the lobby of the police station at Mallaig. He'd seen the police car arrive and, once he heard about Bo Duff, insisted on coming along. I was glad for his company.

"We can't get a thing out of him," Devlin said. "He asked for you, Mrs. Hamilton."

Bo sat between two police constables in the waiting room, knees together, big feet splayed outward. His hair hung in lank strands around a face brindled with a growth of beard. He gave me a wobbly, heartbreaking smile, and I saw that the bridge of his nose was raw. A trickle of dried blood ran toward the corner of his mouth. One of his eyes appeared to be turning a greenish black. I felt sick. This was Bo, the gentle giant.

I turned on Devlin, furious. "The police did this?"

Devlin had perched himself on the corner of a gray metal desk. "The deputies found him hiding in his barn. When he saw them, he took off. That's called resisting arrest. A serious offense. They had to subdue him."

"He needs medical attention."

"He got it. He'll be fine."

Frank's hands were clenched. I saw the muscle in his jaw working. "Does he need a solicitor? Is he under arrest?"

"He's not under arrest, but he needs to explain a few things. Like, why did he run when the constables came to take his statement? He can talk, can't he?"

"Of course he can talk," Frank snarled. "And he'll tell you the truth if you care to hear it."

Devlin ignored the jibe. "Wait here, Mr. Holden. No, I'm serious. We'll let you know if you're needed." He turned to me. "This way, please. I'd like a moment."

He led me down a short hallway to a windowless cubicle with a tiled floor, a metal table, and four molded plastic chairs.

I straightened my back and put on my best impression of my mother. The angrier she gets, the more dignified she sounds. "I'm putting Bo's injuries aside for now, Detective Inspector, but I won't forget them. You can't think Bo had anything to do with Elenor's death. It isn't possible. I've never known anyone—*anyone*—with a kinder spirit. He wouldn't harm a fly. And Mr. Holden is right. He won't lie."

Devlin regarded me with something like pity. "Before we begin, you need to know a thing or two. Mr. Duff is paid to plow and grit the island roads. If he followed his regular route last night—and everyone we talked to says his route never varies—he would have passed the Historical Society around five AM. No way he could have missed the body. Get it? The question is, why didn't he call for help?"

My dignity faltered. I'd asked myself the same question. Was Bo protecting someone? I refused to consider the alternative. "I can't answer that, but I'm sure Bo will tell you if you don't frighten him."

Devlin bent over the metal table and fiddled with some kind of recording device. Then he stepped into the hallway and signaled to the PCs.

Bo entered the interview room. His face screwed up. Afraid he might burst into tears, I adopted the super-calm tone I used when my children were overwrought. "The police have some questions, Bo. It's all right to talk to them. I'll stay with you."

He gave me a nod.

Bo and I sat on one side of the table. Devlin and one of the constables sat on the other. The second constable positioned himself near the door. In case Bo decided to bolt again, I guessed.

I took one of Bo's big, rough hands in mine and held it.

Devlin pushed a button on the audio recorder and stated the date, time, and names of those in the room. Then he began. "Now, Mr. Duff. Two constables went to your croft this afternoon. Why did you run?"

He looked at me. "I was scared. Am I in big trouble?"

"You're not in trouble," Devlin said evenly. I could see he was trying. "But we need to know what happened last night. Can you tell us?"

Bo looked at the floor and began to rock.

"For the record, Mr. Duff refuses to answer," Devlin said into the recorder. Then he addressed Bo. "Well, then, why don't I say what I think happened, and you tell me where I go wrong, all right? That will be helpful. You began plowing around four. Is that correct?"

Bo gave him a tentative nod. "Aye."

"Everything was fine until you got to the Historical Society. You saw something. Can you tell me about it?"

Bo stared at the table.

"It's all right, tell me," I said, and released his hand so he could turn toward me.

The corners of his mouth went down. "She was going to yell at me. She was going to say I'm useless again, and it wasn't right because I was doing a good job. I always do a good job."

Devlin almost left his seat. "Are you saying Mrs. Spurgeon was alive?"

Bo's arms flew up as if fending off a blow. His face was pinched and white.

"When was the last time you ate something?" I asked him.

"Dunno."

"He needs a break." I shot Devlin a pointed look. "You can't expect Mr. Duff to answer questions without something in his stomach."

"Stopping the recording." Devlin stated the time. Then he addressed the constable at the door, a young fellow with a thin neck. "What do we have?"

"Tea, coffee, Horlicks," said the constable.

"Anything else?"

"Dougie's wife sent shortbread. Some left, I think."

"How about Horlicks and shortbread, Mr. Duff?" asked the constable.

Bo brightened. "Is it over now? Can I go home?"

"Not quite yet," I said. "But you'll feel better when you've had something to eat."

The deputy returned minutes later with a steaming Styrofoam cup and a chunk of shortbread liberally dusted with powdered sugar.

Bo tested the liquid with his tongue. Satisfied, he crammed the shortbread in his mouth and drained the cup. He looked at me, his mouth rimmed with chocolate and powdered sugar. I fought the impulse to clean him up.

Devlin was looking at Bo as if he were an exhibit in a freak show. I swallowed the lump in my throat. This couldn't be happening.

"All right, Mr. Duff. Let's begin again." Devlin pushed the button on the recorder. "I'm going to ask you an important question. We need your help here. We know you saw Mrs. Spurgeon's body. No sense denying it."

Bo nodded his head warily. An icy hand clutched my heart.

"Mr. Duff indicates agreement. And what did you do?"

Bo was silent.

"Mr. Duff." Devlin's voice had risen. "Tell us what you did."

Bo covered his face.

"It's all right," I said. *But was it?* An alarm bell went off in my brain. "He needs a solicitor. Why doesn't he have a solicitor?"

"We offered—by the book. He declined. And we read him his rights." Devlin crossed his arms over his chest.

"Well, he wants a solicitor now." I grabbed Bo's arm. "Don't say anything. Not one thing, do you hear me?"

Too late. Bo stood, knocking the Styrofoam cup to the floor. His fists knotted at his sides. He took a deep breath, grimacing as he forced out the words.

"I. Hurt. Her."

Then he opened his powdery, chocolate-rimmed mouth and began to wail.

The cubicle erupted. I shrank back as both constables sprang forward, struggling to force Bo back into the chair.

Frank Holden burst into the room, shaking off a policeman who was trying to restrain him. "What's the bloody hell's going on?"

Bo's wails were becoming rhythmic and atonal.

I pushed my way into Devlin's face. "He's going into shock. Can't you see that?"

Devlin stuck his head outside the door and barked, "Call the doc—now. Then Legal Aid. Leave a message. Mark it urgent."

"You cannae mean to keep him," Frank said, visibly astonished as one of the constables fastened a set of plastic handcuff ties on Bo. "Let me take him home. I'll stay with him. I'll bring him back first thing in the morning."

"I'm sorry." Devlin looked like he meant it. "I can't risk it."

Frank lifted his hands. "What do you suppose he did? Ran her over with the plow? Beat her with the snow shovel? You cannae be serious."

Devlin answered in that soft voice that always gets attention. "Someone shot an arrow through Mrs. Spurgeon's neck."

Frank's face turned the color of putty.

The constables led Bo away.

"Are you charging him?" I demanded. "With what—murder?"

"We're holding him tonight," Devlin said, "until the doc's seen him and we hear from Legal Aid. Check back in the morning."

"He's not fit," Frank said. "You can see that."

"The doc will make that call. He'll be treated properly."

Frank pushed a finger into Devlin's chest. "You shouldn't have questioned him. I shouldn't have allowed it."

"Whoa. Calm down." Devlin took a step back. "Neither of you has the facts. Mrs. Spurgeon's body was buried under a mound of snow. Now who do you think did that? The same person who shoveled the walks, perhaps?"

It took a moment for the words to sink in. I swallowed hard. "But Elenor was dead long before Bo started plowing. You said so yourself."

"How do we know he didn't kill her earlier and return later to hide the body? I think that's exactly what someone like Mr. Duff would do. You heard him. He said he hurt her."

"That wasn't a confession." I steadied myself against the table. "He's in shock. He doesn't know what he's saying."

A woman in a black skirt and a white blouse with epaulets tapped on the open door. She held a leather jacket in one hand and a slip of paper in the other.

Devlin snatched the paper and glanced at it. "Gotta go. But before I do, there's something you need to know, Mr. Holden." He shoved an arm into the jacket. "I took your wife's statement this morning, and I've read yours. One of you is lying."

Chapter Seventeen

~

Sunday, October 30

I woke, bleary-eyed and stiff.

Frank and I had remained at the Mallaig Police Station until the police surgeon arrived. Shortly after that, Bo was transported to the Munroe Clinic in Glenfinnan, halfway between Mallaig and Fort William. By the time I returned to Applegarth, it was four AM. I'd fallen into bed, exhausted but unable to turn off my brain. I must have slept some, though, because I'd had another bad dream.

Pulling the Case Western sweatshirt over my pajamas, I went to the kitchen to start the coffee. As it dripped into the pot, I peered out the window. The air had cleared, leaving a pale-gray sky with a scrim of haze. Was Bo awake? I pictured him, alone and afraid. If I could just talk to him, get him to calm down, he might remember what actually happened that night. Maybe he saw the killer and decided taking the blame was safer than telling. Whatever the truth, he needed to tell his story in his own time and his own way. He needed someone to listen, someone who loved him. *Like me.* I hugged Bill's old sweatshirt around my body. How could I not love the man who had risked his life trying to save my husband?

My thoughts slid back to the day my world ended. I was there again, smelling the sea, feeling the trickle of sweat down my back.

With Bill's sailboat bobbing aimlessly, I'd dashed toward the jetty where Bo was scrubbing down an old wooden fishing boat. "It's Bill," I screamed and pointed at the sailboat. "He needs help."

Instantly, Bo started up the small outboard motor and wrenched the boat around, almost swamping it. I could see him in my mind's eye, straining forward, his hand on the tiller. His cap blew off, and the long strands of his hair unfurled in the wind.

I raced to the end of the jetty, planning to dive in fully clothed, but hands stretched out to prevent me. "Nothing you can do, lass," said a woman in a floppy hat. "You'll only make it worse." She was right. The wind had picked up again, churning the waves.

Bo arrived at the sailboat and cut the motor. I saw him lean out of the fishing boat, his long arms reaching for something.

No. Oh, God, no. A crowd was gathering on the jetty. "Call the medics," I pleaded.

When I looked again, Bo was in the water. He held Bill's head in the crook of one arm and reached for the side of the boat. Once, twice. The boat rocked dangerously and slid out of reach. For one heart-stopping moment Bo hesitated, his head thrashing from side to side like a trapped animal. Then he began to swim, scooping with his free arm, jerking forward with every kick.

Voices around me yelled, "Who has a boat? Doesn't anyone have another boat?"

"Call the Harborview," someone cried.

"No. Call 999."

"He's not wearing a life jacket. He'll never make it."

Several men dove in to help, but the sea was too rough and they were forced to turn back. One guy tried to row out on a paddleboard, but he quickly lost his balance and fell. How he made it back to shore, I never knew.

All the while Bo kept swimming. At times the waves covered them completely, and I feared they'd both gone under. I fought with him. Stroke for stroke. Breath for breath. It took forever. Twenty minutes, someone said. As Bo neared shore, others jumped in. They dragged Bill into the shallows and up onto the shingle.

Bo staggered forward, coughing and gasping for air. His lips were blue.

Bill lay on his back. His face was slack. His hair streamed water. The sun caught a flash of gold—his wedding band. Someone blew air into his lungs again and again until the paramedics arrived. Furious activity surrounded the inert body.

Then they stopped.

A massive heart attack, the doctor said later. Bill never had a chance.

I lay next to his body, my arm over his chest. Bo knelt beside me, sobbing like a child. When the stretcher came, a woman made me stand. She wrapped a beach towel around my shoulders.

Someone must have called Elenor, because she arrived as Bill's body was being transferred from the collapsible stretcher to the emergency vehicle.

"No!" she screamed. She bent over him, her fair hair falling across his face. The doors shut and she turned to me, her lovely face contorted with rage. "Those cruel things you said. You broke his heart. I'll never forgive you." And she hadn't. Until that phone call.

The problem was, I hadn't forgiven myself.

The coffee finished dripping with a fizz of steam. I poured a large mugful and swallowed.

The Fort William phone directory had a listing for the Munroe Clinic. A recorded message told me that visiting hours on Sunday were one to four PM. Then I listened to the sounds of a string ensemble—Haydn, I thought—as I waited for someone to pick up. A vase filled with orange-berried branches sat on the red-and-cream-checked tablecloth. I stared out the window, watching the wind bend the trees.

"The Munroe," came a voice at last. "Sorry for the wait. How can I help?"

"My name is Kate Hamilton. The police brought a friend of mine in last night—actually early this morning. His name is Bo Duff. I'd like to visit him later today."

"No visitors during the initial evaluation process, I'm afraid."

"Can you at least tell me how he is?"

"Resting quietly. That's all I'm allowed to say."

I moved the phone to my other ear. "But you have a waiting room, don't you? I could drive over this afternoon and wait until the evaluation is finished."

"We do and you could, but there's not much point. You won't be able to see him. All visitors must be cleared by the police. I believe the policy is family only."

To my horror, I began to cry. "I'm sorry. Bo was my husband's best friend. I'm not going to abandon him."

"Of course you're not." The woman must have taken pity on me. "Look, I'm not supposed to do this, but Mr. Duff's sister is on her way from Perth. If you leave your name and phone number, I'll let her know you're concerned."

I gave the woman my information. "Tell her I'll do anything to help. Anything at all."

I replaced the receiver and sat for a moment, drumming the table with my fingernail. People like Bo are capable of anger. I remembered Matt's face turning red as he upended a train set when the tracks wouldn't stay together. But Elenor's murder hadn't been a flash of anger. Elenor's killer had come armed with a bow and arrow. That meant calculation, and that was the point. Bo was capable of anger, but not the level of calculation required to plan and execute a murder. I knew that. Frank knew it. Getting DI Devlin to know it was another matter.

Now I had an even more compelling reason to find Elenor's killer. I had to clear Bo Duff.

That thought occupied my mind as I dressed. Someone had killed Elenor, face-to-face, in cold blood. A person who could do that wouldn't hesitate to let an innocent man take the blame. I sat on the edge of the bed, replaying Elenor's phone message in my mind for the umpteenth time. She hadn't known she was about to die. Her last conscious thought concerned something she wanted me to keep for her. *Keep, not know.* That meant an object. And then there was that cryptic notation in Guthrie's novel: *HS6uprtgrnlft51bluedn3rd.* Whatever that meant, it was important. Something Elenor wanted to remember.

I thought of a new question. Was Bo Duff even capable of shooting a bow and arrow? I'd never heard him talk about archery.

I picked up Bill's photograph. "I will protect him," I said aloud. "And I will find out who killed your sister."

Was it a trick of the light, or was it disapproval I saw in Bill's eyes?

* * *

"You had another call." Becca Wallace sat at her desk in the reception hall. "Elenor's solicitor from Inverness, Andrew Ross. He wants you to phone him first thing Monday morning."

"Thanks." I tucked the pink message slip in my pocket. "Detective Inspector Devlin said I could get into Elenor's flat today. May I borrow a key?"

"Sure." Becca handed me a set of keys from her desk drawer. A small brass key bore the initial *E* printed on a strip of white tape. Like no one could figure out what that meant. Not the cleverest security measure I'd ever seen.

Becca closed the computer window she'd been using, and the hotel's blue-tartan home screen popped up. "Toss the keys in the drawer when you're finished. You'll find me in the kitchen. Or the library."

Her heels clicked on the polished marble floor.

I watched her go. Becca was bright, competent, polished. Why would she choose to live and work on an island that was, for much of the year, practically deserted? A similar job in Inverness—even Fort William—would pay higher wages, and she'd be closer to her boyfriend,

Geoff. Maybe she had family on the island. Or was there another reason she'd chosen such isolation?

The computer pinged. The envelope flap on the email icon opened.

I slipped into Becca's chair and eyed that open email flap.

I tried not to click on it. I really did.

Call it research.

An email list appeared. I read the subject lines: Booking for Scott Party, Cancel Booking, Christmas?, Genealogy Seminar. I scrolled down, finding more of the same.

Switching to Sent Items, I typed into the search bar the name of the old newspaper: The Hebridean Chronicle. The computer responded unhelpfully, No matches found. Deleting that search, I tried another: Flora Arnott. This time there were seven matches. I opened each one, finding enthusiastic references to Dr. Guthrie's book. One potential guest wondered if she could book the exact room where the ghost appeared.

Still in Sent Items, I began scrolling backward in time. I was about to give up when, in the emails for a year ago August, I found something that caught my attention. The address was Adoption.co.uk, and the subject line read Birth Parents.

I sat back. Had Elenor sent the email, trying to find a baby she'd given up for adoption?

You can't open other people's mail carped the voice of conscience.

Oops. Too late. I'd already opened it—just long enough to read the name at the bottom. The sender had been Becca Wallace.

"Knock, knock. Anybody home?" Dora MacDonald peered around the hotel's front door.

I closed the screen and coughed to restart my heart.

"Kate. Just the person we came to see." Under his navy jacket, Jackie was dressed in dark trousers and a coral V-neck sweater. Dora wore slacks and a matching wool jacket in asparagus green. Not a flattering hue.

"We weren't sure we should come," Dora said, "but we thought you ought to know. In case the police didn't tell you."

"Tell me what?"

"That I was the one who found Elenor's body," Jackie said.

"*You* found her? You're the person who called Mallaig?"

Jackie nodded. "Lovely woman. So sad, so sad."

"Jackie was on his way to Flora's Café," Dora said, taking his arm. "He goes first thing every Saturday for Claire's yum yums."

"Yum yums?"

"Claire's specialty," Dora said. "A glorified doughnut, twisted into a plait and drenched with icing."

Jackie ignored this. "I saw a mound of snow near the Historical Society and—" He spread his hands and shrugged.

"You knew it was Elenor?"

"Not at first. I thought it was an animal caught in the storm. A sheep, maybe, or a big dog. I thought I'd check to see if the poor thing was still alive, but when I began clearing the snow . . . well." He squeezed his eyes shut as if blotting out the image. "My first instinct was to pull out the arrow, but it wouldn't have helped."

"How many people on the island could have done it?" I asked, figuring he would know.

"Lots. For many of us, archery is a lifelong hobby."

"Jackie's a triple champion." If Dora realized she'd just implicated her husband, she showed no sign of it.

"We'll take our leave." Jackie steered Dora toward the door. "Let you get back to whatever you were doing."

What I'd been doing was probably a felony.

The entrance door closed with a thud, sending dry leaves scuttering across the marble floor. Hadn't I read somewhere that killers sometimes report their own crimes for the thrill of taking part in the investigation? Grabbing the keys, I headed for Elenor's flat. If Jackie owned a pair of Mucky Ducks, they were a heck of a lot bigger than size ten.

I pictured Dora's long, narrow feet, wondering if the size tens could have been a woman's size rather than a man's.

Light from the door at the end of the east-wing hallway shone on the oak paneling. As I turned the key to Elenor's flat, something shifted behind me, momentarily blocking the light.

I spun around.

No one was there.

Chapter Eighteen

Light shifts with the ever-changing cloud cover in the Hebrides. I knew that. Yet I'd had the eerie sense of a presence behind me in the hallway.

I didn't like where my thoughts were taking me.

I switched on the lamps in Elenor's flat and instantly forgot about disappearing shadows. The police had left the place a mess. The cushions on the sofa and love seat were skewed. In the bedroom, her once-made bed was a jumble of linens. A dresser drawer stood partially open, revealing the edge of a violet-blue scarf.

Had they found anything significant, and would they tell me if they had?

In the bathroom, the fluffy white rug bore the imprint of large male feet, but the embellished casket was still there. I took measurements with my retractable tape and, using my cell phone, snapped a few close-ups of the marquetry designs before stepping back to take front, back, and side shots. I attached them to a text: MOM, CAN YOU IDENTIFY? 18TH C? MAKER? I included the dimensions and pushed send. No one could touch my mother when it came to research. If references to similar caskets existed, she would find them.

I sat on the edge of the huge claw-foot tub as Devlin had the day before. The casket could be unique, a one-off, but I didn't think so. The maker of this small jewel in wood had been a master craftsman, an artist of the first rank. And just as painters can be identified by their style and technique, so can cabinetmakers.

A shaft of sunlight pierced the wavy old window glass, pinning the casket in a luminous circle. I blinked at the tiny mythical creatures. On Friday they'd seemed to be frolicking in a field of vines, berries, roses—paradise. Today the creatures appeared to be fleeing from an unknown predator, and the vines looked more like brambles reaching out to ensnare their tiny hooves. I fumbled for my cell phone, hoping to capture what I saw, but the light vanished as suddenly as if someone had flipped a switch.

I realized I'd been holding my breath. The ends of my fingers tingled. My face flushed and my mouth went dry. My hand went to the casket. There were no words this time, but what I felt was fear, razor-edged and raw. Fear for the animals or for myself? I pulled my hand away, willing the creatures back to paradise.

An unformed thought floated away, out of reach. Something I needed to know was buried deep in my brain.

This is where everything began. I'll tell you the whole story after the ball.

I locked the door to Elenor's flat and slipped the keys back in Becca's desk. The reception hall was empty. The computer screen was dark, timed out. The only sound was the ticking of the long-case clock.

Images flipped through my brain. The casket. The code written in Guthrie's novel. Footsteps and shadows.

If Elenor had been right about footsteps in the night—and I could hardly doubt her after my recent experience—how was the intruder gaining access? The big front entrance door had a modern locking system and a dead bolt, turned either mechanically from inside or by a key from outside. The rear door to the kitchen had the same mechanical dead bolt, and both doors were lit on the outside by dusk-to-dawn security lighting.

I chewed the side of my lip. If I wanted to get in unseen, I'd find a seldom-used door, a side door maybe. Bill and I had taken a tour of the newly renovated hotel ten years ago. In addition to the wide French doors along the back wall of the dining room (also flooded with security lighting), I remembered a rear door leading to what were called "the old larders," now two large guest suites at the back of the house. And then there were the exterior doors at the ends of the east- and west-wing hallways. The door closest to Elenor's flat was worth a second look.

I returned to the east wing. Forty feet or so beyond the entrance to Elenor's flat, an exterior door led to a covered porch on the edge of the woods. I tried the knob. Locked.

Someone behind me yelped.

I spun around—again. This time, thankfully, someone was there.

Penny Arnott stood with her hand on Elenor's doorknob. She snatched it back and glared at me. "Scared me half to death, you did."

"Can I help you?" I walked toward her.

"Dead," she said pleasantly, nodding her head in the direction of Elenor's flat. "Heard this morning. Can I have a peep?"

"You want to get into Elenor's flat?"

"Stuff in there from the Historical Society." She rapped the door with a bony knuckle. "Shouldn't go to those Dutch people."

"They're Swiss, actually, but that's something the solicitors will have to—" My words faded as I saw Penny's face crumple. The last thing I needed was Penny Arnott in tears. "Why don't you tell me what you're looking for. I'll check."

"Come for tea sometime," Penny said, apropos of nothing. She smiled, baring yellow teeth. "Across from the Historical Society. We're always there, except when we're here."

With a flap of her voluminous raincoat, she was gone.

*   *   *

I found Becca in the library, balanced on a rolling ladder.

"I just had the strangest conversation with Penny Arnott," I said, deciding to wait for an opening on the adoption thing. I *can* play it cool when I have to.

Becca laughed. "Every conversation with the Arnott twins is strange." She slipped a book into place on the top shelf.

"She was trying to get into Elenor's flat."

"Really? Probably still looking for her property." Becca slid the ladder along its polished brass track and began shelving books in a section labeled LOCAL HISTORY.

"Why would Penny think Elenor had her property?"

"Because she probably did. Elenor often brought boxes home from the Historical Society to catalog. Penny came bursting in a few weeks ago, accusing Elenor of taking something Cilla had donated by mistake. Elenor said if Penny was stupid enough to leave Cilla in charge, she deserved to lose it."

"There is a box in Elenor's flat, but it's just old kitchenware. Junk."

"Junk to you, Kate." Becca moved the ladder again. "The twins believe anything connected with the Arnott family is a rare treasure. Would you care to see a tin of their grandfather's tooth powder? They've got one at the Historical Society, along with a badminton set from the thirties, a ball of twine that belonged to Grandmother Arnott, and a pile of fabric scraps some long-dead Arnott intended to make into a quilt. Penny thinks the Historical Society should install a security system."

"I'm surprised the hotel doesn't have a security system."

"Not practical. What if a guest decides she needs something out of her car at three in the morning? We can hardly lock them in."

"You do lock the doors at night, though, right?"

"At ten sharp. But guests have room keys that also unlock the front door."

Pretty casual for a house containing valuable antiques, I thought. Anyone could have taken the keys out of Becca's desk and had them duplicated. "Penny invited me for tea."

"You must go." Becca grinned. "Think of it as a cultural experience."

"One experience at a time. I'm having tea with the Guthries this afternoon."

Becca moved down a rung. "Hand me that book, will you?" She indicated a large, cloth-bound book lying on the table: *Early Residents of the Isle of Glenroth*.

"Someone interested in island history?"

"Always. You'd be surprised at the people who trace their lineage back to the clans driven out in the Highland Clearances. Mostly Canadians and New Zealanders. Later, of course, Captain Arnott granted parcels of land to fifteen Scottish men, all from the shires south of Glasgow. Their descendants come too." She took the book and placed it on a shelf with other oversize volumes. "That's why we hold a genealogy seminar here every fall. People use our library and the one at the Historical Society for research."

"So that's why the Arnotts and Guthries were resented. They weren't Highlanders." This was one part of the story I hadn't heard much about.

"Exactly so. The Arnotts rescued the house and the island from the English, but the MacDonalds wanted their old clan seat back, even though they had no money to purchase it themselves. They considered the house to be theirs by the law of restitution."

That explained the reference in the old newspaper articles to the "point of contention" between Captain Arnott and the local clansmen. It also provided a nice pivot. "Is your family from the island? Is that why you took the job here?"

Becca climbed down and brushed off her short black skirt. "I never had a family. I was an orphan, fostered a few times, never adopted." She shrugged. "This job gives me a place to live. And I like old houses."

"Will you stay on when the new owners take over?"

"To be honest, I'm thinking about leaving anyway. Geoff's taking a position at Holyrood Palace in January. He asked me to marry him."

"Becca, that's wonderful. You're moving to Edinburgh."

"Too soon for confetti. Geoff's an incredible guy. I'm just not sure."

"Sure that you love him?"

"That I'm *able* to love him. He deserves that, don't you think?" She fingered the fall of hair concealing her thin, white scar. "That reminds me. How was dinner last night?"

"Oh, the dinner." I covered my face with both hands.

"It couldn't have been that bad. Tom Mallory is a charming man."

"He is charming, but I questioned him about the murder, and he told me to leave the investigation to the police. I'm afraid I got huffy."

"Come on, let's get out of here." Becca flipped off the lights. "Good luck with Margaret Guthrie today. I've heard tales about that woman."

"Oh? Something I should know?"

"Just that she's a witch. And not quite the invalid she wants everyone to think she is."

I laughed. "Do I need backup?"

"You'll be safe enough." Becca smirked. "Just don't flirt with her son."

That, as it turned out, was excellent advice.

Chapter Nineteen

~

At two fifteen I set out for the Guthries' on the old-fashioned, wide-tired bicycle I'd found in Applegarth's log shed. The Hebridean wind blew steadily, thinning the cloud cover and brightening the sky. Above me, a white-winged gull shrieked and dove. The snow had finally melted. As I passed the hotel, I saw Becca sweeping the stone steps. She held up two fingers in the victory sign.

Tartan Cottage dozed in the woods to the east. Yesterday a white car had been parked there—Tom's rental, I supposed. Today the car was gone.

He was probably avoiding me.

It took less than ten minutes to reach the old stone bridge. I coasted to a halt. Below me, overshadowed by conifers and bounded on the south by a high bank, the Burn o'Ruadh cut a channel through the underbrush. *Ruadh*—the Gaelic name for the red deer that once roamed the island freely. Bill and I had walked the length of the burn on our honeymoon, following the silvery ribbon of water as it rushed headlong from the high point at the island's center toward the sea. Today a thin stream of peaty snowmelt curled sluggishly around rocks, twigs, and clumps of dead leaves.

According to island history, somewhere along that burn on New Year's Day of 1811, Captain James Arnott had been found with a bullet in his head. Self-inflicted was the implication in the newspaper story, but I wondered about that. Had he been murdered too?

Beyond the bridge, a dry stone wall defined a small cemetery. A newer section in back displayed well-tended graves adorned with frost-nipped chrysanthemums. The headstones nearest the road, the oldest ones, were narrow tablets or stone crosses, pocked with moss and lichens. I wondered if Flora and her unborn child were buried there. Probably not. If the island Chamber of Commerce knew the location of her grave, they'd have erected a shrine and charged admission.

On the left, a hundred yards or so past the cemetery, the Glenroth Historical Society occupied a picturesque 1830s stone schoolhouse with a modern board-and-batten annex. Crime scene tape blocked the entrance and marked off the area between the road and a brick walk-way where the stump of an old tree jutted from the soil. An ugly gash in the stump and an obscenely green square of turf were all that remained of violent death.

A group of reporters was milling about, preparing to film. "Wait," one of them called to me. "May we speak with you for a minute?"

I shook my head and stood on the pedals.

The Arnotts' plain forties-style two-story sat directly across from the Historical Society. Devlin was right. If a body had lain there the night of the Tartan Ball, the twins would have had a clear view. I thought I saw a curtain twitch.

Hugh Guthrie and his mother lived south of the village in a lovely house of dark-gray flint. A lacy trim board followed the gabled roof line. I leaned my bike against the wrought-iron fence and walked up the path. The front door stood open, a glass storm door proof against the weather.

Margaret Guthrie must have been watching, because a rich alto voice called out, "Come in, dear. Door's open."

I stepped into a long foyer. On the right a narrow staircase led to a second story. On the left a small fire burned in the living room hearth.

Margaret Guthrie sat by the fire in an upholstered chair. With her powdery pink-and-white complexion and wings of silver hair, she might have been the spokesmodel for a stair lift or a security call pendant. Her wheelchair was nowhere in sight.

"Welcome to *Taigh Mòr*," she said. "We've had quite a morning. Reporters everywhere. Such an intrusion."

"*Taigh Mòr*?"

"The Gaelic name for mansion house. That's what the house is known as locally."

Was she joking? The house was nice, but no mansion. I detected a familiar scent, something old-fashioned. *L'Air du Temps*?

A portrait hung over the fireplace. I recognized a much-younger version of the woman who sat before me. Her hair had been blonde then, but styled much as she wore it now. She'd chosen to sit in a gown of shimmering lapis lazuli, showcasing a pair of creamy shoulders and a youthful décolleté.

I offered my hand, and Margaret imprisoned it in both soft palms. "Sit here, dear." She indicated a ladder-backed chair with a hard rush seat. Her head lolled to one side like a marionette whose string has snapped. "Such a tragedy. Only three years ago you lost your husband, and now you've lost Elenor as well."

"The loss is your son's."

Margaret's smile puckered. "Of course. But Hugh is such a sensitive person, I must ask you not to press him about"—she twirled her hand—"you know."

I didn't know. Was I supposed to pretend Elenor hadn't been murdered, or was she warning me not to mention the unpleasantness at the Tartan Ball? "Mrs. Guthrie, I—"

"Margaret, dear, and Hugh. No need to be formal."

"I don't want to upset your son, Margaret, but I need to discuss the funeral arrangements. He was closer to Elenor than anyone."

She did a slow blink. "I suppose so, although it still surprises me. Elenor could be quite overpowering at times. Of course," she added quickly, "her death is a great loss."

"Is Hugh here?"

"Certainly," she snapped, as if I'd accused her of withholding evidence. "I gave him a task so we could talk for a moment in private."

"Oh?"

"Hugh is vulnerable right now. Can you imagine who the police sent to inform us of Elenor's death? An attractive young woman. She actually left her card and told Hugh to call if there was anything she could do to help. Next thing you know she'll be suggesting they meet for coffee." Margaret fidgeted in her chair. "I do feel guilty about the little contretemps at the ball, though. If I'd known what was going to happen, I wouldn't have . . . well." She cleared her throat.

Wouldn't have bothered? I let her squirm.

"Anyway, I hope I didn't cause offense." Margaret smoothed her skirt.

"Not to me," I said. "You and Elenor disagreed about the wedding plans."

A flash of irritation crossed her face. "That's what I'm talking about. Hugh can easily be bullied into decisions that aren't his own. I was simply making sure he was getting what he wanted. No one knows a son better than his mother."

Margaret crossed her legs. So she wasn't paralyzed. Maybe that's what Becca had meant when she said Margaret Guthrie wasn't quite the invalid she pretended to be. Had the police checked her alibi, or just assumed she wasn't physically capable of committing the murder?

Hugh Guthrie entered the room carrying a tray. He placed it on the coffee table in front of the sofa. "Hello." His turtlelike eyes darted, as if he wasn't sure where to look. If he'd had a shell, he'd have pulled his head in at that moment.

"Thank you, darling," his mother said, "but we need the tray a little closer. Here, perhaps?" She drew an imaginary circle in front of the fireplace.

Hugh moved a table from the other side of the room and placed the tray on it. Slices of a seed cake had been set out on clear pink luncheon plates with integrated saucers. Hugh poured tea, first for me, then for his mother, adding to hers cream and three sugars.

"A little more cream, darling. You know I like a lot of cream. A touch more."

Tea sloshed out, swamping the cake.

"You've filled it too full now," she clucked. "Get a napkin. Paper, not cloth."

Hugh disappeared and returned with a handful of paper napkins. He mopped up and handed his mother the plate.

She rotated it ninety degrees. "Cup on the right, darling. Remember? Now come sit. Pull up so we can have a nice chat."

He inched his chair forward until she signaled her satisfaction.

I'm usually pretty tolerant of other people's foibles, but I was forming a rather intense dislike for Margaret Guthrie. This made me brave enough to contravene a direct order.

"First, let me say how sorry I am." I turned toward Hugh. "I know what it's like to lose someone you love, but to lose her on the evening of your engagement is something no one should have to experience."

He stared at me, goggle-eyed.

"It's an outrage," Margaret said, filling the silence. "To think a woman can't take a walk at night without getting mugged. A gang from Glasgow, no doubt."

I was about to say that what had happened to Elenor was a little more serious than mugging, but I stopped myself in time. The police obviously hadn't shared the cause of Elenor's death with the Guthries. Weren't they curious? I took a bite of my cake.

"Has a date been set for the services?" Margaret asked.

"Not yet, which is partly why I'm here." I turned again to Hugh. "I'd like to help. If you agree, I thought we might have the funeral at the, ah, church in the village." The islanders called it the Wee Free, but I couldn't bring myself to say that. "I know how difficult it is to think about these things, but it has to be done. The sooner the better, in my experience."

Hugh's face turned pink. "I'm not up to making decisions. Whatever you decide is fine."

"Of course. If that's what you want."

Margaret Guthrie's face wore a Cheshire-cat smile and the air of someone getting not only the cream but the whole cow.

A young girl in Goth gear came through a door at the far end of the room. She peeled off a black leatherette jacket and held up a striped cloth sack. "Got everything on the list, Mrs. G." Her hair had been dyed black, hacked into chunks, and spiked with gel. Under a spackling of pale makeup, the girl's face was angelic. The incongruity was made perfect by dimples that appeared when she spoke. "Oh, hello," she said to me.

"Kylie, this is Kate, Mrs. Spurgeon's sister-in-law. Have you heard the news?" Margaret's voice dripped with the horror, or the thrill, of delivering bad news. "Elenor Spurgeon is dead. The police aren't saying, but we think it's murder."

The girl turned even whiter under her pale Goth makeup. "D'they know who did it?"

"No one from the island, I'm sure. We're devastated, naturally. Elenor was Dr. Guthrie's friend."

"Poor Mr. G. What do you want done today? Anything special?"

"There is something," Margaret said, looking uncertainly from me to Kylie. "But I'd need to explain."

I jumped at the opportunity. "Please, go. In the meantime, Hugh can show me the house."

"Well, don't be long." It sounded like a command.

Hugh retrieved a folded wheelchair from behind a curtain and helped his mother transition.

I followed him into the hallway.

"The house is Baronial Revival, a style popular in the late nineteenth century. It reflects a reverence for the past and Scottish culture."

I could see him lecturing in the classroom. "Who named it Taigh Mòr?"

"My father's idea. Embarrassing, really. Makes the place sound far grander than it is."

"How long has your family lived here?"

"My parents purchased the property in 1954, shortly after they were married. I've only recently returned. Mother needed care and was opposed to leaving the house. I took early retirement. "

The hallway ended in a television room furnished with a small sofa and two loungers. The curtains were drawn. Hugh flipped on the lights. "My parents added this room in the sixties, before Island Preservation instituted stricter regulations."

One wall was covered with family photographs. I pointed to a studio portrait of a heavy-jowled man in a dark suit. "Your father?"

"Sheriff at Portree for forty years."

"Sheriff?"

"You'd call him a judge. In Scotland, sheriffs deal with the majority of the criminal and civil court cases." All the photographs, I noticed, were of Hugh's parents, together and separately, at a variety of social events. Not a single photograph of their son.

He shifted his weight. "There isn't much more to see, really. Kitchen and dining area through that door. Two bedrooms and a bath upstairs.

A bedroom and bath off the downstairs hall—Mother's suite, so she doesn't have to climb stairs. Very little inside is original except my office."

"I'd love to see your office." Anywhere away from Mommie Dearest.

Hugh opened the door to a wood-paneled room near the staircase. Two chairs faced an Adam-style fireplace. On a pedestal near the window stood an enormous begonia plant. Hairy brown rhizomes crawled toward the window as if attempting a slow-motion getaway. I could sympathize.

Hugh placed his hand on the mantel. "This is the original paneling and fireplace, and this is my father." He indicated a portrait above the mantel. "Painted, as you can see, in this very room."

The portrait was a companion to the one in the living room. The thick-jowled man I'd seen in the family photos wore black judicial robes and the traditional off-white horsehair wig worn in court. He sat on the edge of a leather-top desk, one hand on a stack of books. Behind him, on the mantel, a statue of a Lady Justice wielded the sword of justice and the scales of truth. Lady Justice was still on the mantel, and the desk still occupied the center of the room. On the desktop was a small laptop computer and a glass paperweight.

"I started reading your book last night," I said. "It's very good."

"Thank you." He shifted his weight again. His expression had changed, but I wasn't able to read it.

"I hear you're working on a sequel. Have you decided how you'll deal with Flora's murder? I assume there was an investigation. Maybe contemporary records."

"I never talk about a work in progress," he snapped. Then he seemed to wilt. "Forgive me. I'm not myself."

"I understand. I really do. When someone you love dies, your whole life changes, but the universe spins along as if nothing has happened. It's very disorienting."

Goggle-eyes again. Had I lapsed into Hungarian?

If Hugh Guthrie had hidden depths, it would take a spelunker to find them. What had Elenor seen in him? It couldn't have been his trust fund. Elenor had money of her own. Maybe she fancied being the wife of a local celebrity, or maybe she'd gotten bored with running a hotel. She never had possessed a long attention span.

"Will you continue your work at the Historical Society?"

"Of course." He straightened his shoulders and appeared to pull himself together. "We're making an inventory of our holdings. Elenor would want me to complete the project."

Having found a topic of interest, I held on. "Elenor spoke of thefts at the Historical Society. The staff at the hotel thought she was imagining things."

"No, it's quite true. We started noticing things going missing several months ago. Random things—a box of photographs, a hand-woven blanket, a gun. The gun worried us, but it showed up again the day after it was taken. As if it had never been gone. Most of the items showed up again, although I have to be honest, we're so disorganized, we might not have noticed except we're in the process of cataloging. It was almost as if someone were playing a game, seeing what they could get away with."

"What did the police say?"

"Elenor wouldn't report it." He picked up the paperweight and shifted it from hand to hand as if gauging its weight. "She said the culprit would eventually give himself away."

"But he hasn't?"

Hugh shook his head. "Not surprising. Our security's pretty lax. We try to staff the museum with volunteers, but it's not always possible in the off-season. People come and go. There's a bell on the door, but most of us have tuned it out by now."

"How many volunteers do you have?"

"More in summer, but if you mean regulars, there's myself and Elenor." He set the paperweight on the desk. "Agnes MacLeod and the MacDonalds. That's five. And the Arnott twins. Seven total."

"Could the thefts be connected with Elenor's death?"

"Why should they be?" He looked genuinely baffled.

"Who besides Elenor has access to the museum after hours?"

"Look, I've been through all this with the police. Are you implying one of our volunteers killed Elenor?"

"I'm not implying anything. I'm trying to understand why Elenor went to the Historical Society the night of the ball. You must have asked yourself that question."

"Of course I have," he said irritably. "And a hundred others." He wiped his forehead with the back of his hand. "Forgive me. I'm really not myself. There are two sets of exterior keys. Elenor had one and I have the other, although we loan our keys to volunteers occasionally. We keep another set, for the locked exhibits, in the desk. I'm afraid we're not careful about that either. As I said, we're not well organized."

"I've never seen the museum. I know it meant a lot to Elenor."

"The police said we can get back in tomorrow. Stop by if you like."

A petulant voice drifted in from somewhere beyond the door. "Hugh? Where are you? I need to speak with you immediately."

His shoulders sagged. "I'll be right back." He left, shutting the door behind him.

I stared at the neat desktop. Wasn't he supposed to be working on the new book? Where were his notes, outlines, drafts, sticky pads with bits of research? He claimed in the forward to *The Diary* to have done extensive research. Where were his reference books?

None of your business scolded that prim little voice of conscience.

Too late—again. I'd already opened the right-hand drawer.

The drawer was filled with correspondence. The letter on top (I couldn't help seeing it, could I?) was from Hugh's publisher, a contract for two volumes of *The Diary of Flora Arnott*.

In for a penny. I flipped quickly through the pile, reading snatches while keeping my ears open for footsteps and one eye on the door.

A letter dated the previous June read, *May we remind you, sir, that your contract was for two books. With the success of the first volume, we believe a second should come out sooner rather than—* I stopped reading, thumbing forward in time.

A letter written in mid-August complained, *Have you forgotten, Dr. Guthrie, that your book claims to be Volume One? We've been patient, but I believe we deserve to know when a draft of Volume Two will be forthcoming. Remember that you are under contract.*

Had Guthrie even begun to write the new book?

Hearing only silence, I opened the center drawer, finding several pens and a brass letter opener. That wasn't all. Stuffed toward the back was a clear plastic bag holding several round blue tablets. I held the bag to the light. The imprint of *S193* was clearly visible. Eszopiclone tablets. Like Elenor's.

A scraping sound on the other side of the door startled me. Then the doorknob turned.

I shoved the baggie in the drawer and closed it.

Then I did something dumb. Really, really dumb.

I ducked under the desk.

You idiot, I told myself, stating the obvious.

I heard the door open and the sound of wheels on wood.

I curled myself into a ball and held my breath. If Margaret left before I passed out, there was a chance I could—

The wheelchair squeaked into my line of vision. "Looking for something in particular or just snooping?" Margaret Guthrie was seriously annoyed.

I shot her a look of dazzling innocence. "Admiring the dovetail joins. An antique dealer's affliction, I'm afraid. We can't resist." The lie came more easily than it should have, but this was Margaret Guthrie, who could kill with her eyeballs alone.

"Too bad you have to go so soon." She crossed her arms over her ample chest. She didn't look pleased.

Or convinced.

Chapter Twenty

Dusk was settling on the island when I pedaled down the long drive toward the hotel, alive and unscathed. Not a phrase I use often.

Things hadn't ended as badly as they might have. With Margaret Guthrie looming over me, I'd scrambled awkwardly from beneath the desk, mumbled something about the delicious cake, and beat a swift retreat.

The humiliation had been worth it.

If Elenor had been sharing sleeping pills with her fiancé (illegal, of course), it might explain why she'd been asking the doctor for more. And, even more tantalizing, someone really had been stealing things from the Historical Society.

Stealing them and putting them back.

I walked my bike over the gravel parking area. Tartan Cottage was still dark, and there was still no car. Maybe Tom had checked out. Nothing to do with me, of course. I'd have dinner in the cottage, read more in Guthrie's book, and get a good night's sleep for once.

I found Nancy and Frank in the kitchen. Frank stood with his back to the sink. Nancy slumped at the oak table. I got the impression they'd been arguing and remembered that one of them had lied on their police statement. I'd forgotten about that. As much as I liked Nancy, I had to admit she'd been cagey about the night of the ball, and there'd been something behind those clear gray eyes when she denied having a clue about the identity of Elenor's killer.

Frank nodded and resumed his scrutiny of the floor.

Nancy tucked her hair into place and stood, smoothing her skirt. "Detective Inspector Devlin phoned. He said to call him back if you got in before five. Nothing urgent."

It was almost five thirty. I'd phone him in the morning. "Did Bo's sister call?"

"She has not. Frank's been trying to contact her as well."

"Would you mind if I had dinner in the cottage tonight?"

"Not a'tall, lass." Nancy opened a drawer and pulled out one of her snowy white aprons. "Mr. Mallory won't be joining us either. I'll send Sofia with a tray, shall I? Six thirty?"

"Perfect." I wanted to ask why Tom wouldn't be having dinner that night. Instead I said, "Any news about Bo?"

"They've assigned a public defender," Frank said tersely. "Probably some eejit fresh out of university who doesn't give a—"

"*Frank.*" Nancy stopped him.

I refrained from comment. In my experience, most recent law school graduates still wore the shiny halo of truth and justice for all.

I walked the bike back to Applegarth. The sky had cleared. The sun's dying rays laid a shimmering path on the dark surface of the Sound.

In the cottage, I slipped out of my shoes. Applegarth was beginning to feel like home.

At six thirty sharp, Sofia arrived with a tray of dishes covered with silver domes. Nancy had sent beef stroganoff with apple cobbler and ice cream for dessert. I sighed. Lean Cuisine for me when I got back to Ohio.

"Please to put your tray on the bench outside when you are finish." Sofia turned to leave.

"Stay for a minute." *A little tact wouldn't hurt.* "I've been trying to get a sense of Elenor's life these past weeks. I'd like your impressions."

"Is not my business." Sofia clasped the metal domes to her chest like armor.

"But it is your business. The sale of the hotel affects everyone."

Sofia shook her head. "I am just a maid." Her accent was thickening.

"But you were upset." The words flew out of my mouth before I could stop them. "So upset you spent the night in Tartan Cottage."

The metal lids rattled. "Who tell you?"

"Mr. Mallory, but only to give you an alibi."

"Yez, okay. I was upset that she sells the hotel. Now she is dead. Is nothing to do with me." Her eyes were liquid pools of fear.

"Sofia, if you know something, you must tell the police."

I reached for her arm, but she recoiled as if I'd slapped her.

Clutching the lids, she fled from the cottage.

I'd blown it. Plain and simple. Instead of gaining Sofia's confidence, I'd frightened her, and she was obviously already afraid. About what, I'd probably never know now.

In an attempt to feel better, I finished my apple cobbler and practically licked the bowl.

I felt worse. If I stayed on the island much longer, I'd have to buy a pair of elastic-waist pants.

I gave up and got ready for bed. It was only eight, but the day had taken a toll. Every question raised others. Every clue deepened the confusion. Agnes had denied leaving the hotel the night of the murder. A lie, I was sure of it. The Holdens had lied, too—one of them anyway—and Nancy had taken great pains to convince me that she and Frank had gotten along just fine with Elenor. The Guthries were distinctly odd. Not that it made them murderers, but they were odd. The Arnott twins were beyond odd. Jackie and Dora MacDonald were question marks. And then there was Becca.

The adoption thing had been flitting around the back of my mind. Did Becca have some reason to believe her birth parents came from Glenroth? Or—I was riveted by a new thought—could Becca be Elenor's daughter? My imagination picked up speed. Maybe it was Becca who met Elenor at the Historical Society and confronted her with proof that she was her biological daughter. Maybe Elenor denied it. Or laughed at her and—

I shook my head. It was all mist and froth. What I needed was something solid, something I could build on, like Elenor's insistence that I read Guthrie's book. Clearly the book was meant to be the preamble for a story she planned to tell me, the cause of her fear and the reason she had called me for help.

I washed my hair, dried it with a towel, and combed it behind my ears. After slathering on a layer of face cream a salesclerk barely out of puberty had promised would make me look twenty years younger, I slipped into my flannel Mickey and Minnie pajamas, the ones the kids had bought me years ago at Disney World. Some people have comfort food. I have comfort pajamas.

Snuggling into the duvet, I opened *The Diary of Flora Arnott*, but instead of reading, I laid the open book on my chest.

My list of things to do was multiplying like rabbits. Call DI Devlin. Talk to the pastor of the Wee Free about Elenor's funeral. Contact a funeral director. Stop by the Historical Society for the promised tour. If Bo's sister didn't call, I'd have to drive into Glenfinnan to track her down at the Munroe Clinic. I had to make an appointment with Elenor's solicitor in Inverness. And, oh yes, if there was time, I would also check out the jewelry store where Guthrie had bought that ring.

I should have written it all down.

I'd begun to read when I heard the crunch of gravel outside. The sound of a car door was followed by a sharp rap on the door. "Kate, it's me, Tom."

Cripes. "Hold on." Springing out of bed, I dashed into the bathroom and toweled off the face cream. Finger combing my still-damp hair, I threw the robe over my pajamas. After smoothing the duvet and plumping the pillow, I opened the door, a little breathlessly.

Tom stood on the porch, one hand in the pocket of his waxed field jacket. He rubbed his chin. Had he come to apologize for his rudeness at dinner?

No, he had not.

"I've been at the police station in Mallaig all day. May I come in? I have news."

I opened the door wider. He ducked his head as he came through.

Double cripes. Why hadn't I thought to roll up the legs of my pajamas?

The sitting area in Applegarth Cottage consisted of two overstuffed armchairs, a low table, and a well-stocked bookshelf. Tom took the chair nearest the window. I took the other, tucking my legs as far under the chair as I could manage. With luck, he wouldn't notice Mickey and Minnie.

"Devlin said not to bother returning his call," Tom said. "He asked me to give you an update."

"On Bo Duff? Have they completed the evaluation?"

"Not yet, but there's a hearing scheduled sometime next week."

"A *hearing*?" I snapped and immediately felt guilty. Shooting the messenger never helps. "I'm sorry, Tom, but this whole thing is a mistake. Something traumatized Bo that night, and the sooner he gets back to his familiar environment, the sooner he'll be able to remember what that was. Maybe he witnessed something. Maybe he can identify the real killer." I'd leaned so far forward on my chair that I almost slipped off. I sat back. "I'm not going to let the police railroad him, I swear."

"Devlin's not out to railroad anyone. I'm not a legal expert, but I doubt Bo's confession alone will stand up in court. They'll need corroborating evidence."

"Bo didn't confess!" I threw up my hands in exasperation. "How many times do I have to repeat that before someone listens?"

"Kate, I hear you. But if Bo is deemed competent, and if he continues to insist that he hurt Elenor, they will have to take him seriously."

"What if he's deemed mentally *in*competent?"

"I don't know. But if he isn't guilty, there won't be corroborating evidence."

My toes prickled. I wiggled them to get the circulation going. "You've read the statements. What do you think?"

"I think Elenor made a lot of people angry." He reached into the pocket of his jacket and pulled out my cell phone. "They've finished with it."

I took the phone and checked for messages from Christine. There were none. "So what's the update?"

"Preliminary tests came back. Elenor's blood contained a high level of sedatives. Sleeping pills."

"Really?" Sleeping pills were becoming a theme. "Why would she take pills before going out? How long does it take for sleeping pills to kick in?"

"That depends—on what she took, how much she took, if she had food in her stomach, if she was in the habit of taking sedatives. I'm no expert. If you give me your mobile number, I'll text you when I learn more."

I watched him write down the number, thinking I should probably tell him about the pills in Hugh Guthrie's desk. Except he'd ask how I found them, and I had no intention whatsoever of telling him that.

"There's also an update on the boot prints. Seems Mucky Ducks are popular on the island. So far they've located several pairs in size ten. The Arnott twins have a pair that belonged to their father, but they've been stored in their shed for years. A maternity ward for mice, apparently. Hugh Guthrie used to have a pair, but he gave them to the village charity shop a while back. And there are a couple of size tens right here at the hotel. They keep them on hand for guests."

I thought of the wellies Nancy had loaned me the night of the ball. Good thing I didn't wear size ten. "If I were guilty, I wouldn't leave my boots hanging around for the police to find. I'd put them in a rubbish bin somewhere or toss them in the lake."

"You have a criminal mind." He shot me that disarming half smile.

I stretched my legs, realizing too late I'd forgotten all about the pajamas.

Tom stared at the grinning Mickeys and Minnies. "Did I wake you?"

"Just reading." Tom's wife had probably worn fabulous lingerie.

He leaned toward me, frowning. "You've got something on your upper lip. And there, on your chin."

I shot up and dashed into the bathroom.

The image in the mirror made me flinch. No makeup. Smudges of dried face cream on my face. Damp hair sticking to my head. Flannel Disney pajamas so old I could practically sell them in the antique shop. *Good grief.*

I wiped my face with a towel.

He stood when I returned. "I'll say good night, Kate. Let you get back to your book."

After he'd gone, I climbed into bed. Had Devlin really asked Tom to give me an update? I had only his word for that. What did I know about him anyway?

Chapter
Twenty-One

After settling in for the night—for good this time, I hoped—I picked up the diary and began to read.

From mid-March to July of 1809, Flora's household was awhirl with preparations for her journey to Glenroth, no simple matter in the eighteenth century. Friends and relatives descended on Hazelbank almost daily to bid Flora a fond farewell. Her father kept out of the way, pretending that his threats of the previous winter had been no more than fatherly concern. Her grandmother alternated between spurts of activity and bouts of depression:

> *Grandmother is forever calling for my presence, first cling-ing to me & weeping because I am to leave her & then scolding because I am not as unhappy as she. She says I will break her heart, but in truth I am longing to be away! Dear Gowyn will be my companion. She faces her future in the Hebrides with the courage of a martyr bound for the flames. I wonder what Capt. Arnott will think when I arrive like a merchant ship laden with treasure. He says I am dowry enough, but in that opinion he cannot be entirely truthful.*

At last, on the first of August 1809, two months before her six-teenth birthday, Flora Young and Gowyn Campbell set sail from

Greenock, Scotland, on the *Venture*, a three-masted cargo ship bound
for Galtrigill on the Isle of Skye. In addition to Flora's trousseau, the
ship carried furniture, tools, whiskey, and molasses, plus eight additional passengers bound for the tweed mills on the Isle of Harris.
With rough seas and many stops along the coast to load and unload
cargo, the journey took fourteen days. Guthrie's description was har-
rowing. All the passengers fell ill. The food, what Flora and Gowyn
could keep down, was inedible. Sanitation was poor to nonexistent. I
found myself skimming, eager for Flora's reunion with James.

On the fourteenth of August, the rocky coast of Skye was sighted.
On the fifteenth, the *Venture* docked at Galtrigill.

15ᵗʰ August

    *We have arriv'd! As our ship entered the harbour, I was
giddy with anticipation. Gowyn & I searched the quay & at last
we saw dearest James. He bowed, flourishing his hat in the most
charming manner possible. He is handsome as ever, tho perhaps
not quite so elegant. Gowyn remarked upon it & I was quick to
remind her that we are no longer in society. James brought with
him six men, four horse-drawn waggons, & a small curricle. We
stayed two nights at Castle Dunvegan, a fearsome sight rising
from the barren rock. The current Laird extended every courtesy
& regaled us with tales of the visit by Dr. Johnson & Mr. Boswell
during his father's tenancy as Chief of the MacLeods. Gowyn
vows she will rather die than set foot again on a ship of any
description.*

17ᵗʰ August

    *Yesterday we set forth much refreshed. Soon, however, we
were overcome by the muggy climate & devilish biting insects.
The curricle is open to the weather & the roads, no more than
vague tracks marked out by sheep & cattle, shockingly rutted.*

We make slow progress as we are often requir'd to mend the wheels of the carts or carriage. Gowyn is mute with apprehension & I too am sensible that life in the Hebrides will be quite unlike the one I have resigned.

James is tanned by the wind & sun. He wears leather breeks & a sturdy waistcoat of tweed, eminently practical in this inhospitable climate. His men treat him with a deference that those who do not know his true character might mistake for fear. With one of the men he appears to be on terms of some intimacy. The man's name is Joseph, a young negro of perhaps 17 or 18, I presume from the Indies.

The Capt. rides a fine horse & keeps near the curricle. Gowyn insists I guard my reputation, so I smile at him from behind my fan like a proper gentlewoman. I shall not take the liberty of calling him James until we are alone, if ever we are to be alone. Gowyn takes her role as chaperone quite to heart. I shall not be surprised if, after the wedding, she follows us into our bedchamber.

We rest for the night at Ullinish, at the inn where Dr. Johnson & Mr. Boswell stopped also. The fare was edible but the beds as rank as the stews in Glasgow. We spread our plaids over the straw & stopped our ears against the scuttling behind the skirt board. The Capt. raises our spirits with the promise of clean beds & a great feast.

18th August

To-day we boarded a barge with 8 oarsmen for the journey along Loch Harport to Drynoch. After our days in the curricle, Gowyn happily broke her vow. Our hearts soar'd, for the loch is very like the Clyde inlet near Greenock. Shall I admit to feeling a wee bitty homesick?

To-night we put in at Bualintur where we shall be met by

our horses & waggons. Here we rest at Ian MacKinnon's Tavern be-fore making the final journey to Glenroth. In four days' time I shall bathe in a copper tub & sleep in a carved Mahogany bed. Never has the prospect seemed more welcome.

19ᵗʰ August, Evening, Ian MacKinnon's Tavern
    To-night an event of a most disturbing nature occurr'd. Gowyn & I were making ready for bed when we heard below us a fearful commotion. Believing some poor soul was injured or ill, I—being still in my gown—ran part way down the staircase & witness'd a violent altercation between Capt. Arnott & one of his men, a Highlander, judging from his speech. Altho taller than the Capt., this man receiv'd the worst of the blows. His nose gushed blood & one eye was swollen shut. The young negro, Joseph, pulled the Capt. away whilst several others dragged the poor man from the inn. The horror I felt cannot be described. I must have cried out, for the Capt. spied me as I fled to my chamber.
    "What has happened, Miss?" Gowyn asked upon my return. "Nothing of importance," said I. "Only there was a fight among the men."
    I did not tell her about James. Indeed I would not credit it myself had I not witnessed with my own eyes a side of his character so entirely altered from that which I have known. I wish to God I had not seen it.
    To-night I shall not sleep.

20ᵗʰ August
    Dear Mamma once said that a misty night leads to a clear day. The truth of this I have now experienc'd. As we were making ready to depart, James, comprehending a certain coldness in my address, took me aside & explain'd that what I had witnessed was not as it seemed. It was, in fact, a matter of honor, a matter,

dear diary, involving my-self! The Highlander made an ungen-
tlemanly remark & James was bound by honor & sentiment to
defend my reputation. "These men are little more than savages,"
said he, "unused to the presence of a lady." At that moment his
countenance was seized with some powerful emotion & he grasped
my hand, saying, "My darling, you are a perfect angel. Soon I
shall be the happiest of men."

Am I not the happiest of women? To-morrow I shall see my
new home!

I closed the book feeling uneasy, as Guthrie had no doubt
intended I should. Perhaps the episode at Ian MacKinnon's tavern was
meant to foreshadow some revelation to come in the sequel. Had Guthrie's research pointed to one of the captain's own men as Flora's
killer—the Highlander perhaps? It wouldn't do to ask him. Guthrie
insisted he never talked about a work in progress.

How had the real Flora Arnott felt, leaving Hazelbank and everything familiar for what must have seemed a wilderness? Guthrie por-
trayed her as adventurous and brave. Was that entirely true?

I marked my place and closed the book. Grief and loneliness,
always prowling at the edge of my consciousness, had crept in with
my thoughts. At home in Jackson Falls, it would be almost six PM. I
picked up my cell phone and dialed.

"Hello. This is Linea Larsen."

"It's me. Are you in the middle of dinner?"

"Dinner can wait."

"What are you planning to do tonight?"

"I thought I'd watch *To Catch a Thief* on Netflix. I've always liked
that one. Cary Grant reminds me of your father."

I smiled. My father hadn't looked anything like Cary Grant, but
maybe it wasn't looks they had in common.

"You called me for a reason," she said, "What's happened?"

I told her, taking my time and outlining everything I'd learned.

"Will they charge Bo with murder?"

"If he's found competent to stand trial, and if he continues to insist he hurt Elenor. Convenient for them." I heard the bitterness in my voice.

"And if he isn't found competent?"

"I don't know. But he can't—or won't—defend himself."

"Whom do you suspect?"

I groaned. "That's the problem. I could make a case for any of them. The Holdens are hiding something, although I can't imagine Nancy harming anyone. Then there's Agnes MacLeod. She gave up everything, believing Elenor would make her a partner. Maybe she'd had enough of Elenor's mistreatment. Or maybe the sale of the hotel pushed her over the edge. And I can't stop thinking about Becca. But if Elenor really was her birth mother, wouldn't she be showing some emotion?"

"How about someone outside the hotel?"

"Well, if the new owners tamper with the hotel's Jacobite theme, the MacDonalds stand to lose money, but then so do most of the islanders. Besides, the hotel was already sold, so I don't see what Elenor's death would accomplish."

"What about the fiancé? You said he didn't seem thrilled at the prospect of marriage."

"He didn't, but if he killed her, the motive has to be more complicated than ending an engagement. Have you found anything on the casket yet?"

"Still looking. I'll text you. By the way, what's this English detective like?"

"Nice enough. Good-looking. I think he's won a few hearts on the island."

"Not yours."

"Of course not, but he could be helpful. He's working with the Scottish police. They've asked him to keep me informed."

There was an eloquent silence. My mother was wondering if the police really did that sort of thing. I'd been wondering that too. "What about Elenor's money?" she asked.

"I thought of that. Maybe Agnes was the beneficiary, and Elenor was going to change her will in favor of Hugh Guthrie. But it must have been the first thing the police checked. I'll find out more when I meet with the solicitor."

"There are more powerful motives than money, Kate."

"Like what?"

"Like passion, pride, revenge. Even loyalty. You will be careful, won't you? I couldn't bear it if something happened to you."

I thought about those words as we said good night. In all the losses my mother had suffered in her life, I'd never heard her say *I couldn't bear it*.

She was right about motives, though. Maybe a connection between Elenor and Flora Arnott was fantasy after all.

Two murders separated by two centuries? A long time to hold a grudge.

Chapter Twenty-Two

⁓

Monday, October 31

By Monday morning the news was all over the island.

Elenor Spurgeon had been shot through the neck with an arrow. Bo Duff had confessed to something (exactly what wasn't clear) and was now in a mental clinic in Glenfinnan. And Elenor's blood, when she died, had contained enough sedatives to render her defenseless if not actually unconscious. I learned this at eight fifteen when Nancy called and woke me up. Frank had been to Flora's for yum yums, finding it rife with rumor and speculation.

The collective island consciousness was grasping the unthinkable: Elenor's murderer had to be one of them. No more speculation about off-islanders and homicidal maniacs. Even Margaret Guthrie would have to give up her gang-of-thugs-from-Glasgow theory.

For once the sea was calm. The trees looked freshly washed.

Today was Halloween. My mother would have a ball, passing out the candy bars I'd left on the kitchen counter. I could hardly believe only two days had passed since we had learned of Elenor's death. So much had happened.

I poured myself a cup of coffee and called the Munroe Clinic. The nice woman I'd spoken to earlier wasn't on duty, and the person answering the phone refused to tell me anything, period. Frustrated,

I called the funeral home Nancy had recommended and made an appointment to speak with the director the following morning. Finally I phoned Elenor's solicitor in Inverness. He wasn't in. Would I care to leave a message?

"My name is Kate Hamilton. I'm Elenor Spurgeon's sister-in-law. I was hoping to see him today or tomorrow about her will."

"Good heavens," said a deeply shocked voice. "If Mrs. Spurgeon has given you permission to delve into her affairs, perhaps she would care to make the appointment herself."

"I'm afraid that won't be possible," I said smoothly. "Mrs. Spurgeon is dead."

Did I mention I can be snarky?

An intake of breath. "I wasn't informed. Hold, please. I'll need to check his appointment book." I heard pages turning. "He has an opening tomorrow, twelve thirty."

"Nothing today?"

"He's in court until noon. After that he's booked solid." She gave me the address in Inverness. "Tomorrow, twelve thirty. Park in the lot across the street. We validate."

After ending the call, I noticed a text my mother must have sent the previous evening. She may be in her seventies, but she knows her way around technology: CHECKING 18TH C SCOTTISH CABINETMAKERS. NEED CLOSE-UPS OF THE BANDING AND FEET. I pictured her bent over her laptop, a pencil in her teeth, having the time of her life. If she lived in Jackson Falls instead of Wisconsin, we could run the shop together. I'd asked her to move in with me several times, but she'd always refused. "I wouldn't do that to you," was the reason she gave, but I'd always suspected it had something to do with the charming widower she'd met, a retired physician.

At nine thirty I walked to the main house.

Sofia was snapping green beans. Nancy was clearing up from breakfast.

"I can't understand it." Lines of exhaustion pulled at Nancy's face. "Why would Elenor overdose on sleeping pills? It must have been an accident."

Sofia muttered something under her breath and snapped a bean.

Becca appeared in the doorway. She looked as tiny as Elenor in a fitted black leather jacket, black leggings, and a small cross-body handbag. Family resemblance? Her face wasn't shaped like Elenor's, though, and her dark hair was the opposite of Elenor's white-blonde. Of course she might have taken after her father. Whoever he might be.

"Need anything from town?" Becca asked.

"No," Nancy and Sofia said in unison.

Frank came through the back door. "Car's running."

"See you later?" Nancy reached out to touch him, but he pretended not to notice. Whatever stood between them remained unresolved.

Becca followed Frank out the door. Sofia disappeared into the dining room.

Nancy poured two mugs of coffee and carried them to the table by the hearth. "Come sit, Kate." She pushed a plate of yum yums toward me, taking one of the sugary twists herself. "They've no reason to go into Fort William today, but it gives Becca a chance to meet Geoff for lunch. It can't be fun for her, stuck out here with no one her own age."

My thought exactly. "Someone from the hotel goes into Fort William every Monday?"

"Friday, too, if the house is full or we're having a function."

"Always Frank and Becca?" I selected one of the yum yums and took a bite. Amazing.

"Agnes usually goes along, but she isn't up to it today."

I chewed thoughtfully. That meant someone from the hotel—Becca, Frank, even Agnes—could have mailed those threatening letters, once a week, in Fort William.

Nancy stared at the pastry in her hand as if it had appeared there by magic. She put it back on the plate. "Did you know Geoff's asked Becca to marry him?"

"She told me. Do you think she'll say yes?" I polished off the last of my yum yum and washed it down with coffee.

"Hard to tell with that one." Nancy added a splash of cream to her mug. "Becca reminds me of the pup Frank and I adopted from the shelter when we were first married. Poor wee beastie could never trust us. We found out later it had been mistreated."

"Was Becca mistreated?"

"She's hinted as much. I've wondered about that scar."

I'd wondered about it too. "How was she orphaned?"

"Her mother gave her up at birth. Without even seeing her, I gather. Becca pretends it was for the best, but rejection and loss leave scars. The invisible ones go deep."

I thought about my own invisible scars: losing my brother Matt, my hero, when I was five; losing my beloved father when I was in high school; losing Bill, the love of my life, the father of my children. Each of those losses had come like a sucker punch, without warning. I'd never thought of myself as emotionally disfigured.

"What will you do today, dearie?" Nancy blew across her coffee and took a test sip.

"I thought I'd have another look at Elenor's flat. As executor, I'll probably have to provide an inventory." It took every ounce of personal discipline I had not to mention the casket. I'm not good at keeping secrets.

Nancy repositioned the tortoiseshell combs in her hair. "Well, come back later for a bite of lunch. I'm on my own today."

I stopped in reception for the keys. The drawer wouldn't close, so I rattled the contents and slammed it shut.

That brought a thud. Followed by the sound of running feet.

I raced toward the east wing, reminding myself that ghosts don't run.

The door to Elenor's flat swung on its hinges. No one in sight.

I ran for the door at the end of the hall, finding it firmly locked. I peered outside. No dark figure booking it toward the woods.

Someone had broken into Elenor's flat—piece of cake, given the slapdash security at the hotel—but how had he managed to disappear into thin air? Other than pushing past me toward the front door (I would have noticed that, right?), the only exit was through the door at the end of the hallway. And that wasn't possible because, like other doors at the inn, this one had a dead bolt. Whoever-it-was would have had to stop and lock the door from the outside with a key. Even if he or she had a key, there hadn't been time. But that wasn't the most important question.

What was this person doing in Elenor's flat in the first place?

As soon as I walked through the door, the answer became obvious. The contents of the cardboard box lay scattered on the floor. I dashed into the bathroom, my heart pounding like a silversmith's hammer.

As I feared, the casket was gone.

*   *   *

"I couldn't tell if it was a man or a woman."

I stood in the reception hall with Nancy and DI Devlin. "I heard Elenor's door slam—at least I think it was her door—and then footsteps running. I didn't actually see anyone."

"You say the person just disappeared?" Dark circles under Devlin's eyes told me he hadn't been getting his full eight hours of beauty sleep.

"In a puff of smoke, for all I know."

Nancy shivered and wrapped her arms around her body.

"Were you aware Mrs. Spurgeon had a valuable chest in her flat?" Devlin asked her.

It's not a chest; it's a casket. Saying stuff like that out loud is about as popular as correcting people's grammar.

"I didn't know." Nancy's voice quavered. She clasped her hands, flexing and unflexing her fingers. "Elenor was keen on privacy. Only Agnes and Sofia were allowed in her flat."

"Excuse me," I said in small voice. "I think I saw someone in the hallway yesterday, too."

Devlin pressed his fingers to his forehead as if I were purposely giving him a headache. "Would you care to tell me about it?" Exaggerated patience.

"I got here around ten. Becca was at her desk. The MacDonalds came to offer their condolences, but they left pretty quickly. Penny Arnott came shortly after that. She said Elenor had something that belonged to her. A box of kitchenware, I think. But Penny didn't get inside the flat. After she left, I thought I saw a shadow behind me, but no one was there."

He scribbled something in his little black notebook. I pictured him writing *Completely loopy. Hallucinating.*

He snapped the notebook shut. "When was the last time you actually saw the casket?"

"After Penny left. I went in to take photographs."

At that moment, Tom came through the front door and shook off his jacket. "I reached Frank on his mobile. He and Becca will be back soon."

Nancy took a breath and blew it out.

Just then Agnes came limping down the staircase. "Sorry," she said. "Had to throw on some clothes. What's wrong?"

"A valuable antique is missing from Mrs. Spurgeon's flat," Devlin said. "A small chest with inlaid designs."

Agnes's eyes flicked. "Well, I never saw it."

Devlin made another note in his black notebook. "How would

someone leave the east wing without going through reception or the door at the end of the hallway?"

"They couldn't," Agnes said. "There isn't another way."

"Are you sure?"

"Of course I'm sure."

Devlin looked at me. "And you're positive the intruder didn't get past you and run out the front door. Or up the staircase."

"I would have noticed."

Agnes glared at Devlin. "I hope you're not accusing *me* of stealing the antique."

"I'm not accusing anyone," Devlin said. "We'll notify local dealers and pawn shops, but we'll have to search the house."

"You won't find the thing in my flat." Agnes shot him a defiant look and hobbled off.

Why was she being so defensive? And why was she limping?

Devlin slid the notebook into his breast pocket and snatched up his jacket.

He was about to leave when Frank and Becca burst through from the kitchen.

Frank took Nancy's hand. "Tom said there's been another theft."

"I must go." Devlin shrugged into his jacket. "Mrs. Hamilton will explain."

There wasn't much to tell. When I got to the part about the intruder vanishing, Frank put his arm around Nancy's shoulder. "Come on, Nancy. Let's go home."

They left holding hands.

Becca pulled her handbag strap over her head and peeled off her jacket. "This disappearing ghost thing is going to frighten Nancy."

"I never said there was a ghost," I protested. This was how stories got started.

"They must have been good parents, Frank and Nancy. I envy their daughter."

Just the subject I wanted to talk about. "It must have been hard, not knowing your parents. Do you have any information at all?"

I followed her into the kitchen. Becca opened a ceramic jar on the counter and pulled out one of Nancy's homemade biscuits. "Want one?"

I shook my head.

She took a bite and chewed for a moment. "My mother was very young, still in school. That's all I know."

That didn't sound like Elenor. According to Agnes, Elenor would have been in her twenties when the pregnancy occurred. "Do you have a name? A place?"

"The names are sealed. I was born in Ayr. Taken from the hospital to an emergency care home, then to a children's home run by the church. Later I was fostered."

"Good foster homes?"

"Not the last one. The social worker had me in counseling, not that it helped. You turn the page and go on, don't you." She took another bite of biscuit. "I've never told anyone that before, except Geoff. We talked about it the night of the ball, the night he proposed."

I tried to appear nonchalant. "Did you and Geoff stay on the island the night of the ball? I heard the ferry stopped at eleven." *Subtle as a brick through a window.*

"Maybe you'd like to read my police statement." Becca's eyebrow arched. "I think I agree with Tom. You should leave interrogation to the police."

"I'm sorry, Becca. None of my business."

"No, it isn't." She gave a halfhearted shrug. "But I'll tell you anyway. Neither Geoff nor I had any reason to harm Elenor, if that's what you're getting at. We left the island at nine thirty and stopped for coffee at the pub near the ferry terminal in Mallaig. Not the most romantic setting for a proposal, but Geoff said he couldn't wait. One of his neighbors saw us on the steps to his flat around eleven. The police confirmed it." She retucked her hair behind her left ear. "We couldn't have made it back to the island if we'd tried."

I apologized again. Even Penny Arnott would have handled that conversation with more tact. But at least I knew the truth: Becca wasn't Elenor's daughter, and she couldn't be her killer.

One suspect eliminated. I supposed that was progress.

Outside, the air was crisp and autumnal. The pines cast long shadows on the path. I found my notebook and reread the questions I'd written out Saturday night.

Who knew the casket was in Elenor's flat? No one, as far as I could tell.

Did Agnes hear footsteps in the night? Agnes wouldn't hear a fire alarm in a library.

What caused Elenor's mood to change on Wednesday? No clue.

Is Nancy hiding something? Probably, but no idea what.

Why did Elenor go to the Historical Society, and whom did she meet there? Dr. Guthrie might have an idea about that. I hadn't had a chance to ask him on Sunday, nor had I asked him about *The Hebridean Chronicle.*

He'd offered to show me around the Historical Society.

Then again, after my fiasco of a visit to his house, he might shoot me on sight.

Chapter
Twenty-Three

With nothing else planned, I decided to risk a visit to the Historical Society. I might learn something helpful. If Guthrie let me in. The good news was he didn't know I'd found sleeping pills in his desk—or letters from his publisher indicating the draft of the second book was overdue. The bad news was his mother had caught me snooping and had probably told him I was a devious and prying person.

No comment.

Once again, Agnes was hovering at the end of the drive near the letter box. I waved. What was that woman's fascination with the mail delivery?

Since the weather was clearing, I decided to walk to the Historical Society via the forest path, a shortcut that curved through the woods before joining the main road west of the stone bridge—the route, according to Becca, Elenor would have taken the night of the ball.

Walking quickly, I reached the Historical Society in less than twenty minutes. The crime scene tape was gone. The door stood open. Dora MacDonald was wiping down the frame with paper towels and a spray bottle of blue liquid.

"Hello, Kate." She set down the spray bottle and wiped her hands on the front of her thick corduroy jumpsuit. "Jackie and I are truly sorry about Elenor. We weren't friends—I must be honest—but we've known the Hamiltons all our lives. Jackie and Elenor went out in high school. I had quite a crush on Bill at one time." Her hand flew to her mouth. "Oh, dear. I shouldn't have said that."

"I'm not offended." I smiled. "I didn't meet Bill till he was in his thirties. I knew he'd had girlfriends."

Dora relaxed. "Anyway, Jackie came along, and that was that. Everything works out for the best."

The statement, innocently spoken, felt like a punch in the gut. Bill and I were supposed to travel, have grandchildren, grow old together in our lovely house in Jackson Falls. "Is Dr. Guthrie here?"

"He's in the office. I said he shouldn't come in today, but you know men." She winked.

I did know men. That was the problem. My story about the dovetail joins had been terminally lame. Hugh Guthrie probably wouldn't shoot me, but he might throw me out.

A bell sounded as I stepped on the mat inside the door.

Guthrie's arm was inserted up to the elbow in an enormous rolltop desk. He whipped it out, looking as guilty as a teenager caught fiddling with a pop machine.

"Is this a good time to have a look around?"

"Of course. I need a break anyway." He straightened his back and winced. "Cleanup will take some time. Fingerprint powder is everywhere."

"I see that."

"I'm sorry about yesterday." He took a ragged breath. "Mother."

"Yeah, me too."

We let it drop. Nothing like a common enemy to seal an alliance.

The Historical Society occupied a large square room with a high ceiling covered in pressed tin. Oak bookshelves lined three walls. The fusty smell of paper and old leather mingled with a hint of glass cleaner.

"A charming setting," I said.

"Yes, it's perfect." He came out from behind the counter. "The main structure was built in the mid-1860s and used as a primary school until 1932, when a larger, more modern facility was constructed in the village. After 1932, the building was used as a petrol station until 1954, when it was purchased by Dr. Walter Arnott and donated to the newly formed Glenroth Historical Society."

The canned speech flowed easily. Either Hugh Guthrie had adjusted to the death of his fiancée with breathtaking rapidity, or the difference I saw in him today had more to do with his environment than his state of mind. No mommy around to cramp his style.

I followed him toward a large platform on legs.

"What you see is a three-dimensional map of the island as it existed in 1849."

The contour map simulated the island's geography. A narrow blue gash—Burn o'Ruadh—ran crossways from the center of the island to Cuillin Sound, where a tiny boat bobbed in a blue acrylic sea. On the north shore, toward Skye, tiny stacks of fake peat indicated the blanket bogs. A key gave the compass points and identified the major buildings. Glenroth House resembled several Monopoly hotels glued together. Neither the Lodge nor the cottages had existed in 1849, but the Coach House and a building labeled SUMMER KITCHEN (now a storage building) were represented by their own blocks. A rectangular block behind Glenroth House was labeled KIRK. Bill had shown me the foundations of an old stone chapel, incorporated now into the formal gardens. Next to the kirk, a space defined by dotted lines was labeled OLD GRAVEYARD. Bill hadn't mentioned that. That was probably where Flora and her unborn child were buried, close to home.

"I understand your library has a section devoted to island history," I said.

"We've been collecting resources for a number of years."

"I've always wondered about the island legend—that Bonnie Prince Charlie spent his final night at Glenroth House before sailing back to France. Don't some history books say he spent that last night in a cave on the Isle of Skye?"

"Elgol," Guthrie said. "But that was his last night on Skye. Historians claim he spent his last night in Scotland in a cave south of Arisaig on the mainland. I believe that's true, but if you tell anyone I said that, I'll deny it." He huffed a laugh. "Local legend insists Charlie had planned to spend that last night at Arisaig, but the Duke of Cumberland got wind of it, so he and his men crossed the Sound in a small boat and made their way to Glenroth House."

"Owned at the time by the MacDonalds."

"According to the story, the laird took him in, fed him, and let him sleep in the finest bedroom. At dawn, Charlie and his fellow fugitives made their way to Loch Nan Uamh on the Isle of Skye, where they met the French frigate *L'Heureux*."

"Does your library contain accounts of his stay in the islands?"

"We have a copy of Dr. Johnson's *Journey to the Western Islands*. He and Boswell interviewed Flora MacDonald. Most of our books belonged to the Arnotts, donated to the museum when the house was sold to your husband's family. Half the volumes are scientific in nature. Not especially valuable today except as curiosities."

Several thousand books, I estimated, were shelved there, most marked on the spine with a series of numbers in white ink. "Does your collection include old newspapers?"

"No. Newspapers need specialized care, which we can't provide. Are you interested in historical journalism?"

"Actually," I said, pushing the envelope, "I wondered if you had consulted any contemporary accounts of Flora Arnott's death as part of your research for the book."

"None exist as far as I know." He looked like he was telling the truth.

We walked toward a set of double doors, leading to the modern board-and-batten extension I'd seen the day before.

"The Annex houses the museum. Behind that is the Collections Depot. Fancy name for a storage shed with a garage door."

"Something happened at the hotel today," I said as we crossed into the museum. "Someone broke into Elenor's flat. A valuable antique is missing." I watched his reaction.

"I heard." He frowned. "Detective Inspector Devlin asked me if I knew anything about a small marquetry casket."

"Had Elenor told you about it?"

He blinked and rubbed the side of his nose. "I believe she did mention it."

"Did she say where she found it?"

"No." He wiped his mouth.

The sound of breaking glass came from the Collection Depot.

Guthrie rolled his eyes. "What's she done now?"

I followed him toward the sound.

Penny Arnott stood over the shattered remains of a glass vase. "You again," she said, seeing me. She stepped away from the glass shards.

"Hello, Penny." I decided not to be offended—you make allowances for loonies, don't you?—and turned my attention to the museum. No wonder Agnes had called it a flea market. The place was stuffed with items of every description, displayed, as far as I could tell, in no order whatsoever. Suspended from the ceiling was a huge sign that read FILLING UP? ASK FOR ESSO.

"The Esso sign dates from the forties," Guthrie said, "when the building was a petrol station and garage. We acquired most of the old automotive tools as well. And this"—he indicated a full-size wooden statue of what was obviously meant to be Bonnie Prince Charlie in all his tartan finery—"stood for a century outside the apothecary in the village."

"He's wonderful." I ran my hand over the polychrome surface. The image was cartoonish, but I recognized the source—the romanticized portrait by John Pettie, depicting the Young Pretender emerging from the shadows at Holyrood to set up his court. "You should have him appraised by someone specializing in folk art. He's solid, hand carved out of a tree trunk. See? You can see a bit of the bark on the base."

"We need to stabilize him with ceiling wires," Dora MacDonald said. "Kiddies are tempted to climb." She began sweeping up the remains of the vase with a broom and dustpan.

Glass display cases on legs filled the center of the room. Atop one, featuring a collection of antique patent medicines, lay an abandoned feather duster.

"You were meant to be dusting," Hugh said to Penny.

"I *was*." Penny grabbed the duster. "Thought I better check the donations. Police might have damaged something, the fools."

"Looks like you're the one in danger of damaging things."

Penny shot him an evil look and attacked an ancient sewing machine with the duster.

One of the glass cases held a collection of vintage pocket watches, none especially old or valuable. I leaned over the case to inspect them.

"Careful," Dora said. "That one's got a wonky leg. The one nearest you, on the right."

"As you can see," Hugh said, "our displays are in poor condition, and the collection isn't well organized. Our goal is to pare it down, putting the most important items on display and either storing or disposing of the rest. We're making an inventory. Jackie MacDonald is putting it all on the computer so we'll have a database to work with in the future." Hugh pulled a handkerchief from his pocket and wiped his face. "Of course, there's little of real value here."

Penny *tsk*ed. Loudly.

Hugh sighed. "Our collection has great *historical* value in regard to the settlement of the island, certainly, but except for Charlie and a few first editions, the only items of monetary value are the weapons."

Several of the glass cases featured weaponry. In one, flint and bone arrowheads had been mounted on black velvet. Another contained a collection of knives, swords, and claymores—the traditional two-handed Highland sword. The weapons were old but, like most of the items on display, in poor condition. In the center of the case, however, I saw something special—a fine, narrow-bladed dagger, highly embellished. The label read CEREMONIAL HIGHLAND DIRK. CA. 1800. The blade was beveled, about eight inches long and chased with a scroll-like design. The grip was made to resemble a Scottish thistle, carved in an interwoven basket design, adorned with silver brads, and topped with a large faceted cairngorm, the golden gemstone prized by the Scots.

Guthrie took a key chain from his pocket, unlocked the cabinet, and lifted out the dirk. "This is our most important piece. It's quite remarkable." He ran a finger along the edge of the blade. "Hand-forged steel, still sharp enough to cut meat. We had an expert on Highland weaponry here last year. In the right hands and within range, it's as deadly as a gun."

I shuddered, picturing the dagger lodged in poor Gowyn Campbell's back.

He must have read my mind. "One just like this was used to kill Flora's companion. Not a nice way to go." Guthrie replaced the dagger, locked the cabinet, and returned the key chain to his pocket. "This is the gun I mentioned, the one that was stolen and returned." He drew my attention to another glass case featuring a modern-looking handgun. The label read WEBLEY MK III .38/200 CALIBER SERVICE REVOLVER, 1943. Next to it, an open box held copper bullets packed in tight formation. "The gun belonged to Doc Arnott."

"Army Medical Corps. Korean War." Penny stabbed the air twice with her duster for emphasis.

The bell on the front door rang. "Anybody home?" Jackie Mac-Donald strolled through from the schoolhouse. "Put me to work, people. No task too menial, no challenge too great."

Penny shoved the duster at him. "I'm off. Time for tea." She glared at me. "Coming?"

"I'd love to." I still hadn't asked Guthrie about Elenor's trip to the Historical Society the night she died, but this might be my only chance to learn if the twins had seen or heard anything other than what they'd already told the police.

I thanked Guthrie and ran for the door.

* * *

I practically had to jog to keep up with Penny. "I didn't meet Bill until he was in his thirties. What was he like as a boy?"

"Nice lad. Never cared for her."

"Elenor? Why not?"

"Stuck up. Thought she was queen of the island."

She probably did. Usurping the rightful twin queens?

We'd reached the Arnott's crumbling concrete path. The house was the type built after the Second World War, cinder blocks clad with rough cast and trimmed with wood. Everything screamed for paint. Quite a comedown from Glenroth House.

In the parlor, Cilla Arnott sat on a threadbare velvet sofa like a life-sized doll, her feet propped on a needlepoint stool. She and Penny were dressed alike again, in matching pleated skirts and white blouses with Peter Pan collars. "I wasn't expecting company," Cilla said. "Delightful surprise, of course."

I chose an armchair upholstered in dingy, rose-sprigged needlepoint. Penny pulled up a hassock covered in wedges of burgundy and beige leatherette held together by electrical tape.

Cilla beamed at me. "Pen and I have tea and biscuits every afternoon." She scooted forward until her small feet touched the floor.

"Did you bake them?" I realized with horror I'd unconsciously adopted the tone one might use with a child, but neither Cilla nor Penny appeared to notice.

"Oh no," Cilla said. "I'm hopeless in the kitchen. Penny's the domestic one."

Man, that was hard to picture.

Cilla left the room, and I prayed she wouldn't take long.

"Our parents," Penny said, indicating a framed studio portrait on a side table.

From the clothing and hairstyles, I guessed the photograph had been taken in the early 1960s. The twins resembled their parents, but not in the way I'd have guessed. Mrs. Arnott was square jawed, at least a head taller than her husband, and except for a pair of black cat's-eye spectacles, the spitting image of Penny. Cilla, on the other hand, had clearly inherited her father's genes. Doc Arnott was short and plump with Cilla's vacant blue eyes and a dimpled chin.

Cilla returned with a tray holding a blue flowered teapot, three mismatched cups and saucers, and a plate of cookies with burnt edges. "Molasses biscuits, our favorite," she said. The tray wobbled.

Penny jumped to her feet. "Let me take that, dear. Too heavy for you."

Everyone has a redeeming quality. Penny's was a rather touching concern for her sister.

While Cilla poured, I examined the room. Several framed medical certificates hung on the wall left of the fireplace. Opposite, on the right, a shadow-box frame displayed what looked like instruments of torture but were probably medical tools.

The twins didn't mind clutter. Every surface in the room was occupied by curios. Porcelain ladies twirled in lace-trimmed ball gowns. Ceramic kittens tumbled with balls of yarn. A clutch of birds huddled around a marble birdbath. Glass bowls brimmed with artificial fruit. And clowns. Some misguided Arnott had started a clown collection.

I took a bite of my cookie, tasting charred flour.

"You can see the value of our heritage," Penny said, "you being an antiques dealer."

"Penny and I are the caretakers now," Cilla said. "Sadly, the last of the line."

"The last of a line," Penny said, sweeping her arm perilously close to a pressed-glass pitcher, "running back to ancient Scotland. Cilla and I are the direct descendants of—"

"Robert the Bruce." Cilla completed the sentence.

I tried to look impressed. *On their mother's side, no doubt.* If the photograph was any indication, Mrs. Arnott could have led the charge against England and been home by tea time.

"Our ancestor, Colonel Abraham Arnott," Penny told the ceiling, "had the courage to support the clans in their battle for the Succession. Joined up with Lord Drummond."

I followed Penny's gaze to the ceiling, where a large crack snaked from one corner toward the central light fixture. I hoped no one sneezed. The whole thing might come down.

"Such a handsome man, the colonel," Cilla said dreamily. "We have his portrait here somewhere. Or is it across the street, Pen?"

"Mmm."

"How fortunate that you live so near the Historical Society," I said, cleverly turning the conversation to the night of the murder. "I bet you notice everything that goes on over there."

"We don't spy," Cilla said primly.

"But you can't help seeing things, can you?" I began to sweat. "Lights going on and off, people coming and going. The police were grateful for your sharp eyes the night of the murder."

"'Twasn't me," Cilla said. "I was sound asleep. Penny got up to—well, she got up and just happened to take a wee peek outside. That's when you saw lights, right, Pen?"

"What?" Penny was scrabbling through a drawer in a china cabinet.

"Lights at the Historical Society."

"Mmm."

"Did you see anything else?" I asked.

"Like what?"

"I don't know. Like a person or a car?"

"Nope. Ah, here it is." Penny shoved a folded newspaper in my hand. A copy of *The Islander*, a daily paper specializing in local events and Tesco coupons. The headline read ARNOTT TWINS CARRY ON FAMILY TRADITION.

"My goodness," I said. "You were in the newspaper."

"On telly, too," Cilla added. "With Dr. Guthrie, when the book was published. Such a charming man, the presenter. Scottish, naturally."

Penny swiveled in my direction. "Did you know Scotsmen played key roles in world history? American presidents like Alexander Hamilton and James Monroe. Captains of industry like Andrew Carnegie and Andrew Mellon. Writers like Robert Burns and Sir Walter Scott. Scientists and inventors like Alexander Graham Bell. The conservationist John Muir and—"

"Sean Connery." Cilla again. "What a dreamboat." She was on her feet, prowling the room like a child on a scavenger hunt. She removed a shaving brush from its brass-and-porcelain stand. "This brush was used by our grandfather every day of his adult life."

"Except the day he died," Penny corrected her. "Didn't bother to shave the day he died."

I tried to think of an admiring remark, but Cilla's attention had already drifted to the china cabinet. "Grandmother Arnott served tea on—Pen, what happened to the—"

Penny ignored her. She was stuck on the subject of Great Scotsmen. "Our finest British heroes were born in Scotland. We should insist on memorials."

Cilla clasped her hands under her chin. "I can hardly wait to see the statue of Captain Arnott. Should he be standing or sitting, Pen?"

"Standing, naturally," Penny said. "Man of action."

"Do you think they'll show him in informal dress?" Cilla's cheeks had gone pink. "His shirt open? Maybe his gun broken over his arm?" She picked up a lace doily on the china cabinet and frowned at a large brownish stain.

I've fallen down the rabbit hole. "I almost forgot," I said, trying to make it sound like an afterthought. "You were looking for something the other day in Elenor's flat, and I—"

"What about it?" Penny demanded.

"I just thought if I knew what you were looking for, I could return it to you."

Penny arranged her face in an approximation of a smile. "I overheard what you were telling Dr. Guthrie about the theft at the hotel. What was taken?" She cocked her head to one side like an intelligent spaniel.

"A small chest." Since DI Devlin had mentioned it to Dr. Guthrie, I figured it was no longer a secret.

"Interesting," Penny said.

"I think Elenor was going to sell it."

"Fascinating."

I was beginning to lose the thread of the conversation. "Nothing of yours was taken."

"The whole estate is ours," Penny growled. "Or should be,"

Cilla waved her little hand. "We don't blame your husband, Kate—of course not—but when our father sold the house, he was in a bit of pickle, moneywise. The Hamiltons took advantage of him. They stole our inheritance."

The conversation had veered into treacherous waters. "That must have been difficult for you." I meant that. Over the years I'd helped plenty of families dispose of treasured heirlooms to pay for college tuition or a staggering medical debt. No wonder the proposed statue of their ancestor was so important to the twins. No wonder they cherished shaving brushes and tooth powders. Their dignity and these small artifacts of the past were all they had left. "Agnes MacLeod said you were in your early teens at the time."

Penny scowled. "Agnes should mind her own business."

"She's the one the police should question about Elenor's death," Cilla said. "I heard them arguing, Agnes and Elenor. A real shouting match. Elenor kind of shoved her, and Agnes said, 'That's the final straw'—something like that, anyway—and 'You'll be sorry.'"

"When was this?" I didn't like what I was hearing at all.

"A few days ago."

"Did you tell the police?"

Cilla pressed the stained doily to her cheek. "I just remembered."

"Never mind about that now." Penny snatched the newspaper out of my hand. "I'm sure you'd like to see the media clippings about Dr. Guthrie's novel."

"I'll get the scrapbooks," Cilla said.

I'd all but abandoned hope of ever being allowed to leave the Arnott house when deliverance arrived like the deus ex machina of Greek drama. My cell phone pinged—a text from Tom: WHERE ARE YOU? EVERYTHING OKAY?

"Oh dear." I turned the corners of my mouth down. "I'm needed at the hotel."

"No," Cilla pouted. "Can't you even stay to see us on *Good Morning Inverness*? We've got the DVD."

"Not today. But thanks for the tea and biscuits. I hope I'll see you again."

"Bound to," Penny said. "Funeral."

Outside I took a deep breath. First the Guthries, then the Arnotts. The Glenroth islanders were obviously the victims of chronic inbreeding.

I replied to the text: BACK IN 20 MIN. HAVE THEY FOUND THE CASKET?

No, came the immediate reply.

Nᴇᴡs ᴀʙᴏᴜᴛ Bᴏ?

Hᴇᴀʀɪɴɢ sᴛɪʟʟ sᴇᴛ ғᴏʀ Tʜᴜʀs.

My heart sank. Somehow I had to talk to Bo. I had to convince him to confide in me, and to do that, I'd have to go through his sister, Brenda. Would she appreciate the help or resent my intrusion? Would she even agree to talk with me?

I pressed my lips together and picked up my pace. I couldn't wait any longer for her to call me.

If you can't get the bull's attention, wave your red cape and get ready to run.

Chapter Twenty-Four

I stopped at Applegarth to freshen up and grab a slice of Nancy's whole-grain bread with raspberry jam. It was almost two PM, and all I'd had to eat since breakfast was a cup of weak tea and half a burnt molasses cookie.

My plan was to drive to the Munroe Clinic. If Brenda was busy, I'd wait. As long as it took. This time when I called the clinic, I got the woman I'd spoken to before, the nice one. "I did give Mr. Duff's sister your information," she said, lowering her voice. "Listen, she's meeting with the psychiatrists at four. If you want to catch her, come around four thirty."

I checked my watch. Two fifteen.

I was locking the cottage door when I saw Tom walking up the flagged path. He looked sheepish, a new look for him.

"Hullo, Kate. I thought I might drive into Inverness this afternoon. Care to keep me company? We could have dinner there and be back by nine."

"I can't. I'm sorry." I dropped the key in my handbag and stepped off the porch. "I need to find Bo's sister."

"You're driving to the clinic?"

"It's just half an hour beyond Mallaig on the A830."

"Well, then, how about driving into Inverness tomorrow?" He looked at the sky. "They say it will be a fine day."

I tried not to look astonished. Was he asking me for a date?

"I've been meaning to see Inverness while I'm here. The river, the castle, maybe do some shopping." He shifted his weight.

"I have an appointment with Elenor's solicitor in Inverness tomorrow. Twelve thirty."

"Brilliant. We'll have to get an early start if we want lunch. Meet you at the hotel at seven fifteen?"

I hadn't actually agreed. "I want to stop at the jewelry store where Dr. Guthrie bought the engagement ring. In case I need an appraisal. You might not want to wait."

"I don't mind. In fact, is it all right if I tag along today? I won't interfere, I promise."

He wasn't making it easy to refuse, but then I really didn't want to refuse. I clicked open the car doors and grinned at him. "Come on, then."

Maybe Tom was like me. When I'm swamped at the antique shop, I fantasize about a lake, a recliner, and a good book. When I'm actually at the lake, in the recliner, I can read for about a half hour. Then I'm done. I need to move.

We drove north toward the village. Where the road forked, a sign pointed left: GLENROTH ADVENTURE CENTRE & CAMP. ONE MILE.

"Let's drive in," I said. "We have time."

The birch-framed sign read GLENROTH CAMP. HIGH ADVENTURE SINCE 1924. We passed a tennis court, a series of soccer fields, and an archery range. Beyond that, the road divided around a massive signpost. Cabins to the right and left. Visitor parking straight ahead.

"Do you have summer camps in England?" I asked.

"I suppose so. I spent summers with my Uncle Nigel in Devon. Summer camp in a castle."

"A *castle*? Your uncle lives in a castle?"

"A small one." He shot me that half smile and his eyes crinkled.

What an attractive man. A pebble of guilt dropped in my heart and lay there accusingly. I'd hardly thought about Bill all day.

We pulled into a circular parking area. Directly ahead was a massive wood-and-glass structure, identified by another birch-framed sign as the dining hall. Farther down, along the lakeshore, a boathouse rested on a foundation of dark Hebridean stone. A young man, blond with a crew cut, strode toward the boathouse, hefting a red kayak on his broad shoulder. He stopped, lowering his burden as Tom and I approached him across the expanse of lawn.

"Do you mind if we look around?" I asked.

"Reporters?" He gave us a wary look.

"No, just curious. My husband was a camper here years ago."

He grinned. "I'm the facilities manager. If you wait till I unload the kayak, I'll unlock the dining hall for you. It's worth a look."

"Let me help." Tom grabbed the kayak's handle at the stern.

I followed them down the gentle slope. The lower level of the boathouse was a storage area for sporting equipment, much of it relating to archery. Bows, canvas quivers, and armguards hung from the walls on wooden dowels. Ventilated metal bins held arrows, all with the distinctive red-and-yellow fletching. I felt faintly queasy.

"Archery is the main sport here." The young man slotted the kayak into a rack with several others. As we left, he threaded a padlock through the door hasp and clicked it shut.

"You keep the archery equipment locked up?" I asked.

"I thought you weren't reporters."

"We're not," Tom said. "She knew the woman who was murdered."

"Then I'm sorry. But if you think the arrow that killed your friend came from camp, you're wrong. The sport shop in the village sells them by the hundreds. I told the police this morning. It's an island thing, not a camp thing."

We'd arrived at the dining hall. The young man unlocked the double doors.

The structure was huge with a vaulted ceiling and shiplap paneling. Picnic-style tables lined up in rows beneath tartan banners emblazoned with the names of Highland clans. A bucket and sponge sat on one of the tables.

"The yearly purge." The young man mopped his face on the sleeve of his sweatshirt. "Several hundred kids come through here every summer, all with sticky fingers."

Tom had wandered to the far wall and appeared to be examining a group of framed photographs. Photos dotted every wall of the log structure, hundreds of them, most in color, some in black and white.

"Kate, come have a look," Tom said. "Guess who was Senior Boys Champion of 1973?"

One photo showed a much younger and slimmer Jackie MacDonald posing with a bow and arrow. He looked like a young Johnny Weissmuller—broad shoulders, dark wavy hair, straight white teeth. No wonder Dora—and Elenor—had been smitten.

"And now this one." Tom drew my attention to a black-and-white image farther along the wall. A blonde, sixteen or seventeen, arched her back as she drew her bow. The label read MARGARET PARKER, SENIOR GIRLS CHAMPION, 1951.

Unmistakably Margaret Guthrie.

* * *

"That's one question answered." I pointed the car toward the main road, reminding myself to keep left. "Arrows with red-and-yellow fletching are as common on the Isle of Glenroth as pebbles on the beach."

The sky was brightening. Tom pulled down the visor. "Means, motive, and opportunity, the classic elements of crime. If such arrows are readily available, then everyone on the island, in theory, had the means. Right now the police are checking opportunity. Whose statement doesn't add up, whose alibi can't be proved. What they need is a motive. Once they know the *why*, they're a long way toward finding the *who*."

"That's my point." I hit the steering wheel with the flat of my hand. "Bo Duff had no motive. His response to being fired would have been shame, not rage."

"I don't disagree," Tom said mildly. "So who did have a motive?"

I pictured him calmly disarming a maniacal gunman. "As far as I can tell, most islanders would have cheerfully wrung Elenor's neck. She acted in blatant self-interest without giving a thought to anyone else."

"You mean the sale of the hotel."

Light bounced off the windshield. "Tom," I said, shielding my eyes, "what if the motive for Elenor's murder is something no one knows about yet?"

"Then how do you explain the threats?"

"Oh, someone wanted to scare her out of selling the hotel, all right. But what if that had nothing to do with her death?" I held up my index finger. "One, Elenor was afraid. Two, she said everything began with the casket. Three, now it's missing. Four, she insisted I read Guthrie's novel. I just need to connect the dots."

He gave me a look that said *leave dot-connecting to the police* but refrained from saying so. He was starting to know me.

We passed through the village toward the ferry terminal. The press cars had finally departed. Tom shifted in his seat and attempted to stretch his long legs. "Sometimes it helps to come at a problem from a different angle. Instead of asking why Elenor was killed, let's ask why she went to the Historical Society. Whom did she meet there?"

"Jackie MacDonald? He had a crush on Elenor when they were teenagers. Maybe he couldn't stand the thought of her marrying Hugh and met her that night to talk her out of it." I was only half serious, but he took it a step further.

"Would Dora cover for him?"

"Ah, but Dora wouldn't know. With all that champagne, she'd probably passed out."

"Maybe she found out Jackie and Elenor were having an affair. She sobered up and—"

"Stop it." I had to laugh. "You make it sound like one of those cheesy soap operas."

"Now those we do have in England. Not that I admit watching them."

I turned right onto North Shore Road. Tom clutched the armrest.

"Sorry," I said, slowing down. "Lead foot."

"If we were in England, I'd have to arrest you for speeding."

"I have a perfect driving record, I'll have you know. Except for the odd speeding ticket. And last Friday when we almost crashed."

"Almost crashed?" He gave me an innocent look. "I have no memory of that."

Beyond the low-lying peat beds, we could see the ferry terminal, the "roll-on, roll-off," as the locals call it.

"Have the police considered Dr. Guthrie?" I asked. "Isn't the husband or boyfriend usually the first suspect?"

"What motive? If Guthrie was the killer—and I'm not saying he was—Elenor must have had some hold over him, something that made her a threat."

I'd thought the same thing. You don't kill someone to get out of an engagement. "What did the Guthries say about the night of the ball?"

"Same thing everyone said—'went straight home and stayed there.' Margaret Guthrie claims she's a light sleeper. Her son couldn't have left the house without her hearing."

"What about Margaret herself? Becca Wallace implied she isn't as much of an invalid as she wants people to believe. We know she can shoot an arrow. At least she could."

"But she doesn't drive. She could hardly make it to the Historical Society in her wheelchair."

"She could try." I pictured Margaret Guthrie motoring down Bridge Street with a longbow over her shoulder.

"How about the Arnott twins?" Tom said. "Maybe they were plotting to get Elenor out of the way so they could move back into their ancestral home."

"I can almost believe that. Except they wouldn't get the house, would they? The hotel belongs to the Swiss investors now."

"Okay. So assuming the murder was committed by someone close to Elenor, who's left?"

"The staff of the hotel, I suppose. Becca and Geoff can prove they were off the island when she was killed. That leaves Agnes, the Holdens, and Sofia."

Tom tried to cross his legs and gave up. "Means, motive, opportunity. They all had means and opportunity. Who had the strongest motive?"

"I don't know about a motive, but I'm pretty sure Sofia's hiding something."

"Like what?"

"No clue. You seem to have influence. Ask her."

He rubbed his ear thoughtfully. "And the Holdens?"

"Detective Inspector Devlin said one of them lied on their police statement."

"I'll check that out."

"I could make the best case for Agnes MacLeod. She'd banked everything on Glenroth House. Elenor promised her a partnership. The sale of the hotel would have been the ultimate betrayal. Maybe Agnes stole the silver tray—and the casket, too. Payment due for years of abuse." I wanted to tell Tom about the wet purple gloves, but it felt like piling on. Besides, I couldn't imagine Agnes killing Elenor in cold blood. "The problem is, I don't want it to be any of them. Oh dear. I wouldn't make a very good policeman."

"First rule of the job, Kate. Never get personally involved." A line of trees deepened the shadow along his jawline. "Only sometimes we do."

We'd reached the terminal. The ferry was in the process of off-loading. Away to the south, a bank of clouds was building over the mountains of Rùm.

"Anyone we've left out?" he asked.

"Just you." I turned my head to watch his face.

One corner of his mouth went up. "What's my motive?"

"Give me a minute. Okay, you fell hopelessly in love with Elenor and went mad when she rejected you. Or"—I was getting into the game—"you were hired by that Swiss company to bump her off so they could get the property at a reduced price. Or . . . sorry, that's the best I can do for now."

"What makes you think I can handle a bow and arrow?"

"Can you?"

"Nope."

We bumped onto the ferry access and took our place in line. "So who doesn't have an alibi?"

"Everyone *has* an alibi, Kate."

"Someone is lying."

"Yes, someone is lying." He was serious now. "And it isn't a game of Clue. It's a real murder with a real murderer, and until we figure out why Elenor was killed, we can't be certain he or she won't kill again."

* * *

The Munroe Mental Health Clinic, just east of Glenfinnan at the northern end of Loch Shiel, was a small facility catering mostly to outpatients but housing a limited number of men and women in urgent care suites.

Tom agreed to wait for me in the car. Policemen don't tend to put people at their ease.

The waiting room was decorated in cheerful colors. A refreshment station offered a selection of biscuits and an automatic coffee and tea dispenser.

"I'm looking for Bo Duff's sister," I told a woman with an ID badge and a pager clipped to her belt. "Her name is Brenda."

"There she is. Right over there."

A woman with a barley-colored helmet of hair emerged from a door labeled CONFERENCE ROOM, followed by two men in white coats. They shook hands, and the men strode briskly down the hall. Brenda's eyes darted around the room as if she wasn't certain what to do next. Brenda didn't resemble her brother in the least, except for her height. Even in flat shoes, she had to be six feet tall.

I walked over and introduced myself.

"I got your message." Brenda bit the corner of her upper lip. "I should have called, but things have been pretty hectic."

"How is Bo?"

"Calm. Just not talking. The evaluation is complete. The court has appointed an advocate. Very competent, I'm told."

"If it helps, no one on the island believes Bo is guilty."

"I appreciate that. I really do." Brenda squared her shoulders. "But I have to face facts. Even if Bo isn't charged, it's not realistic for him to live alone anymore. I knew the day would come." She pressed her lips together.

This was exactly what I'd feared. "But Bo gets along well. Everyone on the island looks out for him."

Brenda shook her head. "The doctors warned me that sometimes, with cognitive disability, a traumatic event upsets the equilibrium. They talked about stressors, heightened reactions, behavioral compensation." She shifted the large tote bag she was carrying to her other arm. "Do you mind if we sit? I'm feeling a bit light-headed."

We chose a sofa near a window overlooking a pleasant walled garden. Outside, a man in a heavy coat sat on a bench near a fountain.

Brenda slid her tote bag to the floor. "There's a facility in Perth, not far from where I live."

"But Glenroth is Bo's home. He lives independently."

"Not really. The money our parents left him ran out a few years ago. Bo incurred debts. Not his fault. My husband pays his bills now. He's been good about it, very generous. We never had children, you see. Bo's condition is genetic. We weren't willing to take the risk." She looked away. "I saw what it did to our family. To me."

She'd been ashamed of him, and now she was ashamed of herself.

A nursing sister approached Brenda. "Would you like a wee visit with your brother now? Don't stay long. He needs his rest."

"Let me come with you," I said. "Please, Brenda. He might talk to me."

Bo's room was at the end of a wide hallway with a shiny tiled floor and walls painted a cheerful yellow. He sat, fully clothed, in a lounge chair. Through the wide window, Loch Shiel stretched toward the south. Bo's face was shaven, his hair clean and tied back with a band. His nails were trimmed. I sat near him on the edge of his bed. "Hello, Bo. It's me, Kate."

He blinked. A sign of recognition?

Brenda watched us warily from across the room.

I put my hand on Bo's arm. "Remember when you tried to help Bill? I want to help you now. Will you let me? Could we talk about the night Elenor died?"

He flinched.

"I know you didn't do anything wrong. You wouldn't, ever. But something happened, and I need to know what it was so I can help you."

Bo's shoulders hunched. He began to rock, his lips moving soundlessly.

I leaned in. "Did you see someone that night? Has someone threatened you?"

A low vibration began deep in Bo's chest and came out in a moan, wretched and pitiful, like an animal caught in a trap.

"I'm calling the nursing sister." Brenda ran from the room.

My eyes filled. This was my last chance. It might be Bo's last chance, too. I took his hand. "It's all right, Bo. Whatever happened, it's all right. I don't blame you. Just please tell me."

His lips moved again. This time I heard.

"I. Hurt. Her."

Brenda burst into the room, followed by two male attendants and the nursing sister in her blue smock. "Please leave." The nurse signaled for the attendants. "This isn't helping," the sister told me in a tone that would brook no argument.

She was right. Brenda was sobbing. I was sobbing. Bo was rocking. The attendants were trying to get him into bed.

"Just go." Brenda grabbed my arm and pulled me into the hallway. "The truth is the truth, however hard it is for you to accept."

"Your brother didn't kill Elenor." I wiped my eyes. "He just didn't, and I'll do whatever it takes to clear him." I wanted to take her by the shoulders and shake her until she understood. Instead I ran for the exit.

"What happened?" Tom jumped out of the car and came around to meet me.

I shrugged out of my jacket, tossing it into the back seat. "Brenda thinks Bo is guilty. She's talking about institutions."

"I'm sorry."

"Everyone's sorry, but they're letting it happen anyway."

"At least you're trying."

"Yeah, right. I just made things worse."

Tom was silent. What could he say?

Thunder rolled in the distance. I pictured the shame on Bo's face. *I. Hurt. Her.*

The words Frank had spoken that night at the sheriff's department sliced through my certainty like a flick knife. *He'll tell you the truth, if you care to hear it.*

We said little on the drive home. Tom flipped on the radio, filling the silence with, of all things, American country music.

An hour later I dropped him near Tartan Cottage.

"Don't blame yourself, Kate. You've done all you can."

"Thanks," I said miserably. "I know you're trying to help."

He unfolded himself from the car. "Will I see you at our table in the library?"

"I had nothing to do with that. You're safe."

He leaned down, one hand on the door frame. "Is that a good thing, do you think?"

"Is what a good thing?"

"To be safe."

Chapter
Twenty-Five

The storm passed south of the island without a drop of rain.

After showering and changing clothes, I felt marginally better. I'd cruised through a cavalcade of emotions: fear, anger, guilt, acceptance, and finally a kind of pale optimism. I wouldn't be allowed to see Bo again, but that didn't mean I had to give up. If the real killer was found, and if Bo could be made to understood what had really happened to Elenor that night, his confusion might lift. He could still recover. I had to believe that.

In the library a log fire crackled. Nancy had prepared a lovely chicken cordon bleu with cranberry rice and fresh green beans. Tom and I sat at the table in front of the fire again. Tonight our conversation deliberately excluded murder, hearings, and institutions, a pact we'd both agreed upon.

"How did you get started in the antiques trade?" he asked.

"I grew up in it. My parents were collectors first, then dealers. When I was fourteen, they opened a shop. I worked there after school."

"Getting an education."

"I never thought of it like that. It was just how we lived. It never occurred to me that other kids couldn't read the marks on antique silver or that most people bought brand-new furniture. 'Our things have a history,' my mother used to say, 'so much more interesting.' We had a life-sized marble bust of Marie Antoinette in our entryway. She terrified my friends."

"You'd get on well with Uncle Nigel. He has a ten-foot statue of Winged Victory in the great hall. Quite fierce. As a child I worried she might speak."

Tom told me about his summers in Devon—the brooding moor, the narrow sand beach at Teignmouth, the shaggy donkeys that roamed the village streets. I told him about my grandparents' farm in Wisconsin—picking corn in July, finding a litter of kittens in the barn, the gentle old collie dog who protected me from the snappy, ill-tempered geese. We talked about our children and the impossible task of being both mother and father. I told him about my brother's death at age eleven.

Over dessert, a cloudlike pavlova with a drizzle of raspberry syrup, Tom showed me a photograph of his wife, Sarah, standing in a sea of blue flowers. Along the bottom of the photo, someone had printed *The Bluebell Walk, Brede High Woods*. The photo was taken, Tom said, a week before the diagnosis of cancer. Sarah was slim and fair, an English rose. She smiled into the lens, unaware of the shadow of death looming over her.

I didn't have a photo of Bill in my handbag. When Tom walked me back to Applegarth, I showed him the framed photograph from the bedside table.

"Nice chap?" he asked, handing the photo back.

"Very."

"I'm glad." He bent down to kiss my cheek, and I took in the faint woodsy scent of his aftershave. "Good night, Kate. Sleep well. You really are doing all you can."

When he'd gone, I got ready for bed, but instead of climbing into the big empty space, I curled up in one of the overstuffed chairs and watched moonlight dance on the silver sea. I touched my cheek, remembering Tom's scent and the slight roughness of his stubble.

How ironic. The only man I'd been physically attracted to since

Bill's death lived on the other side of the ocean. And of all the single men I knew, the ones my well-meaning friends kept tossing in my path, Tom Mallory was the only one irrevocably out of the running.

I undressed, climbed into bed, and settled in to finish as much of Guthrie's book as I could.

Flora set foot on the Isle of Glenroth, according to Guthrie, on the twentieth of August, nineteen days after she and Gowyn had watched the harbor at Greenock recede into the mist. Once they reached the island, it took a full day to travel from the peat bogs on the north to the southern tip of the island and Glenroth House. Flora was filled with praise for the house and the beauty of the lake and woods. Even Gowyn seemed more cheerful, now that the long and difficult journey was over.

With no full-time clergyman on Glenroth, a traveling minister from Inverness was prevailed upon to perform the wedding ceremony. As his circuit schedule did not permit a visit to the island for another ten days, Flora and Gowyn were settled into temporary quarters in the east wing. Agnes's flat?

The early autumn weather was glorious, breezy, and fair. Flora and Gowyn spent their first days on the island unpacking, exploring the estate, and getting to know the captain's servants. Besides Joseph and the men—most of whom worked in the fields or with the livestock—there were a coachman, a groom, and a stable boy. The household was managed by a married couple, the Frasers from Aberdeen, who had been with Captain Arnott in the Indies. They supervised two housemaids, a scullery maid, and a boy called "Wee Ian," whose job it was to light fires, kill rodents, and black boots.

Mrs. Fraser was a sturdy woman, reserved, a wonderful cook. Mr. Fraser was the typical dour Scotsman, his vocabulary limited to "Aye" or "Nae" with an occasional grunt indicating something in between—or more commonly, as Flora put it, disgust. If they ever made that movie out of Guthrie's book, Frank and Nancy could play the parts to perfection.

Most interesting to me was the reference to Bonnie Prince Charlie.

24th August, Isle of Glenroth
  The clansmen remaining on Glenroth, those who have not emigrated to the New World, scratch a living from the sea & the rocky soil. They remain faithful to the Stuarts & revere this house where, they say, the Young Pretender spent his final night in the Hebrides. This morning I found a bunch of wild flowers on the steps. Mrs. Fraser says this is a frequent occurrence, to honor the one they consider their rightful king. Some of the locals, she says, resent the Capt. as he is not a clansman. This is quite unfair as he has done much to raise their lot.

As August turned to September and the wedding day drew near, Flora's optimism was tested.

1st September, Glenroth House
  I am being watched. This, I assure you, dear diary, is no girlish fancy. When I enter a room, conversation ceases. If I go to the yard with apples for the horses, the eyes of the stable hands follow me. The Capt. is as ever, attentive, kind, solicitous for my well-being, but the atmosphere amongst his servants is strained & I cannot make out the cause. Gowyn does not see this & so I say nothing for fear of planting troublesome thoughts in her head. But with you, dear diary, I must tell the truth.
  I perceive nothing amiss in the girls Susan & Janet. They are too busy making love to the young Highlanders who have come to help with the harvest. The Frasers are scrupulously civil but regard me with a reticence I find puzzling. Mr. Fraser rarely addresses me & when he must, he averts his eyes. Often I catch Mrs. Fraser observing me in secret. Perhaps she thinks

me too young & inexperienced to be mistress of a great house. Or she is concerned for her authority once James & I are married.

There is one other I must mention, the young negro Joseph. At times he appears as if he would speak but does not. He may desire no more than to wish me joy but fears I will not welcome it. I would confide in James, but casting suspicion without cause is unjust. Perhaps I am imagining this after all.

2nd September

I am greatly perplexed & much distress'd. To-night I found an envelope on the table in my chamber. I open'd it and read this: 'Ask him about his wife.' There was no signature. Can the author of this letter mean James?

I turned the page, my heart in my throat, when I heard a sound, so indistinct I wondered if I'd imagined it. I sat up in bed, narrowing my eyes to focus on the darkness beyond the circle of lamplight. A small white patch on the floor near the front door appeared to shimmer and float.

Someone had pushed something under my door. Was this a prank? Could someone have guessed I'd be reading about Flora's anonymous letter and thought it would be funny to spook me?

I flipped off the light and crept out of bed. Snatching the square of paper by an edge, I carried it into the windowless bathroom, where I shut the door, turned on the lights, and stared at the carefully formed block letters.

DESTROY IT NOW OR ELSE.

Or else what? It sounded like a playground taunt. Now that I thought about it, all the threats had sounded childish, as if written by someone playing the part of a villain. One thing was clear: this note was intended for me. But what was I supposed to destroy?

I switched off the bathroom light and made my way in the dark to the nightstand where I'd left my cell phone.

Childish threat or not, my fingers trembled as I punched in Tom's cell number.

Voicemail. I didn't leave a message.

I scrolled through my calls and found DI Devlin's number.

* * *

"You didn't see anyone?" Devlin sounded sleepy. I'd probably woken him up.

"No," I whispered, feeling my way around the fireplace. "The thing is, I don't have anything to destroy."

"Are you certain of that?"

I thought for a moment. "Elenor mentioned something she wanted me to keep for her. Remember? In that phone message. The note writer might think I have it, but I don't."

"Is the cottage locked? Curtains drawn?"

"I just checked." I climbed into bed and drew up the duvet. "Do you think *it* could mean the casket? Am I supposed to destroy the casket?" I was still whispering.

"If so, the writer doesn't know it's been stolen. Are you feeling safe? I could drive out there. Where's Tom?"

"I tried to call him. He didn't answer. Look, the note was meant to deliver a message. I got the message. There's nothing you can do tonight."

"You sure? I can be there in forty minutes. If the ferry's running."

"No need. I'll drop the note off tomorrow at the police station in Mallaig."

"We'll have it analyzed. And while we're on the subject of notes, we learned today that the note you received at the ball and the threat letters sent to Mrs. Spurgeon were written by different people. Something about the slant of the printing and the number of strokes on the capital E."

"*Two* people on the island are sending anonymous threats? That's weird."

"Yes, it is. We also learned Mrs. Spurgeon had a safe deposit box in Inverness. She signed in on the afternoon of October twelfth and then again, for the last time, on the morning of the nineteenth. The box is empty. The clerk remembers her leaving with a small tote bag."

Wednesday again, the day Elenor had phoned me in a panic. "So the notation in Guthrie's book had nothing to do with the safe deposit box."

"No, but there's more. A boat captain fished something out of the sea this afternoon. Ready for this? A Mucky Duck, size ten. We found its mate near the first pier, weighted down with a rock."

I'd predicted that but refrained from saying so. I could hear his delight. Rubber wellies were hard evidence, not insubstantial things like theories and impressions.

I heard a muffled yawn. "I'll try to reach Tom," he said. "Tell him to have a look around, make sure no one's lurking."

"Any news on the casket?"

"No, and I'm not holding my breath. Try to get some sleep now."

Good advice, I thought as we disconnected. Until I remembered what I'd just read: *Ask him about his wife*. Man, talk about a cliffhanger. The wedding would take place in four days.

I switched on the bedside lamp and grabbed Guthrie's book again.

Tomorrow I will find James & ask him what this means. Regardless of the outcome, he deserves an opportunity to explain.

3rd September
I awoke early & dressed as usual, concealing the note in my reticule. 'Where is the Capt. this fine morning?' I asked Mrs. Fraser, feigning cheerfulness.

'In his study, I believe, miss,' said she.

I walked quickly, my heart pounding, & knocked on the door. 'Capt., may I enter?'

'Of course, dearest,' said he.

A fire blazed in the hearth. He was writing a letter. Without speaking a word I lay the note be-fore him & watched his face turn pale as death, confirming my fears. He stood abruptly, overturning his chair. 'The devil take it' he roared, ripping the paper to shreds & casting the pieces on the fire.

'So it is true,' I said coldly. 'Where is this wife you have concealed from me?'

Oh!—the look on his face I cannot describe. 'She is dead, dearest one. Now come & sit by my side. I shall tell you everything.'

This is the tragic tale: When James was twenty-five, his father sent him from the Indies to Scotland for a bride. There he met & married a distant cousin, Cecily. Twice she was found to be with child but brought to bed early & deliver'd of a stillborn son. Hoping to restore her health, James determined to carry her to the islands, but on the voyage she fell overboard, whether by mishap or design he never knew.

'I thought to spare you this sadness, my dear,' said he wretchedly. "I should rather have trusted your strength & sense. Can you forgive me?'

'With all my heart,' I said, drawing him to my breast. 'We shall never speak of it again unless it is your express wish.'

'You know me perfectly, my love. Now there is nothing betwixt us. And when we have our own son, I shall take you both to the Indies."

I rejoice, dear diary, knowing I will bring him happiness & if I can give him the son he desires, my joy will be complete. My former complaints now appear foolish and soon mended. I am certain all those in the Capt.'s employ will accept me, even (dare

I hope?) love me as I shall endeavor to love them. My handwriting is very ill for I have come to the end of this book. This strikes me as fortuitous, for when next I write, it shall be in a new volume & I shall be the new Mrs. James Arnott.

I'd come to the last page of the book and the final implied question: who in Captain Arnott's household hated him enough to murder his pregnant wife?

If Guthrie didn't finish that sequel soon, his readers might storm the publisher.

The wind was picking up. From a distance came another low rumble of thunder. It might rain after all. I switched off the lamp and settled into the downy pillow. The only sound was the ticking of the clock on the mantel.

Flora's life had ended at the tender age of sixteen. The child she carried never took breath, never felt the warmth of the sun or heard the tenderness of his mother's lullaby. Silly as it was, I felt a pang of sorrow for this girl I never knew. And an equally pointless impulse to warn her: *Watch your step. Trust no one.*

Two hundred years too late.

Who killed Flora Arnott? One of the local clansmen? Joseph, the ex-slave who fled that night? The Frasers? The writer of the note found in her chamber? Flora's murder was never solved. Had Guthrie discovered new facts about an old crime, and was that what Elenor had meant by a *big surprise*?

The thought tiptoed in so quietly I almost missed it. Elenor had tucked the original accounts of Flora's death in Guthrie's novel. She wanted me to read them before she told me her story. Could it have been *Elenor*, not Guthrie, who discovered the identity of Flora's murderer? Is that why she wanted my advice?

Is that why she was killed?

Chapter Twenty-Six

࿇

Tuesday, November 1

During the night, a line of storms passed over the island, clearing the air and bringing the suggestion of Indian summer—Scotland's equivalent of it, anyway. The islanders were used to the changeable weather. "Winter one day, summer the next," Nancy had told me.

At six, when I'd woken, I'd had the sense something was missing. Then I'd realized. No wind.

Now, sunlight, the first real sunlight I'd seen since arriving on the Isle of Glenroth, spilled through the French doors and pooled on the kitchen's wide-planked floor. I dropped my handbag and jacket on the table in Applegarth's kitchen, ready for the trip into Inverness with Tom.

My early-morning conversation with the funeral director had been less painful than I'd anticipated. Elenor would be buried in the old cemetery, not far from where she died. He'd suggested a simple oak coffin and I'd agreed, although I felt sure Elenor would have opted for the "Regal Bronze" top-of-the-line model.

With no time for breakfast, I grabbed a quick cup of coffee and thought about the idea I'd had the night before, that a long-forgotten injustice could reach out from the grave to take a life today. I supposed Flora's death could have current legal implications, like the loss of property rights or inheritance issues. That seemed far-fetched, but then I knew nothing about Scottish law. I did know there were other families on the island—not only the Guthries and Arnotts—who could trace their lineage back to those fifteen settlers who arrived in 1809. And then there was Jackie MacDonald, whose clansmen had felt cheated out of their sacred family seat. How would the sale of the inn affect them?

According to the handwriting experts, Glenroth boasted not one but two anonymous note writers. That suggested two separate motives. I pondered the latest note again: *DESTROY IT NOW OR ELSE.* Did someone believe Elenor had given me proof of some ancient injustice that, if revealed, would spell disaster for them today? Without evidence, or even a place to look for evidence, I wasn't about to share my theory with Tom or DI Devlin. They'd say I'd gone off the deep end.

Maybe I had.

The note lay on the kitchen counter. I folded it and tucked it in the outside pocket of my handbag next to the baggie of purple wool. I was assembling a little evidence locker of my own.

After changing into black skinny jeans and a long-sleeved white shirt, I checked my cell phone for messages. Still no word from Christine. I keyed in her number and texted WHAT'S GOING ON? PLEASE CALL. But instead of pushing send, I erased the message and wrote another. CALL SOON. NEWS HERE TOO.

Now that might get a response. Christine can't abide a mystery any more than I can.

Grabbing my handbag and denim jacket, I set off for the hotel. It was almost seven fifteen.

Tom had been right about the weather. The early-morning air was crisp, but the sky was a cut-glass blue and the sea that color of turquoise Bill had always talked about. The gravel path sparkled in the bright sun. I felt a curious mixture of anticipation and apprehension. Among the bare trees along the path, a single beech clung stubbornly to its coppery leaves. A breeze set them fluttering and a few lost their grip, windmilling to the ground. Is that what I'd become—a dormant tree, clinging to the dead leaves of a past season? Bill and I had never talked about the fact that one of us would die first. We'd never spoken about death at all, and we'd definitely never spoken about remarriage.

Reality check. Tom Mallory would return to England in a few days, and I'd return to Ohio. End of story. The outing was no more than a much-needed break from murder suspects and threatening notes. I should seize the day, or at least enjoy it while it lasted.

A small red van with a sign saying ROYAL MAIL circled toward the post box. A hand removed something and replaced it with a thick packet. The driver angled his head out the window. "Early delivery today. Dan's got the flu." He'd taken me for an employee.

As he drove off, I heard a voice behind me, calling my name.

"Kate?" Agnes stood on the back porch in her blue working smock. Her mouth turned down. "Postie's here already?"

"I'll get it," I called, but she'd already darted into the kitchen.

The mail packet was bound by a heavy rubber band. On top was a plain white envelope addressed in block letters to Elenor Spurgeon. Someone would have to explain that she—

Block letters? I stopped walking. A fourth threat? I checked the postmark. Like the others, the envelope had been mailed in Fort William. But not on a Monday this time. This letter had been posted on Friday, the day of the Tartan Ball.

Using only my fingernails, I pulled the envelope free and dropped it in my handbag.

A moment later Agnes came rushing out of the house, buttoning up her cardigan. She met me at the foot of the porch steps. "I'll take that." She snatched the mail packet, pulled off the rubber band, and sorted through the stack once, then again more slowly. "This is the lot?" Her forehead wrinkled. "Are you certain there's nothing left in the box?"

"Nothing." I wasn't lying. The letter was in my handbag.

"I'll just have a wee look." Agnes stumped down the drive.

The truth hit me like a slap in the face. Agnes *knew* a fourth threat letter was coming. That's why she'd been hovering over the letter box since Saturday.

I felt for the baggie of purple wool in the outside pocket of my handbag. This time I'd make Devlin listen to me.

A rich, yeasty aroma met me as I opened the back door.

"Morning, Kate." Nancy was alone, rolling out pastry. Her hands were covered with flour. "Did you get things arranged with the funeral director?"

"What? Oh, yes."

"You're getting an early start. What's on tap for today?" She brushed back an errant curl, leaving a smudge of flour on her cheek.

"I'm going into Inverness with Tom."

"A grand day for it." Nancy smiled into her dough. She placed the lump in a large ceramic bowl and covered it with a tea towel. "Come sit, lass. Coffee? Toast?"

"Not today, thanks. Tom should be here any minute." I moved to the sink and pretended an interest in the garden.

The first three threatening letters had been posted on a Monday, the day the staff of the hotel went into Fort William for supplies. "Nancy," I said, turning around, "Did someone from the hotel go into Fort William the day of the ball?"

"Aye. Elenor went to the salon, remember?"

"I mean someone else, earlier."

"Becca and Agnes went in around nine to pick up the champagne." Her tone was guarded. "Why d'ye want to know?"

"Ready?" Tom appeared in the doorway, saving me from explanations. That man had a miraculous sense of timing.

As soon as we'd shut the car doors, he said, "All right. Tell me what happened last night."

I shook my head. "Never mind about that now. There's been another threat letter." I told him about the plain white envelope and Agnes's fascination with the mail delivery. Then I told him about Agnes's purple knitted gloves.

"Where's the letter now?"

"In my handbag with the wool sample. I tried not to touch it."

"Good. Chances are the writer took care not to leave fingerprints, but you never know. Criminals aren't terribly bright."

"Agnes is bright, but she doesn't have much of a poker face. She's been waiting for that letter since Saturday."

"We'll drive to the police station now." He pulled onto the main road and headed north.

I buckled my seat belt. "Do you think Agnes sent the threats herself?"

"Or knows who did. She probably assumed Elenor destroyed the previous threats. If she could get rid of this one before anyone saw it, no one would ever have to know."

"And connect the threats with her." I took a deep breath, remembering that determined little face.

"You're doing the right thing."

"Then why do I feel guilty?"

We arrived at the Mallaig police station just before eight, only to be told that DI Devlin was on his way to Police Scotland's Forward Command Base near Stirling, expected back in the morning. DS Bruce sealed the purple wool and the letter in evidence bags, and I wrote out a brief statement.

Back in the car, Tom left a message on Devlin's cell phone.

I refastened my seat belt. "I've as good as accused Agnes of murder and signed my name to it. I feel like a traitor."

"Come on, Kate. Agnes knew about the threats. She's going to have to explain herself."

I watched the pavement slip smoothly under the wheels. "I should feel relieved. If Agnes was involved in Elenor's death, Bo will be exonerated."

Tom braked behind a slow-moving truck. "There's something you need to know, Kate."

I didn't like the tone of his voice. I braced myself.

"Devlin rang me early this morning."

"And?"

"The police traced the phone call Elenor received the night of the ball to a telephone box at the Gas and Go near the ferry terminal."

"Can they tell who made the call?"

"No, but one of the islanders passed that way about eleven fifteen that night. He saw a pickup truck."

"Did he get a license number?"

"He didn't need to. He recognized the truck."

I knew what he was going to say.

"It was Bo's truck."

"And *that's* supposed to prove Bo killed Elenor?" My frustration boiled over. "Has it occurred to anyone he was just getting gas? I suppose they'll use this against him at the hearing."

"The judge will consider all the evidence."

"Except they don't *have* all the evidence, and they won't have until Bo speaks." I smacked the armrest. Tom flinched, probably wondering if I was going to smack him next. I slowed my words, trying to sound reasonable. "This didn't have to happen. If the police had treated him more carefully in the beginning, he might have—" I cut off the sentence with a gesture and began again, exercising every ounce of self-control I could muster. "Bo might have been able to help, Tom. He might have seen something. He's not a killer. I'd stake my life on it."

Tom was listening. Or making a good show of it. Another technique in a detective's tool kit?

"Just listen, Kate," he said in that super-calm tone of voice you use when your children flip out in public. Now I did want to smack

221

him. "The police now know that Elenor called you the night of the ball from a mobile phone, one she bought on Wednesday. The clerk remembered her. She asked him to explain the basics of dialing but nothing else."

"Elenor bought a cell phone?" I turned to face him.

"The provider records show she made two calls—one to her solicitor, Andrew Ross, and one to you. The call to you was her last."

I burst into tears.

Tom nearly pulled the car over.

"No, I'm all right. I'm sorry." I wiped my tears with the backs of my hands.

"Tell me about last night," he said. "The note pushed under your door."

I was in the middle of telling him when I remembered I'd forgotten to drop the note off at the police station. I took it out of my handbag, unfolded it, and held it up.

He glanced at it. "And you have no idea what you're supposed to destroy?"

"Not unless it's the casket." He was studying me with a look I hadn't seen before. At least not on his face.

Traffic slowed and he had to jam on the brakes. "Sorry."

"Where were you last night, Tom? I called your cell phone. You didn't answer."

"Took a walk, shut off the mobile. When I got back to the cottage, Devlin's message was waiting for me. I checked the grounds. Your lights were off, so I didn't bother you."

For the first time I took in the mountains, carpeted in amber gorse and dotted with spreading islands of cinnamon-colored bracken. After Fort William, we hooked up with the A82 heading north. I was feeling calmer. The road wound through small villages and forests, following the Great Glen, the geological fault line running from Fort William in the south to Inverness in the north. For thirty miles or so, we skirted Loch Ness. And yes, I did keep one eye peeled for Nessie, the monster—or friendly plesiosaur—reputed to lurk in its murky depths. He was hiding.

"Let's get back to what we were talking about yesterday," I said. "Means, motive, and opportunity. Everyone assumes one person is responsible for everything. Suppose two people were involved, even three or four. Someone was threatening Elenor. Someone wrote the notes to me. Someone met Elenor at the Historical Society. Someone killed her." I tucked my hair behind my ears. "But not necessarily the same person."

Unfortunately, I was making a good case for Bo's guilt, but if Tom picked up on it, he didn't say so. Instead he said, "Agnes could be protecting someone."

"Yes," I said slowly. "And that means she could be in danger."

*   *   *

As we entered Inverness, signs funneled us toward the city center and the High Street shopping area. Tom pulled into a pay-and-display parking area. The pedestrian zone was crowded with people relishing the unexpected warmth. We passed a kiosk selling T-shirts. One featured a cartoon of Nessie and the caption BELIEVE IN YOURSELF.

"I checked the weather back home in Suffolk," Tom said. "Cold and rainy. People will be huddled under umbrellas, dreaming about their holidays in Spain." When he smiled, his eyes looked almost amber. The sun picked out the silver strands in his hair.

I nearly collided with a chalkboard advertisement.

He laughed and tucked my hand in his arm.

Since neither of us had eaten, we decided on a late breakfast. We chose a gray stone pub with a red door. The hostess showed us to a wooden table in a sunny, glassed-in porch. I ordered scrambled eggs and a pot of tea. He ordered a full Scottish breakfast—eggs, sausage, bacon, tattie scones, the works.

Our food came quickly. I spread the red-checked napkin on my lap and pulled my chair closer to the table. "What will Agnes think when she realizes I took the letter?" I winced. "And the purple wool?"

"People with nothing to hide don't lie."

"I wish we knew what the latest threat letter says." I took a bite of my eggs and put the fork down. "I've got to get my mind off Agnes. Talk to me. Tell me more about Uncle Nigel."

"Well, Nigel is my mother's older brother. He'd like you. You have a lot in common."

"He collects antiques?"

"He doesn't collect them, Kate. He lives with them, things passed down in the family for generations."

"You weren't kidding about the castle thing?"

"It's a manor house, but it looked like a castle to me as a boy."

I thought about that. When I was a child, castles had existed in fairy tales and Disney movies. Nothing I was ever likely to see in person. "Are you and your uncle close?"

"We're quite fond of each other. I told you I spent summers with him in Devon. My mother worked, and it was a chance for me to get out of the city. Uncle Nigel has always been kind to me, very generous. When I went up to Oxford, he paid the fees."

"What's he like?"

Tom laughed. "They say England breeds eccentrics. Nigel is one of a kind—witty, opinionated, unconventional, charming. He's almost seventy and has a penchant for fast cars, French wine, and pretty women. He never married, but he's always had what he calls his 'lady friends'—most over sixty by now. He bought one of them a ring once. Naturally she thought he meant to propose, and—"

It was obviously a favorite family story, slightly exaggerated over the years. By the time Tom got to the part about the lady's son bearding Nigel in the library and asking what his intentions were, he had me laughing so hard I almost snorted tea up my nose.

We'd finished eating by eleven fifteen. The waitress pointed us in the direction of Paterson & Son, Jewelers. "Three blocks south," she said. "Turn right on Lombard. Look for the navy awning."

Small shops and cafés lined the street. An enterprising busker on stilts juggled oranges and apples. The sun warmed my neck. I reminded myself that in three days Tom would be back in Suffolk, out of my life.

The navy awning of Paterson & Son, Jewelers, shaded a plate-glass window displaying an eye-popping array of jewels. I pushed the entry button and a security guard buzzed us inside. A young woman met us at the door. "Welcome to Paterson's," she said, eyeing my ring-less left hand. "How may I help?"

"I'd like to ask about a ring purchased for my sister-in-law, Elenor Spurgeon."

The woman blanched. "We heard about her death. Shocking."

"Are you the one who sold Dr. Guthrie the ring?"

"Oh, no. That was Mr. Paterson, Senior. He prefers to handle important clients personally."

"May I speak with him?"

"He isn't in at the moment, but he has an appointment in the store at one thirty. He should be free after that. Say two o'clock?"

With half an hour to kill before my meeting with the solicitor, Tom and I decided to explore a gourmet food shop. He bought a tin of whiskey fudge for his mother plus a bottle of white wine, a package of Scottish oat crackers, and a selection of artisan cheeses.

Wasn't Nancy feeding him enough?

We walked west, then followed Castle Street down toward the River Ness and the solicitor's office. Couples strolled past, walking well-behaved dogs and less-well-behaved children. In ten minutes we'd reached the bronze statue of Flora MacDonald, shielding her eyes from the setting sun as she gazed west toward the isles and the death of dreams.

My phone beeped, and we stopped to sit on a bench. "It's my mother. About the marquetry casket." I cupped my hand against the sun and read:

> 1ST QTR 18TH C, A PERSIAN NAMED IBRAHIM QAZVINI ARRIVED IN EDINBURGH. SPECIALIZED IN MARQUETRY. ONLY 4 PIECES KNOWN TO EXIST. ONE IN THE V&A. ONE ABOUT SAME SIZE AS YOURS SOLD 5 YEARS AGO IN HONG KONG FOR HALF A MILLION POUNDS.

I handed the phone to Tom.
"The Victoria and Albert?" he whistled. "An invitation for theft."
"And a motive for murder."

Chapter
Twenty-Seven

The offices of Ross & Marcum, Solicitors, occupied the entire top floor of a red sandstone building not far from the river. A private elevator opened into a waiting room furnished expensively in cool neutrals.

A woman with hair dyed a startling shade of burgundy commanded the prow of an L-shaped desk. She stabbed at her computer before peering over the top of leopard-print eyeglasses. "Do we have an appointment?"

I bit back a snarky remark about the *we* and said, "I'm Kate Hamilton, here to see Mr. Ross."

Tom touched my shoulder. "There's a coffee shop across the street. I'll wait for you there. Take your time."

I followed the receptionist into the inner recesses of Ross & Marcum. A well-dressed man with a silver mane of hair welcomed me into a large glass-walled office. "I'm Andrew Ross." He extended a gold-ringed hand. "Welcome."

Ross's office looked out on the river and the squat red castle that houses the Inverness sheriff's court. A massive desk and credenza exuded corporate opulence. In one of two leather side chairs sat a man with fiery red hair bristling from his scalp like copper wool.

"This is Stephen Trask," Ross said, "Mrs. Spurgeon's accountant.

I've taken the liberty of asking him to join us. Some of what we have to discuss today involves him."

Ross offered me a seat before settling himself in his desk chair and rocking back to reach a large manila envelope on the credenza behind him. He extracted a bound document and handed it across the desk. "This is a copy of Mrs. Spurgeon's will, executed twelve years ago when I handled the purchase of your husband's share of the property on the Isle of Glenroth. The terms are simple. The assets in Mrs. Spurgeon's estate are to be divided equally among her brother, William Hamilton, her nephew, Eric Hamilton, and her niece, Christine Hamilton. When your husband died, his share devolved to the remaining beneficiaries—your children."

I swallowed hard. Were Eric and Christine about to become overnight millionaires? "How large is the estate?"

Ross's chair squeaked. "That's why I've asked Mr. Trask to join us. Our task is made simpler by the recent appraisal of the hotel in preparation for the sale. Stephen, perhaps you would give Mrs. Hamilton an overview of Elenor's financial position."

This time he'd called her *Elenor*. How friendly had they been?

Trask gave a dry cough. "Apart from her personal possessions, Mrs. Spurgeon owned virtually nothing. In the years since her late husband's death, she managed to spend nearly all of his considerable fortune. If the hotel is sold, the proceeds will be barely sufficient to pay off a mortgage on the property taken out five years ago. With her outstanding bills and other commitments, Mrs. Spurgeon's estate will amount to—this is an estimate, you understand—less than twenty thousand pounds."

Good thing I hadn't gone for the pricey bronze casket. "What do you mean *if* the hotel is sold?"

Ross rolled a gold pen in his fingers. "A week ago, Wednesday the nineteenth, I received an email informing me that the Swiss company had accepted the terms of sale. There were details to iron out, but a week later—last Wednesday—I received a PDF copy of the agreement for Elenor's signature. She would have stopped in yesterday to complete the sale."

I blinked at him. "You mean Elenor hadn't actually signed the contract? But she said—" The sentence died on my lips. Elenor had never been fussy about the truth, and she would have considered the contract as good as signed anyway. "What happens now?"

Ross pointed the gold pen at Trask.

"As executor," Trask said, "you are authorized to fulfill any contracts made by Mrs. Spurgeon. In the interest of preserving capital, I'd say the sooner the better. The Swiss people could change their minds."

Ross removed a packet from his desk and handed it to me. "The court has prepared a brochure to help you with your duties. Don't let it overwhelm you. I'll register the death as soon as we get the medical certificate." Sunlight from the window fell on his silver mane, producing a halolike aura. "You will provide a list of assets—an inventory. I'll go into that in a moment. After all outstanding bills are paid, we'll have a final decree. There will be no death duties to pay, unless Mrs. Spurgeon had assets we don't know about. To begin the process, we need your signature."

Ross called in his receptionist to act as witness along with Trask.

Trask said, "I've prepared instructions for the inventory. They're in the envelope as well."

"What do I include?"

"It's all in the envelope. Furniture, artwork, jewelry, antiques—that sort of thing."

Like the marquetry casket. Except it was missing.

"As I mentioned before," Ross said, "the hotel's furnishings were included in the sale. All but the attic. Elenor specifically exempted the attic. Take a look. See what's up there. We can arrange for a local appraiser if you'd like."

"I'd like to complete the sale as soon as possible. I guarantee my children don't want to run a hotel in Scotland together."

Ross was making notes on a yellow pad.

"How did Elenor get herself into such a mess?" I asked.

"She was unusually private about her financial affairs," Ross said. "When I found out she was in trouble—two years ago—I advised her to seek professional help. That's when Mr. Trask became involved."

"Her record-keeping was nonexistent," Trask said. "When I finally untangled the mess, it was clear the hotel had been losing money since the beginning. Far too much was spent on renovation. She seemed to believe her resources were unlimited. I explained that if she continued at her current rate of expenditure, she would exhaust her entire fortune in a matter of years." He settled back in his chair. "She chose not to take my advice."

"This spring," Ross said, picking up the thread, "I convinced Elenor that keeping the hotel was no longer an option. She had to sell or face bankruptcy. That got her attention. The sale price wasn't what I'd hoped for, but we were fortunate to find a buyer at all."

I thought about what I'd said to Tom, that Elenor had acted in blatant self-interest. That wasn't precisely true. She'd had no other option.

Ross tapped the yellow pad with his pen. "Frankly, I've wondered if that was her motivation for marrying again. Dr. Guthrie is said to be a wealthy man."

"He bought her a very expensive ring," I said. "Is the ring part of the estate?"

"Interesting question, which might change my earlier comment about death duties." Ross balanced the gold pen on his index finger. "The ring should be hers, although there are some legal decisions regarding an engagement ring as a commitment to fulfill an obligation she can no longer perform. In that case, the ring would be returned.

The more modern approach is that it was a completed gift, but if Dr. Guthrie wants to argue the point, he could."

"Is that all?" I asked.

"Not quite." Ross opened a desk drawer and pulled out another manila envelope. "On the day of the Tartan Ball, Elenor dropped off a disposable camera. I had the photos developed the same afternoon." He unfastened the clasp and spread a stack of eight-by-tens on his desk. The photos showed the marquetry casket from every conceivable angle. "She asked me to make inquiries about selling the chest in London. I emailed the photos to a dealer I know there."

"Why London?"

"She said she didn't want local attention."

"The casket is missing," I said. "Stolen."

Ross raised an eyebrow. "Well. I'll have to advise the London dealer. I'm told you do appraisals yourself. I'm curious. Do you have an idea of the value?"

"Half a million. Maybe more."

Ross dropped the pen.

*   *   *

I stood on the sidewalk behind the law offices, clutching my manila envelopes and wondering how much time the job of executor would really take. A dark brick building on the corner housed a community theater. A bulb-lit sign announced the current production, *The Importance of Being Earnest*. A classic, one of my favorites.

Three years ago I'd been Kate—wife, mother, daughter, friend. I'd known my lines by heart. Then the curtain fell, and when it rose again, I'd found myself in a new play, without script or cues. No choice but to stumble along. That's what I'd been doing for three years. Stumbling along, doing the things expected of me but never feeling right. Yet now, standing on an unfamiliar street in an unfamiliar city,

I felt more myself than I had since Bill died. I was still young—well, relatively young—and healthy. Surely the story of my life had chapters left. There was still time to turn the page.

Like Flora? that irritating little voice reminded me. *Look how well that turned out.*

Tires squealed as a Land Rover claimed a parking spot.

That's when I saw Frank Holden. He stepped out of a shop, squinting into the sun before walking quickly in the opposite direction. The sign over the shop door pictured three gold balls and the words YE OLDE PAWN SHOP.

I raced across the street, my heart pounding with the implications of what I'd just seen.

The coffee shop, *Uncommon Grounds*, was bustling. The espresso machine whined. A steam nozzle hissed. I made apologies as I pushed through a line of customers waiting to place orders. The interior was exposed brick. I found Tom sitting near a small Victorian fireplace, converted from coal to wood. He'd rocked his chair back, one foot balanced on the opposite knee, his cell phone to his ear. He ended the call and looked up. "How'd it go?"

"I just saw Frank Holden coming out of a pawn shop." The words tumbled out. "Do you think *he* took the casket—and the silver tray? Maybe he's the one Agnes is protecting."

"That was Devlin on the phone. He's on his way back from Stirling. They've decided to take Agnes in for questioning. They should arrive on the island by four at the latest."

I gaped at him, picturing Agnes being marched away from the hotel in handcuffs. My voice wasn't working properly. "Did Devlin tell you what the threat letter said?"

"'Stop the sale or die.' Do you still believe the sale of the hotel had nothing to do with Elenor's death?"

The irony of it hit me—hard. "But the sale wasn't final, Tom. Elenor was going to sign the contract today."

He gave me a sharp look. "Who on Glenroth could have known that?"

I groaned. "Probably Agnes. But she doesn't benefit from Elenor's death. She's not a beneficiary, and the hotel is mortgaged to the hilt."

"She might not have known that part." Tom downed the last of his coffee and snagged his jacket from the back of the chair. "Let's get on the road. We can make it back by three thirty if we hurry."

Call me a chicken, but that's exactly what I didn't want. "Let's stop at the jeweler's first. I really *do* want to talk to Mr. Paterson. And I really *don't* want to be there when they take Agnes into custody."

Chapter Twenty-Eight

~

Mr. Paterson, Senior, was a nattily dressed man with a jeweler's loupe clipped to his eyeglasses. When Tom and I arrived, he was hovering over his client, a middle-aged woman in leather pants and a mink bomber jacket.

The young salesclerk we'd met previously seated us in an office with chocolate-brown walls and chairs covered in wool tattersall. Five minutes later, Mr. Paterson bounced in. "Now," he said, rubbing his hands together, "what can I do for the two of you?"

We told him and his smile faded. "The police came on Saturday. They showed me a photograph and asked if it was the ring I sold Dr. Guthrie. I recognized it immediately. We don't sell rings like that every day."

"Did Dr. Guthrie choose the ring?" I asked.

"They chose it together on—" He tapped his forehead as if to jog his memory. "Well, it must have been the nineteenth. A Wednesday, I believe."

Wednesday again. The day Elenor's mood changed so dramatically. I was beginning to understand why. First she'd learned the hotel had a buyer, saving her from the humiliation of bankruptcy. Then she and Hugh Guthrie chose that enormous diamond ring. She must have felt like she'd won the lottery.

"We ordered the stone and setting from our wholesaler in London."

Mr. Paterson bounced on the balls of his feet. "Dr. Guthrie paid rather a large premium to have it delivered in time for the Tartan Ball. The lady insisted. She chose an emerald-cut central stone, nearly flawless, D color, almost six carats." He was rhapsodizing.

"How did the couple seem?" I asked.

"Seem? Affectionate, in love. Well, perhaps Dr. Guthrie was a little nervous, but that's perfectly normal. We keep brandy for the fainters."

Tom coughed.

"Can you tell me how much he paid for the ring?" I held my breath.

Mr. Paterson, Senior, sputtered. "That's private. I'm not sure I should . . . well, I'd have to get Dr. Guthrie's permission before—"

Tom interrupted. "Mrs. Hamilton is the executor of Mrs. Spurgeon's estate. I'm sure you won't force her to file a subpoena."

"Elenor had some fine jewelry," I added. "I'll probably need an appraiser."

His face brightened. "The ring cost £194,278.13, including tax. But Dr. Guthrie didn't pay for it."

"Elenor paid for it?" I grabbed the arm of my chair.

"No, I don't mean that. We collected a deposit, naturally, but Dr. Guthrie took the ring on approval."

"You let him take a ring worth that much money on *approval*?"

Mr. Paterson, Senior, gave a tight smile. "He had to arrange for a money transfer. He signed for it, of course, and the ring's fully insured. Although I must say I was relieved when we learned it hadn't been stolen. The deductible's pretty high."

"So," I said, "the question of ownership isn't relevant."

"The ring," Mr. Paterson said firmly, "belongs to me. Dr. Guthrie is welcome to return it for a refund. Minus the deposit, of course."

* * *

"We couldn't afford a diamond," I said as Tom and I reversed our course on the A83, the Road to the Isles. The late-afternoon sun washed the western sky with lavender, rose, and lemon. At Glenfinnan, the loch was a sheet of hammered silver. I dug in my handbag for my sunglasses and imagined Bo viewing the same scene from his room at the Munroe Clinic. Was he all right? Had he calmed down?

Tom lowered his visor. "Love isn't measured in diamonds."

I wondered if he'd given Sarah a ring. Maybe Olivia wore it now. My mother's ring would go to Eric when the time came. My own ring, a scant carat Bill had surprised me with on our fifteenth wedding anniversary, would go to Christine. If she wanted it.

I examined Tom's profile. His hair curled slightly around his ears and at the nape of his neck. He looked . . . the word *edible* came to mind, and I felt myself blush. Christine had said that about a boyfriend once, and I'd thought it vaguely pornographic. Tom had a small scar on his right cheek, one I hadn't noticed before. I found myself wanting to touch it, to feel the texture of his skin.

My stomach swooped.

"What happened with the solicitor?" he asked.

Closing the lid firmly on distracting thoughts, I told him about Elenor's will and her financial condition.

"Disappointed?"

"Just the opposite." The light shifted as the road bent toward Mallaig. "Money changes things. Usually not for the better."

"Fortunately, I've never had to worry about the temptations of wealth. My mother's family had money, but everything was entailed on Uncle Nigel."

"Entailed? If I remember my Jane Austen, that means passing an estate to the oldest male heir. Primogeniture. Can people still do that?"

"Not as such, but Nigel has no children. An older cousin of mine will inherit the house and land when Nigel is gone. Speaking of houses and land, will the sale of the hotel go through?"

"Unless the Swiss people back out."

"Why would they buy a property that's losing money?"

"I wondered that. They must think they can turn things around."

"Or they know something we don't." Tom grinned. "I watched those old American Westerns on TV. Wasn't there always a hidden oil well or secret diamond mine on the ranch?"

I laughed, picturing a smoke-filled room with a gang of Swiss bankers giving themselves high fives. "I've been thinking about Wednesday the nineteenth. Elenor was in a foul mood that morning. She visited her safe deposit box in Inverness and removed something. Around noon she called me and begged me to come for the Tartan Ball. She was desperate. I could hear it in her voice."

"And she bought a mobile phone, which you say was totally out of character."

"But then things changed. She learned the Swiss people had signed the contract to purchase the hotel. That must have been a huge relief. And she met Dr. Guthrie at the jewelry shop to choose the ring. She'd depleted her first husband's fortune. Now she had a fresh source of funds to work her way through. According to Becca, she returned to the island around four and spent a couple of hours at the Historical Society. At dinner she was a completely different person. Nancy called her 'nice, chatty.' She assumed the danger was over. She'd handled it."

"How can you know that?"

"Because whatever else Elenor was, she wasn't a fool. And she wasn't brave. She didn't like admitting a mistake, but the moment she was in trouble—something she couldn't handle—she'd call for help."

"Wouldn't she be afraid the note writer would carry out his threat?"

"Not if she knew who was sending the threats and decided it was a bluff. Besides, she'd assume that once the hotel was sold, the threats would lose their leverage."

"Bad decision."

"Maybe, but here's the point. If Elenor thought the danger was over, why not call me back and tell me not to come?"

"Wanted to share her happiness with you?"

"I'd be the last person."

"To appraise the casket?"

"No. She'd already arranged to have it appraised in London. She wanted me to *see* the casket and read Dr. Guthrie's book. That's why I don't think the sale of the hotel and the threats were why she wanted my help. I think she'd discovered something about Flora's death and wanted my advice on what to do about it. I think that's why she was murdered."

"And Agnes was involved?"

"I don't know."

Tom slowed. We'd reached the ferry to Glenroth just as it was loading.

I was dreading this. "Do you think they've taken her away by now?" I stared across the Sound toward Sleat. The slick, dark back of a porpoise, or maybe one of the huge gray seals, surfaced briefly, catching the sun's dying rays.

"Probably." Tom pulled onto the ferry and set the brake. Several cars pulled behind us. He changed the subject. "You never finished your story about Frank Holden and the pawn shop."

True. The news about Agnes had put Frank out of my mind. "Seeing him coming out of the pawn shop made me wonder if he'd pawned the silver tray. He knows the police are checking. Maybe he decided to buy it back before the police found it."

"Was he carrying a package?"

I tried to remember. "I don't think so. But if Frank stole the tray, he might have taken the casket too."

The ferry reached the Isle of Glenroth. We drove south in silence.

Was Agnes in cahoots with Frank and Nancy? Maybe Sofia and Becca were part of the plan, too—like *Murder on the Orient Express*. I rejected that theory, but by the time we reached the hotel, a knot had formed in my stomach. Devising theories is easy; accusing someone you actually know is brutal.

Tom nosed the car through the stone columns. The coach lamps flickered.

The knot tightened.

We made the final curve into the parking area. Two cars were parked there, a white police car with yellow and blue markings and Devlin's black Peugeot sedan.

The knot tightened again.

Chapter
Twenty-Nine

～

We found Detective Inspector Devlin in the gathering room. This time, instead of Constable Mackie or DS Bruce, he'd brought a policewoman. She was motherly looking in a no-nonsense way, but her dark uniform sported an impressive row of chevrons.

The hotel's staff, minus Agnes, huddled near the fireplace. Nancy pulled me into the circle. "The police want to question Agnes, but we cannae find her."

"What do you mean?"

"We thought she was in her flat, but she's vanished." Nancy's face was white.

Sofia's eyes were fixed on Tom, shooting him signals in some kind of ocular semaphore.

Devlin whispered something to the policewoman. Then he and Tom left the room.

"We need to get into Miss MacLeod's flat," the policewoman said. Nancy handed her a set of keys, and she headed for the staircase.

Becca's eyes were huge. "They must think Agnes had something to do with Elenor's death. I can't believe that."

"When was the last time you saw her?" I asked.

"She made a phone call around two," Becca said. "I know because I saw her extension button light up."

"Sofia was the last person to actually see her." Nancy turned toward Sofia, but she'd fled from the room. "Poor lass had one of her migraines this morning. I told her to go to the Lodge and lie down. She says she saw Agnes around quarter to three on the forest path, walking in the direction of the road."

I nodded slowly, putting the timeline together in my mind. Tom had received the call from Devlin around one. Agnes couldn't possibly have known the police were on their way to pick her up. Unless someone had tipped her off.

"She cannae have gotten far on foot," Frank said. "Be dark soon."

"She could be lying somewhere, injured, unable to call for help." Nancy untied her apron and pulled the loop over her head. "I'm going to search the house again, top to bottom."

"I'll check the cottages," Frank said. "Becca, find Sofia. Check the Lodge and the outbuildings. Take a torch."

They rushed off, leaving me alone.

Agnes hadn't gone for an afternoon stroll. That was clear. And if she took the forest path, she could only have been headed for the Arnotts' house or the Historical Society. Why she'd go to either place, I couldn't imagine, unless this had something to do with Elenor's death. The Historical Society was where Elenor went the night she was killed.

Tom was right. Agnes had some explaining to do.

* * *

The forest path began at the parking area and curved through the trees past Tartan Cottage and the Lodge before joining the main road. I walked slowly, scanning the surrounding woods.

When I reached South Shore Road, a police car raced past, the light bar flashing. Probably checking to see if Agnes was with the Arnott twins. Unlikely, in my opinion, although if Agnes's destination had been the Historical Society, Penny and Cilla might have seen her. They didn't miss much that happened over there. *Unless*—I stopped walking—unless Agnes decided to make sure she wouldn't *be* seen. In that case she'd have approached the Historical Society from the Burn o'Ruadh rather than from the road. She really might have fallen and sprained an ankle—or worse, broken a hip. She could be lying there in pain.

I walked quickly, making use of what light remained. Soon the sun would dip below the horizon, ushering in the *gloaming*, the word the Scots use for that magical time between sunset and full darkness.

Reaching the arched bridge, I peered over the stone spandrel. Would Agnes risk going down that way? She would if she were desperate enough. I stepped over the abutment, steadying myself on the pier as I slid sideways in the loose gravel. Once down, I followed the burn for a hundred yards or so. The high bank on my left cast deep shadows, limiting my vision, but I could see well enough to know Agnes wasn't there.

As I turned back toward the bridge, I stumbled over something.

A shoe. A sturdy women's shoe.

A shiver between my shoulder blades alerted me to danger. I narrowed my eyes and scanned my surroundings. Something caught my attention, high on the bank, lighter than the surrounding brush. Tucking the shoe under my arm, I picked my way across the stream bed and climbed, using roots and branches—whatever I could grab onto—to pull myself up the slope. Halfway I slipped and fell heavily on my hands and knees.

I pushed to my feet and brushed off my jeans, feeling my palms sting. Climbing again, I dug in with my toes to get purchase. Close to the top of the bank, I stopped and looked.

Oh, no. Dear God, no.

Spanning the crest was the body of a woman. She lay on her stomach, her arms and legs splayed. I couldn't see the face, but there was no doubt.

I'd found Agnes MacLeod.

Call the police. I felt for my cell phone. *Crap, crap, crap.* I'd left it in my handbag.

I climbed the last few yards, knelt beside the body. No pulse.

I swallowed hard, forcing myself to process details. Agnes was wearing one leather shoe. The other foot was bare, the sole, what I could see in the gathering dusk, raw and bloody. The dark fabric of her coat had rucked up in back as the weight of her body pulled toward the stream bed below. Fleshy white thighs ended in a pair of flower-sprigged underwear.

The small indignity was too much. This is how Agnes would be viewed, photographed. I reached into the folds of Agnes's coat to pull it down. My fingers met something cold and hard. I felt the hilt of a blade and a thistle-shaped handle, capped with a cold faceted stone.

The Highland dirk from the Historical Society. Or one exactly like it.

The sound of rustling leaves broke the stillness. I froze.

The sound came again, closer.

Something ricocheted off a nearby tree.

I stifled a scream. *Get out of here—now.* Dropping the shoe, I ran, dodging trees and bushes. Branches caught at my clothing. My hands flew up as something stung my cheek close to my eye. Darkness was closing in fast.

I heard a pop as something whizzed past my ear. Was someone *shooting* at me?

Seeing an opening in the woods, I pivoted, praying I'd found the forest path. My feet slid on the damp leaves, sending me sprawling.

I scrambled to my feet.

Lights blazed ahead. The Lodge.

Focus on the lights. And keep running.

Chapter Thirty

I knocked furiously, hands on my knees as I sucked in air.

The door to the Lodge opened. "My God, Kate, what's happened?" Tom reached out and hauled me inside.

"It's Agnes," I gasped. "In the woods. Dead."

"Bloody hell." He helped me to a chair. "Are you injured? Do you need an ambulance?"

"I'm all right. Just let me sit."

"You're shaking. Put this around you." He tucked an afghan around my shoulders and left the room.

I heard running water and a low phone conversation.

He returned with a warm washcloth. "Let's get you cleaned up before you look in a mirror and frighten yourself to death." He dabbed at my face, streaking the snowy cloth with red. "You're certain she's dead?"

"Very." My heart was still racing, but I was getting my breath back.

"Did you see anyone?"

"You mean apart from the guy shooting at me?" I croaked a laugh.

"My God, Kate." Tom leaned forward to examine my head as if he might find a bullet hole I'd neglected to mention.

I held up my palms, seeing abrasions and more blood. I'd ripped my jeans when I fell, so my knees would be a mess, too. I leaned back and closed my eyes. Not bad, considering I could have been sitting there dead.

"Rob Devlin is on his way. Are you up to making a statement?"

I nodded, wondering for the first time what Tom was doing at the Lodge. "Where's Sofia?"

"Upstairs, asleep." He crouched in front of my chair. "Tell me about Agnes."

"Someone stabbed her with one of those Scottish knives." I shivered involuntarily, picturing the bloody bare foot and rucked-up coat. My teeth started to chatter. "I'm pretty sure it's the one I saw at the Historical Society."

Thirty minutes later I sat at the oak table in the hotel's kitchen. A turf fire smoldered in the hearth, warming my bones. Nancy had cut my jeans off above the ripped knees and washed the raw skin before applying a layer of antibiotic gel and bandages. My hands were the worst, dirt and gravel ground into my palms. Nancy washed them twice before applying the gel and wrapping them in strips of soft gauze.

Becca and Sofia arrived with Frank and made me tell my story again.

Sofia clutched a knitted shawl around her shoulders. Her thick braid was coming undone.

Becca slid in beside me and put her head on my shoulder. "Poor you. Forgive me for snapping at you yesterday."

I gave her a hug.

DI Devlin arrived. One of the constables had found Agnes's shoe—and a bullet lodged in a tree trunk. He listened intently for once as I told my story for the fourth time. "I recognized the Highland dirk because I'd just seen it—or one exactly like it—at the Historical Society."

He sucked in a long breath. "Seems you were right. Two women murdered in the same way as Flora Arnott and Gowyn Campbell can't be coincidence."

"And it proves you're wrong about Bo Duff." I was beginning to feel stronger. "He can't have killed Agnes. He's at the Munroe Clinic."

Devlin didn't respond. Not a good sign. "We'll be back at dawn." He zipped up his jacket. "Until then, I've asked Tom to take some precautions for your safety."

"When are you going to release Bo?" I asked, unwilling to let it go.

"Out of my hands now." Devlin dug in his pocket and handed me Elenor's jeweled key ring. "These belong to you."

The door closed behind him.

Tom carried my half-filled plate to the sink. "We need to talk about safety. Two women connected with the hotel are dead."

Sofia pulled her shawl closer. Nancy took Becca's hand.

Several plans were discussed, all complicated. Eventually it was decided that Sofia would spend the night on the Holdens' sofa in Argyll Cottage. Becca would go to Fort William with Geoff, who was already on the way to pick her up. Tom would sleep on a roll-away in my kitchen. Normally I would have insisted I was fine on my own. Not tonight. Not after hearing that bullet whiz past my head.

Geoff arrived while Nancy was clearing the dishes. He caught Becca in his arms, burying his face in her hair. "I'm all right, Geoff," she said. "I really am."

Sofia's headache was back. Geoff and Becca offered to walk her to Argyll, promising to stay with her until the Holdens were finished at the hotel. Tom and Frank left to set up the roll-away in Applegarth.

I wasn't allowed to do a thing, so I watched Nancy clean up the kitchen.

Twenty minutes later Frank returned and took the chair opposite me at the table.

Nancy spread her tea towel over the edge of the sink and turned to face me. "There's something we wish to tell you."

"You saw me today in Inverness," Frank said.

"Look, you don't have to explain." The last thing I wanted to do at the moment was accuse someone else.

"Aye," Nancy agreed, "but we've had our fill of secrets." She stood behind Frank, her hands resting on his shoulders.

Frank ran his fingers roughly through his hair. "Bo had some debts last spring. He pawned his telly and some of his mother's jewelry. I had to be sure that . . . well, I was wrong."

He looked up at Nancy, and she brushed the back of her hand against his cheek.

"My mother was seventeen when I was born," Frank said. "My father was a soldier. That's all I know. He denied paternity. No such thing as DNA testing back then. My mother's folks disowned her. She ended up in a shelter. An older couple, childless, offered her a place to live. After I was born, we stayed on. I called them Nana and Gramps.

"I was the kid with no father, so I made up stories." He spread his thick, calloused hands. "He was stationed in Canada with the Mounties. He'd been killed in Korea. One time I said he was working with MI6 in the Soviet Union. The kids stopped believing me, of course. Eventually I ran away, found a job in construction. Told them I was eighteen. Nobody bothered to check."

Frank's hair was grizzled with gray, his face and neck deeply creased from years spent outdoors, but at that moment I could see him—smooth-skinned, lean, angry.

"One night one of the men left his toolbox at the job site. I sold it for twenty pounds. Then I began stealing other things, anything I could get my hands on. I was nineteen when they caught me. Served three years, nine months, and five days of a twelve-year sentence. Gramps came to visit every week. He told me my life wasn't over, that forgiveness was possible."

Frank closed his eyes and pinched the bridge of his nose.

"He died a month before I was paroled. Nana moved in with a

niece. My mother was married by that time. She was happy, so I decided to go somewhere no one knew me, start over. Then I met Nancy, and somehow I couldn't lie to her." He reached up for Nancy's hand. "That's why I do what I can for Bo. Payback for the grace I was shown. The mistake I made was keeping my past from our daughter. I never wanted her life tainted by what I'd done, but that meant keeping it from everyone else too."

"We're going to tell her," Nancy said, "in person, as soon as we can."

"So which of you lied to the police?"

"I did." Nancy lowered her eyes. "I told them Frank never left my side that night. It wasn't true."

"I couldn't sleep," Frank said. "I was worried about Bo, wanted to make sure he was all right after the blowup with Elenor. Foolish, because by the time I got to Bo's house, all the lights were out. I didn't want to wake him. I knew he had to get up before dawn to plow."

"But you must have been home long before Elenor was killed."

"We didn't know when she was killed until later," Nancy said. "The police always suspect ex-offenders. I thought it would be simpler to tell them Frank was with me all night. Except I didn't have a chance to tell Frank, and he—" Her eyes filled.

"I accused her of not trusting me." Frank looked up at Nancy. "That wasn't fair."

"Had the silver tray been pawned?" I asked.

"No," Frank said, "and here's the strange part. It's back."

"It's true." Nancy's eyes were wide. "The laundry delivered the linens this morning. When Sofia went to put the napkins in the butler's pantry, there was the tray. As if it had never been gone."

As if it had never been gone. That's what Guthrie had said about the stolen gun at the Historical Society.

* * *

I said good night to Frank and Nancy on Applegarth's porch, giving them each a one-armed hug. Becca was right. They had undoubtedly been wonderful parents.

The roll-away was already made up in the kitchen. Tom had changed into navy sweat pants and a long-sleeved T-shirt that said SUFFOLK CONSTABULARY on the front and TAKING PRIDE IN KEEPING SUFFOLK SAFE on the back.

"You must be exhausted," he said. "Will you sleep?"

"Not if I don't take a shower first. I feel grubby." I held up the bag of first-aid supplies Nancy had given me. "Will you help me rewind the gauze on my hands?"

The steamy shower pounded out the knots in my back and shoulders. I poured a whole tiny bottle of Highland Heather shampoo over my head, almost relishing the sting of the soap on my raw skin. I was alive.

The sight of Agnes's body would be in my head forever. Had someone known the police were on their way and killed her to stop her talking to them? I couldn't answer those questions, but the field of suspects was narrowing. The murderer was getting bolder. Or more desperate.

The pop of that gunshot echoed in my head. Was I simply in the wrong place at the wrong time, or was I now a target?

I rinsed the shampoo from my hair, shut off the water, and stepped out of the shower. After towel-drying my hair, I combed it out and tucked it behind my ears. Clearing a circle in the foggy mirror, I threw vanity to the wind and applied a thin layer of face cream and cherry-colored lip balm. *Why not?* Tom had already seen worse.

Once I'd replaced the bandages on my knees, I layered the waffle-weave robe over my pajamas—my *new* flannels this time (I do have some pride)—and opened the bathroom door, releasing a billow of steam.

Tom was in the kitchen on his cell phone. "Got it. Thanks for letting me know." He clicked off and slipped the phone in his pocket. "That was Devlin. Agnes died from a stab wound to the heart. She would have lost consciousness in seconds."

Did that make me feel better? I didn't know, but I was glad she hadn't suffered long.

While I was in the shower, Tom had arranged the cheese and crackers he'd bought in Fort William on a plate. And he'd opened the bottle of white wine.

This was unique: wine and cheese in flannel pajamas with a man I'd known for five days.

He must have read my mind. "Awkward, I know, but the police don't have the resources to provide security. Besides," he grinned, "I live in a house full of women."

We sat at the kitchen table, and he poured us each a glass of wine.

I took a sip, tasting citrus and oak. "So what did Devlin say?"

"They searched Agnes's flat and took away samples of writing paper and envelopes. They appear to match those used in the posted threat letters."

"So Agnes was the one threatening Elenor after all. It makes sense. She was convinced she'd lose her job if the hotel was sold, and she was losing her security as well. She'd cashed in her pension to offset the pitiful salary Elenor paid her. Agnes risked everything on Elenor's promise to make her a full partner." I took another swallow of wine. "What else did Devlin tell you?"

"They searched the Historical Society. The Highland dirk and the gun are missing, no surprise. So are the keys for the display cabinet. No one admits taking them, and no one remembers seeing the knife after the previous afternoon when Guthrie showed it to you. He says he was the last to leave today, around four thirty."

"Why do you think Agnes was killed?" I layered a slice of spicy cheddar on a Scottish oat cracker and took a bite.

"If I had to guess, I'd say Agnes followed Elenor the night of the ball and saw or heard something that put her life in jeopardy. If the strands of purple wool found on the bush outside the Historical Society match Agnes's purple knitted gloves, I'd bet money on it."

"I know she'd hurt herself. I saw scratches on her forehead."

"Sounds like she panicked. Maybe she was the one who left the main door ajar."

"I agree, but it still doesn't explain how these murders are tied to the murders in the past. And it doesn't explain why someone wants me to destroy something I don't have." I stifled a yawn. "It's like tangled yarn. Find the right thread and the whole thing comes undone."

"Leave thread pulling to the police." Tom corked the wine bottle. "Come. Sit here. I'll help you with your hands."

We sat facing each other. I held up each hand in turn so he could wind clean gauze around my raw palms. He frowned, examining his workmanship. "Too tight?"

"Just right." I met his gaze.

He reached up and tucked a lock of damp hair behind my ear. "You've cut your face." He traced the line of my cheekbone with the back of his finger.

A bubble of pleasure caught in my throat. I leaned into his touch.

He took my face in his hands and kissed my forehead, then my mouth. Warm. Sweet. I felt something inside me starting to melt.

I pulled away.

"I know," he said, smiling wryly. "We're being watched. Sarah and Bill."

The thought so perfectly expressed what I'd been thinking that I wondered if he'd read my mind.

He stood and dropped a kiss on my head. "You need sleep. I'll straighten up."

I climbed into bed, wrapping myself in the duvet. What was it I felt? Pleasure, yes, but something else, too, deeper, more elemental, and tinged with—what? Not guilt. More like disloyalty.

Absurd. How can you be disloyal to a man in his grave?

Sounds drifted in from the kitchen. Tom was checking the doors, closing the window over the sink. The kitchen light went out. The roll-away creaked.

"Call if you need anything," he said. "I'm a light sleeper."

We were separated by the fireplace, but I imagined I could hear the soft rise and fall of his breath. My throat tightened. I touched my mouth, still feeling the pressure of his kiss. I'd almost forgotten what a proper kiss felt like.

The clock on the mantel ticked.

Time, like an ever-rolling stream, bears all its sons away;
they fly forgotten, as a dream dies at the opening day.

I lay on my back and gazed into the inky blackness. Gradually shapes emerged. The fireplace stones, the tops of the chairs, the bathroom door frame.

They fly forgotten . . .

His voice broke the silence. "Do you ever stop missing them?"

I knew what he meant. "I don't know."

"Sarah's been gone four years. Sometimes it feels like yesterday, sometimes another lifetime."

"I'm beginning to forget what Bill looked like. It scares me."

"I remember too well, those last months. She was no more than a skeleton, her eyes huge in her face, pleading with me to do something. For months afterward, I saw those eyes in my sleep. Sometimes I still do."

"At least you had time to say good-bye."

"Yes, at least I had that."

The clock on the mantel ticked.

"Tom, why did you really come to Glenroth?"

Silence. Then, "I lived here once."

"You lived here?" I sat up.

"The summer I turned sixteen. My father was in the RAF,

stationed at Lakenheath in Suffolk. My parents met, married, had me. We moved around a lot. Cyprus, Gibraltar. Eventually my father decided to get out of the military, move back to Scotland. Mother agreed to spend a summer on the island. His family had a croft house here. It's gone now. He said he'd find work. We could see what we thought. They sent me to the Adventure Centre. Interesting to see it yesterday."

"Don't tell me you knew my husband."

"No, Kate. I'd have been there well after he went up to Oxford. I meet Rob Devlin there, though, and we've kept in touch all these years. He's the one who told me about the homeland security conference in Edinburgh. He encouraged me to come back. To lay old ghosts."

"Old ghosts?"

"It wasn't a happy summer. My father had an affair. Mother and I packed up and returned to England alone."

"Why come back now?" Something niggled at the back of my brain.

"I wanted to see if the pictures in my mind were real. And the solitude appealed to me. I'd come off a difficult case. Triple murder. I needed time to think, to decide if I want to stay in the force. The investigation was brutal. There was a child involved, but in the end—"

My breath caught.

There was a child involved. Agnes had said that. Thirty years ago Elenor had begun an affair with a much older married man. *There was a child involved.* Not a pregnancy. A child whose family was ripped apart.

I did some quick mental calculations. Tom was my age. Thirty years ago he would have been sixteen. Elenor would have been . . . twenty-three, working at St. Hilda's, spending her summers on Glenroth.

What effect would an affair have had on a sixteen-year-old boy—a father's betrayal, a mother's humiliation, his world shattered? Had Tom come back to take revenge?

My throat tightened painfully. I covered my mouth to keep from making a sound.

But why would Tom kill Agnes? My mind raced. Had she seen him with Elenor at the Historical Society and threatened to expose him?

No, that couldn't be true. Relief flooded in. Tom was with me in Fort William when Agnes was killed.

Then my brain made another leap.

He had help. *Sofia?*

I pressed my fingertips to my temples. I couldn't think straight with that wretched clock ticking. Thoughts crashed upon thoughts, hardly giving me time to breathe.

Sofia had spent the night in Tartan Cottage. I'd seen the looks that passed between them. I could picture Sofia wielding a bow and arrow—or a knife. Tom *just happened* to be in the woods on Saturday when I'd seen that shadow disappear into the brush. He'd been somewhere on the estate when the note was pushed under my door. Was that why he hadn't answered his cell? Tom was the one who opened the door to my frantic knocking at the Lodge. I'd never asked him why he was there.

I swallowed against the lump in my throat.

Was Sofia really sleeping as Tom said, or had she been out there in the woods with a gun? Why had Tom been spending so much time with me, asking all those questions? My vision blurred. The final wave crashed. Maybe it wasn't Devlin Tom had been speaking to at the coffee shop at all. He might have phoned Sofia, warning her that Agnes was about to implicate him. Telling her to make certain it never happened.

"—and if I have to face that, at least I'm making a difference."

He was still talking, but I'd heard nothing.

Panic surged. *Leave now. Run.* The Holdens' cottage was nearby. If I waited for him to fall asleep—

No. Then he'd realize I'd figured it out. I reached for my phone and tucked it under my pillow. I considered texting my mother, but what could she do from three thousand miles away?

The safest thing was to sit tight and phone Devlin first thing in the morning. Would he believe me? I had no actual evidence of Tom's guilt. He and Tom had been friends nearly all their lives.

"Are you awake?" Tom's voice startled me.

I didn't answer.

"Sleep well, Kate."

Sleep well? I wasn't going to sleep at all.

Chapter
Thirty-One

Wednesday, November 2

I awoke with a start as a half-remembered dream—dark shapes, menacing voices—morphed into the nightmare that was real.

The cottage was silent. I slipped out of bed and tiptoed toward the edge of the fireplace. Tom's roll-away was folded and pushed against the patio door, the linens stacked on top. He was gone. *Good.*

A note lay on the kitchen table: *Good morning, Kate. I'll be at the police station in Mallaig most of the day. Stay close to Frank and Nancy. If you must leave the property, call my mobile.*

He sounded so normal.

My brain was muddled, and my heart ached. It actually ached.

I found my phone tangled in the bed sheets and dialed DI Devlin's cell. He knew about Tom's history on the island, but he might not know about Elenor's role in the events of that long-ago summer. He needed to know. I needed to tell him.

I got his voicemail, left a message, and flagged it urgent.

I dressed quickly and walked to the hotel. Yesterday's sunshine had fled. Clouds hung low in the sky. A stiff wind presaged another storm.

Nancy and Sofia were in the kitchen as usual. Nancy was doing something with pastry. She looked dreadful. "Good morning, Kate. How are your wee hands?"

"Much better." I held them out for inspection.

"Becca's still in Fort William. She'll be back for supper." Nancy placed a mug of coffee in front of me. "Tom stopped on his way somewhere. He made Frank promise to keep an eye on you."

I'll bet.

Sofia was preparing acorn squash. I watched with horrified fascination as she held a large green head with one hand, severing it with the thwack of a butcher knife. After scooping out the seeds, she placed the halves on a baking sheet and slid it into the oven. She touched her forehead. "I go lie down."

"Those headaches of yours are worrying," Nancy said.

And way too convenient.

"Get some rest," Nancy added as Sofia wrapped herself in her knitted shawl, "but make sure your mobile's turned on. If you see anything suspicious, call Frank."

Sofia ducked out, her head bent against the wind.

Nancy covered the pastry with a cloth and wiped her floury hands on her apron. "Frank and I talked last night. We wondered if the murders could have something to do with Elenor's money. It's none of our business, but do you know the terms of her will?"

It was a natural question, and I didn't mind answering. "My children are the beneficiaries. I'm the executor."

"Of course. I'm glad." Nancy rinsed her hands at the sink and dried them with a tea towel. "We did wonder if Elenor had left a wee something for Agnes, poor thing."

"It wouldn't have mattered. Elenor was almost bankrupt."

"Bankrupt?" Nancy looked startled. "No wonder she'd been bothered about money lately."

Yes, no wonder. And according to the accountant, there was

precious little money left. If the hotel had a genealogy seminar booked for November and a full house for the holidays, they'd need to purchase supplies, arrange for extra staffing. "How will you manage until May?"

"Becca will take on the manager's job for now. We'll get local help for anything we cannae handle ourselves. Assuming guests will want to come. I'm not sure I would."

"If you and Frank decide to leave, I'll make sure you get a glowing recommendation."

"That's kind." Nancy looked close to tears. "We'll let you know."

I downed the last of my coffee. I had plenty to keep me busy until Devlin called. "I'm going to make a start on the inventory. Let me know when Tom gets back."

Forewarned is forearmed.

I passed through the reception hall on my way to Elenor's flat. The desk was empty, the phones silent. Maybe Nancy was right. No one would ever want to stay at the hotel again. And if the Swiss buyers backed out—

No. I couldn't think about that now.

The east wing was deserted. No footsteps. No disappearing shadows. I turned the key. Four days since Elenor's death, and the flat had already taken on the stale, airless feel of a place long abandoned. I locked myself inside.

Better safe than sorry.

Terrific. Suddenly I was a font of aphorisms.

I had devised a plan of action. As I did with consignments at the shop, I'd give each item a number, photographing it and recording its description and approximate value. Fortunately, I'd brought the digital camera and tape measure I use almost daily in my work. Andrew Ross's receptionist had given me a new spiral-bound notebook and a package of peel-off labels.

I transferred the box of junk from the dining room table to the floor, making room for my notebook and camera. As soon as Devlin gave the okay, I'd return the box to the twins.

The top right-hand drawer of Elenor's desk was stuffed with receipts. These would go to Stephen Trask, Lord help him. I found a metal ruler in the center drawer and used it to divide several notebook pages into three columns: *Number*, *Description*, and *Approx. Value*.

The living room was as good a place as any to begin. I wrote the number *1* on a label, peeled it off, and stuck it inside the hand-blown glass bowl. In the notebook I wrote *1*, then *Blue and white art glass bowl, contemporary*. After measuring the bowl, I added *12"h × 18"w*. I set the camera and took the picture. In the value column, I wrote *$300? TBD*—to be determined. I'm not an expert on contemporary art glass. Next I cataloged the book on fashion and the glass coffee table.

Two hours later I was on number seventy-two, one of those anti-gravity recliners in sculpted wood and leather. I longed to sink into its buttery folds and take a nap. Instead I massaged the muscles in my neck. Why hadn't Devlin called? Was he ignoring me? I dialed his cell phone again, leaving a second message. Then I tried the police station at Mallaig.

"Sorry, Mrs. Hamilton," said a female voice. "Detective Inspector Devlin is in Inverness today. All-day meeting."

"I've left two messages. It's important."

"Would you care to speak with Detective Inspector Mallory?"

"No. *No*. I'll wait for DI Devlin."

"He has his phone with him. I'm sure he'll call you as soon as he gets a chance."

At noon Nancy brought lunch, that wonderful squash soup again, this time with rounds of puff pastry topped with a layer of chèvre cheese, a slice of tomato, and a sprig of fresh basil. She'd stuck a phone message from the funeral home on the tray. Elenor's service would be held tomorrow, eleven AM, at the Wee Free in the village, followed by a short graveside ceremony. The women of the church were organizing light refreshments afterward and suggested the Historical Society as the venue. A perfect choice. Apart from the hotel, the Historical Society seemed to have been Elenor's main interest in life.

The sky was turning dark. Rain pricked the windows.

I finished every drop of soup and popped the last bite of pastry in my mouth. After shifting the tray to the chest in Elenor's entrance hall, I went in search of coffee.

Elenor had probably never fixed herself so much as a bowl of cereal, but she did have a coffeemaker, one of those single-cup jobs with a tiered holder for pods.

Carrying the warm mug, I wandered into Elenor's bedroom.

The top drawer of Elenor's bureau was jammed with jewelry—totally disorganized but genuine and expensive. Bill had told me once that Elenor had a fine pearl necklace passed down from their grandmother. That should go to Christine, but would she appreciate it? Christine's style at the moment was more biker chic than classic retro. The only thing keeping her from tats and piercings was a needle phobia.

I was working on a set of vintage botanical prints when my cell phone rang. I snatched it up, praying it was Devlin.

It was Frank. He'd been at the Munroe Clinic. Bo's psychiatric evaluation was complete, and the report had been forwarded to the court. The competency hearing would take place as scheduled, at eleven the following morning. Brenda had contacted the care facility in Perth.

I clicked END. Raindrops gathered into rivulets that ran down the wavy old window glass. Tomorrow Elenor's body would be sealed in a coffin and lowered into the earth. Tomorrow Bo Duff would be buried, too, in one kind of institution or another.

I sat on the sofa and plunked the mug of coffee on the glass table.

For all my clever theories, I hadn't found a single shred of evidence to clear Bo Duff of Elenor's murder.

I'd failed Bo. I'd failed Elenor. *I'd failed Bill.*

My eyes filled. I shut them and leaned back against the soft cushions.

Every man I'd ever loved had been torn from me without warning. My brother, my father, my husband. Now Bo. *And Tom?* Thinking about Tom made me physically ill.

I gave in to great gulping sobs. Tears streamed into my ears and dripped from my chin. I'm not a pretty crier.

With a final hiccup, I swabbed my face with my sleeve.

My old friend. Grief.

* * *

I stood at the window in Elenor's flat, watching sheets of rain blow across the parking lot. My tears had dried, leaving my eyes sore and gritty.

Nearly three o'clock and DI Devlin still hadn't returned my call. Should I leave him a third message? Text him?

I dropped into the recliner. Even if Devlin believed me, it was probably too late to save Bo. Brenda had made up her mind. Unless something changed immediately, his fate would be sealed.

My cell phone rang again. Nancy this time. "Frank and I will be at our cottage for several hours. Why don't you come along, dearie? I don't like leaving you there on your own."

"Thanks, but I need to keep working." I clambered out of the recliner as if to prove it. "I want to finish as much of the inventory as I can before the funeral."

"Call us if you need anything," Nancy said. "We're locking both doors on the way out. Don't leave the house."

"Too busy for that." I gave a breezy laugh, hoping I sounded more sanguine than I felt.

My phone was low on power. I plugged it in at the dining room table.

A blustery wind whipped the sodden leaves and hurled them against the windows. I picked up the pen and wrote *#234. Set of six dining room chairs.*

By three forty-five, the living room and dining room were complete. Elenor's bedroom was next. Fortunately I wouldn't have to inventory Elenor's massive wardrobe, but I would have to arrange for disposal. I might try a resale shop in Inverness. Or donate them to a clothing bank. Did Scotland's poor need size 2 designer evening gowns?

The second drawer in Elenor's bureau was filled with lingerie, transparent wisps in silk and lace. I held up what was supposed to be a bra, marveling. Even if charity shops accepted lingerie, these flimsy things might be banned.

On to Elenor's jewelry. I would document and photograph each piece, but a gemologist would have to do the official valuation. I'd as good as promised the business to Mr. Paterson, Senior.

I found a permanent marker in Elenor's desk and, in a kitchen drawer, several unopened boxes of sealable plastic baggies. Pulling out the jewelry drawer, I carried it to the bed and dumped the lot on the pale-blue spread.

I worked steadily for an hour, pushing thoughts of Tom Mallory and Bo Duff out of my mind. I was getting good at compartmentalizing.

I found the pearl necklace in a dark-red clamshell box with MAISON CARTIER PARIS printed across the top in gold lettering. The pearls were high quality, a lustrous cream with lovely pink undertones. The clasp was Art Deco—late 1920s or early 1930s—gold with small diamonds.

After photographing the necklace, I returned it to the clamshell box and sealed it a quart-size plastic baggie. I wrote the inventory number in permanent ink on the label strip.

Elenor's jewelry would add substantially to the value of her estate—unless it had to be sold to cover her debts. That remained to be seen, but if the police found the missing casket, my children's inheritance might double or triple. Eric would do something sensible like pay for his doctoral degree. I didn't want to think about what Christine would do with that much money.

Someone knocked. Probably the Holdens, come to tell me they were back.

I ran to open the door.

Tom stood in the hallway, his head and shoulders flecked with rain. "Nancy says you've been working all day. How's it going?" He stepped past me into the room, shedding his rain gear.

"Making progress." I forced a smile. Was I acting normally? I couldn't tell. "Would you like a coffee?"

"No, thanks. I've had enough coffee to last a lifetime. I have news. Can we sit?" He took a seat on the sofa, stretching his long legs under the coffee table.

I faced him on the love seat, eyeing my cell phone on the dining room table and trying to look relaxed.

"More toxicology results came back this morning," he said. "In addition to alcohol, Elenor had two different sedatives in her system when she died. One was her own sleeping tablets, the bottle on her dressing table. But there was another compound as well, a different medication entirely. Tablets matching that compound were found in Agnes's flat."

I frowned. "What does that mean?"

"It means Elenor took—or was given—some of Agnes's sleeping pills as well as her own."

I remembered what Nancy had said about Elenor's memory issues. Weren't sleeping pills said to be a cause of early-onset dementia?

"Are you saying Agnes drugged her?"

"Easy enough to do. Slip a few tablets in a hot drink, mask the taste with spices." Tom met my gaze, calm and cool.

263

Was he speaking from experience? He'd left the Tartan Ball right after Elenor. If he had followed Elenor to her flat, he might have—

"Where's Detective Inspector Devlin?"

"In meetings all day. He asked me to give you the update."

Was that why Devlin wasn't responding to my messages? *Don't bother returning her calls. I'll be seeing her later.*

A headache was building between my eyes. Looking relaxed is stressful.

"There's something else, Kate. I wanted to tell you in person."

That didn't sound good.

"The police searched Bo's shed this afternoon. They found arrows concealed behind an old refrigerator. One of them was fitted with a multiple-blade broadhead. Same as the arrow that killed Elenor. I'm afraid that's evidence."

I jumped to my feet. "But everyone knows Bo's shed is never locked. Someone probably planted those arrows to implicate him—the one person on the island who can't defend himself. It's cruel. It's absurd. Bo was in custody when Agnes was killed."

"The police understand that, Kate, but you said it yourself—there may be two murderers."

"Maybe there are." I clenched my jaw. "But one of them is *not* Bo Duff."

He stared at me. "What's wrong."

Careful. "I'm sick of this. That's what's wrong. Bo is being set up, and why the police can't see that is beyond me." I gestured toward the door. "Look, I need to finish here. Do you mind leaving?"

He opened his mouth to speak but shut it. Taking his jacket, he left.

I stood at the window and watched him drive away.

A thought danced out of reach. Something about the island and—

No, it was gone.

Speaking to DI Devlin felt more urgent than ever. I left a third message on his cell phone. All I could do.

I started on the jewelry again but found I no longer had the patience.

The only task remaining was the attic. I'd already decided to count the boxes and number them, making sure they were well sealed. Then I'd open as many as I had time for. If any furniture looked valuable, I'd take photographs. Hiring a local appraiser was fine, but if there was anything up there from Flora's time, I wanted to be the one to find it.

Blast. What was my brain trying to tell me? Something about the past, the island?

Then it came. That book on island history. I'd forgotten about that. Before the Tartan Ball, someone had been looking into island history.

I found Becca's cell number on a list near Elenor's phone. When Becca picked up, I asked, "That big book about the Isle of Glenroth— do you remember who was looking at it?"

"Sure. Tom Mallory. He was interested in the families who came with Captain Arnott. I told him there were additional resources at the Historical Society."

I thanked her and disconnected. Why would Tom be interested in the island's settlers?

I dialed the extension for Nancy and Frank's cottage.

Nancy answered. "Everything all right? I sent Tom over to see how you were getting along."

Thanks a bunch. "Everything's fine. I was wondering how many of the families who settled here in 1809 still live on the island. I thought you might know."

"You mean besides the Arnotts and the Guthries? Well, there were the Murchies, but they sold the pharmacy and moved south last year. The Moffatts own a flower shop in the village. They left in mid-October to spend the winter in Spain. There may be others. I'm not sure. Why do you want to know?"

"Curiosity. Probably wasting my time."

I replaced the receiver, feeling hopeless. I was wasting my time. Family names change with marriage. I hardly had time to trace gene-alogies. Nor could I ask Tom the names of all the females in his family line. I was missing something, the one puzzle piece that would make the picture clear.

Outside, the storm howled. A downspout rattled. From some-where above me came the creaking of wood. Just the shifting of an old house, but it did sound eerily like footsteps.

I squared my shoulders. I'd had my fill of ghosts, lies, and attempts to frighten me. I really had.

If someone was up there, I was going to find out. Once and for all.

Chapter
Thirty-Two

I scrabbled in Elenor's hall chest for a flashlight.

Someone had been sneaking into the hotel—I'd witnessed that myself—but how?

The why was easy. Everyone knew the silver tray had been found in the attic. Why not assume there were other treasures up there as well? Had Tom come back to avenge his mother and reclaim some valuable antique that belonged to his family? For a moment I wondered if the attic was where Elenor had found the marquetry casket, but that wasn't possible. She'd refused to go up there. More importantly, the casket's condition was too fine to have spent years in a place where the temperature and moisture levels fluctuated with the seasons.

Lightning split the air, followed by the rumble of thunder. Armed with the flashlight, I started up the main staircase. The third step squeaked. *Yikes.*

If this were one of those B movies, I'd be shouting: "Don't go up there, you idiot."

Well, an idiot I might be, but I was an idiot with a bad temper and no other options.

When I reached the third-floor landing, I ran my hand along the right side of the wall as I'd seen Bill do. The fourth panel clicked almost soundlessly and popped out an inch or so. I pulled it open and saw a narrow staircase rising into blackness. I climbed, steadying myself on the wall and praying Becca had told the truth about spider webs. At the top, I paused to listen. The beams and rafters creaked in the wind like the bones of an old woman.

"Who's there?" My voice cracked.

Good thing there was no response. My only weapon was a mini Maglite.

I shone it in a wide arc.

Oh my golly. Boxes, once neatly sealed and stacked, had been ripped open, their contents strewn over the diagonal planking. Sheets had been pulled off the old furniture and left in piles.

Moving forward, I kept one eye on the floor so as not to trip and the other on the massive hip rafters that slanted downward. I directed the beam of light methodically around the large, open space.

I almost missed it.

Tucked into one of the eaves, partially concealed by a supporting timber, was a small carriage trunk. My flashlight shone on studded leather hide, a high-domed lid, and what looked like hand-forged banding and hinges. Late eighteenth century was my guess. Excellent condition.

Moving closer, I saw I was wrong. Someone had forced the latch, damaging the hide and leaving flakes of oxidized iron beneath the smashed plate and locking mechanism. Recently done. Crouching, I lifted the domed lid, supporting its weight as I swung it back to rest on the attic floor.

Folded inside the trunk was an old quilt, skillfully pieced, a geometric pattern in red and white. That rang a bell. Hugh Guthrie mentioned a quilt in his novel, one that Gowyn pieced, using the red calico from Flora's old summer dress. Even if the quilt wasn't connected to Flora, it should be conserved and displayed in the museum. I touched the delicate fabric and felt something solid within the folds.

Propping the flashlight on the beam, I lifted out the bundle and laid it on the floor. Wrapped inside the quilt was a framed portrait about eighteen inches square. I focused the light for a better look and felt an instinctive flash of anger. The canvas had been vandalized, sliced through from corner to corner. But not recently. The torn fibers were stiff and dark with age.

Even in its present condition, the image was compelling. A young woman sat in three-quarter view, her face turned to fix the viewer's gaze with grave, black-lashed eyes. Her dark hair was parted in the middle. Ringlets framed her face. She wore a pale-yellow, high-waisted dress with a square neckline. A red paisley shawl was draped loosely over her shoulders. One small hand lay palm up in her lap. The other bore a heavy ring and rested on a dark object in the lower left corner. I moved the light closer. The object resolved into a rectangular block, covered faintly with tiny creatures and a checkered banding.

I gasped. The marquetry casket. The woman in the portrait had to be Flora Arnott.

I lowered my other knee to steady myself.

Who hated Flora enough to slash her portrait? Her killer?

My thoughts spun wildly. Flora Arnott. Glenroth. Guthrie's novel. The link I'd been looking for was the casket. But where was it now, and more to the point, how had the thief spirited it out of the house?

According to Agnes, there were only two exits from the east wing—either through the doorway to reception (I'd been blocking the way) or through the door at the end of the hall (which was locked). *Unless*—I felt a frisson of excitement—there was a third way out, a way not even Agnes knew about.

I followed the logic, step by step, as my mother had taught me.

The east-wing hallway, like the hallways on the second and third floors, was paneled with oak, installed sometime in the late eighteenth or early nineteenth century. The paneling on the third floor concealed a hidden access to the attic.

Could there be something similar in the east wing? Why hadn't I thought of it before?

Leaving the portrait, I practically slid down the three flights of stairs.

Reaching the east wing, I began with the panels closest to Elenor's flat and moved methodically toward the end of the hall. I pressed each panel, finding nothing.

I was a third of the way back, working on the opposite wall, when I heard a faint click. My heart stopped. A panel swung open to reveal a dim passageway lined with shelves.

There, on one of the shelves, sat the marquetry casket.

Following the passageway would have to wait. Puzzling over why the thief had stashed the casket there would have to wait, too.

I'd just had an astonishing thought.

I ran with the casket to Elenor's flat and set it on the dining room table. I turned the key and opened the lid. Closing my eyes, I ran my fingertips over the faded red leather.

There it was—a blip.

The light was against me. Tipping the casket on its side, I shone the flashlight. A tiny hole appeared in the morocco, the edges slightly worn. I'd seen something like that once in an antique tea caddy with a hidden compartment. The hole gave access to a wooden spring lock, released by a metal bodkin.

Fresh out of bodkins. I looked around for a substitute.

Of course. The paper clip I'd stepped on earlier. Elenor must have discovered the hole, recognized what it was, and used the paper clip as a tool.

I retrieved the clip and, tipping the casket again, inserted the end of the wire into the tiny hole in the leather. I held my breath and pushed. Something gave way. The molding on one side popped, and I caught a musty, slightly fishy odor that reminded me of the cheap leather handbag I'd bought once in an open-air market in Spain.

Fitted within the base of the casket, perfectly concealed by the molding, was a shallow drawer, about two inches deep. The drawer was empty, but it hadn't always been empty.

Like the main compartment, the hidden drawer was lined with red morocco leather, but here, protected from the light, it was as red as blood. Except for a dark, ugly stain—I grabbed the ruler—roughly rectangular, about eight inches by five.

I sat back and let my brain work.

You put something in a secret compartment because you don't want anyone to know it's there. Something important or precious. And unless what you hide is weightless, a shift in orientation would betray its presence, as Guthrie's book had on Saturday when I tipped the casket to look for markings. Unless you pack the extra space with wadding.

Using my lighted magnifier, I examined the interior of the compartment again.

The first things I noticed were several fragments of yellowed paper that looked suspiciously like newsprint. Could this be where Elenor had found the newspaper accounts of the deaths in 1810? In the absence of a better theory, I'd go with that one.

The second thing I noticed was a shred of buff-colored fiber caught in one of the sliding dovetail joins. *Yes! Wadding.* I love the antiques business.

Examining the stain more closely, I saw that it was old. The edges were uneven, with the deepest color toward the center and the edges lighter and sort of fluted. I knew from experience that meant moisture, the source of the musty smell. Something wet, or at least damp, had been stored in the compartment. The fishy odor suggested poorly tanned leather.

I'd told Tom on Monday that all I needed to do was connect the dots. Except there weren't many to connect then. Now, with more dots, a picture was forming.

When Elenor had shown me the casket on Friday, I'd asked her where she found it. She'd said, "That's the secret." I pictured her touching the casket.

This is where it all began. I'll tell you the whole story after the ball.

Elenor's story began with the casket. She'd found the hidden compartment and something inside more valuable—or dangerous?—than newspaper clippings. In her final phone message, she'd asked me to keep something for her. She'd used the word *hidden*.

Where would Elenor hide something valuable? Possibly in her flat, except the police had gone over every inch of the place. Short of pulling up the floorboards, there was nowhere else to look.

Where else? The obvious place was her safe deposit box. And, yes, the bank employee remembered Elenor leaving on the nineteenth with a small tote bag. She'd taken something away, and she'd gone from there to the Historical Society.

Light dawned.

That's what *HS* meant. Not Hewie Spurgeon—the Historical Society. That's where Elenor went the night she was killed, the night she left the message on my cell phone.

Need you to keep something . . . hidden . . .

My brain leapt from dot to dot like a gazelle.

Elenor had found something in the casket, something she wanted to keep secret until I arrived because she needed advice. She'd hidden it, first in her safe deposit box and then at the Historical Society.

Guthrie's book lay on the towel-draped table in the bathroom. Retrieving it, I turned to page 112. *HS6uprtgrnlft51bluedn3rd.*

I copied the code into my notebook. Scooping up my jacket, my cell phone, Elenor's Burberry umbrella, and the flashlight, I turned out the lights and locked the door.

If you had any sense, you'd call for help, carped the voice in my head.

"Shut up," I said out loud. What had being sensible ever gotten me? Besides, who would I call? Devlin (even if he answered his phone) wouldn't believe me. I certainly wasn't going to call Tom. Nancy and Frank would insist I call the police, and that would take time.

Time was the one thing I didn't have. If I waited sensibly until morning, the hearing would take place and Bo Duff would be taken to jail or remanded to an asylum.

I couldn't fail him now, not when the answer lay so close. Rain was falling in sheets, but I didn't care. For the first time since Saturday morning, I had hope.

I was rushing out the door when Nancy appeared in the hallway from the kitchen.

She stared at the umbrella. "Where are you going?"

I arranged my face in a smile and lied.

Chapter
Thirty-Three

❧

The rain came at an angle, soaking my jeans to the knees. I tipped Elenor's Burberry umbrella forward and felt an icy trickle hit the back of my neck and slither down my spine. I could have taken the car, but the Holdens would have seen the lights and tried to stop me. This was something I needed to do alone and now.

When I reached the stone bridge, I dimmed the flashlight. Below me, the ribbon of Burn o'Ruadh curled, black as old blood. I kept going, following the bobbing circle of light at my feet.

The Historical Society was dark. Good. I felt for the lock, fumbling with Elenor's key. The door opened and I stepped inside, nearly jumping out of my skin as the bell chimed.

Crap, crap, crap. The last thing I needed was the Arnott twins rushing over to make sure I wasn't damaging the family treasures. I peered over my shoulder. No curtains twitched. No faces appeared at the window.

The flashlight cast a narrow beam around the room. This wasn't going to work. I needed to see. I felt for the wall switch and the lights blinked on. If Penny and Cilla came over, demanding to know what I was doing, I'd tell them . . . well, I'd think of something.

I started with the rolltop desk. Sometimes old desks have hidden compartments, too. I tried all the variations I knew—pressing on panels, feeling for levers, trying to slide pieces of trim to one side or the other. Nothing. I opened each drawer in turn, finding only a box of Kleenex, a half-full bottle of whiskey—Glenfiddich, no less—and a stack of paper cups. Was Guthrie a secret drinker? Dropping to my knees, I checked beneath the desk and behind it to see if something had been taped there. Nothing was.

Pulling out my notebook, I read the code again: *HS6uprtgrnlft-51bluedn3rd*. Several patterns were obvious—a series of numbers (6, 51, 3), what might be orientations (upright, left, down?), and colors (green, blue, red—or did *3rd* mean third?).

That didn't help.

I decided to write it out another way. Turning to the next page in the notebook, I wrote *Historical Society* and under that *6 upright green*. I looked around for six of anything standing upright, green or otherwise. Nothing. But maybe Elenor meant "up right" instead of "upright." She hadn't been careful about spacing. She knew what she meant.

Crossing out *6 upright green*, I wrote *6 up right green*. Under that I wrote *left 51 blue*, and then *down 3 red*. It sounded like a board game, a series of moves you might make with a game piece—places to land and go from there. That made sense.

The contour map table had lots of green and some blue, representing the sea. Maybe the colors led to a certain location on the island. A brilliant thought, except there wasn't a speck of red on the map.

A green-and-blue vase on the visitor counter held a sparse bouquet of red silk geraniums. I pulled out the flowers, finding a penny and some dust.

What would Elenor have noticed? Well, the books. The room was lined with books, most bound in shades of brown and black but some in other colors as well. I took the notepad and read the numbers again—6, 51, 3. Elenor had written *6 up right green*.

A large green cloth book lay flat on the bottom shelf. That didn't fit. No way to go *up* to the bottom shelf. But there was another green book near me, at shoulder height. I pulled it out. The title was Latin, something about flowers—*Flora*, a compendium of the wildflowers of the Hebrides. Coincidence? My heart quickened.

I counted the shelves. The green book was on the sixth shelf from the bottom, on the right-hand side of the bookcase. I fanned through the pages, finding nothing but an old bookplate with the owner's name written in elaborate copperplate: CHARLES EDWARD STUART ARNOTT, 1889. Some people just won't let go of the dream.

The next set of directions presumably started from that point: *left 51 blue*. I counted to the left and—my golly, the fifty-first book was blue. Beautiful bonnie blue. A medical textbook from Doc Arnott's days at university. I examined it carefully, finding only faded underlining in pencil, and replaced it on the shelf.

Following the pattern, the final set of directions read *down 3 red*. It must mean "down three shelves," but the books weren't precisely lined up. I counted down three shelves and—sure enough—a book bound in a sort of coppery red sat just out of line. This had to be the end point of Elenor's directions.

The Steam Locomotive, Its Failures and How to Deal with Them was a slim volume published in 1927, a primer with questions and answers. What interest could Elenor—or Doc Arnott, for that matter—have had in locomotive steam engines? I turned the book upside down and shook it to see if anything would fall out. Nothing did. I flipped through every one of the eighty-three pages to see if someone had written a note. No one had. I checked the binding to see if someone had slipped something between the backing and the spine. Nope.

I frowned. The book was small enough to fit in the hidden compartment, but it wasn't old enough, and it wouldn't have left a stain. Another dead end.

Use that good brain of yours, I heard my mother's voice say.

Okay, if the book itself wasn't the important thing, what was? The only unusual feature was the size—tall and slim—but the spine had been pulled forward so it matched the depth of the books on either side.

Leaving a space behind.

I pulled out several more books and bent to look, my heart in my throat.

Something was there. Reaching in, I pulled out a bundle of old and deeply stained homespun fabric, held together by a very modern rubber band. I removed the band and unfolded the cloth. Inside was a small handmade book, bound in split, bark-colored animal hide. A single word had been hand-tooled in gold on the cover.

Diary.

* * *

I carried the diary to the rolltop desk and opened the cover with care, so as not to dislodge the hand-sewn pages. The handwriting alone placed it as early nineteenth century—Spencerian, right-slanted, faded tea-colored ink. The first pages were badly stained and illegible. After about ten pages, I could begin to make out words and phrases.

I knew the voice.

13th November
What I have suspected is now certain! When I think of the joy I shall . . .

A large stain blotted out several lines.

'When the child is born, you will sail with me to the Indies' said he. 'You must promise me a son, Flora, an heir to . . .

Flora was pregnant.

The next paragraphs were impossible to read. I flipped the pages, reading what I could.

> . . . *confined to my chamber . . . very ill . . .*
> . . . *solicitous for my health. Mrs. Fraser assures him this will pass, but James seems . . .*
> *Perhaps the deaths of his first sons has . . .*

> *2ⁿᵈ December*
>   *James insists I remain in my chamber. He will not hear of my going . . . no one is allow'd to visit except Mrs. Fraser. I fear he may be . . .*
>   *. . . A fortnight has passed since last I laid eyes on him. Why does he not come to cheer me? What have I done to . . .*

The first fully legible entry was dated mid-January. Flora must have been three or four months pregnant.

> *13ᵗʰ January 1810*
>   *James no longer comes at all. Perhaps it is my growing belly that repulses him. For my health he has every regard. I am allow'd dried fruits & vegetables with a thin broth & and an egg every 3 days. Mrs. Fraser makes a kind of tea from chamomile & crushed oyster shells, but I believe this makes my sickness worse. No one else, not even Gowyn, is allow'd in my chamber. Oh! I am lonely & sick at heart. How shall I survive 'til my lying-in? Perhaps solitude plays tricks with the mind, but I can only conclude James no longer loves me. My hope is that once the bairn has safely arriv'd, he will return to himself.*

> *17ᵗʰ January*
>   *At long last I am better. Still James does not come to me, nor Gowyn. I feel like a prisoner.*

21ˢᵗ January 1810

Events of such a disturbing nature have transpir'd that I am barely able to hold my pen. This morning Mrs. Fraser brought me tea as usual. 'Your husband has gone to Glasgow on a legal matter, madam, & is not expected to return 'til the end of the week,' she inform'd me.

I thanked her for her kindness & waited for her to take her leave as usual, but she did not. Instead she began to weep.

'Whatever is the matter, Mrs. Fraser?' said I.

She merely shook her head. Then, taking a letter from the pocket of her apron, she placed it in my hand. 'Read for yourself, madam,' said she, 'and you will understand.'

The letter was dated a month after the wedding. I shall not reproduce the entire contents, but the final lines are burned on my soul.

'My darling James, I wait patiently for your return, knowing I must endure our separation a while longer. By summer you will be in my arms again & I promise all will be well. Your little Rosamund sends you a kiss. I remain yr most affectionate wife, Maria Amalia.' Folded within a twist of paper was a lock of dark hair, tied with a ribbon of palest yellow.

'What can this mean?' I cried.

This is the story Mrs. Fraser told: My husband, if that is what he must be called, has a wife in the Indies, a woman called Maria Amalia of mixed Spanish & Arawak blood. She has given him a daughter, Rosamund, who is not yet five years of age. A vast fortune is entailed upon the Capt. with one stipulation: that he produce a lawful male heir of Scottish blood.

I am not the first to be used thus. His cousin, Cecily, unable to bear a living son, was—my hand shakes as I write—cast into the sea, while onboard the ship carrying them to the Indies. He rid himself of her as soon as she was no longer of use. When my child is born, this will be my Fate as well.

'Do not imagine you will escape, madam,' said Mrs. Fraser. 'You may board the ship, but you will not arrive in the Islands. You must leave this house or forfeit your life.'

'Why do you and your husband not leave him?' I demanded.

'Because, I am ashamed to say it,' she sighed. 'Mr. Fraser has a price on his head. If the Capt. suspects any disloyalty, Mr. Fraser will be taken up & thrown in prison.'

'What of Gowyn?'

'She is banish'd from the house & made to work in the dairy, madam. We send news of you when we can.'

'And Joseph?'

'Ah, Joseph. Have you not suspected? Joseph & his sister Rachel are his slaves. Joseph bears a deep hatred for the Capt., but if he takes his freedom, his sister will pay the price.'

'Oh! Whatever shall I do?' I cried, throwing myself on her breast.

'Do not distress yourself, madam. Think of your bairn. This letter must return to its place. After that, we shall see what can be done. I give you my solemn promise. Mr. Fraser & I will not allow you to be harmed.'

I must keep this diary well hidden. My only hope is escape & if I die in the attempt, I shall consider it not loss but gain.

I stared at the page in horror. The handsome Captain James Arnott, soon to be memorialized with a statue on the Glenroth village green, had been a slave owner, a bigamist, and a murderer.

And that wasn't all. The novel Dr. Guthrie claimed to have so meticulously researched was no work of fiction. It was the actual diary of Flora Arnott, volume one. The crumbling book in my hands was volume two.

I turned quickly to the final entry.

2nd March 1810

 Gowyn & I leave at first light under the protection of an itinerant peddler known to the Frasers & paid well for the service. We shall travel north on horseback as far as the turf beds, then by boat toward the Pt. of Sleat & Arisaig. Someone is to meet us on the road near the bay & conduct us from there to a kinswoman of Mrs. Fraser near Inverlochy. From thence I know not, only that we shall reach Gretna in some days. From there the border is but two miles. Gowyn & I shall be in England in a fortnight.

 We take only a small valise, my beautiful casket & a few pieces of silver to sell for our bread. How I shall provide for us after that I know not. I only know I shall never return to Scotland. I think now only of my bairn. I feel him move in my belly & rejoice that he is strong. He will never know the truth of his father.

 Mrs. Fraser has packed a trunk which she will forward to us when she is able. Joseph is to create a diversion so that he (I swear never to speak his name again) does not discover our absence until we are safely away. These friends risk their lives for us.

Flora's final words.

I held the little book to my heart. Arnott had obviously discovered the plan and pursued them, disguising the murders as a clan attack. Nothing could be proven now, of course. Except one thing. In presenting the diary as a work of fiction, Hugh Guthrie had perpetrated a fraud.

He must have killed Elenor to save his reputation.

I reached for my cell phone, feeling almost giddy. Tom was innocent. Bo Duff would be safe. Everything would be all right.

Wrong.

I wasn't alone.

Guthrie stood in the shadows near the door to the Annex. He held a tire iron—damn that gas station display. I felt strangely disembodied, as if I were observing the scene from some remote vantage point. We were in a bubble, the two of us, and time had slowed to a crawl.

"Is that the second diary?" Guthrie's voice was as dry as dead leaves.

"Yes," I heard myself say. "I found it."

"I knew it was here somewhere. I couldn't search with those blasted volunteers poking around. I was afraid one of them would find it first."

Keep him calm. Keep him talking. Isn't that what they tell you to do? "So you came back tonight to look. Where's your car?"

"In the bushes up the road. How did you find the diary?"

"Elenor left directions." My hand moved toward the notebook but stopped when he visibly tensed. "I wrote them out. Would you like to see?"

"Read it to me."

I did, explaining the meaning of the code.

His face contorted. "This will ruin me." He gulped air, staring into the mid-distance. "I don't think . . . I don't think I can handle that."

"Wouldn't it be best to admit what you've done, pay back the money, and—"

"No." He took a step toward me, holding the tire iron. "It's not the money, don't you see? It's the shame, the gossip. My academic reputation. That's all I have left."

I wanted to say he should have thought of that earlier. "Where did you find the first diary? I'd really like to know."

He dragged a fist across his mouth. "Four years ago. The twins donated a box of old books to the Historical Society. Not part of the library, just some old books tied up with twine in bundles of five or six. Cilla must have packed them because Penny wouldn't have been so careless. There it was, the diary, in one of the bundles. The fabric cover was torn. Most of the pages were loose. I recognized the importance immediately."

"Where is it now?"

"Hidden in my closet. I couldn't bring myself to destroy it. The curse of the historian." He gave a mirthless laugh. "At the time, the head of my department was trying to push me out. I hadn't published anything for years, and the number of students interested in ancient stone circles wasn't sufficient to justify an entire course. I thought the diary would be a chance to vindicate myself—local history, popular appeal. Originally I planned to edit the diary, get the twins' permission to publish. When I probed, I realized they didn't know the diary existed. That's when it occurred to me I could publish it as my own work, a work of fiction. No harm, I thought. A bit of local history to sell in the island shops. I had no idea it would become so popular.

"You can't imagine the pressure." He gestured with the tire iron. "Not only the pressure of producing a sequel, which was never going to happen, but the pressure of interviews, book signings. I never wanted to be famous." He groaned and slumped onto a battered metal footlocker.

"Why did you agree to a sequel in the first place?"

He looked up. "The first diary ends before the wedding. The publisher said that wouldn't fly—I had to include the wedding day. I tried writing it, but I couldn't reproduce Flora's voice. So I told them I'd planned a second volume, beginning with the wedding day and ending with Flora's death."

"You didn't know there was a second diary?"

"Not until the Tartan Ball."

How long could I keep him talking? Someone at the hotel would miss me. Eventually. "You found the carriage trunk in the attic, didn't you?"

"What attic?" The corners of his mouth turned down. "What are you talking about?"

Whoa. Guthrie wasn't the one who'd done the damage in the attic? "Never mind. Tell me about Elenor."

He groaned again. "When the book took off, her attitude toward me changed. She asked me to take her to dinner. She started talking about the life we could have together—travel, adventure, a new start. I honestly don't know how it happened. I know I never proposed, but after a few weeks, it was simply taken for granted we'd get married. I was bewitched, and the best part was escaping from my mother. Elenor promised to handle everything."

"But wasn't she expecting a sequel, too?"

"Of course, but I figured I wouldn't have to deal with that for a long time. I even thought of scenarios—a ransomware infection, losing the entire manuscript and having to start over. I was sure something would come to me."

"Then Elenor found the second diary."

He nodded. His face was pale, but his grip on the tire iron looked secure. "About a month ago, Elenor told me she'd found a small chest at the hotel, something special. She was going to sell it in London, so the twins wouldn't make a fuss. The problem was I'd already seen the chest in the Collections Depot. Bo Duff brought it with some boxes from the Arnotts. I knew Elenor stole it, but I kept my mouth shut, like the coward I am."

Elenor must have seen the casket and realized its worth. The money she'd get from selling it would tide her over nicely until she got her hands on Guthrie's trust fund.

His lip curled in disgust. "After that my eyes were opened. Elenor would be worse than my mother. I started fantasizing about disappearing. I even considered faking my own death, but I couldn't figure out how to pull it off. At the ball, when Elenor told everyone I'd finish the new book soon, I knew it had to end." He looked up, his eyes blazing. "It will end." He struck the floor with the tire iron. "Tonight."

I flinched, imagining what that metal rod would do to my skull.

"So you were the one who phoned Elenor that night. How did you get out of the house without your mother hearing?"

"I put a sleeping pill in her nightly drink. Elenor had given me a few of her pills for my insomnia. Once Mother was snoring, I drove to the Gas and Go. Bo Duff was filling up his truck, so I pulled behind the building and waited. After he'd gone, I called Elenor from the phone box and told her we had to talk. She wasn't pleased, I can tell you, but I insisted. She said we had to meet at the Historical Society so Agnes wouldn't know. It was after midnight when she arrived. I told her I couldn't go through with the wedding. She could keep the ring. A steep price to pay, but I needed a way out. That's when she told me about the second diary."

"She threatened to expose you."

"No." He looked truly baffled. "She said we'd get married as planned, and I'd publish the second diary as the sequel. She joked about the sensation it would create. 'They'll think you discovered the truth in your research,' she said. 'That ridiculous statue won't be raised on a pedestal—it'll be tarred and feathered.' And she laughed and laughed.

"She told me she'd hidden the diary somewhere safe—I figured it was here—and I could begin work on the sequel as soon as we were married. She even suggested we move the wedding up. She got out the bottle of Scotch we keep in the office and poured a toast. That's when I knew I was trapped. Either face ruin or spend the rest of my life under her thumb."

"So the Mucky Ducks the police found in the lake are yours."

He nodded miserably. "One of the toes melted in a bonfire. Mother will recognize it immediately."

"And Agnes?" I still held my cell phone. I moved my thumb, feeling for the reset tab on the side. *Push. Swipe. Find the phone icon.* Could I dial 999 without looking? Would he notice?

He groaned again. "Just when I thought I was safe, when all I had to do was find the second diary and destroy it, Agnes phoned. She said she had information that would implicate me. Was that yesterday?" His forehead glistened with perspiration. "I agreed to meet her in the woods near the creek. She told me she'd followed Elenor the night of the ball and heard our entire conversation."

"What did she want?" I gripped the phone. I'd pushed buttons, but were they the right ones?

"Money, of course. Two hundred thousand in cash to keep her mouth shut. But the more she talked, the more I realized she hadn't heard anything. When I challenged her, she said, 'It doesn't matter. All I have to do is tell the police you were here.' She was right, of course. And I knew it would never end. She'd demand more and more." He moaned, covering his face with his free hand.

"Killing me won't help."

His head shot up. "What?"

"I've recorded everything." I held up my cell phone, praying the bluff would work. "I recorded your confession, and I'm emailing it right now to my mother in Ohio." I pushed a random button and tried to look triumphant. "She'll call the police. You won't get away with it."

"Get away with it?" His face twisted. He bent his head, and his shoulders began to shake.

Was he going into shock? Was he falling apart?

No, he was laughing. "You think *I* killed Elenor and Agnes?"

"You didn't?"

"Of course not. What do you take me for?"

"Why are you holding a tire iron?"

"For protection. When I saw lights, I thought someone had broken in again." He wiped his eyes and stood. "Look, I know this has to come out. I must go and prepare Mother." He dropped the iron with a clang and disappeared into the Annex. Without the diary.

For a moment I considered the possibility that Guthrie was delusional. If he wasn't the killer, who was? It had to be someone who stood to lose as much or more if the truth about Arnott came out.

Then I knew. Everything—the footsteps in the night, the missing items from the hotel and the Historical Society, my cottage searched, the disarray in the attic, the secret passageway.

I picked up my cell phone and scrolled to the number of the police station in Mallaig. I'd begun to dial when the door opened.

Penny Arnott stepped deftly over the mat. She pointed her father's army revolver at my chest. "Hang up and give me the diary."

Chapter
Thirty-Four

❧

I pressed END and held up the phone for Penny to see.

"Slide it to me on the floor." Her eyes were shiny marbles. "Now the book." She closed the space between us in two long steps. Keeping the gun trained on me, she pocketed the phone and the diary. "Thanks. Saves me a lot of trouble."

Maybe playing dumb would work. "Dr. Guthrie killed two people over that diary, Penny. Don't you think we should call the police?"

That cracked Penny up. She threw her head back and hooted, her lips stretched over a tangle of yellow teeth.

"What's so funny?"

"You." Penny was still chuckling. "Doc Guthrie didn't kill anybody."

"How do you know?"

Penny cocked her head like a turkey vulture spotting a fresh carcass. "Because I did. You're not as smart as you look."

I'll give you that one. What now? Penny did like the sound of her own voice. "How did you know about the diary?"

"Found it in that fancy little wooden chest. Pack of lies."

"That was clever, Penny. Most people wouldn't have discovered the secret compartment. And the little chest is called a casket." Impending death is no excuse for sloppy terminology. "Where did you find it?"

"Didn't *find* it anywhere." Penny's eyebrows formed an angry line. "Belongs to us. Elenor stole it."

"Why didn't you destroy the diary as soon as you discovered it?"

"I was *going to*," Penny screeched. "Decided to burn it in the fireplace, but couldn't do that with Cilla around, see? She'd want to know what I was doing. She'd insist on reading it. Couldn't let that happen. Cilla idolizes that man."

Was she talking about Captain Arnott or Hugh Guthrie? I stared in amazement as a tear rolled down Penny's cheek.

She swiped at the tear with the revolver. "Before I got my chance, Cilla gave the thing to the Historical Society."

I remembered Becca's story about Penny bursting in and accusing Elenor of taking something Cilla had donated by mistake. "Why would Cilla donate the casket to the Historical Society?"

"For the new Arnott display. Girl's not Mensa material, in case you hadn't noticed. Have to watch her like a hawk."

"So that's why you wanted to get into Elenor's flat. You knew she had the casket and hoped she hadn't found the diary yet."

"Wrong. Knew she'd found the diary when she said the doc's second book would be a big surprise. Poor wee Flora." Penny sneered. "Liar is more like it. Traitor. Back-stabber. Turned poor Captain Arnott's servants against him. Got what she deserved."

"Penny, have you read the diary? As soon as the baby was born, Flora would have had a tragic accident. Arnott murdered his first wife. He already had a wife on the plantation. That's bigamy. Not to mention that he bought and sold slaves on the side, and almost certainly murdered Flora and Gowyn."

Penny's face turned an ugly shade of fuchsia. "Shut yer gob!" Balls of spit exploded from her mouth like grape shot. "You think I'll allow the name of Arnott to be dragged through the mud?" She gestured wildly with the gun. "They'll take away our statue. Break Cilla's heart." She took a menacing step toward me. "I won't let that happen."

I took a step back. "I see your point. You had to do something."

Penny's lips curled horribly. "You're a liar too. You'll tell."

She's completely mad. "How did you know Elenor was here the night of the ball?"

Penny shrugged. "Heard the bell, saw the lights—like tonight. Agnes was here, too. You didn't know that, did you? The wee scunner was watching them through the window, so I snuck around to the other side. Elenor told the doc he had to publish the second diary. Agnes got spooked and ran off. The doc left, and Elenor started back to the hotel. 'Cept she wasn't doing so well. Collapsed by the stump. That's when I showed myself. She said the doc doped her."

Guthrie hadn't mentioned giving her drugs, but I wasn't in a position to argue the point.

"Told me to call for help." Penny flashed me a canny grin. "I said, 'Sure thing.' Went home, got the bow and arrow, and . . . whaaaap." Penny mimed a bow, cocking the gun back like an arrow.

I swallowed hard.

"Did you use a bow and arrow because of Flora?"

"No. First thing to hand. Forgot to ask where she hid the diary, though. Been trying to find it ever since—me and the doc." She chuckled, making it sound like a game of Hide the Thimble.

"You're the one who broke into my cottage the night of the ball. You put the note in my pocket and the one under my door. *DESTROY IT OR ELSE*. You stole the casket, and when you found the hidden drawer empty, you thought Elenor had given *me* the diary."

"Why else would Elenor invite you to the ball? She didn't like you."

Penny might be crazy, but her logic was impeccable. "You used the secret passageway to come and go without being seen. Clever."

"Cilla and I used to play hide-and-seek in there. No one could ever find us."

Of course. That's how the so-called ghost of Flora Arnott could vanish into thin air. No wonder Elenor was spooked. No wonder she thought she saw the ghost. "But why leave the casket in the passageway?"

"Couldn't take it home with Cilla there, could I? Besides, someone might have seen me carrying the thing. Planned to come back for it later, at night, when things calmed down."

"But why did you have to kill Agnes?"

"Don't you get it?" Penny tapped her temple with the gun. "She heard Elenor telling the doc about the second diary. I watched Doc Guthrie meet Agnes in the woods. She wanted him to give her money or she'd spill the beans. Couldn't risk that. So I waited till he was gone and—*thwack*." Now the gun was a knife. "She tried to run, but I got her."

Poor foolish Agnes. She hadn't heard a thing.

"Saw *you* there, too." Penny made a face. "When you found her."

"You shot at me."

"Never was a great distance shooter." She grinned and aimed the gun. "Now, at close range I never miss."

"When did you decide to use the Highland dirk?"

"When the doc showed it to you at the Historical Society. Made sense. Use the same weapons used back then. Throw people off the scent."

I cringed. I was running out of questions. "Who taught you to use the dirk?"

"Father. Taught me all the old Highland ways. Hobby of his. Used one of his old arrows on Elenor. Nice touch, don't you think?"

"And you planted the arrows in Bo Duff's garage."

"Easy peasy." Penny actually looked pleased with herself.

If I hadn't had that gun pointed at my head, I'd have slapped her. "What about Dr. Guthrie? Won't you have to kill him too?"

"He won't tell. Have to give all that money back, for one. He'd be ruined. Might even go to jail. Any more questions?" Penny waggled her head like a fond parent who knows her child is stalling at bedtime.

Oh, man. Could I drag this out long enough for someone to realize I was missing? "Are you the one who took the silver tray from the hotel. And the things from the Historical Society?"

"Certainly not." Penny looked almost prim. "That was Cilla. Only borrowing anyway. I put 'em all back."

Well, Penny's standards were unique. Murder? No problem. Kleptomania? Now that was embarrassing. "Um, tell me more about the Arnott family. What happened to James Arnott's son?"

Penny chuckled again, a deep throaty sound I found deeply disturbing. "Time's up," she snarled, and pushed the gun into my chest. "Turn around. Through the museum and out to the burn. That's where they found poor Captain Arnott. Shot through the head."

So that was it. My death would be the third and final recreation. First a bow and arrow, then a Highland dirk, now a gun. "You won't get away with it, Penny. Someone will hear the shot."

"I'll say I caught you breaking in. You attacked me. I had no choice." Penny prodded me with the gun. "Start walking."

We moved through the double doors into the museum. At least Penny wouldn't risk shooting me there. Might damage the precious Arnott memorabilia.

"Hurry up," Penny growled.

I shuddered, imagining the bullet tearing through my skull. Would Penny finish me off there or leave me bleeding to death? My children would be orphans. My mother would be left with no one to care for her in her old age.

Father, into Thy hands I commit—

Then I remembered that wonky leg.

The glass case of pocket watches was just ahead. I pictured Dora MacDonald with her bottle of Windex.

Which leg?

Right front corner. Yes, that was the weak one.

As I passed the case, I put the palm of my hand on the right front edge and pushed down hard, at the same time kicking out the wonky leg.

I leapt out of the way as the case came crashing down in an explosion of glass.

Watches skittered across the floor.

Penny screamed as she fell into the shards of broken glass. She still had the gun, though.

I ducked behind the Bonnie Prince and heard a pop as part of his belted plaid shattered.

Another pop and his sporran exploded. *Ouch.*

How many bullets did that revolver hold?

Penny scrambled to her feet. She was bleeding, but she held the gun with both hands.

Thud. A bullet lodged somewhere in Charlie's wooden body.

A few more seconds and my cover would be useless.

Instead of panicking, I felt a white-hot coil of anger inside me. My life was *not* going to end because some crazy woman didn't want to lose a statue. Eric and Christine were *not* going to have both parents die on the Isle of Glenroth. I was *not* going down without a fight.

Penny stepped closer, snarling with rage.

Wedging my back against the wall, I put my feet on Charlie's back, and pushed hard.

The statue tipped.

"Whaa—?" Penny fell backward, twisting out of the way as the statue landed with a boom and a crash of splinters. The gun went off. Sparks flew as the bullet severed one of the chains holding the Esso sign.

The sign swung like a pendulum into Penny's head. I heard a sickening crunch.

Everything happened at once.

An enormous dark shape careened into Penny on the floor. Strong arms scooped me up. *Tom?* As we rushed for the door, I caught a final glimpse of Penny, howling like a banshee, her head gushing blood. Standing over her, holding the gun, was—*Jackie MacDonald?*

Tom swept me outside. "Thank God, Kate. Thank God." The faint woodsy scent of his cologne was utterly sweet. He kissed me, and I felt tears, whether his or mine I couldn't tell.

Lights flashed. A siren screamed. Devlin's black Peugeot skidded to a stop, followed by two police cars and an emergency response vehicle. Someone clamped an oxygen mask over my face and I let them do it, thinking how nice it would be to sleep in Tom's arms.

Not yet.

I lifted the mask, feeling a jolt of pain. "Check on the Guthries. I'll explain later."

Chapter
Thirty-Five

Tom sat with me in the Accident & Emergency ward at the hospital on Skye. The place bustled with activity. Computer displays flashed. Nursing sisters scurried in and out, yanking curtains open and closing them again. From somewhere in the distance, a baby cried inconsolably.

My cubicle smelled like disinfectant. I thought of Bo. A nurse had cleaned blood from my face and hands, leaving the damp cloth in a kidney-shaped pan. A splinter from the wooden statue of Bonnie Prince Charlie had grazed the fleshy part of my right arm. A doctor had cleaned the wound, immobilized my arm, and given me a shot for pain. As soon as he signed the release papers, we could leave.

Tom blinked once and took a breath. "Seeing Penny with that gun, Kate, knowing there was nothing I could do that wouldn't put your life in further jeopardy . . . I couldn't have saved you. Thank God you had the presence of mind to do what you did."

More desperation than presence of mind, but why refuse a compliment?

He took my good hand and kissed it. "Fearless Kate."

I shook my head. "A long way from fearless."

"All right, then. If crazy women with guns don't frighten you, what does?"

"Heights. I have a fear of heights. And spiders."

He laughed.

A head appeared around the privacy curtain. Rob Devlin held a bouquet. He stood at the foot of my bed looking sheepish. "You okay?"

"I'm fine. What happened to Penny and Hugh Guthrie?"

"Haven't heard about Guthrie yet. Miss Arnott was transported to the district hospital in Inverness. She suffered multiple cuts, a concussion, and a pretty deep gash on her head. She should make a full recovery, physically anyway."

"And Cilla?"

"We sent a female constable. She called in to report they were drinking tea and looking at scrapbooks." He held out the bouquet. "I hate to admit it, Mrs. Hamilton, but you were a step ahead of us the whole time." He tossed Tom a set of keys. "Your car's in the lot. Near the kiosk." Then he pulled an envelope from inside his jacket and handed it to Tom. "I think you'll both find this of interest."

"What's in the envelope?" I asked when Devlin had gone.

"Something to read on the ride home."

"I just remembered. What was Jackie MacDonald doing at the Historical Society?"

"When you didn't show up for dinner," Tom said, "Frank and I went to search. Jackie met us on the road and insisted on coming along. We thought Guthrie was the killer. You can't imagine our shock when we saw Penny with that gun."

"Oh, I think I can."

"When the statue fell, Jackie dove for Penny. In case she tried to get off another shot. I just wanted to get you out of there."

"Penny's sturdy. I'll say that for her." I laughed and winced. The pain shot was wearing off. "She survived Charlie, the Esso sign, *and* Jackie MacDonald."

"Don't sell Jackie short. Under that bulk is the body of an athlete." We were silent for a moment. "You shouldn't have gone alone, Kate. Why didn't you call me?"

I told him everything.

"I didn't want to believe it, Tom. It made me sick. But once I figured out Elenor's affair with your father, I couldn't dismiss the possibility that you'd returned to the island to take revenge."

"Not revenge. Setting things right. I'd decided to confront Elenor. Figured she should take responsibility for what the affair did to our family. I never got the chance."

"And then you were always hanging around. I couldn't figure out why."

"Couldn't you, indeed?" He gave me that half smile.

"Why were you reading up on island history?"

"Oh, that. My father's mother was a Maxwell, one of the Lowland families who came to Glenroth with James Arnott. I was curious."

"And what *is* going on with you and Sofia? Why were you at the Lodge the night Agnes was killed?"

"Sofia's here illegally, Kate. She came on a temporary work permit fifteen years ago and never left. She told me the night of the ball. She's been terrified that the new owners of the hotel—or the police—would look into her background and deport her. I've been working with Devlin on her behalf. I went to the Lodge to give her the good news."

"That she won't have to return to Bulgaria?"

"She can stay, perhaps permanently. As a member of the Romani community, she can claim persecution." He stood. "I'm going to see about breaking you out of here. Nancy's got food ready at the hotel, along with plenty of questions."

Chapter
Thirty-Six

I sat with Tom and the remaining hotel staff at the oak table in the hotel kitchen. A turf fire simmered in the hearth. I was going to miss that toasty smell and the bone-warming heat.

Frank had propped the portrait of Flora Arnott on the counter, along with the red-and-white pieced quilt. Nancy served hot, sweet tea and a buttery round of shortbread. I broke off a massive wedge and tucked in. Tomorrow I'd regret the calories. Tonight I didn't care.

While Tom and I were at the hospital, Frank had located the secret passageway and followed it down a narrow staircase to the cellar. From there the twins could come and go through a wooden bulkhead door concealed in the bushes. They'd been using the passageway for years, keeping the hinges well oiled so they could slip in and out silently.

"I'm sure that's why Elenor was terrified as a child," I said. "She must have seen one of the twins and thought it was the ghost of Flora Arnott."

"There goes the legend," Becca said.

"Oh, no. The legend just changes. Now it's a story about a greedy father, an evil man, and a young woman who should have lived to write lots of diaries. It's about a loyal friend and a child who never got the chance to live."

"Do we know what's happened to Hugh Guthrie?" Nancy asked.

"Devlin called on our way back from Skye," Tom said. "Guthrie locked himself in his office with a bottle of whiskey and sleeping tablets. The police were about to break down the door when he came out. Stumbled out actually. He'd consumed a lot of whiskey but nothing else. He confessed to stealing the diary and passing it off as his own work."

"What would he have done if Elenor hadn't been murdered?" Nancy asked. "Would he have gone through with the wedding?"

"Probably, " I said. "And she would have held his forgery over his head forever. I almost feel sorry for him."

"Do you think he would have paid Agnes all that money?" Becca said.

"No choice," Tom said. "Guthrie told the deputies Agnes had written out a sort of confession. She called it her 'insurance policy,' in case Guthrie threatened her or refused to pay. The police found it in her desk and gave us a copy. Kate and I read it on the ride home."

"So who *had* been threatening Elenor?" Becca asked. "Was it Penny?"

"Agnes," I said, earning a few shocked looks. "She'd eavesdropped on a phone conversation between Elenor and her solicitor. If Elenor sold the hotel, Agnes faced a future with no home, no job, and no money. Knowing how superstitious Elenor was, Agnes hoped to frighten her into stopping the negotiations."

"Agnes went to Elenor's flat after the ball," Tom said. "In the guise of helping her sleep, Agnes fed her a hot toddy laced with two sleeping tablets. Apparently Elenor got chatty when she was under the influence, and Agnes hoped to learn something she could use to her advantage. She didn't know Elenor had already taken two of her own sleeping tablets."

"But why did she follow Elenor?" Becca asked. "Was she trying to find the second diary?"

"She didn't know about the diary," Tom said. "When Agnes saw Elenor leave the house, she panicked. She knew the sedatives would be taking effect, and Elenor wouldn't be safe out there in the storm. As angry as she was, she didn't want Elenor to die. So she followed her to the Historical Society and watched through a window as Elenor met Hugh Guthrie. She was trying to hear what they were saying when she lost her balance and fell into a bush. Fearing she'd be discovered, she ran all the way back to the house."

"That's hard to picture," Becca said. "No wonder she was limping the next day."

"When the police arrived in the morning, the first thought that entered Agnes's head was that she'd killed Elenor with the concoction of sedatives and alcohol. She assumed the police had come to arrest her."

Nancy sighed. "How's Margaret Guthrie taking it?"

"Stoically," I said. "She's disowned her son completely."

"What will happen to Bo?" Nancy asked.

"All charges dropped," Tom said. "He'll be released tomorrow into Brenda's care."

"I've offered to pick them up at the clinic in the morning," Frank said, speaking for the first time.

An uneasy silence fell on the room. We all had the same questions: could Bo ever recover from the trauma he'd experienced, and what would Brenda decide about his future?

Nancy whisked away my empty plate. "Time for you to get some sleep, lass. There's a funeral tomorrow."

DI Devlin came through the door from reception, carrying the casket. "I thought you might appreciate a final look, Mrs. Hamilton." He placed the casket on the table and handed me the paper clip. "I'm sure we'd all like to see the secret compartment."

Everyone watched as I released the spring lock and the drawer popped open. "This is where Flora Arnott concealed her second diary, proof of her husband's guilt. He probably never knew it was there."

As the others marveled, I laid my hand on the old wood and held my breath.

My fingertips tingled. My cheeks grew hot, and my heart thumped. Was there something more, something yet to be discovered?

I watched as Frank slid the concealed drawer in and out. For the first time, I noticed that the hidden compartment didn't span the full width of the casket.

I slid my hand, palm up, into the secret drawer, feeling my way along the underside of the main compartment. At the back, almost beyond the reach of my fingers, I felt some sort of pin. Without really knowing why, I pushed on it, and the drawer popped completely out.

"Hand me my handbag," I told Tom. Grabbing my flashlight, I bent down and peered inside. "Something's there. Help me tip it."

In the end we had to shake the casket before it gave up its secret, a tiny papier-mâché snuff box, the lid painted with the image of Bonnie Prince Charlie.

"*Jings*," Nancy said in a reverent voice.

I held my breath as I opened the hinged top.

Curled inside was a lock of red hair. And a scrap of paper, on which was written in a slanted, flowing hand, *Thank you & farewell. Charles Edward Stuart. 19th Sept 1746.*

For a moment no one spoke.

Then I started to cry.

Chapter Thirty-Seven

～

Thursday, November 3

The morning of Elenor's funeral, the Glenroth islanders awoke to a layer of frost on trees, hedges, and postboxes. Before dressing, I called my mother and filled her in, glossing over the part about Penny's gun. I'm not sure she bought it, but she listened as usual without comment. Then, when I'd said all I intended to say, she spoke. "You always were a special child, Kate. So bright and curious, and such a compassionate heart. Remember all the stray animals you took in?"

"I remember the baby owl." I laughed. "He started hooting, and Dad took him to that barn where he could have his fill of mice."

"You were my treasure. You still are. I'm so grateful you're safe."

"I'll see you tomorrow night. I love you, Mom."

We disconnected. I took a forkful of scrambled eggs and watched Nancy bustle around Applegarth's luxe little kitchen. She'd stayed the night to help me with the awkward tasks of dressing and undressing with one arm in a sling. She held two slices of bacon over the skillet. "A second helping?"

"I'm sure I'll explode—so, yes, and maybe another bite of toast."

Some people overeat to compensate for pain. I overeat to celebrate not being killed.

Tom arrived. Nancy set a place for him at the table and made a discreet exit.

"Devlin called." Tom steadied my mug of coffee as I lifted it with my left hand. "Brenda's with Bo at the Munroe. Getting him ready to go home."

"Has he said anything about that night yet? Does he know what happened?"

"He's still confused, but from what they've been able to piece together, he saw Elenor's body near the road, but he couldn't stop the snow plow in time. He didn't hit her, but the snow spray smacked her hard, and when he realized she was dead, he assumed he'd killed her."

"Didn't he see the arrow?"

"If he did, it didn't register. He was in full-blown panic mode by that time, and concealed her body with the snow he removed from the walkway. Then guilt set in. Apparently his father had drummed two things into his head—first, never hurt a woman, a good thing considering Bo's size and strength, and second, don't hide your mistakes."

I sighed. "I'd feel better if I knew what will happen to him now."

"Brenda will stay with him at the croft house for a few weeks. What happens ultimately is up to her."

"And Penny?"

"She'll face charges, but she'll almost certainly be declared mentally incompetent and sent to an institution."

"I can't see Cilla living alone, but the marquetry casket rightfully belongs to the twins. If it's sold, she'll be able to live in sheltered comfort the rest of her life." I downed the last of my coffee. "That leaves Hugh Guthrie."

"I'm not a solicitor, but if Guthrie can return the money he took fraudulently, his publisher might agree not to prosecute."

A sudden twist of emotion colored his face. "I really thought I might lose you, Kate. Do you know what that did to me? I care for you deeply." He put up a hand. "No—don't say a word. Life's too short not to tell the truth. We both know that."

I put my hand on his cheek. He took it and kissed my palm.

My insides went all wobbly. I swallowed, hoping my voice wouldn't let me down. "We'll talk later. The funeral begins at eleven."

Even a funeral couldn't spoil my joy. Tom was innocent. He was a good man. Gratitude overwhelmed me. And something I'd thought I'd never feel again.

Perfect timing as usual. Tomorrow he was flying back to England.

* * *

About forty people attended Elenor's funeral service. Most followed the procession from the church to the island cemetery. Since the Historical Society was a crime scene again, the funeral meal was moved to the church hall.

"Grand turnout." Nancy handed me a fork and a gigantic slice of chocolate cake. "Every family still on the island is represented."

"With two exceptions." I cut off a wedge of cake. "This must be the first island gathering in more than two centuries with no Arnotts and no Guthries."

The fellowship hall was crowded. Sofia looked almost happy in an exotic beaded blouse and long bottle-green velvet skirt. Becca seemed preoccupied with clearing plates and rearranging the buffet table.

The MacDonalds were chatting with Tom. I joined them. "Thank you for what you did, Jackie."

"Nothing a'tall, dear lady." Jackie saluted.

"One of his old rugby moves." Dora beamed. "He used to mow 'em down like grass."

A door opened. Frank entered from the parking lot, followed by—*oh, my*—Brenda and Bo Duff.

Men pumped Bo's hand and clapped him on the back. Women hugged him.

Bo found me and broke into a big grin. "Hey, Mrs. Bill. I didn't hurt her. I didn't hurt her at all. Did you know that?"

"I did know that, Bo. I always knew that." I stood on tiptoes to give him a one-armed hug and burst into tears. That was happening to me a lot lately.

Bo bent down to look at me. "What's wrong? Are you sad?"

"No. I'm very, very happy." And I cried again.

"Come on," Tom said, leading Bo toward the buffet table. "Let's get a piece of Nancy's cake in you."

I squeezed Brenda's hand. "I know you'll do the right thing. Just remember, Bo has a place on the island. He always will."

"I'm beginning to realize that. It's just that I promised my parents I'd protect him."

"He might need more support one day, but wouldn't it be better to let him have his freedom as long as possible?"

Frank and Nancy had joined us. "I could use some help at the hotel," Frank said, "until the new owners take over. Lots of work for Bo. After that, we'll see."

Peace settled on Brenda's face.

Tom caught my eye from across the room and shot me that charming half smile.

"A bonnie man," Nancy said. "He's taken with you, lass."

I couldn't help smiling. "What did Frank mean by 'after that, we'll see'?"

"We've decided to join our daughter in Dundee. Not immediately. We'll wait until the new owners take over, but time is precious. We don't want to miss watching our grandchild grow up."

"And Becca?"

"I don't know about the hotel, but she turned Geoff down."

"Oh, Nancy. I hope she isn't making a mistake. Real love doesn't come along every day."

"That it does not." She held my gaze for a long moment.

"It's not the same and you know it."

"Oh, aye?"

"Tom has a life in England. My life is in Ohio. It's wrong."

"What's wrong is living in the past." Nancy gave me another pointed look. "Don't let your yesterdays define you, lass. Learn that lesson now before it's too late."

I was about to respond when my cell phone rang. "Sorry. I have to take this."

Nancy started to move away.

"No, stay," I caught her arm. "It's my daughter."

"Mom, are you okay?" Christine's voice was so clear she might have been in the next room. "I called the antique shop and got Grandma. She told me about Elenor and all the other stuff. It must have been horrible."

"I'm fine. Sore arm is all."

"What are we going to do about the hotel?"

"Don't worry. I'm signing the contract of sale on my way to the airport. Miss you, honey."

"Same here." Christine moved on. "Listen, Mom. I won't be coming home after Michaelmas term. That's what I wanted to tell you. Tris and I have been offered internships. Isn't that amazing? He's going to study medieval construction techniques at a guildhall. I'm going to one of the nearby estates to work in the family archives. Perfect, right?"

"In England? Where?"

"A village called Long Barston. We've got a place to stay and everything. It's real cool—a converted stable. There'll be other students from other universities. We're all doing internships. We'll be there for a month, from the beginning of December to the fifth of January. You can come for a couple of weeks, right?"

"Where is this Long Barston?"

"Northeast of London. Suffolk."

"You're spending December in *Suffolk*?"

Nancy just smiled.

Chapter Thirty-Eight

❧

After the funeral, I changed into jeans and the Magdalen College sweatshirt. I'd taken off the sling. I really didn't need it.

The noontime sun had melted the frost. I breathed in the clear, cold air.

As I passed Glenroth House with its turrets and crenellated battlements, I couldn't help feeling that, this time, I never would return to the island. Bill was gone. Elenor was gone. So was Agnes. Soon the Holdens would be off to Dundee, and even though Becca had turned Geoff down, I couldn't imagine her remaining on the island alone. Besides, she might change her mind and marry him after all. What would happen with Bo, I couldn't say, but he would need more care one day soon, and Brenda was ready to provide it.

Within the space of a week, everything had changed. I had changed.

Time like an ever-rolling stream . . .

An unknown future lay ahead of me, but that didn't matter because one thing was clear: the past was gone.

I might not be able to envision the future, but I had one. I did.

Another thought dampened my euphoria. I also had a present, a here-and-now. And with that came responsibilities. I had a business to run, people who depended on me.

On that note, I headed for Tartan Cottage.

Tom's clothes were laid out on his bed next to a backpack and a small wheeled suitcase. He'd changed into jeans, too, with a shirt in blues and browns.

"Want to take a walk?" I asked. "There's supposed to be a grave-yard behind the house. I'd like to see if I can find it before I leave the island."

"And so you shall." He smiled and shrugged into his waxed cotton jacket.

Tom ducked his head as we passed through a wrought-iron arbor leading to the garden. "Do you think the second diary will ever be published?"

"With the tale of literary fraud, double murder, and a lock of Bonnie Prince Charlie's hair? You're kidding, right? It would be an international best seller." I flashed him a smile. "Of course, getting Penny and Cilla's permission to publish might prove tricky."

The foundations of the old kirk began in the formal gardens. Beyond that, in a grove of poplars, concealed by brush and tall grass, were the remains of a ruined graveyard. Small blocks of dark stone, perhaps ten or twelve, lay broken and mostly sunken into the soil.

"These stones are older than the upright tablets in the old grave-yard." With my good arm, I tried to wiggle a dark stone jutting at an angle. Even with Tom's help, the stone wouldn't budge.

Tom tried several others before finding one that could be freed.

I brushed off the surface, hoping to read the inscription. "Ironic," I said, sifting through a mass of stone flakes. "They chose sandstone—easily carved but prone to weathering. No one will ever know for sure who lies here." I examined a few flakes, looking for carved letters but finding nothing.

Tom had moved a few yards away. He crouched near the base of a magnificent oak. "Kate, come have a look." He was clearing moss and lichens from a small rectangular block of the local gray limestone, the same stone used to build Glenroth House. An inscription emerged, cut by an inexpert hand but as sharp as the day the stone was laid:

Here lies Joseph
Born 1791? Died 3rd Mar 1810
John 15:13

I reached for Tom's arm. "I know that verse. *Greater love hath no man than this; that he lay down his life for his friends.*" I pointed to the date. "Look. March third. That's the day Flora and Gowyn tried to escape. Joseph was going to create a diversion."

Tom blew out a breath. "Seems there were four murders that day, and Arnott never faced justice for any of them."

"We don't know that. I've wondered if James Arnott's death was really suicide, or if someone—Mr. Fraser, for example—decided he'd done enough harm? Regardless, he faced a greater justice."

Tom pulled me to my feet and gathered me in his arms. We stood without speaking. Then he took my hand, and we walked back toward the house.

Before reaching the arbor, Tom stopped and turned to face me. "Come to England with me, Kate. I want to spend time with you, know you better. I want you to meet my family. I want you in my life." He pulled me close and kissed me with such passion I nearly swooned.

Always wanted to use that word.

I caught my breath. "You said we should tell the truth, so here goes. I've never felt this way about anyone." I looked at the hand that used to hold my wedding ring. "Not even Bill. I loved him dearly, Tom, but I've never met anyone like you."

That was true. Bill had been kind, predictable, safe. With Tom, there was an intensity that both intrigued and disturbed me.

Tom traced the line of my lip with his finger. "Go on."

"But I can't simply walk out on my responsibilities—to my children, my mother, my work." The look on his face nearly broke my heart, but I had to finish. "Your life is in England. Mine isn't. We're separated by a great big ocean."

"Not at the moment." He drew me to him again, folding me in his arms. "It could happen, Kate," he murmured into my hair. "We just have to let it."

Oh, how I wanted to believe him. "But why cause ourselves pain? You're not going to move to the States. I'm not going to move to England."

"We don't have to face that yet. Come to England. Just for a visit. We need time together. We'll figure it out." His face darkened with some powerful emotion. "Please don't say no. Please, Kate."

I rolled my eyes at him in mock exasperation. "Oh, all right. I'll come in December."

I'd tell him about Christine and the internship later. I know— I'm bad.

I made a face, and he started to laugh. "Come on, you. Let's spend our last few hours together."

A sudden breeze made the leaves flutter.

I could almost feel a page turning.

Acknowledgments

I want to thank Inspector Lynda Allan at the Portree Police Station on the Isle of Skye and Detective Inspector Richard Baird of Police Scotland's South Highland, Western Isles & Shetland Command, for answering my questions about policing in Scotland. This book could not have been written without the support and encouragement of many generous friends—from my awesome critique partners, Lynn Denley-Bussard, Charlene D'Avanzo, and Judy Copek, to all those who read and commented on my manuscript at various stages, especially Mary Graf, Charlene Ehrbar, Grace Topping, and Dorothy Leal. I'm deeply grateful for my fellow authors at Buckeye Crime Writers; for my agent, Paula Munier; for my editor, Faith Black Ross, and the crew at Crooked Lane books; for my sons, Dave and John; and most of all, for my husband, Bob, who deftly avoids encroaching hedgerows, rogue pheasants, and opposing vehicles while driving me down single-track roads all over the British Isles.

Soli Deo gloria.